*"And the LORD God said unto the serpent, Because thou hast done this, thou art cursed above all cattle, and above every beast of the field; upon thy belly shalt thou go, and dust shalt thou eat all the days of thy life:*

*And I will put enmity between thee and the woman, and between thy seed and her seed; it shall bruise thy head, and thou shalt bruise his heel."*
~ Genesis 3:14-15 KJV

*"How art thou fallen from heaven, O Lucifer, son of the morning!"*
~Isaiah 14:12 KJV

### *Other works by Lucas James*

*I Am Simon Black*
*Paradise*
*Ultraviolent*
*A Quiet Fury*
*She Called Me the Devil*
*I Never Saw the Spiders*
*Don't Call Me Lucky*
*Psilocybin Skies*
*Something Beautiful*

The following is a work of pure fiction;
any similarities to any persons, living or dead,
are purely coincidental and should not be interpreted
otherwise…

*This work is dedicated to the following people:
Kyle, Brittany, Maddy, Josie, Jess, Erika, Liz,
Wayne, Crystal, Shope, Jimmy, CJ, Kaspar,
Tom, Kris, Lauren, Grace,
Mackenzie,
and Jade*

*Step into the Sound*

# Chapter 1

## River Sound County Prison
## Hannover-Fist, Ohio
## May 8th, 1997

"They don't let you play guitar in prison."

Jasmine Garcia listens to my words with a worried look. She's standing just outside the iron bars separating me from the rest of the world. I'm standing there in a black suit with no tie like I'm going to a funeral, looking at her through dark glasses.

Everything is shades of gray – it's a condition called "achromatopsia." I've had it since I was a little kid. Lights are brighter than hell and everything is black and white – everything except the color red.

For some reason, I could always see red.

My theory is that it's because it was my favorite color, so when the cone cells in my eyes started to degenerate and die off, my mind committed that wavelength to memory, and my brain in turn used what little bits of my cones remained to focus on the color red.

If it was dull or I wasn't paying attention to it, I didn't notice it – like the inside of people's mouths or when someone's face blushes. But Jasmine's bright red lipstick stands out to me like a beacon in the fog.

Then I say, "I think that's the worst part. All I want to do is play and they gave me a goddamn harmonica." I try to smile. So does she.

"You don't seem too terribly nervous," she says, hugging herself and lightly gripping one of the iron bars. Her voice is like honey spilling out – even when she speaks, there's a melody to it. She might be one of the most beautiful women I've ever seen, too. Maybe even too beautiful. If I had to guess, I'd say her skin is golden brown and her eyes are the color of sweet tea. Dark dreadlocks hang over her shoulders and bright streaks cover her bangs, hanging over a face carved by an artist.

If it were up to me, I might never look at anything else.

"Nervous?" I breathe, then lean against the bars with my hands in my pockets. "Of course I'm nervous. It's a murder trial, Jazz."

She reaches through the prison bars and touches my arm. "It's almost over. Carl said they don't expect the trial to go on after today. Yours is the last testimony."

Wryly, I pull a frowning smirk. "Saved the best for last."

Jazz shoots me a somber look, then pulls her hand away. I take mine out of my pockets with an uneasy sigh and grip the bars, leaning my head against them, staring down at the gray floor. Jazz does the same; our heads just barely touch and I wonder if the floor is gray to her, too.

After a moment, her fingers start drumming a rhythm on the iron bars. I recognize the beat; it's one of ours.

My fingers rap along with hers and we both pick up intensity. Then she sings, starting high and wavering her voice until she ends on a lower note in a somber, melancholic tune, repeating the pattern again in the next line.

*"If my devils ever leave meeee, then my angels will as well,*

*Find my penance here in Countyyyy while I'm climbin' outta Hell…"*

I join in almost a low hum, adding my timbre to her voice.

*"And your karmaaaa, when it finally comes around,*

*You can make a deal with the Devilllll, and get into the ground,*

*Or you can sing along with your angelllls, and step into the sound…"*

Jazz finishes off with one more refrain as my voice diminishes.

*"Step into the sound."*

At that moment a man's authoritative voice announces as he strolls into view of the temporary holding cell they've got me in, separated from the rest of the prison: "Lyric, it's time."

The correctional officer gives Jazz a look and another guard comes over to escort her. She looks back at me. "I'll see you in the courtroom, Donovan. It's gonna be okay."

Just like that, she's out of sight. A moment later, the iron gate slides open loudly and the CO puts me in handcuffs and leg shackles.

***

"It's gonna be alright, Lyric," Carl Hoskins says. We're sitting in a small office, waiting for the trial to commence. There's only a few minutes left. "We've got solid evidence exonerating you from Huck's murder. No jury in their right minds is gonna find you guilty."

"Except that I killed him," I reply dourly.

Carl lets out a sigh and runs his fingers through his short, buzzed hair slicked back with pomade. Almost every time I've seen him he's got on suspenders and slacks. Today he's got on a red tie, that way I can focus on him better when I'm on the stand. He gets up and paces around while he thinks aloud. "It isn't just about *what* you did, it's about *why* you did it."

"Yeah, which boils down to the difference between the death penalty or life in prison."

"Death penalty ain't gonna stick," Carl argues. "Too many extenuating circumstances. Prosecution is pushing for life. We've been through this, man."

"I'm dead either way. You die in prison, you got the death sentence. I don't care what they call it." Anxiously I start picking at my beard. My fingers twist around a hair and it falls out. It's white in my palm; I'm not even thirty yet and I'm going gray.

"Just relax, alright?" Carl sighs heavily. "Get up there, tell your story, and what will be will be."

I try to give him an optimistic look but it's not in the cards; I've got a nothing hand. Then the door opens and the bailiff walks in. "The court is ready."

With lead in my feet, the bailiff escorts me by my handcuffed arms as Carl follows us into the courtroom. The place is packed; damn near everybody I know from New Freedom is here. Colton Rust, the owner of the Clawhammer Tavern; Lorraine Jones, the bartender; several of the people I've spent my nights drinking or playing music with, and a horde of people here to watch me burn. Save for Rust and Lorraine and the people I used to drink with or work with, the majority of the faces scowl at me like I'm the Devil. Reporters all sit in the front rows of the prosecution's side.

Toward the end of a bench in the back, I spot Red Sutherland and my heart twinges with guilt. He isn't scowling at me. He just has a stoic look on his face underpinned with heartbreak, subtly leaking through.

I really didn't expect him to be here.

Then I spot Jazz walking in through the large main entrance of the courtroom. My body warms and freezes at the same time when I look at her, strolling in with a mesh fabric scarf flowing past her neck and a light denim jacket over a patterned dress. She gives me a look like she's praying for me when she takes a seat on the first bench behind the defense table. I'm not sure who we oughta pray to anymore – not sure I ever was – but I think I'm praying in my head.

Nervous as hell, I stand there while the bailiff uncuffs me and leads me and Carl to our table. On the other side of the aisle is the prosecution team. There's three of them – a man not much older than me, a woman about the same age, and an older man. The old guy is the lead prosecutor, and that cold look in his eyes tells me he wants to see me burn, just to warm them up.

As soon as we sit down, I turn to Jazz and whisper, "*Thank you.*"

It's not long at all before the judge shows up, but you could have told me I sat there for a year and I'd have believed it. "All rise," the bailiff says loudly. We all do as we're told. "Honorable Judge Thomas presiding."

The judge gathers his bearings and announces in a deep voice that carries naturally, "You may be seated." My legs are shaking as I sit down and I hope nobody notices. Judge Thomas then says, "We will go ahead and resume proceedings for the case of Donovan Lyric versus the State of Ohio. As a reminder to the jury, the defendant has been charged with resisting arrest and three counts murder in the second degree. I would like to ask the media here as well not to take any photographs of the jury members. If you have any devices such as a cellular phone or a pager, please turn them off."

It was wild to me that the phrases *murder in the second degree* and *please silence your cell phones* could be uttered practically in the same breath. *The banality of the judicial system.*

Then the judge looks at Carl. "Mr. Hoskins, I understand that you would like the defendant to take the witness stand?"

"Yes, your Honor," Carl says as he rises to his feet.

"Very well; the court summons Donovan Lyric to the stand."

There's lead in my feet again and a heavy rhythm as I walk, like drumming a blues song on the courtroom floor. I seat myself in the stand. Carl approaches a lectern and begins speaking. "I would just like to begin with a reminder to the jury on the nature of my client's appearance; please bear in mind that he has a congenital medical condition which requires the use of protective eyewear. If he could, I'm sure he'd love to see you in the light."

The jury and a portion of the court audience murmur a collective chuckle. I might chuckle too if it weren't for the sick feeling in my stomach.

Then Carl addresses me specifically. "Mr. Lyric, we've heard the testimony of several character witnesses regarding the events that led up to the night of May 17th, 1996. Can you, in your own words, starting from the night you were charged with assault, tell the jury what happened?"

"Objection, your Honor," the prosecutor jumps up. "The question is asking for a narrative."

"Sustained," Judge Thomas says quickly. "Counsel, please rephrase your question to the defendant."

Carl takes a deep breath. In my head, I'm playing a tune on a six-string with my beating heart as a metronome.

*Just step into the sound.*

Then Carl looks at me and says:

"Donovan, in your own words, could you tell the jury what happened the night Huckleberry Singer died?"

# PART I

# Chapter 2

## River Sound County Sheriff's Department
## New Freedom, Ohio
## May 17th, 1996, 1:00 A.M.

In my mouth I tasted copper. My tongue searched my teeth, looking for the damage. Probably came from Huck's fist when he clocked me a couple hours ago.

I spat onto the floor of the jail cell.

Suddenly the gray popped out with a little bit of red.

There's nothing to do in jail. Nothing to look at but brick walls and a brick ceiling, with a big pane of bulletproof glass for the cops to watch you through. You just gotta sit there on that cold metal bench and wait for them to let you out. It's an adult daycare, reserved for the most reckless of society.

My eyes rested on a black tattoo on the underside of my right forearm. It was a silhouette of the devil, flying out of Hell with sharp wings and spiked tail in the style of a tribal tat. I got two black wings on my shoulders crawling down past my sleeves to match. Meekly, I frowned. I'd gotten them just to piss off my dad four or five years back, when I was in my mid-twenties – he wouldn't ever shut up about God when I was a kid, so I figured I'd give him something to pray on.

Sitting there in that all-too familiar drunk tank, I couldn't help but wonder what that said about *me*.

With a huff, I glanced up at the brick ceiling.

"How're *you* doin' today?" I asked aloud. Nobody ever answered; that's the funny thing about trying to talk to God – you'll never hear a word back, yet we all did it at some point in our lives, no matter what we believed.

I stared up at the ceiling waiting for an answer that never came. Then I let out a sigh and looked back at the spot of blood on the floor. Wearily, I muttered, "How am I doing today?"

Cops shuffled back and forth past the bulletproof window. It was a small cell, only built for a couple of inhabitants at a time. It must have been a blue moon because I was the only one there that night. Usually they mopped up a couple staggering drunks from the Clawhammer after it closed for the evening.

There was a big steel door barring me from the outside world, all metal save for a small foot-by-foot window near its crest. Movies were full of shit; all I ever wanted was a jail cell with iron bars.

Instead, they always locked you up behind one of those metal door behemoths in New Freedom, Ohio, as if you were in danger of breaking out at any minute, ready to punch through the bulletproof window like you were the Man of Steel.

After a moment, the face of my arresting officer appeared in that small window at the crest of the door, then a loud *buzz* pierced my ears and the door slid open.

"Hello, Clarice," I greeted in my best impression of Anthony Hopkins. The cop just gave me a weird look. "Seriously?" I remarked. "*Silence of the Lambs?* Nothing?"

He ignored me. "Mr. Lyric – your ride's here."

I slurred, still a little drunk. "You know, they have it at Blockbuster, I'm sure you would love –"

"Cut the shit, Lyric," the officer grumbled as he sauntered over to me. He stopped and glanced at the spot of blood on the ground with a look of disgust. "Jesus."

"Sorry, I was trying to add a bit of color to the place."

"God," he clicked his tongue, "I can't *fathom* why Huck knocked the shit out of you."

I shrugged as the cop pulled me up forcefully by my arm. "Guess he didn't like my set."

Then he escorted me out of the cell and down a hall toward the reception area.

I could see Jasmine standing there waiting for me, her bright red lipstick burning brightly in a field of white.

Suddenly I felt bad.

"I'm innocent!" I yelled dramatically, clasping my hands behind my back and pretending like I was trying to break free. Jasmine's head snapped toward me with a wild look of surprise. "Innocent, I tell ya!"

The cop let go of me with a grunt as we reached the front desk, then I pulled out my hands with a grin to show the lack of cuffs. She broke into a grin and shook her head at me.

"See?" I smirked.

"'Innocent' and 'going home tonight' are two different things, Lyric."

My smirk faded as I watched her grin evaporate when she looked closer at me. She took her thumb and smudged it against the corner of my mouth. Gently, I pushed her hand away. "I've been hit harder than that before, Jazz. I'll be fine."

"Trust me, I'm aware," she gave me a look.

My face fell guiltily and I averted my eyes for a second. Then the receptionist said, "Your arraignment will be on Monday the 20th, 9:00 A.M. in Magistrate Swinton's courtroom. Don't worry, you'll get your own copy."

"Well that's good because I'm obviously too drunk to remember," I replied casually as I looked at the piece of paper.

The receptionist began to giggle uncontrollably. She was in police uniform – I wasn't used to seeing that kind of expression above a badge. She was pretty, though. "Sign here, Mr. Lyric," she responded and slid another paper across the countertop. I scrawled my name down haphazardly and slid it back to her. "Is that a stage name?" she asked curiously.

"No," I shook my head, sort of amused. "Fair assumption, though. My great-grandfather came here from Ireland – Donovan Lee Rick the First. When he told the man at the immigration center his name, his accent was so thick that it sounded like 'Donovan Lyric,' so that's what the man wrote down. Apparently, my great-grandpa liked it better that way."

"Wow," the receptionist smiled broadly. "Well, he made the right decision."

I held her look for a second. One second longer and I probably would have scrawled down my number for her right on the release forms. But I could feel Jazz's eyes impatiently boring into the back of my skull, so I said,

"This is actually my vocalist, Jazz," as I gestured toward her. "You should check out one of our sets sometime. We play at the Clawhammer a couple times a month."

"That seedy little bar in town?" she cocked her brow. "I thought that place was just for sleazy drunks."

I gave her a sly look. "What – do I not seem like the type of person it attracts?"

The receptionist looked away coyly as she flipped through paperwork. "No, you seem exactly like the type."

"Oof, ouch," I clicked my tongue, then leaned onto the counter. "I can still count on seeing your face in that crowd of sleazy drunks next time though, right?"

"Maybe," she smiled despite trying not to. Then Jazz spoke up impatiently.

"Do we need anything else?"

The police woman began to blush. "Nope, you're all set." She handed me my discharge paperwork.

My lips pulled a frown as I stared down at the paper in my hand. It said in big, bold letters: ASSAULT; DISORDERLY CONDUCT.

"Well that sounds familiar," I remarked to myself. Then I looked at Jazz. "Is my baby okay?"

Her face became flustered and she sort of shrank, then her expression changed and she rolled her eyes with a grunt. "You mean your guitar?"

I grinned. "What, you thought I meant you?"

Jazz turned and I followed her out of the doors of the River Sound County Sheriff's Department into the warm mid-spring night. Jazz looked back at me as we walked to her utility van. "God forbid you care about anything other than that instrument."

"Jazz, we both know I'm nothing without it. It's my *life!*" I gestured dramatically to make her giggle.

"Shut up," she laughed. "I'm mad at you – you're not allowed to make me laugh."

"Oh, come on," I sped up and stopped in front of her. She stopped too and gave me a cross, expectant look. "You know damn well Huck started it."

"Yet you're the one getting charged – is that how this works?"

"It is when Huck is dating the sheriff's daughter," I argued.

"Well then maybe you shouldn't have *slept with* that sheriff's daughter," she gesticulated animatedly. "Notice all this karma coming around?"

"Oh, come *on!*" I rolled my eyes. "Alita was just *waiting* for that opportunity. If Huck's gonna be pissed off, then he should be pissed at her, too. I haven't even talked to her in almost two months. Besides, I was drunk – it's not like I did it on purpose."

"When *aren't* you drunk, Lyric?"

"I don't know – usually I wake up sober, if that counts."

"Yeah – at twelve o'clock in the afternoon," she laughed again, almost uneasily.

"Well if I stop at seven in the morning then…."

She raised her eyebrows and stared at me.

"Okay," I breathed. "Maybe I could stand to cut back a little."

"A little?" Jazz scoffed with an incredulous smirk as she resumed walking. "If you cut back a *little*, you'd still be drinking half a fifth a day."

"It keeps life interesting."

"Is that what you call getting thrown across the bar?"

"Well it definitely wasn't *not* interesting," I half grinned to myself as we reached Jazz's red van. She painted it that color so I could spot her better. It suddenly dawned on me that we were outside at night, so I popped off the glasses. Street lights were a pain to look at, but I could handle it. I went on: "When most of your best stories come out of a bottle of whiskey, it's hard to put the book down."

Jazz unlocked the van and gave me a look. "Yeah, but so do most of your worst – think there might be a correlation there?" Her stern visage broke into a slightly worried little smile as she got in the van. I walked around the back and opened the double doors.

*Oh, thank God.*

Lying flat on the bed of the trunk was my guitar – a sleek black beauty with a classic body that I'd had since I started playing a few years back. I dabbled with the piano as a kid, then dropped music entirely for years. Huck and Jazz were the reasons I picked up an instrument again. My guitar bore scars and scuffs from years of playing while intoxicated. A black denim jacket – at least, I think it was black; I never asked if it was just dark blue – laid next to it, with all of my daily inventory piled on top: There was a pack of cigarettes, a knife, lighter, and a small wooden container called a "dugout" that housed about a gram of weed and a metal pipe made to look like a cigarette.

Jazz always made an effort to keep my things safe when I got into trouble. I tried not to show up to jail with anything more than my wallet, keys, and the clothes on my back. Never know what they might decide to confiscate just because you pissed them off.

Quickly, I stuffed my belongings in my pockets and threw on the jacket. Then I furrowed my brow, shut the doors and got in next to Jazz.

"Hey, why didn't you put my guitar in its case?"

She played dumb for a second, then exaggeratedly went, "*Oh*, I'm sorry, I didn't think it would bother you. You know, since you threw the damn guitar on the floor anyway." I huffed my breath and Jazz continued animatedly. "See, when *I* have something that I value, I like to take *care* of it – like *my* guitar or my life or my future."

"I do value those things, but I think they need tough love sometimes," I joked.

Jazz laughed and shook her head as she turned over the engine. "You're stupid. You know you have other guitars, right?" With the windows down, the van rolled out of the parking lot onto the streets of New Freedom, while Roy Orbison belted out *Oh, Pretty Woman* from the radio.

"Yeah, but I only have one of *that* one. It was my first guitar – it's special."

"Real quick, what was the name of the first girl you kissed?"

I puffed out my cheeks and let out the air.

Jasmine busted out laughing. "See, you don't even remember!"

"Yeah, because I'm pushing thirty."

"I've got three years on you and I can still tell you who *my* first kiss was!" Jazz laughed with a bright smile and red lips.

Finally, I grinned and said, "Her name was Christina."

"But it wasn't special," Jazz remarked.

I shrugged. "Not really. I was fifteen – I took the first chance I got."

"But the guitar is special just because it was your first?" she gave me a knowing look bordering on a smile.

"Something like that."

Her smile stretched out and she said, "I don't think that's true. I think you just don't like change."

"What, and you do?" I rejoined with a playful scoff.

"I happen to enjoy change very much."

"Like hell you do. You've been stuck here for just as long as I have, Jazz. You don't want things to change, either. I *know* that I don't. At least I can admit it."

Jazz gave me a bemused smirk, then turned her eyes to the road with her beaming headlights. I couldn't help but stare at her for a second. Consciously, I turned my head to look out my window.

We were quiet for a moment, then Jazz said: "I like you better when you're sober."

"I'll be sober in the morning."

"That's not what I mean," she looked at me. "I mean *sober*."

Guiltily, I shrank into my seat.

She turned her eyes back to the road then continued. "You're always better when you're sober. You're nicer, you play better, you're funnier; when you're sober, it's like you're walking in the light. When you drink...."

I gave her a curious look. "What?"

"I don't know... It's like you're walking with the Devil."

"The Devil on my shoulder and an angel on the other," I muttered, then let out a strained sigh. "I don't like being sober, Jazz. It's a nightmare. All people ever do is congratulate you and ask how long it's been, and you have to pretend to be proud of yourself or strong or like you wouldn't end that conversation right there just for a shot of tequila and some salt. It's too much."

"You were sober for seven months, that *has* to count for something."

I shook my head. "No, I don't think it does. I tried, and found out the hard way that sobriety isn't in the cards for me. It's a nothing hand."

"Oh, bullshit!" Jazz rejoined. "You're the one in control of your destiny, Lyric. Nobody else. Not Huck, not the sheriff, not even God. You are." She held the look on me for a minute. "If you don't realize that soon, then it's gonna be too late."

Silence struck our voices and the only sounds I could hear were coming from the quiet crackling of the radio. I looked out the window so I wouldn't have to see the disappointment in her eyes.

New Freedom was a small town, almost as small as it gets. There were a couple other towns within spitting distance; Driftwood, Killdevil, Ashville, Hannover-Fist. That last one was further away than the rest of them – a solid thirty or so minutes away, all the way at the top of River Sound County. That's where the real court was, not the small-time magistrate bullshit. Hannover-Fist was a little bigger, too – the first stop on the inevitable trail of gentrification leaking into southern Ohio, slowly, spanning decades.

The rest of the towns, you could pass right through them and not even know it. Go west, you'll hit Driftwood; south, you'll pass through Ashville in the blink of an eye; up north a couple minutes' drive, you'll be in Killdevil, the oldest town of the bunch; and then there was New Freedom on the east, just a couple miles from the River Sound Dam and the West Virginia state line. Sometimes I'd think back to the Book of Genesis, when God sent Adam, Eve and the serpent all east of Eden, and I'd wonder to myself if they wound up in New Freedom, too.

Collectively, New Freedom, Driftwood, Killdevil and Ashville made up what we all called Southern Sound County. That's where I lived, that's where I grew up, that's probably where I was gonna die.

I was fine with it.

It was 1996, but Southern Sound County decided the fifties was a good enough place to stop.

We rolled by the small shops condensed on Garden Street, the second-to-main road going into town; New Freedom Deli, Marvin's Auto Shop, The Cigar Cabana, and a general store just called The Goods. I knew the owners of most of them; knew most of the patrons, too. Then there was the Blacktop Grille – a place I used to work at until things took a turn for the worst with me and Huck. He was one of the cooks there. Jazz worked there, too, waiting tables when she wasn't working in a garden or helping deliver babies as a doula. I hadn't been back since things came to a head. Every time I glanced at it, I had to shake off that unplaceable sense of loss.

So I quit looking at it. Instead, I looked up the street toward my favorite place in town.

Take the first right onto Water Street and you'll see the Clawhammer Tavern in the middle of the first block, right across from a train platform with a bunch of fancy dining cars and a bright red engine parked on the tracks.

The Clawhammer was a dive bar with an emphasis on music. The owner was an interesting guy. Retired military police, undercover – apparently he had left some demons and bad deeds in his past. He didn't talk about it much, but you could tell he was always thinking about it. Colton Rust was his name – I think there was something to that. He was a man carved out of iron that turned into rust, passing the time with a drink and his strings, just waiting to die. Almost never saw him without a drink in his hand; never saw him get cross with someone who didn't deserve it, either.

He was one hell of a musician, probably the best one in town. Graduated from Peabody when I was still playing with toy soldiers in the yard. Me and Jazz would hang out at the Clawhammer and jam out for hours at a time while he sorted and displayed his eclectic collection of instruments.

God smiled on me at least once in my life because I got a house right up the street from it.

Go to the next intersection at Garden and you hit North Bethel Street. Take a left down that road, my house was a couple down on the right, between a hardware store and a funeral home. Keep on going and you'll hit Main Street, with the only gas station for a few miles.

As the van crawled down Garden Street, Jazz abruptly asked, "So wait – are you the fourth Donovan Lyric?"

"Third. It skipped a generation. My grandpa's name is 'Donovan' but he named my dad 'Samuel.'"

She gave me a bemused smile. "What, your grandpa wasn't a fan of Donovan the First?"

"Not particularly," I replied humorously. "Apparently Donovan Lyric the First was something of a bastard."

Jazz cocked her brow with a wide grin. "Oh? Did he womanize and get into bar fights, too?"

"Probably," I laughed. "But I'll never know. My grandpa never met the guy."

"What? Why?"

"Spent his life in prison."

"Wait – really?"

"Yup," I replied nonchalantly as I thought back to the stories from my childhood. "I know he was a musician, though. My great-grandma used to tell my grandpa that –" I started imitating a bit of a southern drawl, "– his daddy would sit there in prison, pickin' and grinnin' on his *gui*tar every day." I paused for a moment while Jazz studied me. "I doubt it was true. I think she just didn't want him picturing his dad sitting in prison, rotting away."

"Jesus," Jasmine breathed. "I mean, it could be true – why wouldn't it be?"

"They don't let you play guitar in prison." I glanced at her with a hint of mischief. "Believe me, I've tried."

Jazz tittered and said, "You've never been to prison. Jail doesn't count."

Immediately, I belted out a line of vocals imitating twangy new-country music: *"Well they sent me to jail, but I call it prison, 'cause the only thing I want is the only thing I'm missin', I –"*

Jazz cut me off with a playful shove to the shoulder. "Stop it, I already have a headache and this isn't *Rock-a-Doodle*," she laughed. When her smile faded, she asked, "So what did he do, anyway?"

I rolled my window down and pulled out a cigarette with my lips. "He shot a man. Killed 'em."

The van silently filled with smoke as Jazz turned left onto North Bethel Street. In a moment, we were parked in front of my house. We sat there for a moment, then Jazz huffed.

"What?" I asked.

"I don't know," she said, almost frustratedly. "I just don't like the idea of there being a murderer in your family."

I sort of scoffed. "There's a lot of violent men in my family, Jazz. The Lyrics are old-world – that's what my dad used to say. 'World's gonna break you if you don't let it know you'll break it first.'"

"And that doesn't worry you?"

I furrowed my brow. "What do you mean?"

"You're talking about 'breaking the world' – when do you break the *cycle?*"

Then I scoffed with a laugh. "Break the cycle? I'm not an abuse victim, Jazz. I mean – I am, technically I guess… but that's just life."

"You think it has to be that way?"

There was a pause.

Jazz continued. "We're not as young as we used to be, Lyric. The older we get, the more it hurts when we fall down. That's why you gotta learn how to keep your balance when you're young. It's easier just to stay off the ground."

"You know I love it when you speak in rhyme."

She shook her head and rolled her eyes with a reluctant smile. "What I'm saying is –"

"I know," I interjected. "The longer you play with fire, the more likely you are to get burned. But I'm not my great-grandpa, I'm not my grandpa, and I'm not my dad. We cool down a little bit every generation, I think."

"Going off the fact that you threw a barstool at a guy tonight," Jazz rejoined, "I'm not so sure it's tapering off as fast as you think it is."

I averted my gaze out my window and frowned with the corner of my mouth, then took a long drag from my cowboy killer. "I don't wanna hurt anybody. It's just a hard world we live in. Someone points a gun at you, you gonna turn the other cheek?"

"No," Jazz said, "but I don't think I'd let it get to that point in the first place."

I clicked my tongue and snuffed my cigarette in the van's ashtray; Jazz didn't like it when I tossed my cigarette butts on the ground. "Well, so far I haven't." Then I opened the door and got out, holding it open while I leaned in and talked. "Thanks for bailing me out."

"It was a zero dollar bail," she told me, slightly amused. "They were just sequestering you for the safety of the public."

"That's me, Mr. Goddamn Dangerous," I rolled my eyes.

"Knowing you?" Jazz laughed. "Maybe it was the right call."

She winked at me and a small grin flashed at the corner of my mouth as she held her smile at me, then I felt my face starting to turn red. "Well, luckily I have you. Thank you. I mean it."

She sort of wryly smiled at me, then I rounded the van, pulled my guitar out of the back and strapped it over my shoulder. Jazz propped herself out of the window, hanging with her elbows over the bright red door. "Get yourself some rest – we're picking up our set where we left off tomorrow."

"We finally doing an encore?" I asked.

"Sure are," she replied chipperly, "so I hope you didn't break your hands tonight. Be real hard to finish the set with a busted fretting hand."

"Set don't matter much to me, long as you're there," I winked.

"Shut up, Lyric," she laughed and shook her head curtly. "Get some sleep."

I smiled to myself. "You too."

As I turned to leave, Jazz stopped me. "Oh – wait!"

"Hm?" I swung back around, slowly walking backwards toward the concrete steps of my porch.

"I forgot to ask you – why did he shoot him? Your great-grandpa – why'd he shoot that man?"

Lightning flashed in the sky and I glanced up at the dark clouds for a second. I could have sworn there was lightning every night in that town, but it never seemed to rain.

"Nobody knows," I admitted, staring up at the sky. "I think he just wanted to watch him die."

# Chapter 3

My house was shitty. It was like a mobile home with the facade of a house. Wearily, I sauntered up the concrete porch steps as Jasmine's bright red van became a distant dot in the night.

Then all I saw was gray.

With a sigh, I fumbled with my keys and pushed open my front door. It opened right into the living room. On the far wall straight across was a swinging door that led to the kitchen. Go through it and directly across from that was the door to the bathroom, and to the left right before the bathroom was my bedroom door. That was the whole thing, that was the whole house. The rent was still too much goddamn money for what I was getting, as cheap as it was.

In a flash, I flipped on the lights and everything was bathed in red; I used red-dyed bulbs when I was home alone. There was a normal soft white lamp in every room for when people were over, but I always used the red lights. When everything's covered in red, I don't even notice that it's the only color I can see. It's dimmer, too, so it's easier on my eyes.

My keys clanged as I dropped them on a small end table by the door. Wearily, I dragged my feet over to the window on the side wall with an old, beat up air conditioner unit sticking out. A dial was missing from the front; I grabbed a pair of needle nose pliers and squeezed the metal bit inside the unit, turning it with a loud *crank* until the machine kicked on.

Then I swung my guitar around in front of me and set it on its stand beside two other guitars – both also black, one being acoustic and one electric. To be honest, I couldn't remember the last time I played either of them. Hell, I wasn't even sure the other electric even *worked* anymore.

Jazz was right; I was nothing if not resistant to change.

My living room was decorated pretty sparsely; there were vinyls on one shelf, cassettes and CDs on another, and a record player on the coffee table. I set my sunglasses down beside it. My musical taste was somewhat eclectic, if admittedly a little mainstream. I listened to everything from Elvis to Nirvana. My shelves were a monument to music history – The Beatles, The Rolling Stones, Black Sabbath, Queen, Eric Clapton, Van Halen, Jefferson Airplane, Bush, Johnny Cash, Metallica, NWA, The Cranberries – all of it.

There was a heavy CRT television with a small screen resting on top of an old wooden entertainment center, with a small crack underneath that I constantly lost shit under, and a big black VHS player on the shelf below the TV. I only owned a few VHS tapes – three of the dozen or so were *Star Wars* movies I had grown up with. Half the time I went to watch them, I changed my mind halfway through rewinding it.

Movies were great to me when I was younger, but the older I got the more it just felt like all I was doing was vegetating when I put in a video tape. Just as well, I still had my old Nintendo from the eighties, like I might pick it back up some day and pretend to be a teenager again. Every once in a while, I would run through *Super Mario Bros.* and relive those memories. But it was always fleeting, evanescent as nostalgia tends to be.

My real passion was resting on its stand next to me.

I fished through the fifth pocket (or the coin pocket) of my jeans and pulled out a bright red guitar pick, picked up my guitar, then reached over and grabbed the cable snaking away from my amp. It plugged into the instrument with a satisfying *click* and I flipped it on. At first I always kept the gain low – no distortion, just the clean sound of electric steel from my fingertips.

Lightly, I strummed a few chords and tuned the thing to E standard with my electronic tuner, then set it back down on its stand so I could saunter into the kitchen and pour a glass of bourbon. My back hurt, my body hurt, everything hurt. Maybe Jazz was right, I thought as I took out my dugout and lit the pipe – I was a little old to be getting tossed around in bar fights. With a deep exhale, billowing smoke, I took a drink from the warm liquid in the glass.

Corn liquor went down sweet, with a burn like silk going up in the smoke.

My mind flashed back to screaming at Huck earlier in the bar. "*Get a hobby and go FUCK yourself! At this point you've probably got as many intrusive thoughts about me during sex as SHE does, you fucking scrub! Oh – and in case you forgot where my apartment is, just ask your girlfriend! She remembers!*" I was so angry everything was a blur. As the bouncer took me out to the cops after the fight broke out, the last thing I remembered was screaming at Huck: "*10 North Bethel Street – do your fucking worst!*"

"Christ," I mumbled aloud as I stared down at the bourbon, embarrassed of myself. "I really overdo it when I'm angry."

With my drink in hand, I stumbled back into the living room and fell into the couch as I got high. My guitar found its way back into my fingers, then I leaned forward and dragged a small, brown, plastic rectangular device toward me across the top of the coffee table – my cassette recorder. It had an opaque plastic top so you couldn't see the tape rolling, and big clicky buttons that made satisfying mechanical *clacks* when you pressed them down.

My thumb pushed down the button to record and the tape started turning.

Every night when I got home, I'd sit there and play while I let the tape pick up whatever came out. My best ideas always came when I forgot it was recording; the tapes I bought were thirty minutes per side, standard for the time. After each half hour, I'd flip the tape and do it again.

Half the time, I ended up recording over it the next day. Usually, if something was really worth playing again, I'd remember most of it. Mostly the cassettes were to make sure I didn't create my magnum opus while I was too drunk to remember doing it.

For a while, I sat there getting stoned and drinking away the pain in my jaw. I let my fingers play whatever they wanted and closed my eyes.

Inside my head is where the magic happened.

Ever since I was a kid, if I shut my eyes and focused on music, I could remember what colors all looked like, every single one of them. In my mind's eye I watched a little yellow light dancing, making shapes like a laser pointer through a long exposure lens. It drew abstract art like a sprite buzzing around excitedly.

And the longer I kept my eyes closed and listened to the music, the more sprites there were.

Slowly, I began to turn on the distortion.

After a while, there were dozens of sprites – each leaving glowing trails behind them as they drew out shapes in every color, like skywriting in the dark. I watched as one of the lights zigged and curved up and down to the rhythm, drawing out the intricate shape of a leaf where every stem and every vein was a different color, all connecting like cosmic arrows in space. The lights drew trees, fields, clouds and stars; they made odd shapes and random patterns, smoother ones for the melodies I would strum and harsh, chaotic ones when I turned on the distortion. For hours in my head, the lights danced with me while I played.

I think I flipped the tape over three times before I finally passed out.

\*\*\*

When I opened my eyes they were stabbed by the sun. My hand shot out and grabbed my sunglasses off the coffee table, then quickly put them on over my bloodshot eyes. My guitar laid haphazardly on the floor and my glass was knocked over beside the record player, spilling out what little whiskey remained while I slept.

Half asleep, I grabbed a record off the shelf, let it spin against the needle on the turntable and listened to the warm crackling sound spilling out as Elvis serenaded my morning. Then I put on a pot of coffee and stumbled into the bathroom. A red light illuminated it dimly, and for a second every day I would forget I was colorblind.

Before side A was finished, I was showered and grooming myself half-dressed, running gel through my wet hair and studying the man looking back at me in the mirror. A black cross hung from my neck, and the sharp black wings on my shoulder caught the light; sometimes I forgot they were there. Even in the dim redness, I could point out the spots of gray in my beard. *Dad went gray at thirty-five, let's see if I can beat his record*, I thought dourly.

Steam poured through the kitchen as I stepped out of the bathroom and gripped the handle of my refrigerator to grab half-and-half for the coffee. But I paused for a second. My eyes rested on a crude drawing stuck to the fridge with a button-sized sticker.

It was a caricature of myself, drawn out poorly in pen with little care given to detail, wearing the same outfit I always wore. *Lyric* was written inside the most uneven heart you'd ever seen, and every time I looked at it, I couldn't help but grin. The hostess at the restaurant I used to work at drew it for me one afternoon, I think as an attempt to satirize my appearance – kind of skinny, always dressed in black, and she had given me a neck like a fucking giraffe – but I thought it was the funniest shit in the world when she did it. She was just a kid, maybe fifteen when she drew it, and there was something endearing about it. I think she thought I would hate it, so I kept it out of spite.

It had been nearly two months since I left that place, and now every time I saw it, I couldn't help but feel a little lachrymose.

*Christ, how quickly we fall from grace.*

My expression soured, so I quit looking at it and opened the fridge, made my coffee and finished getting dressed.

Standing over my dresser in the bedroom, I rifled through a stack of plain black T-shirts, until one caught my eye with a bit of red. It was the only shirt I had that wasn't plain black or plain white – I wasn't a fan of labeled clothing and I didn't like to broadcast my interests through my wardrobe. This shirt was the one exception: it was black like most of the rest of them, but in the center was a ruby red *Superman* logo across the chest.

My sore jaw and raging hangover made me feel not a whole hell of a lot like a superhero, and when I glanced down at the devil tattoo on my arm, holding that shirt, I couldn't help but notice the irony. But I think that's why we liked characters like Superman, or Jesus for that matter, I mused as I glanced at the cross hanging from my neck.

I wasn't a Christian by any stretch of the imagination. I viewed Jesus the same way I viewed any other ancient philosopher, like Socrates or Lao Tzu – as a mortal man with a pretty good moral compass. But I needed something to remind me to do better, to be better, and the cross wasn't cutting it that week.

Superman's symbol was much more appealing to me.

I was a big fan of the comics and the first couple of movies growing up, though I hadn't seen them in years. I couldn't remember the last time I even *touched* a comic book. But there was always one line in the first film, a Richard Donner picture from 1978 simply titled *Superman*, that stuck with me – when Clark Kent finds the Fortress of Solitude and discovers that he's an alien named 'Kal-El,' a name the two Jewish creators of the character derived from the Hebrew word 'kalel,' meaning 'voice of God.' His birth father tells him:

*"They can be a great people, Kal-El; they wish to be.*
*They only lack the light to show the way.*
*For this reason above all, their capacity for good,*
*I have sent them you... My only son."*

That scene played out in my memory as I stared down at the red *S* enclosed in a diamond, like a crimson serpent in a sea of blacks and whites and grays. It had been nearly a year since I wore it last – the last time I wore it, I was surrounded by a field of sunflowers with a beautiful woman. Maybe a part of me just didn't want to tarnish that memory.

"What the hell, why not," I mused aloud, pulling the shirt over my head. "It's been long enough."

For a while, I sat on my couch listening to the tape from last night, skipping back and forth to the parts that I liked, trying to remember how in the hell I played it.

One of these days, I might find that secret chord David played that Leonard Cohen and Jeff Buckley were talking about, and Lord hallelujah I'd be so drunk when it happened that I'd forget it in the morning.

With a frustrated huff, I popped out the cassette, got up, put on my jacket, stuffed the cassette into my jacket pocket then grabbed my guitar. It was unwieldy without the case, hanging loosely behind my back so I tightened up the strap. As I stopped by the end table and grabbed my keys, my hand hesitated.

My mind flashed back to the murderous rage in Huck's eyes last night – it probably mirrored my own. If he confronted me on the street instead of in a bar, that fight might not have ended with the cops showing up. It might have ended with one of us in the ground.

A breaking point was near.

*I shouldn't, but… what if?*

Quickly, I opened the small drawer within it. There was a .38 caliber single action revolver tucked inside next to a box of bullets. It used to belong to my father; he made damn sure I knew how to use it.

My hand halted for a moment, then I picked it up, checked the safety, and tucked it in my belt behind my back, hiding it with my shirt and jacket.

Then I closed the drawer and opened the front door.

There was a young woman standing on my porch, looking anxious.

I knew her face immediately; she was gorgeous – absolutely stunning. She was made with mousey features and a look of perpetual innocence, undercut by a brush with sorrow. She always seemed sad, even when she wasn't. Her eyes were bright, shielded by circular wireframe glasses. The way her hair caught the sunlight told me it was probably strawberry blonde, and bright red lipstick colored her lips like Marilyn Monroe. She wore an acid washed denim jacket over a black blouse and jeans, with a deerskin purse around her shoulder.

All the beauty in her face was stricken with guilt and fear.

I stopped in the doorway as the bright white light of the sun stabbed my eyes through my sunglasses. "What are you doing here, Alita?"

"Can we talk?" she asked, biting her fingernail.

"If it's about the fight with Huck last night, then no," I responded as I pushed past her and shut my door.

She followed me down the porch to the sidewalk. "Lyric, I'm sorry!"

"There's nothing to be sorry about," I dismissed indifferently as I turned the corner up an alley by my house. "You fucked me over. Simple as that."

Alita took a few hurried steps and caught up with me. "He pried it out of me, Lyric. I didn't want to tell him."

"Then maybe you shouldn't have." My car came into view, parked in front of a standalone garage halfway down that section of the alley. It was a bright red '81 Monte Carlo that I rarely ever drove. My vision problems classified me as legally blind; I was allowed to drive during the day since I could see mostly fine, but my license was restricted after dusk.

Of course, I mused darkly, it was daylight out when I gave it that nice bit of damage to the front bumper. Shamefully, I pushed that memory away.

"You don't know what he's like when we're alone," Alita said quietly.

Suddenly, I stopped in my tracks and peered at her. Her face was pulled tightly and she was still biting her nail. The sleeve of her jacket dipped just below her wrist and I saw a touch of darkness on her skin.

Without asking, I took her by the forearm and pulled up her sleeve. Her arm was covered in bruises.

Alita yanked her arm back and grabbed the sleeve with the same hand, clutching it over her wrist. Quietly, she murmured, "He didn't mean to…."

I could feel my blood starting to simmer. "What, it was an accident?" I scoffed. "Alita, those bruises look like they were one step away from a radial fracture. That's not an accident."

She sort of dropped her hands in frustration and patted her thighs forcefully, then held her palms out to her side exasperatedly. "Well what the hell did I expect? We broke up for six hours and I fucked his friend behind his back. I probably deserved it."

"The hell you did," I spat. "Alita – you've gotta get away from him."

"And do what?" she bemoaned. "My dad fucking loves the guy. He wouldn't even believe me – he never does. He thinks I'm crazy. Half the town thinks I'm fucking crazy."

"Just tell him the truth." Then I looked at her arm. "*Show him* the truth."

Her eyes widened fearfully behind her glasses. "Donovan, do you know what my dad would *do* to him if he found out?"

"The right thing, probably. Me and your dad don't see eye to eye on most things, but I think this might be the exception."

Alita shook her head. "You don't understand. He would *kill* Huckleberry if he found out that he hit –" Her words stopped dead. Shamefully, she averted her eyes to the pavement.

For a moment, I studied her. "How long?"

She frowned meekly. "Not that long... It was just screaming and name calling for a while, but it's been... getting worse since you left the Blacktop. Like he's even more suspicious now because he can't keep tabs on you. I figured maybe if I told him the truth, then... Then maybe he'd calm down. Like maybe it was the not-knowing that was driving him insane." She glanced down at her wrist. "Turns out, knowing is worse."

Anxiously, I let out a breath. "You can't stay with him, Alita. Especially not now that he knows what happened with us." I turned away and cursed under my breath. "Fuck... I knew it was a mistake. I knew I should have turned you away, just let you sleep in your fuckin' car at the church parking lot again...." Then I looked at her and suddenly I felt guilty when I watched her face fall. "I don't think I ever could."

"We were hammered, Lyric," Alita argued. "Neither of us would have done it if we were sober."

"I don't know if that really matters anymore."

Her eyes fell shamefully to the pavement and she hugged herself tightly.

I said, "We are what we do. And what we did – what I did – it was fucked up. But Christ, Alita..." I took her arm again and pulled up her sleeve. "That doesn't mean you deserved *this*."

She let me hold her arm there for a moment, then gently pulled it back. "Can I stay with you tonight?" she asked solemnly. "I'm gonna see Huck later. I don't know how it's gonna go, but I've gotta tell him that I can't live like this. I already moved most of my stuff to my car when he left for work... I don't think I'll survive another night with him... Not like this."

Tightly, I pulled a frown and stared down the alley. I didn't want her to come over. I didn't want to see her and have to think about all the ways I fucked over Huck, I didn't want to be her shoulder to cry on, I didn't want to be her goddamn savior. I was no white knight and I sure as hell wasn't Superman.

But I said, "Okay. Go ahead and swing by after me and Jazz are done with our set at the Clawhammer tonight. I oughta be home sometime around eleven."

Her face broke out with relief and she threw her arms around me. "Thank you," she exclaimed breathlessly.

She held it like that for a minute, then I gently pushed her away. "On that note, I've got shit to do," I said, resuming my walk toward the Monte Carlo.

"What's on the docket?" Alita asked.

"Gotta go buy a new guitar case," I pointed my thumb at the guitar on my back. "At this point, I think I need a spare."

Alita sort of giggled, her mood elevating slightly. "I'm actually kind of amazed how many times you've walked out of that bar without actually putting your guitar away."

"To be fair, I was escorted out by the cops last night, so...." I half shrugged and Alita gave me a mischievous stare.

Then, when she looked at the car, her face fell. "What the hell?" she gasped.

I turned my head and saw what she saw.

My car was flat to the ground. All four tires had been slashed.

Anger and tension swelled inside of me. Alita asked aloud, "What happened?"

*Son of a bitch.*

"I guess Huckleberry stopped by."

# Chapter 4

## River Sound Dam, June 14th, 1995
## Eleven months ago

Alita's palms rested on the concrete barrier of the dam as we stood there, watching the River Sound ebb and flow. It was part of the Ohio River, bordering West Virginia, but this particular length of water had its own special name. Guess the settlers a few hundred years ago never bothered to see how long the damn thing actually was, and didn't realize it was all the same river.

The dam kissed the riverbend, and allowed intermittently a small amount – relatively speaking – of water to seep through into the reservoir for Southern Sound County. From that reservoir shot off creeks and streams and forests and seemingly-untouched habitats for the creatures of the earth to roam. The streams ran down all through the woods surrounding New Freedom and its adjacent towns, only drying up once you got toward Driftwood, where the land turned to fields of crops and farms instead of miniature rivers and creeks and forests.

Alita looked at me and I looked at her. Heart-shaped sunglasses covered her eyes. The sunlight gleamed off her hair like it was liquid, flowing and spilling over into an aura around her. You could have told me she was an angel sent there to tell me not to jump and I would've believed you.

"This is my favorite place in the world," Alita said.

"Well, the view is gorgeous," I winked behind my shades.

She sort of batted her eyes at me behind hers, then looked back out over the river. "You've really never been up here before?"

"I'm afraid of heights," I admitted as I nervously looked over the side of the dam. Trees bloomed on both sides of the river, stretching out as far as the eye could see. That stone wall kept the water at bay, corralling nature like it was something to be controlled instead of accepted.

Alita smiled and said, "You're not gonna fall."

I glanced at her again. "Maybe I am."

She blushed and became quiet. The only sounds we could hear were from the water. My eyes scanned the dam up and down; River Sound Road, the fastest way out of Sound County. Less than a mile down the road, past the dam, you hit the state line where another bridge crosses into West Virginia.

After a minute, Alita suddenly spoke.

"Oh, I have something for you." Quickly, she reached into her purse and pulled out a thin paperback novel. "Here."

"What's this?" I took it.

"*The Prophet*," Alita answered. "You said you were starting to write lyrics. This book was always my biggest inspiration when I used to write poetry. You should read it."

Bemused, I looked it over. "I'm not a big reader, but maybe I'll give it a crack." Then I looked at her. "You say 'used to' like your best years are behind you," I teased.

"Maybe they are."

"Alita, you *just* turned twenty-seven."

She half smirked and said, "What if I don't make it to twenty-eight?"

I shook my head with a grin. "Okay, Janis Joplin."

"Okay, but what *if?* Then my best years *are* really already behind me. Ever think about that?" Her ruby lips stretched into a smile and I could feel my heart throb for a second.

"Okay," I laughed, "if you don't make it to twenty-eight, then I'll write a song about you. Call it *Twenty-Seven For Life.*"

Alita laughed into her hand and peered at me. "Why does that actually sound good?"

"Because you have no taste," I smirked.

She gave me a feigned-stern look, then returned her attention to the river.

"I could stay here forever," Alita said softly. My legs wobbled as I looked over the edge.

"As nice as that sounds, I'm starting to feel like I'm *really* gonna fall over," I chided playfully. She turned and looked at me with a tight, playful frown and crossed her arms. I shrugged with a grin.

"Fine," she said, uncrossing her arms.

I smiled and said, "Come on, let's get a drink."

We turned and walked over to my bright red Monte Carlo, standing out sharply against the black and white trees gleaming from the sun. She got in the passenger side and we were on the road. After a minute, I spoke.

"So did you get things worked out with your dad? You know, with the whole living situation?" Her landlord raised her rent for the third time in as many years. Alita daylighted as a hotel maid for slave wages while she tried to get her own apprenticeship at a tattoo parlor in Hannover-Fist; neither of them were effective at paying her bills.

She's the one who put the Devil on my arm and the two black wings on my shoulders crawling down below my sleeves.

"Yup," she replied in a flat tone. "We're peachy."

Suspiciously, I cocked my eyebrow. "You sure about that?"

"Well I won't be living there, or taking anymore of his goddamn money, so I think our relationship is about to become the best it's ever been." Her voice was sour, cynical, bitter.

"You moving in with Huck?" I asked, trying not to let my inflection rise.

"No."

I'd be lying if I said a part of me wasn't relieved. "Why not?" I asked. "You've been dating for, what, like three or four years now?"

"I just... I don't want to, Lyric. I love him but sometimes I can't stand being around him." She leaned against the door and let the air hit her face as we sailed down the road. "He's so paranoid. It feels like all we do anymore is fight."

"About what?"

"Literally everything. We got into a screaming match over a pair of *shoes* yesterday."

I couldn't help but laugh. "Well that's stupid."

"Yeah, tell me about it." She sighed deeply. "And he's constantly asking me where I'm going and where I've been. It's really fucking draining."

"Why doesn't he trust you?" I asked.

"Take a shot in the dark, Lyric. I'll give you a hint – it has to do with my old 'career.'"

For a moment, I fell silent. Then I asked, "How are you gonna afford your own place? Forgive me for saying this, but I know you don't have jack shit saved up, and I don't foresee the hotel giving you much of a raise."

She shrugged in feigned carelessness. "I'll go back to clubs and street corners, I don't care. I'll make my own way."

I let the air out slowly. "Alita, you're better than that. You shouldn't put a price on your body."

"Now you sound like *him*."

"Well shit – you *really* wanna do that?" I retorted.

"No," she responded. "I hated doing it and I hated the people I did it for. Nevermind that it would prove Huck right about me – he already thinks I'm a whore."

A disquiet fell over us. Then I said, "You're not a whore."

"Yeah, well…."

I looked at her. "So where are you staying then? You can't afford a new place."

She went silent. I knew what that meant.

"Alita…."

"It isn't that bad, Lyric. I prefer it over living with people."

"You can't live in your fucking car, Alita," I replied frustratedly.

"Why not? That's what I did in Colorado."

"You have more options than that. *Better* options."

"What, my dad's house? Huck? Am I just gonna hide upstairs in the Clawhammer?"

For a moment, I didn't say anything. Then:

"You can stay with me. At least until you get enough money saved."

Alita didn't say anything for a moment, either. For a while, it was just the sound of the wind at our backs and the classic rock coming out of the radio, the sunlight gleaming off her heart-shaped sunglasses. Quietly, she said, "Maybe I wouldn't mind that."

My eyes were fixated on her for a moment. We didn't say anything else until we got back to my house. "I'll be back out in a minute," I told her as she sat in a chair on my porch.

"I'm timing you. One-one-thousand, two-one-thousand...." she grinned.

"Your beat's a little fast," I replied with an endearing smirk, then ran inside and grabbed a six pack and my guitar, dragging the amp to the door, then returned to the porch.

"Ooh, you're playing?" Alita beamed.

"A little bit." I took out my lighter and popped off the bottle caps, then handed her one of the beers. "Cheers," our bottles clinked together. Lightly, my fingers strummed across the strings of my guitar, idly wandering around, searching for a melody. Then I asked abruptly, "You really prefer living in your car over with people?"

"One-hundred percent," she replied, taking a drink. "People are judgy. People don't get me. Everybody thinks I'm crazy but all I feel like I ever do is respond to the way people treat me." She looked at me. "I mean, if half the town treated *you* like a villain, what would *you* do?"

I let out a sigh and mulled it over for a second. "I don't think people see you as a villain, Alita."

"They treat me like one."

I half shrugged. "That's karma. When you drink too much – which you do – you have a way of exploding on people. Most people don't get what they did wrong, so to them you just seem… unhinged." I took a drink and she stared at the porch shamefully, angrily. "Don't get me wrong – you're *definitely* unhinged."

Her frown broke into a begrudging laugh. "Shut up!"

I smiled at her. "For what it's worth, you've always made sense to me. I don't always agree with what you do, but I always get it. Even living in your car. It's freeing. It's the most independent you can ever be, in a way."

She didn't say anything for a while as she looked me over, sipping her beer, droplets of condensation sliding down in the heat. Then, quietly: "Thank you."

We went through a six pack and a half as the day gave way to twilight, the placid sounds of New Freedom meshing with the melodies from my guitar. After a while, she said with a sigh, "I've gotta get going. Huck's gonna be around soon and he'll lose his shit on me if he knows I'm still hanging out with you."

"What?" I asked in sharp surprise. "Why?"

She sighed frustratedly. "I don't fucking know. It's like every time we hang out without him, he thinks there's something going on. I think he thinks you have a thing for me."

Guiltily, my face flushed. "That's just...." My voice trailed off and I felt my face turning hot.

Alita looked right through me. Then, she gave me a very subtle look and said, "I'm supposed to meet him at the Clawhammer in a few; you wanna come with?"

I scoffed. "What, he's not gonna get angry?"

"He has no right to, so I don't care," she proclaimed as she stood up. For a second I hesitated, then I got up too, opened my door and tucked the guitar, the amp, and the rest of the beer inside my house.

"Let's go," I said when I came back out.

We walked down North Bethel Street a block and a half to the Clawhammer Tavern on Water Street. It was an old brick building standing three stories high with white wood trimmings and cross-framed windows. White railings led up a dozen brick steps with a brick patio, and a large awning that read: CLAWHAMMER TAVERN.

The sound of 1960s rock kissed our ears as we walked into the building. The Clawhammer was a musician's bar – even the name of the place was taken from a playing style for the banjo, one of the swear-to-god dozens of instruments Colton Rust could play. The door opened into a room featuring one pool table, with a set of stairs on the side that led to Rust's living space on the second and third floors. The pool room led back to the larger bar area. There were a few patrons seated at the wooden bar snaking along the back wall toward a single door that led to the patio out back. Alita followed me up to the bar.

The woman behind the bar gave us a smile as we sat down. She was average height, mid-thirties, medium-dark hair cut to her shoulders, with kind eyes and a kind smile, but she knew how to take care of herself. Legend had it that her husband was a Soviet expatriate, but I never knew if that was true or not.

"Oh hey," Lorraine greeted us with a slightly upward inflection. "What are you guys up to?"

Alita answered, "We were just up at the River Sound Dam, came back and had a few drinks on the porch while Lyric played a bit." She looked at me with a smile, then back to Lorraine. "It was relaxing."

My face flushed as Lorraine peered at me skeptically. "Sounds magical," she remarked with an amused look. "Whatchu drinkin', baby?"

"Silver Bullet," Alita said.

"Bulleit – neat."

"Stressful day?" Lorraine gave me an incisive look as she took out a bottle of Coors Light for Alita and a rocks glass for me.

Flustered, I muttered, "Something like that."

After a moment, our drinks were in front of us and we sat there listening to the Moody Blues on the jukebox for a while. A familiar, gremlin-looking old man sat a ways down the bar. I caught him eyeing us up, and he called out,

"How you doing, Lyric, Alita?" in his croaking, throaty, ancient voice.

"Every day, same as the last, Rick," I replied disinterestedly.

Old man Rick was a frequent face around town, but he was probably the dirtiest pervert in Southern Sound County. He would get shitfaced and start going on and on about girls he wanted to fuck, and he didn't care if they were of age or even willing. Lorraine told me all about his drunken confession to her at the Clawhammer – "She was living with me and she wouldn't put out," he told her one night, then leaned in close and said, "So when she was sleeping… I took what I fuckin' *deserved*."

I coulda killed him for that, just out of principle. But that wasn't my job. It was either God's or the Devil's, and I wasn't sure which one I should pray to for it but believe me, I was praying.

"Hi, Rick," Alita waved politely. She didn't know what I knew; most people didn't.

His eyes lit up eagerly. "How's your day going, beautiful?"

She smiled back, staying cordial but keeping a distance. "Wonderful as always." She turned her attention away before he could continue, and the two of us sat there listening to the music together.

Each second that passed, it got harder not to tell her what was on my mind. Huck would be there any minute, and as soon as he was, the dynamic would change.

It was now or never.

"Alita –" I began and her head snapped toward me. But before I could speak, another man's voice cut me off.

"Hey, good lookin'."

We both turned to see Huckleberry Singer standing there, thumbs hooked around the straps of his backpack. His hair was short and dark, and his chin was penciled in with stubble down his neck. Cracked and crooked teeth lined his smile – the trophies of years of fighting and cigarettes. Tattoos covered his arms and he stood a couple inches shorter than me, but he was built like a boxer. His light tie-dye T-shirt clinged to his sweat and he held his look at Alita as if he were posing. She beamed at him. "Hey yourself," she said.

I stood up and greeted Huck. "What's good, man?"

He clicked his tongue and let out a breath. "Not shit, brother. I gotta get off this fucking bike," he laughed, wiping sweat from his brow. "Shit's gonna kill me in this heat."

I laughed too and said, "How long till your car's back on the road?"

Huck shrugged and replied, "Don't really fuckin' matter till I get my license back, does it?" We chuckled and he added, "Fuckin' daddy government reaching its hand into your pocket like, 'oh, what's this? Money? I'll take that, thank you very much. Only two thousand more dollars until we give you your shit back.'" He chortled with a touch of cynicism as he sat on the other side of Alita. "Fuckin' two thousand dollars in child support, give me a fucking break," he laughed bitterly. "Kid don't cost *that* fuckin' much."

*Like you would even know*, I thought to myself. Instantly, I felt guilty for that. Maybe his kid's mom really was taking him for a ride, maybe that two-weekends-a-month custody he had was overly punitive. What the hell did I know?

So I didn't say that. Instead, I said, "That's Big Brother, for you. Keeps us on the grind while they're all up there, sitting pretty and fine."

"Write that one down," Alita grinned.

Huck teased her: "What, you gonna sing it? You finally learn how to carry a tune?" Lorraine laughed to herself as she set a pint down in front of him.

Alita laughed playfully and said, "Shut up! I'm not that bad."

Me and Huck simultaneously wavered our hands and went, "Ehhhh."

Alita crossed her arms and huffed, trying not to smile. "I hate both of you."

I grinned at her and said, "No you don't." She returned the look and I think we must have held it for too long because Huck took a drink, then asked:

"So what'd you guys get up to today?" He held the glass in front of his face, taking a sip as he spoke. Most people don't realize it, but that's something we do to hide ourselves. When we lie, when we don't want our emotions to be seen, when we need to keep ourselves from oversharing. The look in his eyes screamed suspicion.

"Went up to the dam," Alita answered plainly. "It was so pretty. The way the sunlight dances off the water and all of the trees, like leaves glistening in burning rain." Her voice trailed off as she waxed poetic.

Awkwardly, I turned my attention forward so I wouldn't look at Huck. He said, "Oh yeah?" But his voice rose sharply. "Sounds romantic." He let out an uneasy laugh.

"Oh, don't start," Alita grumbled.

"What?" Huck recoiled innocently. "I'm not starting anything, babe. I'm just saying that sounded really nice; I wish I could have been there to see it with you." He reached out and gently grabbed her hand, caressing her fingers with his.

Desperate to change the topic, I leaned in and asked Huck, "What were you getting into?"

He half shrugged and said, "Had to sell a few things."

I raised my brow. "You didn't pawn any of your guitars, did you?"

Huck let out a laugh and said, "No – more of the *herbal* wares, if you catch my drift."

I grinned and replied, "The best kind of wares."

But Alita grunted almost involuntarily. Huck looked at her dumbly and asked, "What?"

"Nothing."

He glanced at me; I could have told him what the problem was, but that wasn't my business and I wasn't gonna change that. So Huck asked her, "Babe, are you mad?"

She chewed her lip for a second, then said, "No, I'm not *mad*. I'm just confused."

"Why?"

"Because you said you wished you could have spent the day at the river with me, that it sounded romantic. I invited you, you said no. You said you had work to do today and you couldn't make it until later. By 'work' I assumed you meant – oh, I don't know – your *job* at the Blacktop. You left out the part where the 'work' you had to do was sell fucking weed."

Huck scoffed and rubbed his chin. He picked his words carefully. "It's money, Alita. It's work. It *is* a job. I know you don't *get* that because your daddy helps you out with everything, but I don't have that luxury."

Alita turned on him swiftly. "Did you just call selling grass a *job?*"

Huck's face fell and I swallowed my bourbon in one swig, then flagged Lorraine down for another. Huck stammered at first, then he said, "I need income – and income is income, just ask the IRS. I wanted to go with you – I really did. But sometimes there are more important things." He took another drink and said, venom creeping through his words, "Besides – you oughta know a thing or two about *making money on the side*."

"Oh, go *fuck* yourself!" she yelled loudly, then downed her entire bottle. Something switched in her. Most people couldn't read Alita to save their lives. She was obtuse, complicated, outspoken, and probably fucking crazy. But people said I was crazy, too, and she made sense to me.

I knew where this was going.

"Excuse me?" Huck recoiled angrily.

"What's my favorite place, Huck? I've told you a thousand times. Do you know what it is?"

Huck scoffed again. He went quiet. "This is ridiculous."

*Dude, come on. It's the dam. That's why we went there. Her second favorite spot is the watering hole. How do you not know this?*

Then she said, "The River Sound Dam – go fucking figure, right?" Another moment went by. "I bet you Lyric would have been able to answer that question."

There was a tense calm before Huck finally said, "You know what? Go back to the fuckin' street corner, then. Surprised *that* ain't your favorite fuckin' place in the world." The backdoor opened and Huck's footsteps carried him inside.

Then all was silent save for the sound of quiet crying.

I thought about going back in and consoling her, but I figured that would just make it worse.

My feet resumed walking as I wrestled with the complicated nuances of guilt and love. At a certain point, it's hard to tell if you're poisoning the well or purifying it.

When I got home, I picked up where I left off, playing and drinking on the porch. I must have sat there for hours.

By the time eleven o'clock rolled around, my feet were heavy with liquor and beer and my fingers couldn't find the melody anymore. Just as I stood up to go back inside, I saw the silhouette of a woman walking briskly toward my porch.

It was Alita.

"Hey," I began in surprise, trying to sober up. Her eyes were bloodshot; she was crying. "Are you okay?"

"Can I stay here tonight?" her voice wavered. "Me and Huck just broke up. I know what I said about people, but I don't want to be alone tonight."

For a moment, I froze. My heart pounded rapidly. A glimpse of the future flashed across my mind: I knew what would happen if I said yes. In sobriety, maybe I could have put aside what I wanted and spared myself from the consequences; but when I saw her standing there with her heart on fire like that and tears in her eyes, all I could say was:

"Yes."

# Chapter 5

## New Freedom, May 17th, 1996 12:45 PM

"You sure you'll be okay until later?" I asked Alita as I walked her back to her car parked up the street. She was more shaken by the act of vandalism than I was.

"Yeah..." she breathed, hugging herself tightly. "I just... I need to find a way to tell him I'm done. Without him deciding to change my mind."

"Well if he tries –" I began, but she cut me off.

"My dad's the sheriff, I know, I know. But my dad thinks he's just the shit. Swear to God, he still gets lunch at the Blacktop every Friday just because he knows Huck will be there." Her eyes fell. For a moment, I hesitated. Then I put my arm around her shoulder. "I don't know what my dad would do if he found out, or if Huck *really* hurt me."

I peered through her round glasses and said, "I wasn't talking about the sheriff."

Her head perked up at me. A glimmer of a smile flashed across her face then disappeared. "This isn't the wild west, Lyric. You can't round up a posse and run him out of town."

"Nah, no posse. Just me," I replied as we reached her car. "Hey –" we stopped and she looked at me. Gently, I touched her arm. "You're safe now, okay? I'll take care of you."

She hesitated, then wrapped her arms around me in a hug. "Thank you."

We held it for a moment before releasing each other. "Come by around eleven."

"Will do."

I didn't wait for her to take off before I started down the sidewalk again. Her car rolled past me and she waved, but I didn't return it. There was nothing to be happy about with that shitstorm. I did Huck dirty and so did she, but the man's response was abject failure.

*He grabbed her hard enough to bruise.*

It was almost baffling; I had known Huck Singer for nearly six years, ever since I started hanging out in the bars around New Freedom. He was the reason I started taking music seriously – his voice was average, but the man could play. Then I thought back to that pleading, desperate look he struck right before I heard him screaming at Alita outside the bar.

*How much of Huck Singer is just a facade?*

In a matter of moments, my feet had carried me to the Clawhammer. I stepped into the sparsely populated building that reeked of smoke and tried to put my mind off of Alita and Huck, with my thumb hooked through the strap of my guitar.

Rust stepped down the stairs immediately at the side of the entrance in the pool room. "Hey there, Lyric," he said. His voice had a rattle in it and he spoke with the hint of a southern drawl. A tall man in his early forties, his appearance was perpetually haggard. Dark and unkempt hair draped past his shoulders and a long beard hung from his face. Rust glanced at his watch. "Little early for *you*, innit?"

I shrugged. "Was gonna go get a spare guitar case but some asshole slashed my tires."

Rust raised an eyebrow. "Any idea who it might be?"

I returned the look. "I think you know about as well as I do."

He frowned and nodded sympathetically. "About what I figured. You're a smart guy – you just gotta start staying one step ahead."

"Yeah, well... Lotta good being smart's done me. It's my own damn fault, anyway."

Rust studied me and gathered his thoughts for a moment. "Yeah, figures... In my experience, most people want to be good – we just stumble a lot, and don't know how. Lord knows I've done my fair share of wicked deeds. I suspect ol' Huckleberry's a lot the same way. That's why you gotta give people an example to look at if you ever want them to change. 'Rising above,' I think's what they call that."

"Sounds real simple, Rust," I replied sardonically. "Lemme get right on that. Pretty sure this is what you'd call *fucked up beyond repair*."

Rust gave me a knowing look while he chose his next words. "Could be. Maybe a storm's 'bout to break. Maybe you already done crossed a threshold, and ain't no turnin' back. But you're still in control of *you*. Just face the music when it gets here and I think you'll do alright."

I let out an anxious sigh. "Much as I love music, I don't think it's that simple."

"Sure it is," he replied plainly. "Nobody ever wants to face the music, but sooner or later we all got to. Trick is, when your karma's coming back around, when the music is here... Don't run from it. Just pick up your guitar and step into the sound."

He gave me a slight wink and a nod, patted me on the shoulder, then walked out through the door. For all the years I had known him, I still couldn't figure him out.

When I walked up to the bar, Lorraine was grinning mischievously.

"You have a good night up at the Sheriff's Department?" she asked.

I rolled my eyes. "They only kept me there for a couple of hours – they threw me in the fucking drunk tank for an assault charge. Tell me how that doesn't scream 'personal vendetta.'"

Lorraine shook her head and laughed. "Well, Jed probably heard you hooked up with his daughter. Given the way word around town tends to go about you, I can see why he might not be too keen on that. You're kind of a scoundrel."

"Scoundrel? Give me a fucking break," I breathed as I sat down at the bar and removed my guitar from my back. I laid it down gently across the bartop. "Huck's been with more soul-searching floozies and aimless drunk women than anybody else in this town. If anything, Swanson ought to be more concerned about *him*."

"Yeah, but Huck's a hell of a lot better at lying about it than you are," Lorraine chuckled as she set down a glass of bourbon and a bottle of beer in front of me.

Bitterly, I took a swig of corn liquor and chased it with the beer. "I'm just too goddamn pretty for this town."

Lorraine busted out laughing as she polished a glass. "You sure about that?"

I grinned. "A man can dream." I took another drink and let it settle in my stomach, then asked, "Oh, hey – you didn't happen to see my guitar case lying around here anywhere, did you?"

Lorraine raised her eyebrows and pursed her lips, like holding back amusement, with a face that told me I wasn't gonna like what she had to say.

"What?" I asked.

"Pretty sure Huck took it out to the dumpster last night. Trash came and got it this morning."

I coughed on my whiskey. "What? Are you fucking kidding me? Nobody stopped him?"

Lorraine laughed and said, "What, you mean after everyone watched him throw you across the bar? Yeah, believe it or not, nobody wanted to die on that hill."

"Give me a fucking break," I repeated under my breath. A girl down at the end of the bar caught my attention. She had deep red hair, dyed that way, and makeup plastered over her face. "Oh, God dammit," I mumbled.

She called out with a wicked smile, "Hey, Lyric!"

I tried to smile back and carelessly waved, "Hey, Misty."

She got up and strode toward me, kind of stumbling a bit, already half-way hammered in the middle of the afternoon – but I guess I shouldn't judge; far be it for me to call the kettle black. "Well fancy seein' *you* here," she grinned.

"Yup," I replied without paying her much mind. "Small town."

She giggled exaggeratedly and leaned onto the bar beside me. "Amen to that, handsome. Whatchu got goin' on today? You gonna sit up here and drink it away with me?"

Lorraine raised her eyebrows as she tried to hide a grin. I shot her a look that begged *please kill me* and she mouthed the word *scoundrel* slowly.

"Not the day" I replied casually. "I've got some errands to run, things to do, you know."

"What about the night?" Misty asked coyly.

"No can do, Miss," I said simply. "Gotta date with Jazz and the lady music tonight."

Misty's face changed and she gave me a sharply pissed off look, then scoffed. "Oh, so I'm good enough to fuck but not to spend some goddamn time with?"

I choked on my whiskey and coughed into my hand. Then I looked at her. "Misty, it was one time."

"Oh, fuck *you*, Lyric!" she shouted. "It was twice!"

I made a puzzled look and furrowed my brow as I tried to think back. "Oh yeah."

Misty scoffed again and said, "You're a real fucking asshole sometimes, you know that?"

"Misty, the last time we hooked up, you remember what happened the next day?"

She recoiled defensively. Then she deflected with, "You never called."

"No," I responded, " – well, okay, that too – but *after* I didn't call you? And we ran into each other here?"

She went quiet and crossed her arms. "No."

"Okay, lemme remind you – you stood out in the parking lot *screaming* at me for ten minutes, because, and I quote –" I mimicked her voice. "'You barely even said 'hi' to me!'" Misty frowned and furrowed her eyebrows. Then I said, "Despite the fact that we sat at the same table out back for like *twenty minutes*, you were just so drunk that your short-term memory went out the fuckin' window. Ring any bells?"

She huffed furiously. "You remember what *you* said to *me* the night we made love the first time?"

"Please don't call it that."

"You said – and *I* quote – 'don't ever be afraid to use your voice. There's power in that.' Remember *that*, asshole?"

"Sounds like me, but I can't say I do – we were drunker than hell, Misty."

She pointed a finger at me accusatorily and shrieked, "Well I'm using my voice *now!*"

Painfully, I covered my ears. "I didn't mean for you to take it so goddamn literally!"

She huffed again as she stared at me for a second, then grabbed my glass of whiskey and finished for me, before slamming the glass back down on the bar. "Go fuck yourself, Lyric. 'Cause I sure won't be doing it."

"Glad we're on the same page," I muttered as she stomped away, back to her seat.

Lorraine came over laughing. "You really do know how to pick 'em, Lyric."

"Don't remind me," I groaned. "I'll take another one. Put her next drink on my tab, too."

"What for?"

"Penance."

She laughed with a tight grin and went to grab my drink.

Then the door opened and I turned around. Carl walked in, wearing his normal attire with a red bowtie so I could see him better. Red wasn't good; any time he wore red, it meant he needed to talk to me.

Alongside him was another friend of ours, William Coors. He was forty, just a couple years older than Carl, and had long, wild, light hair pulled back in a ponytail and an equally wild beard. Even without being able to see color, I could tell his beard was streaked with gray. Will was something of a womanizer; it was like his ultimate goal in life was to sleep with as many women as possible after his divorce. The problem was the women he chose ended up being a sacrifice of quantity over quality – strippers, women too drunk to know what they want, wives, girlfriends of friends. One of these days, he was gonna get burned.

They were both laughing and carrying on when they walked in.

With a friendly grin, my mood shifted and I got up from my barstool to greet them both. "What's up, Will? Carl." I shook both of their hands.

Will spoke first. He talked with a calculated drawl and moved with almost meticulous body language, crossing his arms first then gesturing pointedly as he spoke. "You look better than I pictured. I half expected you to be missing a few teeth after what happened last night."

"Word travels fast," I exhaled.

Carl put his hand on my shoulder and said, "It's a small town, Lyric. Someone starts throwing guitars and bodies around the bar, it's gonna get talked about." Then he produced a few stapled sheets of paper from a manilla envelope.

"What's this?" I took it.

"Your plea agreement," Carl replied. "No contest to assault, then they'll drop the disorderly conduct charge. I got the DA to agree to a fine and a restraining order – the fines won't be finalized until after your arraignment Monday."

"A *restraining* order?!" I bleated. "You've gotta be fucking kidding me!"

"Well, you fucked the guy's girlfriend and then jumped into a fight with him. Given who his girlfriend is, I'd say you're lucky all it is is a restraining order. Just sign this and Jed will serve you later."

Angrily, I stared at the legal paper. "Christ, thank God I don't *work* with him anymore. It'd be a real pain in the ass to expedite the line five hundred feet away from the kitchen."

"I'm sensing some resistance here," Carl raised his eyebrow and waved the paper.

Bitterly, I grumbled and spat, "Go ahead, do it. A restraining order doesn't matter if I don't wanna be around him in the first fuckin' place"

I turned around and sat back down at the bar, grabbing my guitar and propping it under the bar next to my stool. Carl and Will sat on either side of me. In a flash, Lorraine had a pint of beer in front of Will and a Red Bull and vodka in front of Carl.

I gave him a glance. "Aren't you working?"

"I'm on lunch," he replied as he knocked back half the glass in one gulp. He smacked his lips and went, "*Ahhh.*"

Me, Will and Lorraine laughed. Will said, "This is actually Carl's secret to being such a good attorney. He's just half way plastered all the time."

Lorraine laughed and said as she walked away, "Half way?"

Will smirked and said, "Dealing with Lyric and Huck's shit? Can't say I blame him." Then he looked at me. "I consider you both to be friends of mine – you obviously more so than him, but I will say that he and I didn't see eye to eye for a while."

Curiously, I asked, "Why's that? Cause you're a foot and a half taller than him?"

Will laughed but it was quickly replaced by a sense of unease. "No, not in the literal sense. A woman I dated a few years ago happened to be an ex of his from a long time ago, and she told me he was an abusive piece of shit. Used to scream at her and get physical, just turning into a raging psychopath until she left him." Will took a long drink. "Allegedly."

Anxiously, mixed with anger, I balled my fist and dug my nails into my own palm. "That sounds about right."

Will then said, "When I moved up here, he made it out like he had changed, but given the ongoing drama between you two, it doesn't seem to be the case."

Carl frowned tightly and finished the rest of the glass. "I'll do another one, Lorraine."

"You want it now or you want me to wait till you're done taking a shit?" she smirked as she came back toward us.

Carl sort of grinned. "How'd you know?"

Lorraine laughed out loud and said, "We've been doing this dance for a *looong* time, Carl."

With a hearty laugh, Carl rose to his feet and wandered off toward the bathroom. Then Lorraine sauntered down the bar to check on Misty and the few other guests. Will glanced at me.

"I'm digging the *Superman* T-shirt, by the way. Good to see a bit of color in your wardrobe, even if it's only red."

"It's the only color I see, so I'd say it's perfect."

"Fair point," he mused. "You hear they're making a new set of *Star Wars* movies? That oughta be something spectacular."

Will was one of the few people in town with the same penchant for nerdy shit as me. "Idunno," I replied. "I feel like they wrapped it up pretty neatly at the end of *Jedi*. I mean, who really cares what Darth Vader's backstory is if we know how it ends?"

"True, true," he tilted his head. "Either way, you can't complain about a new trilogy of lightsaber duels and space battles."

"I guess we'll see about that."

For a moment, me and Will were silent. Then he touched his face and let out a long breath.

I sized him up for a second. "Something on your mind?"

"Yeah, just... Some shit," he said, almost dismissively as he looked down at his pint glass. His fingers idly danced around the condensation forming on the glass.

"Care to be more specific?"

Will let out another sigh. "It's Red. I ran into him on the way here and he was going off about some crazy shit."

Instantly, my curiosity piqued and so did my anxiety. I knew Red and Layla Sutherland had been going through a rough spot lately, and Red... He was the kind of man who was inclined toward dramatic action. To him, everything was black and white – either you're with him, or you're not. You're either in the tribe, or you're the other. He never treated people like the "other," but he was old-world like me – doubly more so, actually. Red cared about everybody on some level, but deep down the only things that truly mattered to him were his wife and their son. He was either six or seven – I was half drunk every time Red brought him up, but there was nothing that man was more passionate about than his family.

Guiltily, I swallowed every drop of beer in the bottle, then waved down Lorraine and she got me another one faster than the last.

The moment she was gone, Will spoke again. "He started accusing me of insane shit, like trying to fuck Layla."

My eyes widened. "Oh, shit – did you?"

79

Will grunted and said, "No, of course I didn't. But he said she told him about all the guys she's hooked up with behind his back. Made me think of what you told me."

The bourbon disappeared from my glass in one swig. It hurt my stomach so I took another drink of beer. "As far as I know, I didn't have sex with her, so there isn't anything to worry about. That was the night that –"

"It's all good, man," Will dismissed casually. "You don't need to tell me the story again. I just figured I'd give you a heads up in case Layla tried to make up some shit or blow things out of proportion just to piss him off."

Glumly, I took another drink from the bottle. "Thanks for the warning."

We were quiet for a moment, then Carl came back from the bathroom. He sat down with an exaggerated *"Whew!"*

"Everything come out okay?" I asked, attempting to forget what Will had told me.

"Rust's probably gonna need a plumber," Carl laughed.

Will grinned broadly and said, "Hold on, I think I know one." Then he turned to look at Lorraine down at the other end of the bar. "Hey, Lorraine!" Her head snapped toward us. "Toilet's clogged!"

Her hands dropped to her sides and she gave Carl a look. "Seriously, Carl?"

Carl busted out laughing and said, "No, the toilet's fine. Idunno what the hell you put in this drink but it's shooting right the fuck through me."

I interjected, "That would be Red Bull and vodka, sir."

We all laughed and, for a moment, I forgot about my troubles. We just listened to the soothing sounds of the sixties and laughed the hour away. Then Carl checked his watch and said, "Welp, back to the ol' grind for me." He slid the DA's plea agreement down the bar and withdrew a pen, clicking it out and brandishing it toward me. "Can I get your signature, rockstar?"

"What can I say?" I mused cynically, taking the pen and signing my name. "I do it for the fans."

Carl smirked and stuck the paper back in its manilla folder. "Good doing business with you, sir."

"I swear to God, half of my disposable income goes right into your fucking bank account, Carl."

He stood up and grabbed my shoulder. "We call that 'karma,' Donovan."

Will then said, "We also call that 'don't stick your dick in crazy.'"

"Like you're one to talk," I rejoined. "You're a textbook sex addict."

Will recoiled a bit. "I wouldn't call myself a *sex addict*."

I raised my eyebrow. "You remember Dina?"

"Christ, don't remind me," Will exhaled humorously.

"That girl invited you and her ex to the same bar on the same fuckin' night," I laughed. "Just to pit you two against each other. And you *still* kept hooking up with her for months afterward. She got off on watching you guys fucking *scream* at each other more than she ever got off on your dick, Will."

"Well, I don't know about *that*," Will smirked proudly. "But suffice it to say, I am a veritable expert on why one should not stick their dick in crazy."

We all laughed and Carl said, "That you are, buddy; that you are." Then he waved at Lorraine and said, "*Au revoir!*"

"See ya, baby." The way she said *baby* was never sexual or flirtatious. It always reminded me of someone's grandma from Tennessee.

Quickly, I pulled out my wallet and set cash down on the bar. "I'm gonna walk out with you, actually."

Will stood up and shook both of our hands. "You outta here?"

"Yeah, I've gotta get through the rest of my day before I can start *really* drinking," I replied as I slung my guitar over my shoulder.

Will chuckled and asked, "You and Jazz playing again tonight? Maybe a full set instead of a violent intermission in the middle?"

"'Violent intermission,'" I echoed. "I like that. Yeah, God willing."

"Cool, I'll try to make it." Will's eyes shot over to the drunk looking redhead sitting at the end of the bar. "In the meantime, I think I'll go see how lovely the little mermaid is doing over there."

I glanced over to Misty, who was taking shooters like her life depended on it. She glanced back and raised her middle finger at me. Then I said to Will, "Trust me – bad idea."

Will raised an eyebrow. "She as crazy as she looks?"

"Crazier," I replied.

Will sort of grinned and stroked his beard. "Perhaps I spoke too soon about not putting one's dick in crazy, then."

My eyes rolled into the back of my head. "One of these days, you're gonna get burned."

He just grinned. "We'll see about that."

Lorraine called out to me and Carl: "Have a good day, you two."

Then I turned and smiled. "Don't worry – I'll be back with the sunset."

With that, me and Carl walked through the pool room and out the door. He and I lit cigarettes simultaneously as we stepped out into the bright daylight, painting New Freedom as a glowing field of white. "Christ, it's fucking bright out here."

Carl looked at me and said, "When *isn't* it?"

"Fair."

We headed down the steps and Carl got into his old Volkswagen sedan. "Need a lift anywhere?" he asked. I had told him about how Huck slashed my tires. He said he couldn't do anything about it except tell me to call my insurance provider.

"Nah," I breathed. "Think I'm gonna go for a walk down the trail. I should be fine without my car for a few days – I don't really have shit to do, I just know if I sit in there all day I'm not gonna be able to play tonight."

"Ah," Carl clicked his tongue. "Yeah, I wouldn't recommend pissing off Jazz."

"I've already disappointed her enough, I think. Last thing I wanna do is break her heart." My eyes averted away from Carl's, like I suddenly realized I was broadcasting the way I felt.

Carl gave me a knowing look and said, "Well, then I'd recommend maybe cutting back the shit. You know she doesn't like it when you drink. And she doesn't date addicts."

I scoffed. "Wagon, off the wagon, an addict's an addict. She knows me too well – I don't stand a chance in hell with that one."

Carl grinned and said, "Maybe in another life."

Then he got into his car and drove off.

His words rattled around as I walked back to my house to drop off my guitar. *Christ, I hope we don't have to come back and relive this shit again.*

As I walked down Water Street and hit the intersection at Garden, I suddenly stopped. You could see the Blacktop Grille from there, with its neon sign illuminated even in the daytime.

It was Friday.

Huck worked Fridays.

It might have been the bourbon or it might have been the memories, I'm not sure which. But fury began to boil inside me again. It had been over a month since I worked there, over a month since I'd gone there at all. Jazz, Huck and I all worked there together once upon a time.

*How about one for old time's sake?*

# Chapter 6

## The Blacktop Grille, March 4th, 1996
## About a Month and a Half ago

"Huck, I need fries down," I called in the kitchen. "Three fries all day."

"You got it, brother," Huck's voice came from the other side of the line. It was a long, bright room, hotter than Hell. Flames shot up from the grill and grease jumped out of the fryer. Huck opened the freezer next to the fryers and pulled out a large bag of frozen french fries. The oil screamed as they plummeted in. "Mother *fuck!*" Huck cried out, flicking his hand to fling off the hot oil.

I peered at him through the window with an amused smirk. "Looks like they're trying to escape." Guilt undercut everything I said to him; It had been months since what happened with Alita happened, and he still didn't know.

She and him had reconciled the very next day.

It was like they had never even broken up, but what happened with us still happened.

Huck turned around with a grin stretched out over his stress-beaten face, carved with worry lines from years of poverty. That was something I related to. We had both grown up poor. In a way, it was endearing.

"Fuck 'em," he replied, still grinning. "I hope they feel pain."

We both laughed and the other cook, Hyde, came walking down the line. "I'm ready to go on that salmon if you wanna put up the burger." Hyde was shorter, always wore a baseball cap and had both of his ears pierced. One time he told me it was so nobody could crack a joke about it being the "gay ear," and Huck said back, "Pretty sure with you, they're both the gay ear."

Once upon a time, we had a fun gig there.

Huck turned over the burger, didn't press it down so it wouldn't lose its flavor, and put it up in the window. I glanced over it for a second and checked the handwritten ticket CJ had given me. "Huck... I need bacon on that bacon cheeseburger." A bit of annoyance leaked through my voice. I'd gotten so used to saying that phrase that it became a running joke between me and Hyde. Huck's nickname at the Clawhammer was an endearing "Fuck-you Huck," both for his crass attitude toward society and occasionally caustic spats with drunkards who didn't know any better. His nickname at the Blacktop between me and Hyde was "can-I-get-bacon-on-that-bacon-cheeseburger Huck."

Didn't quite roll off the tongue so well, but nobody's ever accused me of being a poet before.

"Shit, my bad." Huck corrected the mistake quickly, but Hyde still made a remark.

"Quit dickin' around and you won't miss shit like that."

Huck clicked his tongue and said, "Fuckin' fryer oil jumped out at me, sorta threw everything off for a minute." He grinned but there was an underlying extra emotion to it, like a creeping fear of being seen as weak or incompetent, and a desperate need for that not to be the case.

"Uh huh," Hyde replied, not turning his head as he pulled a salmon filet out of the six foot tall broiler.

Huck's face fell slowly and I thought back to the screaming match he'd had with Alita after we went to the dam, how he had acted so cool about it while subtly giving her the third degree, then erupting when he thought nobody could hear. That devil-may-care attitude went out the window as soon as nobody was watching. *What's really going on in your head?*

In a moment, both of the items were plated up and I turned my head down the line to call out the entryway to the bar: "CJ! Pick up!"

A minute went by and nobody came back to get the food. With a grumble, I grabbed both plates. Huck made an amused comment: "Make sure you let him know he's gotta tip you out now."

With a grin, I took the food out to the restaurant, but I could never shake the odd feeling of knowing there was an underlying resentment toward me, yet he would never address it. My grin vanished as I stepped out to the floor.

Maybe the resentment went both ways.

It wasn't a huge place – bigger than the Clawhammer, but not by a hell of a lot. It was top of the class as far as atmosphere and ambience, though. The lighting was tastefully low, with neon beer signs and sports memorabilia hanging everywhere. There were a handful of tables on one side of the restaurant, then a big horseshoe-shaped bar made of black marble back against the wall in between the front door and the patio door on the side. It was only five in the afternoon on a weekday and the place was already half full.

Wearing the black button down and slacks uniform of the place, Jazz walked by me with a mischievous smile as I stepped out of the kitchen with the plates, her dreadlocks held up in a bun with a headwrap. "You the food runner now?" she grinned.

"For you? Always," I winked behind my sunglasses. Jazz shook her head and smiled to herself as she walked to a table and greeted them. Then I spotted Will and Red at the bar. Eagerly, they waved me over.

"There he is," Red greeted as I set the burger down in front of him. He was a big guy, early forties, dark hair buzzed military style and a thick beard with a gray chin. His skin had a tone like he was half or a quarter Native American. He wore dark red flannel almost all the time; it helped him stand out to me. He stood up and we grabbed each other's hand and patted one another on the back with the other.

"Shoulda known it was you two," I said as I shook Will's hand. "You order the same damn thing every time."

"Best burger in town," Red grinned as he sat down.

"Practically the only burger in town," I rejoined. "Ever since Huck jumped ship from the Clawhammer – Rust *still* hasn't replaced him. Steep competition, right?"

They both chuckled, then the bartender sauntered over. "Thanks, Lyric," he said, keeping an eye on the Cleveland Indians' pre-season baseball game playing on one of the TVs mounted above the bar.

"No problem, CJ," I replied, glancing at the game. CJ was built like fucking Hercules. He had short dark hair and a pleasant demeanor. For being strong enough to crush most people, I'd never even seen him give a man a cross look. Most he ever got was annoyed. He moonlighted as a college student breaking into the medical field. He didn't want to be a rich doctor or a profiteer, though. He wanted to work with people, with patients, because he knew he could help them.

Young as he was, he was a good man.

CJ grinned up at the TV and thought aloud, "Man, they're gonna kill it this season."

"Yup, and we'll be right here, watching from afar," I responded.

He kind of sighed and said nonchalantly, "Just a couple of guys workin' at a bar." Then he looked at a check lying on the bar at an empty seat. "'Oh, don't worry man, I'm a great tipper,'" he said in a mocking voice as he rolled his eyes.

"What, he stiff you?" I asked.

"May as well have – left me a dollar on a thirty dollar tab."

"Damn, ouch."

CJ balled up the check and threw it away. "Like, it's one thing if you're gonna leave a shitty tip, but don't pull that whole 'sorry I'm a pain in the ass, but I tip well' thing. I hate it."

"Right?" I said, then added: "Plus, even if you *do* tip well, that doesn't mean you get to be a pain in the ass. I'm not a whore; you don't get to spit in my mouth just because you paid me."

CJ busted out laughing. "I needed that." Then he glanced at Red and Will, who gave us strange looks as they chuckled through bites of food, and said, "Sorry, sometimes we get a little retarded here at the Blacktop."

I grinned at Red and Will, "You guys enjoy. I'll be at the tavern when I get off if you're around."

"More than likely," Red replied with a sigh. "Layla is acting like a fucking crazy person again, so I'm not trying to go home any time soon."

Guiltily, I winced.

"Just... Keep your head up, man," I patted him on the shoulder. "It'll either get better or it'll be over. Either way, this is gonna pass, too."

Red nodded solemnly, then said, "Thank you, brother," as Will nonchalantly dug into his salmon.

"Damn, fliss is ghood," he spoke through bites. Red laughed with a bit of disgust on his face, then I turned around.

Immediately, I was startled.

"Jesus *Christ!*" I exclaimed. A girl was standing there grinning at me. "Fucking announce yourself next time, you sneaky little fuck."

The hostess held her grin and said, "Lyric, I'm hungry."

I rolled my eyes and replied, "Should have eaten at school, then."

"I'm a senior – I don't stay the whole day," Makenna complained. She was seventeen with long, straight hair that caught the light almost perfectly medium – if I had to guess, I would say her hair was brown. Her eyes looked almost white to me, meaning they must have been blue. She was one of the brightest people I'd ever met. She used to do math for fun when she started at the Blacktop – a straight-A student who earned the honor roll every time.

But that isn't what made her smart. She could read people.

She almost always picked up the same stuff about people that I did – little moments where somebody does something vaguely odd or says something stupid and it sort of flies by most people, but she would always give me a glance and try not to grin.

She was still young and naive, though; tomorrow was her eighteenth birthday, and when it hit her, things were gonna change rapidly. The world would try to break her if she let it, so you gotta let it know you'll break it first.

And there was always somebody looking for the next beautiful young woman to exploit.

"You couldn't figure out how to make lunch yourself?"

"I was busy!" she whined.

"Parents couldn't feed you? I can do this all day, kid."

She frowned with the corner of her mouth. "Well my dad pulled one of his famous disappearing acts, and my mom is mad at *me* for it for some reason, so...." Suddenly, I felt guilty. "Can you get me some fries?"

"You're not fifteen anymore," I replied with a frustrated sigh. "You can get them yourself."

She glanced toward the open way into the kitchen apprehensively. "They scare me back there."

"Didn't you spend like a year as an EMT?" I asked. "How are *line cooks* the thing that scares you? You used to treat literal gunshot wounds."

"I only did that for college credits! It's not like I did it for fun!" She glanced toward the kitchen again. "Those guys are scarier than dying people."

"Bullshit – you've talked to Huck tons of times."

"Hyde scares me!"

"So don't make eye contact – his vision is based on movement, I hear."

Her face fell and she gave me an exaggerated pouting look. "Please?"

It worked every time.

I grumbled and rolled my eyes behind my sunglasses again. "Give me a few minutes. I'll have Huck drop another side for you."

Makenna clasped her hands together and grinned. "This is why you're my favorite."

"Goddamn better be," I grumbled to myself irritatedly as I started back toward the kitchen.

"Hey!" Makenna yelled after me. I stopped and turned around. "Also…" she held out her palm expectantly. "You have a new tape?"

Quickly, I fished into my jeans pocket and pulled out my cassette tape from the previous night's practice session. I was seven months sober and my playing had improved significantly, but I still didn't think I was anywhere close to where I wanted to be yet. "Here. It's not exactly my best work, but listen to your heart's content." I handed her the cassette and she took it eagerly.

"When are you gonna do an album?" she asked.

"Never," I replied as I resumed walking.

"Haven't you written like nine songs? Just put them on one tape and send them to someone."

"Don't care, still not doing it."

"Well Hope also thinks you have to."

"Oh, well in that case – I still don't care." Then I stopped again and turned around. "Speaking of – where is she, anyway? I thought she worked today."

Makenna's face suddenly became written with guilt. "She lost a couple shifts."

"What?" I exclaimed. "Why?"

The girl grabbed her arm in a self-comforting gesture and replied, "Her parents found out that we had liquor at prom last weekend. They called in and asked Rachel to have her taken off the schedule for a while so they can *ground* her ground her." Rachel was our boss.

CJ called out from the bar, "See – I told you this place is just too damn fun." She looked back at him with a grin, but my face was donning a look of concern.

"You weren't drinking, were you?"

Makenna turned back toward me and shook her head no. "I mean, I did a little when we got back, but I was the DD so I didn't drink anything at prom."

I sighed through my nostrils with a modicum of relief. "Good. You're smarter than that – smarter than most of this town. Don't ruin your shot at M.I.T. or Boston for pointless memories you're not even gonna remember. Trust me on that one."

Makenna smiled wryly, then said, "I told her it was a bad idea."

Then I glanced back at the kitchen – I'd been on the floor way too long. But before I resumed walking, I asked, "How the hell did you two even get your hands on liquor in the first place?"

Makenna's face tightened and she looked at me with a conflicted expression. "I shouldn't answer that."

I looked at her sharply, suddenly suspicious. "Makenna, who bought you liquor?"

She kind of huffed. "It isn't even that big a deal – I told her we probably shouldn't, but he said he would get it for us and she figured we wouldn't get caught. Besides, you used to drink *way* more than any of us, so –"

"'He?' Who's 'he?'"

Makenna's eyes fell. "Huck." My face must have done something concerning because she immediately grabbed my forearm and said, "You can't tell anyone. I don't want to get him in trouble."

My body began to shake with anger. Instinctively, I wanted to doubt her, but Makenna wouldn't lie to me – especially not about something that serious. *Maybe I'm just overreacting. Maybe this is more of that old-world fire and brimstone coming out. Maybe I'm the crazy one for thinking it's as serious as I do.*

Then she said, "We asked other people and they all said no."

*Or maybe I'm not.*

I pulled my lips in a frown and thought for a moment. "Huck is thirty-five; you know why a thirty-five year old man buys a sixteen and a seventeen year old girl liquor?"

Makenna studied my face for a moment, then slowly replied, "Out of the kindness of his heart?"

"No. Unless the man is a member of your family, or a de facto member of your family, the list of reasons is pretty short. Best case scenario, he doesn't care if you or Hope got hurt driving back from prom. Medium case scenario, he wants you to think he sees you at the same level of maturity as himself. That you're on equal levels, that you can do all the shit adults do. *All* the shit adults do." I gave her a stern look; she understood. "Worst case scenario," I went on, "he wanted you to invite him to drink it with you after prom. That's how men take advantage of girls like Hope and girls like you. You're smart, but nobody's immune to manipulation. Be careful around him."

"But he's dating Alita," Makenna protested. "It's not like he would try and sleep with us."

I shot her a look. "Actions speak louder than words."

Makenna kind of frowned and nodded. Then I let out a sigh, trying to keep myself even keel.

"I'll have your fries out in a minute."

Her demeanor brightened up and she said, "Okay," then bounded back to the host stand.

My body was still trembling as I went back into the kitchen. Hyde was on the line, but I didn't see Huck. He must have been out smoking.

*What the hell is the matter with him...* I dropped a side of fries into the fryer and went back to the other side of the line, leaning with my palms against the narrow, gleaming metal table that stretched from the fryer to the broiler.

Jazz walked into the kitchen after a minute with a concerned look. "What was that all about?" she asked, looking me up and down. "You're shaking."

"Nothing," I replied staunchly. "I'm not at liberty to say and I'm really trying to honor that."

Jazz screwed up her face as she pulled a small salad out of a fridge behind us. "Is it about Makenna? She in trouble?"

"Not yet," I frowned. "Hope is, though. Apparently they snuck liquor into prom and Hope's parents caught her drunk."

Jasmine's eyes widened. "Well who the hell gave those girls alcohol?" she demanded. "They *drove* themselves – do you know how dangerous that is?"

"Of course I do," I snapped softly, "that's why I'm so fucking mad about it."

Jazz recoiled a bit.

"I'm sorry," I said immediately. "I'm just trying to stay cool."

She touched my forearm gently, her hand covering the silhouette of the devil drawn there. Then the sound of the fryer oil bubbling to the top hit my ears, so I rounded the corner behind the line and pulled out the basket, dropped the fries in a metal bowl and tossed them in salt.

As I returned next to Jazz, Huck came walking in from the back. "Much better," he said with relief as he returned to the grill and the fryer. He looked at Hyde. "Man, I don't know how you go the whole fuckin' day without a cigarette."

"Because I'm an adult," Hyde rejoined playfully, masking genuine irritation.

Huck took it on the chin, then noticed the bowl of fries. "We get another ticket in while I was out?"

"No," I replied curtly, trying not to look at him. Jazz gave me a quizzical look – I think she picked up on what happened. I tried to ignore it as I grabbed a pair of tongs and dropped a bunch of fries in a small white bowl. "Makenna!" I called out, anger creeping into my voice.

Almost instantly, she appeared around the corner with a wide grin. "For me?" she asked.

"Obviously," I muttered, sliding her the bowl.

She picked one up and ate it while staring at me with a hint of amusement. "Thank you."

I didn't say anything, just took a deep breath and clicked the tongs in a rhythm to try and soothe the rising anger. My hand reached up and touched the black cross hiding beneath my T-shirt. *Be better; do better.*

But then Huck leaned into the window and my head snapped toward him.

Jazz's eyes flashed like she could see what was about to go down.

"So," Huck began, speaking directly to Makenna in a kind of low voice, "how drunk did you guys end up getting after prom?"

Hyde chuckled to himself as he prepped for the week and Makenna made a mischievous face. "I didn't get that drunk – Hope was the one who became a problem."

Huck smirked at her and leaned in casually. I'd seen him strike that same face and pose a million times picking up women at bars, a million times talking to Alita.

He said, "That's 'cause she wasn't careful," he laughed. "Y'all need a *chaperone*."

Something in me snapped.

I dropped the tongs with a loud clang on the long metal table and looked at him through the window, his arms propped up under the spot where the heat lamps ended. His eyes shot toward me, then I looked at Makenna. "Hey, Makenna," I began sharply, my voice rising, "who was it that bought you guys the alcohol again? It was someone who works here, right?" I asked, feigning ignorance. Makenna's eyes widened anxiously and Jazz grabbed my arm again.

Huck looked me in the eyes through my glasses.

Then I said loudly, "Wasn't it that thirty-five year old piece of shit who just offered to chaperone you next time?"

Everything became silent. Everything except the drumming of my heart in my ears as adrenaline coursed through me.

I wanted to hurt him.

Something about a grown man cruising for young girls just made me wanna scream.

Huck rounded the corner and stood in front of me on the line. Makenna receded away and Jazz held her hands out between us. "Whoa! Whoa!" she said.

Huck ignored her but stopped a foot away from me. "You got a fucking problem with me?" he jabbed his finger into my chest.

That hidden resentment finally bubbled to the surface.

I pointed at Huck with the devil on my arm and snarled. "You *know* what the fuck you did."

Then I turned around and marched out of the kitchen until I burst through the back door. Everything was going fast, everything was getting brighter. All I could see was black and white with red all over.

"Mother *fuck!*" I yelled as I kicked a stack of milk crates next to the door. The top one went flying and hit the pavement with a plastic *crack*.

My entire body was quivering as I pulled out a cigarette with my lips and lit it, desperately breathing in the acrid smoke to calm me down. The back door opened and Jasmine appeared, looking fraught with worry. "You okay?"

There was a moment where I didn't speak – my body was too tense to let me. Then I said, "I'll be fine."

A few minutes later, I was upstairs in the office, on the phone with Rachel the owner. My hands were still shaking. "There *has* to be some kind of consequence for this, Rachel. Hope is sixteen – you know how many kids die driving drunk every year? And that look on his face... If they'd made the offer, he woulda been right there with them. He's a fucking predator, Rachel."

Rachel's voice came through the receiver. *"Jesus..."* She took a long breath. *"Thank you for telling me. Huck denied it, though."*

"Of course he denied it – that's what people do when they commit crimes."

*"Well, Makenna and Hope aren't saying he did it, either, so there really isn't anything I can go on...."* Her voice fell apologetically.

"Fuck...." I breathed. "You *know* he did it, though, right?"

Rachel let out a sigh. *"I don't want to say that I do or that I don't. But I've already talked with Hope's parents about it, and they said they don't need us to fire him or anything since all we have is hearsay."*

My eyes widened. "Fuck what her parents think – the man *works* here. They don't have jurisdiction over that, *you* do. If he's done it once, he'll do it again."

*"I mean, it isn't like he went and drank it with them,"* Rachel said. You could tell she wanted to be more upset, but couldn't without blurring lines.

"Because he wasn't invited!"

*"Lyric, calm down."* There was a pause in the conversation. *"Are you gonna be able to keep working back of house with him?"*

My mouth fell open. "Are you serious? The guy's a certifiable piece of shit –"

*"Donovan!"*

" – so no, I don't foresee a future staring at his crooked fucking smile from across the line. Put me back on the floor, I don't care."

*"Well, we're already pretty staffed up right now, so I don't know how many shifts I can give you. Maybe you could still expo on the days when Huck isn't working? It would only be a couple shifts a week, but...."*

Something clicked when she said that.

"I... I think I need some time away."

There was a long silence.

*"I don't want to lose you. Take as much time as you need to think this through. Reach out if you need anything, Lyric. And hang in there; there really is a light at the end of the tunnel."*

With a heavy sigh, I said, "Thank you, Rachel."

I set the phone down on the receiver and ran my hands through my hair. My body was trembling with anger. When I looked up, Jazz was standing in the doorway. "You okay?" she asked. With a heavy sigh, I let my hands fall flat on the table. I watched them quiver and shake against the woodgrain.

"I need a drink."

"Lyric, don't –"

Wordlessly, I pushed past her and marched out of the office, then out the side door through the patio, walked up the street and into the Clawhammer.

"Well you're here early," Lorraine greeted cheerfully as I walked up to the bar. "Diet Coke?"

"Bourbon."

She raised her eyebrow slowly. "I thought you quit?"

My voice shook when I spoke. "Bourbon. Please."

Hesitantly, she poured a glass of liquor.

I drank it in one gulp.

# Chapter 7

## New Freedom, Ohio, May 17th, 1996
## 2:00 P.M.

That memory played in my head as I stood outside of the Blacktop Grille. I'd been living off of my music and my life savings for the last month, and that place kept on spinning. Rachel said I could come back to work whenever I was ready, but I didn't think that day would come. Huck hadn't gotten any consequences for being a creep, and now he was battering Alita and trying to keep me away with a fucking restraining order.

Sheriff Swanson hadn't served me yet.

*Might as well grab a bite while I wait.*

My gait was swaying as the bourbon from Clawhammer guided my feet. I marched up to the metal gate of the patio, opened it, and walked into the restaurant through the side door. The place was fairly deserted; it was right in that quiet spot between lunch and dinner. There were a few people sitting at the bar – one of them was old man Rick. I kept my distance.

CJ stood behind the black marble bartop washing dishes and organizing everything after the lunch rush. "Hey-hey, what's up, man?" he beamed at me as I sat down at the corner of the bar. "Ain't seen your smiling whites in here in a minute."

"Yeah, well," I replied as I took my guitar off my back and laid it across the bar. "Ain't a whole lot to smile about."

The bartender turned and looked up at the baseball game playing on TV and said, "Tell me about it," as one of the Indians struck out.

I said, "I think I've pinpointed their problem." CJ turned and looked at me curiously. "They need to hit the fucking ball."

CJ laughed and replied, "They were off to a great start the last few games – I don't know what the hell's happening here."

With a shrug, I said, "Couple of strikes don't make a bad season. Game's not over yet."

CJ kind of smiled and slid a menu in front of me as I put my jacket on the back of the metal frame of the chair. "In case you forgot," he chuckled. "What're you drinking, homie?"

"Bulleit, neat."

"Thought you were sober?"

"I was."

Then Rick, around the corner of the bar, leaned over and went, "Rough day?" He let out a raspy cackle.

"Each day the same as the last, Rick," I replied without looking at him. I didn't like that he still went to that place; he'd been something of a problem with the girls there before, and I didn't see it in the future for him to ever stop. People thought he was harmless so he never got barred permanently, but I knew better than that. His confession to Lorraine was never far from my mind.

The man would put his hand on any girl near him – always in a feigned platonic way, but he would hold his hand on their shoulder so long that I couldn't count the number of uncomfortable "please save me" glances I had gotten from the girls I worked with or drank with when he was around.

"Ah, well, what can you do," Rick chuckled as he took a drink from his margarita.

I still didn't look at him as I replied: "You can fuck off and die."

He glared at me and then mumbled something under his breath.

In a moment, CJ slid a glass of whiskey in front of me. "What're you chowin' down on, dude?"

"Huck working the grill today?"

"Sure is," CJ replied, trying to hide a growing smirk.

"Cool – I'll take the filet mignon, extra *extra* well done, but don't burn it and don't butterfly it either."

CJ tried to stifle his laughter as he wrote down the ticket. "You get two sides with that, brother."

"Do a side of cheesy broccoli, roasted and then steamed extra soft – like fucking baby food – with the melted cheese on the side." Then I spotted Makenna at the hostess stand. "And a side of fries."

CJ couldn't stop smiling as he finished writing it down. "You're an asshole, man. A funny asshole."

"My proctologist said the same thing."

CJ and I laughed together as he walked the ticket back to the kitchen. While I sat there, Rust's words about karma and music rattled around in my brain, and I glanced down at my tattoo. A saying I had heard a long time ago popped into my head when I looked at the devil I had branded myself with.

I had written nine songs before; each of them was in the style of a ballad – telling a story, usually taking inspiration from my life. Of the nine, my best were *A Quiet Fury, She Called me the Devil, Don't Call Me Lucky, Psilocybin Skies,* and *Something Beautiful.* They were all sad, in their own right. Some of them were triumphant; all of them were tragic.

But in that tragedy, when I looked back on it, there was power. And it was only through those words that I could ever understand myself, or that the world could know who I am.

Sitting at the bar, I began to feel like I wasn't as sure of who I am as I thought I was.

There was at least one more song left to write.

Suddenly, inspiration struck. I reached across the bar and grabbed a pen and pad of paper, then started writing:

*The barman said 'Your karma, when it finally comes around,*
*When it's time to face up to the music or get into the ground,*
*Just pick up your guitar and step into the sound,*
*Step into the sound.*

*If my devils ever leave me, then my angels will as well,*
*Find my penance here in County while I'm climbing out of hell,*

*And your karma, when it finally comes around,*
*You can make a deal with the Devil, and get into the ground,*
*Or sing along with your angels, and step into the sound,*
*Step into the sound.*

For a moment, I stared at the lyrics on the paper, struggling to hear a tune through the intoxication buzzing in my head. Then I added a few stanzas and still couldn't hear it. Maybe it was the liquor dulling my senses, maybe I just wasn't listening close enough. Maybe there wasn't anything left to write.

Bitterly disappointed, I set the pen down.

In an instant, Makenna was standing between me and Rick. She didn't acknowledge him, but his eyes kept flicking back and forth from her to his drink.

"Well, well, well," Makenna grinned.

"Well, well, well," I echoed. "Miss me yet?"

Makenna grunted and said, "The new expo sucks. Can you come back?"

I grinned almost proudly and replied, "Not a chance in Hell."

"But nobody feeds me anymore!"

With a laugh, I said, "Because you're an adult, Makenna. Just go and get some damn fries. You can fend for yourself."

She narrowed her eyes at me for a minute. Then she noticed the drink in front of me. Her face fell disappointedly. "Are you drinking again?"

"What do *you* think?" My words came out harsher than I meant them to. The look of heavy disappointment in the girl's eyes broke my heart.

"You were doing so well though...."

"Yeah, well... *C'est la vie.*"

A silence fell and I couldn't bear to look at that sad look on Makenna's face anymore, so I looked past her and caught Hope glancing at me from the hostess stand. She averted her gaze quickly.

"She still mad at me?" I asked, nodding toward Hope.

Makenna glanced back for a second, then said, "What do *you* think?"

With a heavy sigh, I took a drink from my glass. Suddenly Hope marched toward me furiously. She was taller than Makenna – only a couple inches shorter than me – and had just turned seventeen maybe a couple weeks ago. Light and wavy hair hung down to her shoulders gracefully; she carried herself well for being as much of a troublemaker as she turned out to be.

Suddenly I felt her fist forcefully strike me in the shoulder. "Hey, goddammit!" I yelled as bourbon spilled onto my hand.

Hope held a fiercely disappointed look on her face. "You deserve it!" she exclaimed. "You're drinking again?!"

I studied her for a second, then took a sip. "Fell off the wagon. It went on without me."

"Hypocrite!" she yelled. "You've always given me *so* much shit for –"

"Hey!" I snapped, cutting her off. Her face went stiff. "I gave you shit because *you* have your whole life ahead of you. If I want to throw mine away, I've earned that right, goddammit."

She huffed her breath and stuffed her fingers in her pockets while Makenna looked between the two of us. Then Hope said, "No you haven't."

Silence was my reply.

She furrowed her brow and told me, "I'm still mad at you."

"Yeah, you weren't exactly subtle," I chided. "I don't expect you to get it right now, but someday you'll understand."

"Understand what?" she rejoined sharply. "That you're a hypocrite? That I shouldn't trust anybody?"

"That I was trying to protect you."

Hope fell silent and Makenna anxiously glanced between us.

Then I said, "Give me the silent treatment all you want, you're still gonna see me for my arraignment on Monday."

Hope's mouth fell open. She was an intern at the magistrate's office. She did clerical work, and sat in on most of Judge Swinton's hearings. It was always small brow, local stuff, but she wanted to be a lawyer someday and damned if she wasn't off to a good start.

Makenna blurted, "You got arrested?"

"You really that surprised?"

Hope stared daggers at me while I took a drink. Then her eyes gave me a once-over and she told me, "Wear something nice."

"Believe it or not, Hope, I wasn't gonna wear the *Superman* T-shirt to see the judge," I remarked with sarcasm.

She glared at me for another moment, then stomped off back to the hostess stand.

With a heavy sigh, I set the glass down on the bar. Makenna glanced at my guitar on the marble bartop.

"Where's your case?"

"This thirty-five year old scrub threw it in the dumpster last night," I commented, playing kind of dumb. "I think he works here."

Makenna grinned, then her expression changed and she held out her palm. "You have a new one for me?"

I reached behind me into my jacket pocket and pulled out the cassette from last night. "Here," I set it in her palm. "I passed out in the middle of playing last night, so side B has about half an hour of white noise and me snoring."

She laughed and said, "Finally, you're doing vocals."

"The hell I am," I laughed back. "That's what our favorite little Mexican angel is for." Eagerly, I glanced over at Jazz across the restaurant. She shot back a smile at me, then turned to speak to another server – a young guy with a mullet and mustache named Jimmy. He was a good kid, if a little too reckless for his own good.

Makenna regained my attention. "Come on, you can't be *that* bad. Am I better than you?" She squeezed her eyes shut and sang half-heartedly, *"Zah-ahm-bay-ay-ay, ooh."*

"God, stop – please," I chortled, almost choking on my bourbon. "Was that supposed to be The Cranberries?"

"You listen to The Cranberries?" she asked in amusement. "Aren't you like thirty?"

"Fuck off, I'm twenty-nine. And good music is good music."

"Tsk tsk tsk," she shook her head and crossed her arms, teasing me. "You know, Jesus was already out there doing his thing by the time he was your age."

"How'd that work out for him?"

She laughed, then noticed the pad of paper with the lyrics scrawled down and pulled it toward herself. "Is this a song?"

"I think it's just a poem, because I can't hear a melody right now to save my fucking life," I complained.

She sort of hummed to herself, then blurted out, "It's sad. It sounds like it should lead with maybe an A minor."

My eyebrows rose. "Since when are you a musician?" I chuckled as I took a drink.

Makenna hummed some more and mapped out a melody with her hand like a conductor, then looked at me and replied casually, "I've been taking music theory classes since I was in the fourth grade."

"*What?*" I asked sharply.

She grinned and said, "Yeah – I play piano, guitar, viola, and the violin."

Dumbfounded, I stared for a second. "How have you never brought this up before? Makenna, music is literally my only hobby."

She almost blushed and said, "You never asked!"

I laughed and replied, "Christ, you're probably a better musician than *I* am, holy Hell. I couldn't even *name* most of the chords."

"How?!" Makenna burst out laughing. "You've been playing for like two years!"

Embarrassed, I took a drink and said, "Three, actually. I'm self-taught and I play electric – ninety-percent of what I do is power chords and riffs." She studied me for a second like she thought I was lying. Then she looked back down at the song lyrics. "Keep it," I nodded toward her.

"Really?"

"If you can write an accompaniment to it. Like I said, you're probably better at it than I am."

Makenna grinned, then pulled off the paper and tucked it in her jeans pocket. "Speaking of good music – when are you gonna start sending your stuff out to labels?" she inquired. "You know, so you can actually get signed."

"Never, Makenna," I dismissed.

"But you're good!" she protested. "I've liked literally everything I've heard you play – what's the problem?"

"That is the problem, Makenna. Fame would kill me."

She rolled her eyes and said, "You don't know that you would get *famous*, you just wouldn't have to live here anymore."

"Why would I want to do that? I like it here."

She gave me a skeptical look. "Are you being serious?"

My face flushed and I laughed embarrassedly. "Yes I'm being serious. I like my life how it is – I wake up whenever I want to, spend my days playing music and being around people I actually know. And people who actually know *me*."

"Yeah, but... You're poor," she teased.

I shrugged. "But I'm happy. I don't care about the money – all I want is for people to listen."

"First off, I don't believe you when you say you're happy, and second... *more* people will be able to listen to your music if you get a label."

"But then it wouldn't be *my* music – it would be the label's. If I write for money then it isn't art and if I write for someone else then it isn't mine."

"But you're smart and you're talented. You shouldn't be here."

I shook my head. "This is where I belong, right here, east of Eden." Then I gave her a pointed look. "You could go on to be far greater than anything I am."

Makenna looked away and Rick's eyes latched onto her as Jazz came walking by. She wiggled her fingers across my back as she settled on the other side of me.

"I take it the search for the missing guitar case isn't going so well?" she grinned.

"Mystery solved, actually – he threw it in the dumpster last night."

Jazz shook her head and laughed. "Can't you guys just act like adults?"

"I didn't do anything!" I protested.

"Other than sleep with Alita?"

Makenna's eyes grew. "You *slept* with her?!"

Irritatedly, I frowned. "It was one time and it was a mistake."

"Uh, *yeah*," Makenna blurted. "*Ew!* She looks like a rat!"

"Hey!" I snapped. "Watch it! I think she's cute."

Makenna smirked proudly and rejoined with: "Well, you're legally blind, so...."

"Hey," Jazz chastised Makenna with kindness and a reluctant grin, "be nice." Then she asked me, "Have you actually tried, you know, *apologizing?*"

"Fuck an apology – how does that change anything? How do words affect what happened?"

Jazz rubbed my back with a knowing look. "You'd be surprised." She gave me a wink, then walked away.

I must have stared after her for a full minute, because Makenna said, "You need a camera?"

"Oh, fuck off."

Rick started laughing at the interplay as he put cash on the bar and rose to his feet. He was short and hobbled, but he didn't let that stop him from making people physically uncomfortable. He latched his hand onto Makenna's shoulder and gripped her with his talons, leaning in close to speak. "Don't worry – she's got *nothin'* on you," Rick said quietly, probably thinking I wouldn't hear him.

Makenna's face froze and she became still, bearing a look of immense discomfort. "Gee, thanks Rick," she replied disinterestedly.

But Rick didn't let go of her shoulder. I could see his fingers furling the fabric of her black shirt with how tightly he was grabbing her. "Well, you know, I could take real good care of you if –" he began, but I cut him off.

Without saying anything, I got up and stepped between them, grabbed his wrinkly old hand and pried it off of her, the spiked tail of the devil in my skin pointing right at his throat. He gave me a look of indignation and I said, "Nobody wants to be touched by you, Rick."

He stared venomously at me as Makenna scurried away the second she was free. "The fuck is your problem?" he cawed in his nasally voice.

"Rick – today's not the fucking day. Don't touch Makenna, don't touch Jazz, don't touch *anybody*."

"She didn't even fuckin' say anything!" he prattled.

"Because she *works* here and you're a customer. It's not an invitation, it's called being too polite for her own fucking good. But I'm speaking for her. *Don't* touch her. Understand?"

Rick glared at me for another minute, then waved his hand dismissively while mumbling swears under his breath. With shuffling feet, he sauntered past the hostess stand and out the door. Bearing a devilish smile, Makenna called out, "Have a nice day!" then hurried back over, laughing. "Wow," she said, glancing between me and CJ.

CJ shrugged and said, "I hate that guy. But what can you do?"

"I could kill him," I muttered.

"Easy, boy," Makenna laughed.

Before I could say anything else, Huck came out of the kitchen holding a plate with a very dark filet, fries and grotesque looking broccoli with the melted cheese on the side. For a second, I had actually forgotten I ordered that.

*Oh yeah.*

He walked over to me with a look like he was already raring to go. "This yours?" he asked pointedly.

I glanced at the deliberately ruined dish. "I'd say it's some of your best work."

Huck dropped the ceramic plate with a loud *clang* on the bar. "You got a fucking problem? Why the fuck are you here?" His chest was heaving angrily. I stood statue-still, yet shook with adrenaline.

"I know what the fuck you did," I pointed my finger sharply at him. "You put your hands on her."

Huck snorted bitterly. "There you go – two fuckin' *nutjobs* makin' shit up about me again."

"I saw the bruises, you lyin' fuckin' snake. I *see* you."

Huck puffed his chest and went, "I'm sorry, are you even *allowed* in here? I seem to recall calling the cops on your sorry ass."

"Yeah, go the fuck ahead, call them again," I retorted. "Fucking coward."

"Yeah? Be *real* hard to play at the Clawhammer with that restraining order tonight once I show up there."

"Won't really matter once everyone knows what an abusive sack of *shit* you are. All it takes is one good song."

Huck stepped forward. "You better watch what the fuck you say."

Angrily, I balled my fist and said, "No. I'm through pulling my punches with you."

He jabbed his finger at me. "Keep your fuckin' mouth shut and your shitty music as far away from me as possible – before I shut it for you."

"What – you too afraid I'm gonna play a song about how hard I *fucked* Alita?"

Without hesitating, Huck launched both palms at me and shoved me back into the bar. Makenna jumped away fearfully and Jazz ran over. Pain shot through my back as I launched myself off the black marble and returned the shove. Huck stumbled backwards, caught his balance, then lurched forward and swung at me. He got me right in the jaw.

"*Huck!*" Jazz cried out as I hit the bar and fell to the floor.

"Fucking *stay* down!" Huck pointed his finger at me furiously.

Dazed, I got back to my feet and spat blood at his feet. The dark floor popped out with a bit of red. "You're gonna have to fuckin' kill me."

Just as he cocked his fist back again, CJ jumped over the bar and grabbed Huckleberry in an arm lock. "Knock it off!" he barked.

Huck tried to wrestle free but he couldn't overpower CJ. After a minute, he calmed down. "I'm good, I'm good."

"We don't fucking fight here," CJ scolded him as he released the lock, even though he was twelve year's Huck's junior. "You're a grown fucking man – act like it."

Huck's arms were shaking as he took a step back. He pointed at me again and said, "You better fucking hope I don't catch you outside of this place. I'm done playin' this game. Quit runnin' your fuckin' mouth and telling the town my business."

We locked eyes for a moment and I couldn't stop picturing the bruises on Alita's arm. "Like I said – you're gonna have to fuckin' kill me."

His eyes narrowed. "Then start diggin' the fucking grave."

With a cold stare, I replied, "I'll make it big enough for two."

Then I picked up the filet with my bare hand and threw it in the garbage.

Huck scoffed and said, "Get help, you fucking drunk." Then he walked back into the kitchen. There was electricity in the air as CJ waited to make sure the situation was settled, then walked around to the opening of the bar. Jazz put her forehead against her fingertips and shook her head. Hope watched with wide eyes from the hostess stand, and Makenna just stood there staring at me with a fearful look of dread.

Suddenly I felt guilty.

I slid the plate of fries to her. "Here," I mumbled. "I just lost my appetite." She shot me a concerned look, but took the plate and scampered away.

Then I threw on my jacket, strung my guitar over my shoulder and said to CJ as I put money on the bar, "Sorry about the mess."

Jazz said abruptly, "You're gonna be functional for the set tonight, right?" She peered right through my glasses.

"Because that looks like it's about your third glass of bourbon by that stagger you have."

"I'll be there tonight. Functional. I promise."

She studied me doubtfully for a moment, then said, "Okay," and walked away.

With my guitar on my back, I walked out the patio door.

A man in a light-colored police uniform and aviators stopped me as soon as the sun hit my eyes.

"Mr. Lyric," Sheriff Swanson proclaimed. "Just the man I was looking for."

# Chapter 8

## Clawhammer Tavern, March 4th, 1996
## About a month and a half ago

"Good god, I can't believe I ever gave this up," I grinned from ear to ear as I raised my glass of whiskey. Lorraine sort of chuckled, but there was a look of worry, almost pity underneath it. I didn't care. I'd been sitting there since I stormed out of the Blacktop. "Here's to seven months of sobriety, everybody."

She glanced around as I downed the bourbon. "Lyric, there's nobody in here."

Old man Rick chimed in from the other end of the bar. "Well I'm here."

"Fuck off, Rick," I replied without looking. "You don't count."

Bitterly, he grumbled and dismissed me with a wave of his hand. Lorraine made a face of amusement and tried not to laugh. "God damn, Lyric."

I shrugged. "Fuck 'em. *Una cerveza más, por favor.*"

Then another voice struck my ear. It was Jazz.

"Shouldn't it be *uno más?*" she asked.

I looked over my shoulder; she was standing behind me, looking concerned and failing to hide it with her fragile smile. "Actually," I slurred slightly, "*un* and *una* mean *a*, like the article. *Uno* means *one*, which so do *un* and *una* technically, but the context is different. *Cerveza* is feminine, so it gets *una*."

She kinda grinned. "But wouldn't *uno* be the masculine version then?"

"You'd think, but nope. They drop the *o*, I think because it's basically implied. Kind of like *yo soy* versus *soy*. You know, like in Beck's one song – fuck, I'm drawing a blank."

"*Loser?*" she asked.

I cocked my brow. "What'd you just call me?"

Aghast, her mouth opened and she stammered, "I – I wasn't –"

Then I cracked a smile. "I'm fucking with you, Jazz."

She huffed, smiled, and shook her head. "I can't always tell with you sometimes."

I went on. "He says '*soy un perdedor*' instead of '*yo soy un perdedor.*' The *yo* is implied." Then I gave her a funny look. "How am I explaining Spanish to *la Mexicana mamacita?*"

She sort of blushed. I couldn't see the red in her cheeks – it was too dull – but they darkened and that always told me someone was blushing. "Yeah, believe me, I'm painfully aware of that," she sort of tittered as she sat down beside me. "I've been telling myself I need to learn Spanish for years, but there's always something in the way."

"Here's to you, Kurt," I raised my Corona. My hand stopped as I went to take a drink. "Oh, hey Lorraine – can I get an orange slice?"

"Sure, baby." She handed me one in a flash and I stuffed it down the bottle.

Jazz eyed me curiously. "Well that's different."

I took a drink then kind of shrugged. "Someone told me that's what Florida people put in it instead of a lime. Fun fact, the lime is just to keep the flies out in Mexico. If they wanted the beer to be lime flavored, then they'd probably just make it lime flavored."

She gave me a bemused, entertained look. "Well if they wanted it orange flavored, wouldn't the same logic apply?"

"Sure. But who cares?"

She laughed in a sort of confused way and shook her head. "Your brain never ceases to amaze me."

"That's what my doctor always says."

She smiled warmly for a moment. But it faded quickly. "I don't like this."

"Don't worry, they have other beers."

"No, smartass. *This*. You drinking again. I don't like it."

"Yeah, well… You can't always get what you want," I replied, turning my attention forward. There was a mirror behind the liquors at the Clawhammer, and for a minute I watched my reflection. I looked… lost. Out of it.

But I looked happy.

At least, that's the lie I told myself. There's a difference between revelry and happiness. The biggest difference is revelry will kill you. Nobody ever died of being too happy, though.

Lorraine came by again and asked Jazz what she was drinking. "Just soda water with a lime, thank you."

"Orange is better," I interjected with a smirk.

"I'll take your word for it," she smirked back. Lorraine set the drink down in front of her. I could feel Jazz's eyes on the side of my face for what felt like forever. "You sure you're okay? Because this doesn't look okay."

Irritated, I huffed. "I told you I'm fine, okay? It was a rough day."

"Believe me, I noticed. You stormed out in quite the fury."

"And I had every reason to."

"Sure, but... You don't think this might not be helping?"

"Of course it's helping," I answered. "I feel better already." I motioned to Lorraine for another whiskey.

There was a moment of silence. Then Jasmine said, "Makenna's pissed at you, by the way."

I turned and looked at her. There was sincerity in her eyes. "I don't care," I responded coldly. "She'll get over it. Let her be pissed. I did the right thing."

"Sure you did," Jazz replied carefully. "But was it the right way to do it?"

I scoffed. "What, should I have written a strongly worded letter?"

"No," she replied cautiously, "but maybe not blowing up in front of everybody and calling him out like that in front of her would have been a start. You put *her* on the spot, too."

"I got mad, okay? What was I supposed to do?"

"I don't know, maybe take a few deep breaths and step away?"

"Yeah, because anybody in *history* ever got anything done by taking a few deep breaths and stepping away," I remarked crassly.

"The Buddha did," she replied confidently. "And I'd say he accomplished a lot more than either of us."

"Oh, give me a fucking break," I rolled my eyes behind my glasses. "Dude grew up rich then stepped outside for the first time in his life and realized 'wait... other people have *hard* lives? Well shit, let me go sit under a tree about it.'"

Jazz couldn't help but laugh despite her staunch disagreement. "Yes, and then when he got up from under that tree, he passed on wisdom that's lived on for generations upon generations."

I blew a raspberry in a juvenile response. "Yeah, and his ultimate piece of advice was to detach yourself from everything that might hurt. Buddhists are cowards. Personally, I'd rather take the pain. It lets me know I'm still alive."

"That what this is? Taking the pain?" she asked incisively, gesturing toward the two containers of alcohol in front of me.

"Sure it is – it's got a burn to it," I replied as I took a drink of whiskey. My ears caught the sound of the door opening behind me and I craned my neck.

Alita walked in.

Quietly, I muttered, "Speaking of the pain."

She strolled over to us and stood beside me for a second. "Hey, Jazz," she waved with a sweet smile. Then she looked at me. "Is it alright if I sit here?"

"I don't know," I replied bitterly. "Ask your boyfriend."

She frowned, then sat down anyway. Lorraine had a Coors Light in front of her in a matter of moments. "Thank you," she said.

"Sure, baby."

In an awkward silence, the three of us sat there for a moment. I mean, I imagine it was awkward for them – I really didn't give a shit. Alone, together, what was the difference? I had my two best friends sitting on the bar right in front of me, not beside me. Bourbon doesn't judge; beer doesn't take you out on fake dates when it's lonely. They just are what they are.

"So –" Alita began, but I cut her off with a sharp look.

"What are you doing here?" I asked curtly. Her face fell. "No, seriously – *what* are you doing here?"

Jazz made a dumbfounded look and said loudly, "Dude, chill!"

"You haven't called me in *weeks*," I went on, ignoring Jazz. "*Now* you show up like you suddenly give a shit?"

Alita's face became crestfallen, then she tightened it back up. "I heard about what happened at work today."

"Small town, word travels fast," I replied, looking straight ahead.

"Yeah, well…" Alita replied, looking almost guilty. "If it makes you feel any better, I gave him an earful about the *stupid* thing he did with those teenagers."

"Stupid?" I turned sharply. "The words I would use are *dangerous* and *predatory*, but yeah, I guess *stupid* sums him up pretty well, too."

I could feel Jazz becoming tense beside me, but I didn't pay her any mind. Alita's face flashed between anger, guilt, and sadness. "Good to see you're drinking again."

"Oh, what the fuck do you care?" I spat bitterly. "Sober, drunk, it doesn't make any difference. Sorry I can't always be there when you need a break from the fucking degenerate you're shacking up with – I hope my rekindled raging alcoholism doesn't get in the way of that."

Then Jazz smacked me on the shoulder. "Uncalled for!" she chastised me.

Then I turned on her. "*That's* what's uncalled for?" I asked with daggers in my teeth. "No, you know what's uncalled for, Jazz?" She recoiled before I even got out the next part. "Your fucking *input* in my life. You aren't my fuckin' keeper, you don't get to sit there and act like I'm on some kind of fucking spiral just because I'm not acting how *you* think I should be acting. You know what? I *like* being drunk. Drunk Lyric calls shit out when he sees it. Drunk Lyric has *balls*. Drunk Lyric doesn't give a flying fuck who he upsets, because at the end of the day, drunk Lyric is usually fucking *right*, and he talks about the shit the rest of this backwater fucking town is too pussy to point out. You don't like it? Then get the fuck away from me."

Jazz sat in her barstool, shocked. Her lips quivered with an amalgamation of indignation and betrayal. After a moment, she said, "You know what sober Lyric never does? He never tries to hurt me."

Then she got up and marched out the front door.

A heavy silence fell over the place, punctuated only by the music. From the corner of my eye, I spotted old man Rick getting up and sauntering toward the jukebox. "Rick," I said loudly without turning around, "I swear to God I will end your miserable existence if you put on a song to fuck with me."

He stopped, then quietly turned around and walked back to his barstool.

Furiously, I took another drink.

"Wow," Alita said plainly after a while. "Bravo."

"Fuck off, Alita. What do you care?"

"Quite a bit, actually," she replied, her voice rising. "And it's unfortunate because I also don't want to sit here and become your next fucking victim."

I took another drink. Without looking at her, I said, "Then you're in the wrong seat."

She stared at me for a second, but she didn't say anything. Instead, she took money from her deerskin purse and set it on the bar, then got up and left. I wouldn't see her again until she showed up at my door a couple months later.

I closed the place down that night.

\*\*\*

*Angels, what have I done?*

Those were my first thoughts as I woke up on my couch the next day with the most brutal hangover of my life. Thank God my shirt was black, because if it had been white then I could have seen the perspiration it was soaked in from the cold sweats overnight. Everything hurt as I sat up and looked around.

*At least I didn't trash the place.*

Aching and exhausted, I rolled off the couch and landed on the floor, then climbed to my feet and stumbled into the bathroom, illuminated by a red light. I almost forgot I was colorblind as I looked at myself in the mirror. My eyes were sunken and my skin was pale, even in that light.

Then I noticed a fist-sized hole in the drywall.

*So much for not trashing the place.*

With shaking hands, I grabbed my toothbrush and doubled over in the sink basin as I tried to scrape the taste of liquor from my mouth, cold water running down the drain and splashing my face as I leaned over. I rinsed and spit, then killed the water and propped myself up by my arms as they trembled, white knuckles gripping the sink.

For a moment, I made eye contact with myself in the mirror, then my gaze rested on the black cross hanging from my neck.

Suddenly my stomach lurched violently and I vomited into the sink.

I just stared at it for a second, then turned the water back on and brushed my teeth again.

And all I could think was:

*This is going to be bad.*

I laid in bed until the sun went down that day, nursing myself back to health with glass after glass of water, trying to make up for each one I'd throw up with another one to wash it down.

By the time I stepped outside for a cigarette after dusk, finally feeling like a human again, it suddenly dawned on me:

I had spent the day alone.

Feebly, I stepped out onto my porch steps and looked up at the sky. In the distance, a single strike of lightning illuminated the darkened clouds. "How're *you* doin' today?" I asked with gravel in my throat from disuse. Then my eyes fell to the sidewalk. "How am I doing today?"

I stood there smoking, hoping a friendly face might walk by to say 'hello,' but no one ever came. So I did the only thing I knew how to do to kill the loneliness.

I went to the bar to have a drink.

Hesitantly, I walked in. It wasn't very crowded, some of the usual faces. I'd hoped the cat had gotten out of the bag that the wagon left without me – it seemed easier than having to explain to everybody when they saw me drinking.

Without greeting a soul, I went to the bar and flagged down Lorraine. "How you feelin' today?" she asked genuinely.

"Like shit. Medicine didn't work so the doctor prescribed a hair of the dog that bit me."

"Bulleit?"

I shook my head. "Not tonight. Just a Corona. Please."

She half frowned in sympathy, then handed me a cold bottle with an orange slice. I thanked her as I took it and went out to the back patio, filled with five or six wooden picnic tables on a concrete slab floor, with the white panel fence surrounding it.

There was nobody out there.

Thankful for that, I sat myself down on top of one of the tables and rested my feet on the bench. It was an odd feeling – I didn't want to be alone, but I didn't want to talk to anybody. Maybe someday they'll have a word for that.

I nursed the beer slowly; I didn't think I could handle more than a couple without throwing up again. My thoughts drifted to the previous night and stayed focused on them for a while. Maybe I should call Alita, I thought. Maybe she didn't want to hear from me. And I definitely owed Jazz an apology for –

*Christ... I don't even remember what I said.*

Then, as if on cue, the patio door opened and I heard the sound of her laughter, along with the coarse sort of chuckle that Hyde always let out. Meekly, I turned my head and looked at them.

Jazz stopped abruptly when she saw me, but only for a second. Hyde spoke first, his face stretching into a wide grin as he jammed one hand in his hoodie pocket and the other held a cigarette. "Well how are you, sir?" he asked humorously.

"Livin' the dream," I replied flatly. He took a seat at the picnic table I sat on, so I got down to sit on the bench across from him. Apprehensively staring at me, Jazz took a seat next to him.

She asked me, "So is it Dr. Jekyll or Mr. Hyde tonight?"

Hyde went, "What?"

Guiltily, I frowned. "She means me."

"*Oh*," he said, taken aback. "You have one too many last night?"

"Something like that," I responded glumly.

"Yeah, something like that," Jazz added sharply as she shifted on the end of the bench.

I looked at her and the face she was wearing broke my heart. "Don't worry," I said, "it's Dr. Jekyll."

"You sure about that?" she questioned. "Because if you keep drinking that potion, it won't be."

Almost defeatedly, I held up the half-drank bottle. "It's my only one so far."

Her eyes narrowed. "So far."

There was a tense moment of quiet. Hyde broke it up. "That was a hell of a display you put on yesterday."

"Yeah, well, he deserved it." Then I scoffed. "I can't believe that happened and *I'm* the one who's on leave."

"Yeah," Hyde responded a little sarcastically, "that's what happens when you *quit*, dumbass. Besides, it's your word against his – it's hearsay versus denial, and if she fired his ass over *your* word then she might have a lawsuit in her near future. Rachel's hands are tied."

"Fair enough. I don't think I quit, just... taking a sabbatical." I took a drag from my cigarette. "But you're right, it's my word versus his, and the girls won't rat him out."

Hyde just shrugged as he drank his beer. "Of course they won't." Then he pulled a devilish, sly smirk. "Who's gonna buy them liquor, then?"

Anger rested in my gut, but I put it aside. "Ah, well... *C'est la vie.*"

"*Touché*," Hyde grinned. He downed the rest of his beer, then said to Jazz, "I'm gonna go get another drink then hit the head – you need anything?"

She shook her head. "I'm good, baby. Thank you."

Then he asked me with a look. "Nah," I replied. "I'm one and done tonight. I just got done throwing up and I don't do encores."

He kind of cackled to himself, then got up and went inside.

Jazz and I sat in silence for a while. I wanted to say I was sorry, but that word sounded so hollow after the way I bit her head off.

So I pulled my dugout from my breast pocket and packed the little cigarette-looking pipe with Mother Nature's greatest gift, then handed it to the woman.

"What," she began skeptically, "is this a peace pipe?"

"Something like that." I held my hand there, refusing to budge.

After a minute, she sighed through her nostrils and took it, along with my lighter. I watched as the black and gray scenery lit up with a deep, yet bright red at the tip of the pipe. The way the smoke left her lips could have been a film vignette from an art museum.

"I'm still mad at you," she said as the smoke flowed carelessly into the air.

I frowned with the corner of my mouth. "I know. You should be."

"You had no right to talk to me the way you did. I don't even know where that came from. All I was trying to do was get you to calm down a little."

Slowly, I nodded. "I know."

She observed me for a second, then handed the pipe back to me. "It doesn't matter what state of mind you're in or what kind of mood you're in," she went on. "You can't treat people like that, Lyric. You can't treat *me* like that. All my life I've had good men become cruel, usually because they get lost in their addictions and then suddenly everyone becomes the enemy when they point it out to them. And your anger, that rage... It's making you cruel. I can't do that anymore, not again."

Guiltily, I swallowed my throat and nodded again. "I know."

"I don't want you to become one of those men I have to leave behind," she said somberly. "Hell, I probably shouldn't even be *sitting* here. I promised myself that I wasn't gonna give people second chances to hurt me anymore; I'm too old and I've seen too much for that now. That's not what I want my life to be about. I promised myself I would turn around the first time I saw a red flag flying instead of going down with the ship."

My face fell and I found myself staring at the woodgrain of the tabletop. *Shit, I really did it this time, didn't I?*

*I guess this is only fair.*

But then she paused, and she said, "But I don't want to do that with you." My head lifted up curiously. She continued. "Maybe I should – I probably should, but... I don't want to. There's something about your mind that just... I don't know, it captivates me. You can be better than that. You *are* better than that. You're a good man. Don't let this turn you cruel."

It took me what felt like a long time to think of how to put my thoughts into words. Then I said:

"I'm sorry."

Her eyes morphed into a sad sort of warmth, and all was quiet but the night. We sat there like that for maybe a minute, until she finally groaned, "Ugh, my feet are *killing* me."

Instinctively, I slid down to the end of the bench to sit across from her. "Here."

"What?"

"Give me your foot."

She laughed for a moment and I just gave her a look. "What, are you serious?" she asked.

"Of course I'm serious," I laughed, finally at ease. "I happen to be pretty good at massages."

In skeptical amusement, she eyeballed me, then hesitantly put her leg across mine. "This better not be one of those weird foot fetish things."

I let out a hearty, belly laugh, and for the first time that day I felt good. "Don't make it weird."

She smiled coyly, then I took off her shoe and pressed my thumbs into the sole of her feet.

The patio door opened and Hyde stepped out. "Whoa," he chuckled. "Don't stop on my account."

With a warm grin, I shared a look with the woman across from me. "Don't worry, I wasn't planning on it."

# Chapter 9

## New Freedom, May 17th, 1996
## 2:45 P.M.

"Just give me the damn papers already," I groaned. "I'm not having a great day."

Sheriff Jedediah Swanson studied me. "What makes you think that's *my* problem?"

"It isn't, but the longer you stand there the more likely it will be."

The sheriff scoffed at me. "What is that, some kind of tacit threat?"

"No, it's a tacit admission that I don't want to be having this fucking conversation," I spat back. The liquor had loosened my tongue. I jabbed my thumb toward the Blacktop. "Your buddy's in there if you wanna go suck him off afterwards."

Swanson clicked his tongue. "You know, that kind of mouth probably qualifies as obstruction of justice."

"I'm not obstructing anything. Give me the damn papers and you can go back to dutifully protecting our community from those evil skateboarding teenagers."

He looked me over for another moment, then I hiccupped. "Huh," he said, "sounds like you're slurring your words a little bit there, Lyric. You been drinking?"

I turned with a sarcastic expression and gestured toward the Blacktop. "Well, I'm pretty sure this is a bar, so...."

He chuckled to himself and replied, "Seems like you've gotten yourself in a bit of a tough spot then, 'cause soon as I hand you this paper you've gotta get off the premises. But the moment you step foot onto that sidewalk, well that's a violation of local ordinance, ain't it? Public intoxication – you got that one on your record yet?"

Finally, I stopped talking.

"That's what I thought," the sheriff smirked proudly to himself. Then he took and unfolded a piece of paper from his belt and handed it to me. "Effective immediately, you're not to come within one hundred yards of Huckleberry Singer. Any violation of this will be a prosecutable offense."

"I don't watch a lot of football, can you give that to me in baseball diamonds?"

He shook his head in disbelief. "That mouth of yours just don't stop, does it?"

"Why don't you ask your daughter?"

Jed's face twisted in a snarl and he took a step toward me. "You little –"

I took a step back with my hands raised. "Alright, alright, I surrender. Jesus. Learn to take a joke." He eyed me with vitriol as I took the paper. "You know Huck's playing you, right?"

The sheriff scoffed and said, "Cut the shit, Lyric. I shoulda thrown your ass in jail when you sailed through that field of sunflowers last summer – you remember what I told you back then?"

Uncomfortably, I shifted in place. "Yeah, I remember."

He went on. "I told you if you started backslidin', or if I started to catch wind you'd become a real nuisance around town, I'd make it my personal mission to make sure you stay as far away from my daughter as possible – sound familiar?"

Bitterly, I let the air out through my nostrils. "Yeah, I reckon it does."

"Well, boy, you're backslidin' – you slide any further back and you're gonna become a real thorn in my side." Then he nodded toward the restaurant. "Man in there, he gave my little girl a place to live."

"I'll give him that – he's a big fan of little girls."

"Shut the hell up when I'm talkin' to you," Jed barked dismissively. "He helped her get her life back on track these last couple-a years, kept her outta clubs and nightwork. Ain't a whole lot you can do to compete with that, is there?" The sheriff lowered his aviators. "What the hell you ever done for her?"

Statue still, I looked him in the eye. "I listen."

He studied me for a moment, then put his sunglasses back on to shield his eyes from the high sun. "Lotta good that's done her. You been arrested twice in the last year, ain't you? Around here, we call that a *villain*. Trust me, Mr. Lyric, I know what a thorn in my side feels like. And it ain't Huck."

"Yeah, well, maybe take a look at your daughter's arms next time you see her. Figure out who the real fuckin' villain is."

With that, I started walking away. Swanson made a puzzled look. "The hell is that supposed to mean?" he called after me.

"Ask Huck."

"Lyric – stop!" he yelled. But I passed through the gate onto the sidewalk and raised up my middle finger at him without looking back.

Suddenly the sound of the metal gate opening and closing behind me hit my ears. "God dammit," I mumbled.

Then the sheriff put his hand on my shoulder to stop me. "Look here, you little devil –"

I swung my arm around and broke free, turning around to look at him. "What the hell is your problem with me, Sheriff?" I asked with an accusatory tone. "I'm about the only person in this whole town who doesn't think she's crazy, but *that* piece of shit –" I pointed forcefully toward the Blacktop, " – screams at her and puts his hands on her, yet somehow *I'm* the fucking devil? Why?"

He stood there and clicked his tongue for a second while he mulled over the question. Then he said, "See, I don't believe a word of what you just said. Huck's a good man; good to me, good to my daughter. He looks out for me and mine." Then he took off his sunglasses and watched me as I stood there gritting my teeth. "He's had his own run-ins with the law, but the love of a good woman changes a man. I was a lot like you when I was younger. Always in and out of trouble, going wherever the wind would blow me. And it was dangerous. *I* was dangerous. You know why I don't like you, Lyric?"

"'Cause I'm just too fucking handsome?"

"'Cause you've got nothin' left to lose. And that..." He paused, staring me down like he was trying to see my soul. "In my experience, that's the most dangerous thing a man can be."

"What?" I spat. "Free?"

"Alone."

For a moment, we looked each other in the eyes. He peered curiously, like he couldn't find the soul he was looking for. Finally, I shrugged my guitar up on my shoulder and said, "There are worse things to be than alone."

I didn't look back as I started walking again. A part of me felt bad for spilling Alita's baggage out in front of her father, but it's hard to keep your tongue stiff when it's been softened with bourbon. *He don't even believe me. He'll walk in there, ask Huck about it, and he'll tell him she's crazy.*

Idly, I reached into my breast pocket for my cigarettes and withdrew an empty pack. "God fucking dammit," I sighed as I reached the intersection of Garden and Water Street. With a huff, I turned left and headed toward Main Street. My eyes scanned over the line of train cars seated on the tracks next to the Railroad Museum, being prepped a little ways down from the platform for that evening's tourist rides.

The passenger cars were all black and gray, but the engine was bright red, and looked about a hundred years old. They restored it with a shiny coat of paint so the borough could give people brief train rides as a tourism gimmick. It would follow the tracks alongside the trail all the way to Killdevil about four miles away.

*Whoop-dee-fuckin'-doo.*

Guiltily, I thought about how that's where Red was living now, out in Killdevil in a new house he built after he and Layla split a few weeks ago. He started building it for his family; now it was just gonna be him. Those thoughts carried me all the way to the Shell gas station. It was a small one, just a couple of pumps and a little convenience store. My guitar clumsily bumped the side of the automatic doors as I walked in.

A woman's voice said to me from behind the counter, "You playin' a set here tonight, Lyric?" I looked up and she was grinning. It was a woman named Liz, maybe in her late thirties with light hair and glasses. She was a regular at the Clawhammer.

I grinned back. "You couldn't afford me."

"Don't you play for free?"

"I play for tips."

Liz laughed and said, "Yeah, I think I can afford you. Cowboy killers?"

"Yes, please."

She grabbed a pack of Marlboro Reds off the rack behind her and set them down, then I gave her cash. The red label of the cigarettes stood out to me. That was half the reason I smoked them – I could always spot where I set them down. She asked, "You gonna be at the Clawhammer tonight?"

"That's the plan. I'm playing with Jazz again tonight."

Liz raised her eyebrows mischievously. "Oh, I've seen you lookin' at her, I *bet* you wanna play with her," she teased.

My face flushed. "Oh, fuck off. I should be so lucky."

Liz grinned then gave me my change. "Well, maybe tonight's the night you are."

I sort of laughed and said, "Doubt it."

Before I turned around, I heard a vaguely familiar small voice. It belonged to a little boy. "Mommy, can we get ice cream?"

"Not before dinner, Daniel."

Immediately, my body froze. I knew that voice.

It was Layla.

I turned around and she stood there holding her and Red's son by the hand, and kind of waved at me with the other. She was a taller woman, at least a few inches taller than me, dark hair with light streaks. She had an almost eager look on her face. "Hi, Lyric."

Guiltily, I grumbled, "Hey, Layla." I stepped aside and she brought a couple of bottled drinks to the counter and Liz checked her out.

"What're you up to today?" Layla asked as she stepped away from the counter. I glanced over and Liz gave me a look that asked, *this one, too?* I did my best to telepathically answer *no*.

"Just killing time before the Clawhammer tonight," I responded as I walked back out the door. Layla and her son followed me.

"When are you playing?"

"Few hours. We start at seven."

Layla smiled and said, "Well maybe I'll come by."

I grimaced. "You don't have to do that." Her face fell and I continued. "Red will probably be there." Then I gave her an incisive look. "Will probably won't."

Layla didn't say anything for a minute. She just kind of stared out ahead as we slowly sauntered down the sidewalk. Daniel was curiously looking at everything, like the world was new – which, to him, I guess it was. Then Layla said, "I've got my own place now. An apartment out in Driftwood."

"You're not staying in the house?"

She shook her head. "It just... It feels too weird without Red, you know? And everything that's happened... I just didn't want to be there anymore."

Sympathetically, I frowned. "That's a feeling I can understand."

"Too bad you're not as close anymore, though. It was nice being within walking distance from everyone." Then she laughed. "At least I'm pretty sure you were close. You'd think I'd know where your house is at after –"

Her words cut short.

She resumed. "After walking you home that night."

For a second, I didn't say anything. "Yeah."

Then she asked, "Are you proud of me?"

My feet stopped. Like a statue, I stood there looking at her. *Why would you ask me that?*

My mouth stammered out, "I... I have to go. Take care of yourself, Layla." Before anything else could be said, I cut across the road through the slowly moving handful of cars and headed down North Bethel Street.

All I wanted to do was forget.

But life has a funny way of reminding you of things.

When I got to my steps, Red was sitting there with a solemn look, his hands clasped together. I began slowly, cautiously, "Hey, man. What's up?"

Red let out a heavy sigh and looked at me. "We need to talk."

# Chapter 10

## New Freedom, August 12th, 1995
## Nine months ago

We were all sitting around a bonfire in Red's back yard. Me, Alita, Jazz, Will, Red and Layla. The sun had gone down and the moon was up and we were all carrying on in revelry and intoxication. Alita sat opposite of me across the fire, and I was between Jazz and Red.

Alita and I had barely talked about what happened between us; it had been two months, and she and Huck were long since back together.

I never had the heart or the guts to tell him what happened. My mind replayed that next morning after our tryst every time I looked at her.

"Well good morning to you," Alita had said as she rolled over in my bed, the air conditioner creaking and groaning as it struggled against the summer heat.

"Good morning yourself," I replied, shielding my eyes from the sunlight breaking in through the blinds. She laid her hand on my bare chest and idly let her fingers roam.

"So... that was certainly something."

I removed my hands from my eyes and blinked twice at the black and white scenery, then grabbed my glasses off the nightstand. "Yeah, so is this hangover," I groaned.

"Oh, come on, I'm sure you've had worse."

"Yeah, and I've also had better." She made a face as I said that. I looked at her and grinned. "Don't worry – I'm not talking about you."

She smirked flirtatiously. "Better not." Then she affected a heavy Brooklyn accent and gesticulated like an Italian mobster from *The Godfather*. "Or next time ya won't be sleepin' wit me, you'll be sleepin' wit da fishes."

I laughed and ran my fingers through my hair. "God you're weird. I dig it." My legs swung across the side of the bed and I sat up in my boxers. The sheets fell as she sat up in the mattress and leaned forward, hugging her legs with her knees covering her breasts. I glanced back and admired the tattoo along on her spine – a phoenix rising out of a fire, surrounded by a few sunflowers. I could actually see the red ink of the bird and the flames, but the flowers were all white to me. My hand traveled up and down her back. "How much of last night do you remember?"

She screwed up her face. "Not a whole hell of a lot, to be honest with you. I remember we put on *Friends*, and then before I knew it, we were acting like more than friends." She smiled sweetly at the end of her sentence.

"What, like really good friends?" I teased. "Dare I say… best buddies?"

She laughed and gently pushed me. "No, sir, you dare not."

I cracked a grin and pulled out two cigarettes with my teeth from the pack on the nightstand, then lit them both with a match and handed one to her. "God, you have no idea how long I've wanted to do that."

"Oh, believe me, you're not as subtle as you think," she remarked in amusement.

Suddenly I blurted, "Now *you're* starting to sound like Huck." Immediately, my gut tightened with guilt. My elbow rested on my thigh and I leaned my head into my hand. "Shit..." I murmured. "The hell are we gonna tell him?"

"Don't know, don't care right now," Alita responded. "I don't want to think about that yet."

"Well we're gonna have to think about it sooner or later."

She looked up at the ceiling. "Hmmm... Later sounds good."

I half scoffed, half chuckled and shook my head. I couldn't expel the sick feeling in my stomach. "Fuck, this is bad," I breathed through smoke.

"I didn't hear a lot of protesting *last night*."

"We were drunker than hell last night," I reminded her. "How am I supposed to stand across the line and look him in the eye after this?"

"It shouldn't matter," Alita argued. "We broke up – I don't belong to him. I don't belong to anybody."

"That doesn't change the fact he's supposed to be my friend. This is shitty all around, Alita."

Her voice rose sharply. "Really? That's your hot take? You got what you wanted out of me and now you *feel* bad?" She scoffed bitterly. "You're a piece of work, Lyric."

Angrily, I rose to my feet and smashed the cigarette in the ashtray. "You know damn well that's not what this is. I *do* want you, Alita – you're on my mind all the time. But I don't know how the fuck we're supposed to come out of this as the good guys. I just had sex with my friend's girlfriend the *moment* she became single – and you just had sex with your boyfriend's buddy. No matter what we do, we're gonna hurt him."

She snuffed her cigarette in the ashtray too and loudly argued, "What the hell happened to the guy yesterday who told me I could move in with him? Huh? How were you gonna explain *that* one to your 'buddy?' Who – by the way – doesn't even *like* you, whether he'll say it to your face or not."

Guiltily, I shook my head and muttered, "I don't know. In due time, I guess."

She tossed her hands up angrily and slapped them down on the mattress. "Oh, cut the shit, Lyric." Then she got to her feet and began getting dressed. "Now you suddenly have a conscience? You don't get to slide back on everything just because you woke up and decided to be a human fucking being today!"

"Well excuse the ever-loving shit out of me!" I retorted. "What's *your* suggestion, huh? What's the next move, Alita?"

She pulled her blouse forcefully over her slender frame. "We tell him what happened, and what will be will be. *Que sera, sera.*"

"Alita, that would *crush* him!" I protested. "We can't do that to him – *I* can't do that to him. I don't care if he gives me mixed reviews, I can't do that. We need to give it time."

"For what? You to change your fucking mind again? Face it, Donovan – you don't want me. You wanted to get your dick wet and I was just your latest fucking conquest."

"God *dammit!* You know that's not true!"

"Then why won't you just take a leap of faith?!"

For a moment, all was quiet. The beautiful woman stood across from me, her lips quivering with indignation.

Then, softly, I replied: "I don't know. I'm scared."

She frowned tightly, then grabbed her deerskin purse off the floor. "Well you can't be afraid of heights forever."

Without another word, she stormed out of the bedroom, through the kitchen and out the door.

For hours, I sat in my apartment, ruminating on what transpired and what to do about it. She was right – if I ever wanted to get what I wanted, eventually I'd have to take the leap.

Just as I threw on my jacket and shoes to look for her at her usual hangout spots, my phone rang.

"Hello?" I answered, picking the handset off the receiver hanging from the living room wall.

"*Hey….*" Alita's voice spoke.

"Oh – hey," I replied, softer than before. "I was just about to come looking for you... I'm sorry about how this morning went."

"*It's fine,*" she said, trying to mask the hurt in her voice. "*You are who are. I shouldn't expect one night to change that.*"

Grimly, I frowned to myself. "Alita –"

"*I need to tell you something.*"

With bated breath, I stood there silently.

*"I talked to Huck today."*

Painfully, I swallowed my throat. "Yeah?"

*"Yeah...."*

"How'd... How'd it go?"

*"I didn't tell him about us, if that's what you're wondering."*

I shook my head. "It doesn't matter."

*"Well, it might now...."*

My brow furrowed. "How come?"

There was a pregnant pause; then –

*"I'm moving in with him."*

As I stared at her through the flames at Red's bonfire a couple months later, I couldn't stop wondering if she would be sitting next to me that night if I had just taken the leap when I had the chance.

"And this guy," Red laughs as he tells a story, "he's supposed to be mixing these two chemicals for the helicopter to spray on the field, right? One of them is a pesticide, and one of them is water."

Will grinned and rubbed his chin. "Oh, God, tell me he didn't."

Red chuckled in his booming voice and said, "Oh, but he did. He's supposed to mix it *one* part pesticide per *ten* parts water – which means we should have enough pesticide for about a dozen jobs from one order. So he's filling the tank with the mixture and then suddenly the pump stops and he taps me on the shoulder and goes, 'Hey, Red, I ran out of the pesticide.'"

Jazz covered her face with her hands and let out an uneasy but amused, "Oh no."

I laughed and took a drink from my bourbon. "Dear God, Red, where do you find these people?"

Red laughed and said, "I think God sends them my way to test me." Everyone except Alita laughed. She was sitting there glancing at me from across the fire. Guiltily, I looked away. "So I ask the guy, 'How the hell did you go through a dozen jobs worth of this shit in one tank? Did they send us empties?' And he goes, 'No, I filled it just like you said. One part water, ten parts pesticide.' I looked at him like, 'Dude, are you trying to kill the fucking planet?'"

We erupted into laughter. Layla said, almost confused, "See I think I would have done the same thing."

Red looked at her with amusement. "What? Babe, how could you *possibly* fuck that up?"

"Because I'd get nervous!" she tittered.

Will said, "You're a smart woman, you'd figure it out."

Layla grinned at him, almost flustered and said, "No, I'm not."

I chuckled and replied, "Eh, don't sell yourself short. I've seen worse."

She shot me a look and went, "Oh, thanks."

It felt like she held the look a little too long so I averted my eyes as I took a swig from the bottle of beer in my hand. I looked at Jazz next to me and she said, "I hate modern agriculture. It isn't even farming anymore, it's figuring out how to kill the land and revive it over and over again to produce massive amounts of crops – most of which just goes back to feeding livestock so they can keep overgrazing fields. It isn't farming. It's necromancy, and it's torturing Mother Earth."

Admiration struck me across the face as I listened to her speak, her words spilling out like music from her lips. "Tell us how you really feel, Jazz," I teased.

She tried not to grin and put on a playful expression. "I'm serious," she laughed. "We were given this place as a gift and what we've done to Her is abusive."

"*Ha!*" Alita suddenly chirped. We all looked at her. "That's rich."

Will formed a wry smirk as he saw Alita winding up and he decided to give her a prod. "Which part, the gift or the abuse?"

Alita scoffed and crossed her arms, staring at me and Jazz through the flames shooting off the timber and kindling. "I don't think this place is a gift. I'm pretty sure we're in Hell."

Red cocked his brow and looked at her with bemusement. "Hell on Earth? Or Hell *is* Earth?"

"Take your pick," she shrugged. "When the Devil whispered 'perfection,' the world became evil." She looked right at me when she said it. Guilt-stricken, I looked away. Almost out of instinct, the devil in my arm reached up and felt the cross beneath my shirt.

Jasmine replied, "I don't think the world became evil. I think the world already had evil in it, and mankind woke up to it."

"Oh, great – we're saved," Alita responded bitterly.

"We're the ones who have to know good from evil," Jazz said. "That way, we can help the people around us figure it out, too."

"Then what? We can all drink a Coke and sing in harmony?"

I peered at Alita through the fire and said, "The Devil never whispered 'perfection.' He whispered 'freedom.'"

Red's eyes lit up and he eagerly pointed at me. "That's a good one, you should write that down."

A little proudly, I smirked to myself. Then the smile faded as I listened to my thoughts. "I don't think I believe in God – this all seems like one big cosmic accident to me, and I haven't come across anything I couldn't explain with science and reasoning yet. But I think about the Book of Genesis a lot... Mostly the serpent and Eve."

Jazz feigned a gasp and went, "You? Not believing in God? What a shocking turn of events this is." Then she smiled and added, "I figured if anything you would follow the ways of the Jedi." There was a wink punctuating her sentence; I found myself blushing and looking away as I smiled wryly.

Will grinned and said, "I think Lyric giving any thought to a book from the Bible of all things is even more shocking."

Somewhat embarrassed, I remarked, "I had a minor in theology in college – I mean, I dropped out, but a lot of it stayed with me. Religion is fascinating shit."

Then Red looked at me and asked, "What's your take on Genesis? I gotta hear this."

I gathered my thoughts for a moment and glanced up at the stars, a field of white dots on a black backdrop. People told me sometimes you could see blue in outer space if it was dark enough outside. There were gas clusters surrounding the Milky Way, and they would shine from the light of the billions of stars passing through them.

I'd never get to see it.

I said, "In the book – especially if you go to older Kabbalah lore –"

Red interjected. "Yes! I knew you knew your shit. Kabbalah, Gnosticism, Hermeticism – humanity figured this shit out a *long* time ago, and we keep trying to remember what we already knew."

"Exactly," I responded. "I don't know how literally you can take any of those stories or texts, but if you go to the more forgotten lore surrounding the old testament, their interpretations of those stories... the archetypes are still around."

Jazz gave me an excitedly curious look and asked, "So what's the real story of Genesis, then?"

"Well, when Phil Collins touched his first drum set –" I joked. Jazz laughed and playfully gave me a love tap on the shoulder. I shot her a mischievous grin, then glanced back at Alita. She was still sitting there with her arms crossed. I continued. "In the book, at least in Kabbalah myth, Adam's first wife was a woman named Lilith. She was made from clay and earth and stars just like him. But she wouldn't be subservient to him, so she left the Garden of Eden. Certain texts claim she went on to have a relationship with Samael, the angel of death and king of demons, the one who punishes the wicked."

Will chimed in. "Isn't that Lucifer?"

I shook my head. "It is and it isn't. It's one of those things where names and characters have changed and morphed over the last few millennia. 'Lucifer' was originally used to describe the king of Babylon, in an allegory equating him with the Fallen One – with the word 'lucifer' meaning 'the lightbringer,' and 'satan' meaning 'adversary,' or 'rebellious.' Interestingly enough, in the Latin translation, 'lucifer' was also used to describe Jesus."

"Talk about a plot twist," Red laughed heartily.

"Right?" I continued. "In Hebrew, the fallen angel was called 'Helel,' which has roughly the same meaning as the Latin word 'lucifer.' And because of the role of the serpent in Genesis, retroactively Lucifer became the angelic part of Samael and Samael became the devil in Lucifer."

Jazz asked, "So what about the serpent and Eve then?"

"I'm getting there," I winked at her. She could always tell when I winked, even with the sunglasses on to spare my eyes the pain of the fire. "So Eve was made from Adam's body after Lilith left, and she and Adam were to take care of the Garden and bask in its eternal glory. But they didn't have free will – at least, Eve certainly didn't. You can't really have free will if you have no knowledge of consequences. Some even think Samael is the one who planted the tree of knowledge in the Garden. So when he saw God's creation – mankind, fashioned in His image and the likenesses of angels – he saw an abuse of Mother Nature. He saw a divine creature in Eve, who was stripped of her divinity. She could have had the divine light, but God saw it better that she stay ignorant and innocent."

Alita remarked dourly, "Then Lucifer fucked it all up."

Pangs of guilt held my breath for a moment, and I glanced down at the dark silhouette of the devil on my forearm, illuminated by the fire. I continued: "So then Samael, Lucifer, whatever you want to call him, came into the Garden and told Eve that she wouldn't actually die if she ate from the tree of knowledge. You could argue that she would have died anyway and God was lying to her, or you could argue that knowledge of death is what makes us die. Either way, Lucifer convinced her to eat the apple. That was the first act of free will, I think – the realization that we can defy God if we want to."

Red asked me, "Yeah? How did that work out for them?"

"That's where it gets super interesting. So if you read the book, the serpent is condemned to crawl on his belly and be seen as a villain for all time – which implies he wasn't actually a serpent when he went into Eden. Adam, Eve, and Lucifer are all cast from the Garden. The way it's described for Adam and Eve makes it sound like the Garden was on Earth, but Lucifer's story contradicts that."

"You mean when he fell to Hell?" Will asked.

"Except that he didn't fall to Hell – he was cast down to *Earth*. To here. And in his anger and rage that Eve would abandon him for Adam, he followed them around for generations, disturbing and destroying their family, and they in turn would crush the head of the serpent for generations to come."

Then Jazz asked, "Why would Lucifer be mad, though?"

I shrugged. "Personally, I think it's because he saw what mankind does with the freedom he gave us. We kill each other, we hate each other, we fuck each other with no regard for sanctity. He took the bet that mankind could be just like the angels if he gave them the chance, but the first thing they did with knowledge was become ashamed of themselves. We might have been angels once but then we died, and this is where God buried us." I looked at Alita through the fire. "So in a manner of speaking, Alita is right about this being Hell – from a certain point of view."

Will chuckled at that last sentence and said, "Okay, Ben Kenobi."

His laugh faded into the night and the circle grew quiet, somber even, for a moment. Then Alita finished her beer with one long drink from the bottle. Darkly, she mused, "Yeah, well... you oughta know." She tossed the bottle carelessly into the fire, then got up and went inside.

Everyone stared at her as she marched up the stairs to the porch. Red asked, "What the hell was *that* about?"

Jazz gave me a concerned look and asked, "Is she okay?"

Will clicked his tongue. "That's little miss crazy for you." Then he stood up. "Well, that's gonna do it for me tonight. Take it easy, everyone. Red, thanks for having me."

"Typical," Red grinned. "A woman starts getting angry and Will instinctively leaves."

Will and Layla laughed. He said, "Sometimes it's the right move." He gave Layla a peculiar look, almost flirtatious, then he wandered off into the darkness. Jazz was studying the side of my face as the fire reflected off my glasses.

"I'm gonna talk to her," she said.

Layla added, "I need another drink anyway so I'll go in with you."

Gently, Jazz placed her hand over mine, gave me a sympathetic look, then she and Layla went inside. It was just Red and I sitting there by the fire then. For a while, neither of us spoke. We just watched the flames dance and nursed our beers and whiskey.

Finally, he said, "I think Layla is having an affair."

"Shit, really?" I asked.

He nodded. "Yeah."

"What makes you think that?"

He let out a sigh. "She's just been… different lately. She's arguing, being distant, always answers the phone when I'm around even if I'm standing right next to it. I don't know, man. Something's off."

Alcohol coursed through me, slurring my words. "I'm sure it's in your head, man. I don't think she would do that to you."

Red looked at me. "She has before."

That was the first I'd ever heard about that. Layla had given me flirty looks sometimes – she did the same with a lot of Red's friends – but I just assumed it was innocent, that she didn't know how she came across all the time. "Shit… I'm sorry, man."

Red took a long drink. Then he asked me, "You think Lucifer regrets what he did?"

For a moment, I stared into the fire, thinking about what happened with me and Alita, and how much that knowledge would break Huck to find out. "Regret? No, no I don't." I punctuated my thoughts with a long drink. "But I think I understand Lucifer's remorse."

We sat there silently enjoying each other's company for another ten minutes or so, then Red groaned and stood up. "I think I need to go to bed. I'm almost at twenty-four hours since my last power nap."

"Jesus, dude," I chortled. "You drank six beers and a quarter of a bottle of whiskey, how are you still standing?"

Red laughed and said, "You drank as much as me, shut the hell up."

I laughed too then stood up and we embraced. The yard spinned as my head rushed. "Thanks for having me over, Red. I appreciate nights like these."

We let go of each other and Red said, "Well don't get *too* hammered tonight or you're gonna regret it tomorrow. Don't *not* get hammered, though," he laughed. "Feel free to keep drinking the whiskey."

With a grin, I said, "There's that freedom again – it'll kill ya."

Red smiled and nodded, then sauntered off inside. For a while, I sat there drinking bourbon and beer, letting my mind wander. Eventually, it began to stumble as the liquor made my thoughts foggier and heavier. Suddenly I realized it had been forty-five minutes and Alita and Jazz were still inside. I assumed Layla went up to bed with Red.

*I should probably go home.*

My feet shuffled through the grass as I picked up the half empty bottle of whiskey and stepped toward the porch. I didn't go up the stairs, though. Instead, I stood beside the house and relieved myself of all the fluid in my bladder. But as I finished and went to move again, I heard a voice from the kitchen window.

It was Alita.

*"He's not this great fucking guy, Jazz. He'll tell you anything you want to hear to get you for a night, then in the morning all bets are off."*

I frowned and strained my ears to eavesdrop.

Jazz said, *"Mistakes happen. You two were both drunk – it's shitty but it isn't exactly surprising. Besides, what about Huck?"*

*"I don't care about that right now. Huck's an asshole, and I wouldn't have done anything if he didn't constantly accuse me of it anyway."*

*"That isn't Lyric's fault. He wasn't trying to hurt you. He's... complicated."*

Alita scoffed. *"Oh my God. You like him, don't you?"*

Jazz was silent for a moment. *"I think he's fascinating. I think he's troubled, but the way his mind works is... it's different. There's something captivating about that."*

Alita scoffed again. *"Yeah, I'm sure it's all totally natural. He isn't playing you to get in your pants or anything. Lyric would* never *do that."*

Another pause. *"I don't think he would."*

*"Jasmine, he's the Devil! He doesn't care about you!"*

*"He's not the Devil. He's a rebel, he's reckless, maybe even sometimes dangerous. But he's not the Devil."*

Alita grunted furiously, then said loudly, *"Whatever. Bite the fucking apple then, Eve. See how well it turns out for you."*

Then I heard thudding footsteps coming toward the door. It swung open as I stayed out of sight beside the wall, and Alita marched down the steps and through the yard.

Stunned, guilty, and angry at myself, I slumped down with my back against the wall. After a minute, I heard a gentler set of footsteps come out. "Lyric?" Jazz called out as she stood in the yard. I didn't move, I didn't say anything. I just sat there to keep myself from pulling another girl out of the Garden.

Alita was right – the apple was poison.

Jazz let out a somber sigh, then took a garden hose and doused the fire. I listened to her footsteps as she walked away.

Then I was alone.

With heavy hands and leaden feet, I got up and grabbed the bottle of whiskey, took a long drink until it made me want to puke, then walked up the porch to return it inside.

*Shit, I think I overdid it.*

The world began to spin and everything became intense and fast – that moment right before you're about to black out. As I stumbled onto the porch, the back door opened before I reached it.

Layla stepped outside.

"Oh, hey, you're still here?" she said with a look. It was somewhere between curious and seductive, and as I eyeballed her change of clothes into a form fitting tank top and revealing pair of shorts, I figured out which.

*I should go home.*

But I didn't.

I returned the look.

"Still here."

Everything else that happened that night became a black spot in my memory.

# Chapter 11

## New Freedom, May 17th, 1996 3:00 PM

My eyes were fixated on Red as he sat with his hands clasped together on my porch. "We need to talk," he said.

Cautiously, I took a step toward him. *Did I do it? Did I really do what I think I did?* Desperately, I strained my brain to think back to that night at Red's place. *What happened after Layla came back?* I knew she made a pass at me, or I made a pass at her, and I knew she walked me home that night. Everything else...

Black.

I asked Red, "What's going on?"

He let out a sigh and rubbed his face. "I was right about Layla having an affair," he began. "I just didn't think it would be so goddamn many of them. Including a friend."

Fearfully, I raised my eyebrow. "Who?"

He looked me dead in the eye. "You know who."

My body went cold. *Oh my God – I fucked her, didn't I?* "Red, I'm so–"

"It was Will."

My words stopped short and I studied my friend's visage. He wasn't testing me, he wasn't hiding anything. He was just hurt and angry. "Really?" I asked. Red nodded. I took a seat next to him on the concrete steps outside my house.

"Layla told me he's been hooking up with her for months. Consistently." Red scoffed bitterly. "You know that son of a bitch actually said to me once when I left for a job: 'oh, don't worry, man. I'll keep an eye on your kin for you.'"

Nauseously, I silently retched. "That's disgusting," I replied. "How the hell can a man say that shit to a friend when he's actively doing *that?*"

"Will isn't a man, he's a coward. He's soft. Literally – I told him to flex one time and it felt like fucking jello," Red laughed bitterly.

I laughed, too. "Believe me, I've noticed."

Red laughed until it faded and the world sank back into his broad shoulders. "I had a panic attack when she told me," he admitted. We exchanged a look and held it for a second, like he was expecting me to make fun of him or I was expecting him to retract his statement. "Standing right there in the grocery store. We were picking up supplies for her new place and we got to talking about it – I knew she had cheated on me, but I only knew about the one guy, her fucking penpal from Michigan she met in – the hell are they called? A chatroom? Then she went through and told me about every guy she fucked while we were together. And I just… It killed me, Lyric."

I let out an empathetic sigh. "Women will do that to us."

"Tell me about it," he groaned.

For a second, I mulled over my thoughts. "She told you about every guy?"

Red nodded. "Yup."

*Then that means...*
*I never slept with her.*
*I didn't let it go all the way.*

Almost with relief, I felt the guilt finally bubbling up to the surface. "You know, I wanted to tell you this a while ago – months ago, actually. But the night after your bonfire, when we were talking about the Devil in the Garden, I asked you if you would rather know it if there were some great truth that could shatter your family, or be kept in the dark to save your bliss."

Red cocked his brow. "And I told you I'd rather be kept in the dark, didn't I?"

I nodded. Then I took a deep breath. "She made a pass at me. At your bonfire that one night over the summer. The night where Alita kind of lost her shit."

"Really?" Red asked, unsurprised.

"Yeah. It was after everyone else had all left and you went to bed. I was putting the whiskey bottle back on your porch and she came out. I don't really remember what all happened, but I know she got... weird. Like being really flirty. Saying shit she shouldn't say. She walked me home that night but I was so fucked up all I have are scattered fragments of memory, like the burned tapestries of the Library of Alexandria. I didn't know how to tell you about it."

Red thought about it for a moment. "I'm not surprised. I saw the way she looked at you, at a lot of my friends." Then he looked at me. "You know Will tried to say she was lying about him hooking up with her? He told me it was actually *you*, and she was just trying to spare you."

"So she lied and said it was him?" I asked incredulously. "Will actually thinks that story would work?"

Red laughed bitterly again. "Yeah, right? And the way she told me they hooked up the first time was... Christ, it was borderline rape."

"Really?" I asked with a pit in my stomach.

"Yup," he said. "He got her in his car to smoke some grass, then just whipped his fucking cock out and started stroking it."

I almost threw up in my mouth. "Jesus fucking Christ," I exclaimed.

"Yeah. He wouldn't put it away and kept telling her to touch it, so eventually, she did."

I let that dark revelation sink in. "What about the other times?"

Red shrugged. "There was always some kind of carrot and stick involved. He'd get her high, get her drunk, just start grabbing up on her without saying anything. And Layla's kind of a shitty human being, so she started going along with it at some point. She liked the attention."

"How long was it going on?"

"He's *still* fucking her," Red blurted.

"Fuck... Wow, that's a terrible friend. I can't believe he threw *me* under the bus, like I'm not one of his only three friends left. I told him about the bits I remembered from that night and asked him what he thought I should do."

"Lemme guess – he told you not to tell me?"

I nodded. "It's my own damn fault I listened, but... It makes a lot more sense now."

For a minute, we sat there listening to the sounds of the wind. I forgot I still had my guitar on me, I was so used to the weight by that point. Suddenly Red said, "I want to get drunk on the train." He looked at me again. "You wanna get drunk on the train?"

"After that discomforting bombshell? Yeah, I could use a drink."

Red grinned, then patted me on the back. "Thank you, brother. I mean it. You're one of the good ones."

"Maybe," I stood up, glancing down at the red *S* on my shirt. "But I could always be better."

It was a delicate balancing act to get my feet in position so the bourbon wouldn't knock me down. I'd had a steady stream of alcohol all day – the goal now was to keep my BAC level at the most, instead of letting it rise before the set began in a few hours.

Red and I walked down to the train platform across from the Clawhammer where eager passengers were lined up at the cars, ready to board. He bought us a couple tickets for the luxury car with the bar in it, and in a few minutes, we were sitting in class.

"Damn, this is stylish," I remarked, looking around. I couldn't tell what color the interior was supposed to be, but all the seats were bright red leather and the bartop was painted to match.

"You ever been on this thing before?"

"Nope. Something about gently rolling toward Killdevil then gently rolling back just never sounded like a fun way to spend my day," I chuckled.

"It's surprisingly relaxing," Red chuckled back.

Then a familiar voice struck my ears. Will said to a woman he was boarding the train with: "This is probably the classiest bar New Freedom will ever get. I mean, how can you not love an old-timey train bar?"

Red's head snapped around and he stared at Will boarding the train while I sat across from him with my guitar in the seat next to me. He was with Misty, the drunk redhead from the Clawhammer earlier. "Easy, man," I urged.

Red breathed through his nostrils like a dragon blowing smoke, and Will made eye contact with us. He said nothing, acknowledged nothing. Just sat down in his seat next to the dead-eyed drunk woman he had picked up. She could barely walk as they stumbled down the aisle.

Red returned his attention to me. "She can't even walk, dude. This is what he does. He gets chicks so drunk they don't know which way is up, then he coerces them or forces them into putting out."

My stomach churned. He was right. That was Will's signature move. "Just watch the bridges burn," I said.

The train started rolling and a rotten feeling sank into my gut. This was a bad idea. Even though his face was calm I could see the fire flashing in Red's eyes. A waitress came over to us, a pretty little brunette who looked like she just started college. "Hi guys, my name is Annie and I'll be taking care of you for our *lovely* train ride this afternoon," she said with a flirtatious smile at the two of us.

Red's expression shifted immediately into a cocky smirk. "See, I knew there was a reason to climb aboard."

The girl and I both grinned and she said, "There's lots of reasons."

I replied, "Just not to travel. Seriously, it might be faster to *walk* to Killdevil."

She laughed and made a mockingly offended face. "Well, then, sir – exit's that way," she jabbed her thumb. Me and Red laughed again. "What're you handsome devils drinking tonight?"

Red shot me a mischievous look, then asked, "Idunno, what's good here?"

Annie's face fell immediately. Servers hated that question – in fact, never fucking ask your server or bartender that question for the rest of your life. The customer is always right in matters of taste, and we don't know what the fuck you like. So be an adult and figure it out on your own.

But I digress.

Before Annie could become genuinely flustered, Red spoke again. "I'm kidding, I'm kidding. I worked at tons of bars when I was younger, I know how much you hate that question." Annie's face broke into a slightly embarrassed smile.

I said, "Two Jack and Cokes, please. Unless you have any actually decent bourbon back there," I winked behind my glasses.

She gave me a cute look, then said, "It's Jack Daniels. Why do you have your sunglasses on? And what's with the guitar?"

Red spoke before me. "Oh, this is my friend... Johnny Cash."

We all laughed. I half expected the girl not to know who that even was. But she asked flirtatiously, "Oh, really? Is this the line you're walking?"

"All depends on whether or not it leads me to that burning ring of fire," I flirted back.

"Actually," Red interjected, "I think we're headed to Folsom Prison."

I laughed again and said, "Yeah, well, maybe that's where I oughta stay."

Annie shook her head while trying not to smile. "Seriously, Johnny Cash. You know we're inside, right?"

"I have a condition – achromatopsia. Total color blindness, photosensitivity. So everything is black and white and bright all over."

"Really? Everything?"

"Everything but the color red."

She studied me for a second, trying to size me up, then simply went, "Interesting," and walked to the next set of passengers, in Will's direction up the car. Red's eyes followed her as her voice let out another, "Hi, I'm Annie, I'll be taking care of you today...."

My eyes followed her, too, as Red rubbernecked, then he and I exchanged glances. We shared the same face for a moment. "She's young," I said. "Gonna guess nineteen, *maybe* twenty by the looks of her."

"Christ, I feel old," Red mused.

"Nothing makes you feel older than realizing you're old enough to be that girl's father," I laughed.

"Nothing makes you feel younger than when a twenty-year-old looks at you like *that*, though," he turned his head again. She was glancing back at us with a smirk.

I averted my eyes self-consciously. "I feel old as shit and young as the breeze at the same time. Not a great feeling."

Red laughed. His eyes were fixed on her as she walked past us again toward the bar behind me. "I don't think I could do it."

"What, hook up with her? Pretty sure you have a shot."

He shook his head. "No, I don't think I could go *through* with it. I'd be too self-conscious the entire time. It would feel good in the moment, but as soon as you're done, I bet that post-nut clarity hits you like a freight train."

"That, and as soon as you're done, she's gonna ask you where you were when Kennedy was shot."

Red busted out laughing, then Annie came back with the cocktails. "Something funny?" she asked with an incisive look, trying not to grin as she wobbled with the movement of the train.

"Lots of things," I replied. She gave me another look, then sauntered back up the train car.

For a minute, I looked out the window at the trail passing us by at a speed slightly faster than a bicycle. We passed an all-too familiar swimming hole just beyond a small intersection leading to a couple houses, and my chest tightened as I thought back to the first time Alita had ever taken me there.

But something else quickly stole my attention.

My ears pricked up as Annie began talking to Will and his date.

Red must have been listening, too, because he downed his drink in one gulp. I could see the gears turning.

"Red, it's not worth it."

He looked at me. "I know, I know. Just every time I hear the sound of his goddamn voice, I want to commit violence. I could *kill* him, you know."

"Yeah? Good luck raising your kid from prison."

Red frowned. "You're right, you're right."

Then Will's voice struck our ears again. "Well if you're the waitress here all the time then maybe I oughta start taking more train rides."

Something in Red's eyes snapped. "Red, don't –"

He turned around in his seat and shouted loudly, "Careful, buddy – I don't think she's twenty-one yet, so your strategy of getting girls so drunk they *pass out* before you fuck them might not work."

The train car went silent. Will looked back at us and did his best to keep a calm demeanor, acting like Red was just an unhinged drunk.

Misty slurred badly: "Whass-he talkin' about?"

Slowly, Will scratched his beard and said to the waitress, "Excuse my former friend back there. He thinks that I slept with his soon-to-be ex-wife."

Red rose to his feet. "I don't think you slept with her. I think you *coerced* her, you fucking diet-coke skim-milk *rapist*."

Tension filled the air so quickly you could have seen lightning sparking off.

Annie stood there looking nervous. Will's fingers were trembling but he tried not to look scared. He stood up and said, "Is now really the time to be doing this?"

Red strode over to him. "As a matter of fact, it is."

I jumped up. "Red, stop!"

Red turned back at me with a look that said, *don't worry, I'm not gonna kill him.*

Misty exclaimed in a shrill voice, "Just fucking hit him already!"

Will exhaled nervously, trying his best to look like a man as he ignored the woman next to him. But he gripped the back of his seat with white knuckles while he stood there. "You're really gonna believe her over me? Red, I mean no offense by this, but Layla is a crazy whore."

Red cocked his brow. "Yeah? You think so?"

Will sort of shrugged and nodded. "I mean, you know she is."

Then Red clicked his tongue. "Yeah, well, I'm kinda fuckin' crazy, too."

Without warning, Red cocked back his fist. "Red, no!" I yelled.

But before my breath was through, Red knocked Will right across the jaw. He tumbled backwards into his seat and his head bounced off the window. Annie screamed and Misty shrieked.

Quickly, I grabbed Red to restrain him. He was a lot bigger than me, so it took all the dedication I had. He probably could have thrown me off without even trying that hard if he really wanted to. But I kept him still.

A man in a vintage conductor's uniform came marching quickly into the car. "What in Sam Hill is going on back here?"

Will stood up with blood leaking from his nostrils. "This man just *assaulted* me!"

Red scoffed and rolled his eyes. "Oh, man the fuck up, pussy."

The conductor looked at me and Red. "This true, fellas?"

Red sighed and said, "It's true: this man is a pussy."

The conductor let out a strained breath through his nose, then said something to Annie. She quickly bounded through the door to the next car, stopping to shoot me a worried look, then disappeared. In a moment, the train slowed to a stop. I looked out the window; we were halfway to Killdevil.

Then the conductor announced, "This is your stop, boys."

With a heavy sigh, Red looked at him and said, "Sorry about that." Then he looked at Will. "Don't ever speak to me again."

Will stood there with a pleading look of fear.

Then, Red and I stepped off the train.

We watched as it went on without us and I let out a sigh.

"And that train keeps a-rollin'...."

# Chapter 12

"Jesus Christ, Red – how far away is this place?"

"Not too much further."

"Whose bright fucking idea was it to build a town on a hill like this?" I bitched and griped. My legs were on fire and my buzz was gone; something about long walks just kills the liquor in you.

Red chuckled as we walked through the streets of Killdevil. "I'm right on Cherry Lane."

Killdevil was even older than New Freedom was, and it showed. The town was built on a slope, with houses packed tightly like sardine cans. They almost looked like row houses, except more colonial. There wasn't a whole lot in Killdevil. There was a bar, a gas station, and the rest were houses. Most of my friends who didn't live in New Freedom, they lived here.

My guitar weighed on my back as we climbed a steep hill with cracked cement sidewalks. "You'd think everybody in this town would be in *great* fucking shape," I groaned as my thighs screamed at me.

Red laughed and said, "Be a man, suck it up."

"Oh, I'm fine," I replied. "I'm just wondering if the heavier members of our community walk or roll here."

Red chortled again and my eyes drifted toward the houses along Main Street. I knew a couple of them. Makenna's house was right on the corner, Huck's place was down an alley, and Will lived on the top of the hill. As we passed Will's house, Red was staring at it.

"Don't burn it down," I advised. "He's got a daughter. Plus, prison isn't worth it."

"Fine example he's setting for her," he remarked darkly. "But I wouldn't go to prison. They wouldn't know it was me."

"After you clocked the man on a train in front of thirty other passengers? Yeah, they might."

Red huffed his breath and went, "Fair." We passed Will's house and the anger subsided. Then Red said, "Even if I got caught, I've got people. I've got places. They wouldn't ever *catch* me."

I smirked, amused. "What, you've got an underground network or something?"

Red shot me a look. "You know I was in the military with Rust, right?" There was a pause, then he went on. "Between him and I, we have people all over the country who can help us out in a bind. Especially the extra-legal kind of bind."

My smirk broke into a grin. "You got a safehouse around here?"

"As a matter of fact, I do," Red laughed.

I laughed, too. "No shit, really?"

"Mhm," he nodded. "Out past the River Sound Dam. It's a couple miles past the West Virginia line, across the second bridge, tucked away out in the woods. Stocked up for a month's supply of food, situated a quarter mile from a stream. Fresh water, plenty of game to hunt, so far in the woods you'd never find it without a map." His face stretched proudly into a broad smile.

"Shit, that's cool," I breathed. "I guess if I'm ever in trouble I know who I'm coming to."

\*\*\*

A couple hours went by where Red and I sat on the porch, shooting the shit and playing music. His new house was empty save for a sparse bit of furniture, but the outdoors was where we would both rather be, anyhow. I did my best not to get stoned but I might have had a scotch or two. Going by the position of the sun dipping below the horizon in the west, I gleaned it must have been about 7:00.

"Hey, you think you can give me a ride back to New Freedom?" I asked Red. "Me and Jazz are supposed to play soon."

"What, you don't wanna walk?" Red chided playfully.

"As fun as that sounds, I don't think I'll make it back in time for my set."

We both chuckled as we got up off his porch. His new house was remarkably similar to his old one. Sometimes I think we do everything we can to slow down change, or to stop it all together. But time is inexorable; it always moves forward, just like a river or a stream. You can never set foot in the same river twice and you can never live a moment again.

Time doesn't wait.

We got into his truck and within a couple minutes, we were back in New Freedom, parking in front of the Clawhammer. Quickly, I scanned the parking lot to get a bead on who all might be in there. Mostly I saw the cars of the regulars, the usual suspects. A part of me was hoping to see Alita's gray sedan, and another part of me was hoping I wouldn't see her at all.

"Hey," Red stopped me as I opened the passenger door. I looked at him. His red flannel popped out at me. "Thanks, man."

"For what?"

"For being honest. For not being Will. For telling me that Layla made a pass at you instead of taking the free ticket out of a tough conversation." Firmly, he gripped my shoulder. "Thank you. I mean it."

Silently, I nodded. For some reason, things still didn't feel right.

Lightning struck the dimming sky as we stepped into the evening air. *Lightning every night, never any rain*, I mused to myself as I swung my guitar over my shoulder. Red and I walked up the brick steps to the Clawhammer Tavern. As soon as we were through the door, music hit my ears. The place was packed; I didn't know how many of them were there to see me but I could have bet most of them were there to see Jasmine. Her voice could fill an auditorium if it were given the chance.

"God damn," Red mused as we walked through the poolroom with the stairway to the second floor. "People really showed out tonight."

My eyes spotted Jazz leaning against the bar, laughing with Lorraine and the other bartender, Madeline. Jazz turned and looked at us, her face still stretched out with a bright wide smile as her lightly colored bangs rested over her forehead, and her dreadlocks fought to escape her headwrap. My heart skipped a beat like she broke my metro-nome. "Yeah," I replied distantly. "I had a feeling they would."

We sauntered into the main area of the Clawhammer with the wooden bar that snaked along the wall all the way to the patio door. I glanced at the corner of the room where amps and instruments were set up. Rust was sitting on a stool with a banjo in his hands, his fingertips moving faster than the Devil's down in Georgia as he struck every note, every chord perfectly. He rattled a melody but Rust didn't really care for doing vocals. His voice was a backup to the strings; he knew how to make that instrument sing.

Jazz turned around and swung her arms around me. "You actually made it!" she teased joyfully.

Red grinned and said, "I almost kept him, but this one's trouble and I don't need it." We all three laughed.

"I told you I'd make it," I responded with a devilish smile.

She returned the look then sized me up. "How drunk are you?"

"A little buzzed, that's all."

She eyed me skeptically as Rust finished his song, and I gestured to Madeline for a bourbon. Jazz echoed, "A little buzzed?"

I leaned over to the bar as Madeline set down my drink. She was a tall girl, stocky and built similar to Lorraine – they were cousins. "Thanks, Madison," I teased.

Madeline rolled her eyes with a grunt. She hated when people fucked up her name. "Bitch, I will slap you," she said.

"Do it, I've been hit harder."

She leaned into the bar and cocked her hand back and I leaned forward to challenge her, our faces only a few inches apart. She stared through my glasses for a second as we held our stances. Then suddenly she dropped her hand and belched loudly in my face.

"Oh, goddammit, Maddy!" I recoiled.

She laughed triumphantly and said, "Don't start none, won't be none," then sauntered off.

I grabbed my bourbon and took a swig as I turned back toward Jazz. She was eyeing me with worry. "I'll be fine," I told her.

A young guy with a mullet and a mustache, standing kind of short, came up and greeted me and Jazz excitedly, carrying a Walkman in one hand and holding one headphone to his ear with the other. He was a guy we worked with at the Blacktop. He made music, too, but he did new age shit and I would be lying if I said it was my style. "Yo!" he beamed.

"What's up, Jimmy?" I grinned back.

"Excited to see you play, dude," he held out a fist and I gently hit it with mine. "'Bout damn time I actually get to see a show."

"Don't hype me up – Jazz is the one bringing this crowd." I glanced at her with a small smile and she rolled her eyes with a laugh.

"Ha haa," Jimmy went excitedly, "I'm pumped, dude." Then he took the headphones and held one half to my ear. "Check this out."

I listened for a moment. It was a techno beat with distorted vocals singing over it. "New song?" I asked.

"Hell yeah, buddy," he grinned proudly. "Cooked this up in the studio last night. Whatchu think?"

"Not my style," I replied, "but it's good – it's catchy as hell."

"Ya damn right it is," he rejoined humorously. "This is gonna make me rich."

I laughed and replied: "It's not about making money, Jim, it's about making music. It's your passion – it doesn't matter if it pays the bills or not."

Jimmy gave me a look and said, "Yeah, well, in case you didn't notice, Lyric – we work at a fuckin' restaurant. I ain't tryna die there. This shit better pop off or I'm just gonna have to throw myself off a bridge."

Jazz's eyes widened. "Or, here's a thought, maybe *don't* kill yourself?"

Jimmy scoffed and his arms dropped. "Goddamn, Jazz, relax. It's a joke."

I laughed at the interplay, then Madeline's voice called out from the other end of the bar. "Jimmy! Come get your fuckin' drink!"

He inhaled air through his teeth and went, "Whoops – forgot I ordered that." Then we bumped each other's fists again and he said, "Good luck out there." He leaned in and held his hand beside his face to shield his words. "Looks like a tough crowd tonight."

"Jimmy!" Maddy yelled again.

Jimmy laughed then bounded away. Jazz and I shared an amused glance.

Then Rust's banjo struck its final chord and the bar clapped. "Thank you, thank you," he said into the microphone with gravel in his voice. "Now that the warmup is done, I hereby cede the stage to my friends Lyric and Jazz." He sort of bowed, then gestured for us to take his spot.

Jazz looked at me nervously as we took our spots. "You're stumbling. Can you even play that guitar right now?"

I sat down on the stool and plugged my guitar into the amp. My fingers fumbled for a second as I strummed a chord to get my bearings. But I found the music.

Then I gave her a look.

"Sure I can."

My fingertips cried out a small section of a guitar solo I had been practicing, and through the grace of God somehow I didn't miss the beat. Red clapped and let out a loud *whoo!*

"Thank you, thank you very much," I said into the microphone, imitating Elvis as Jazz picked up her own guitar plugged into a separate amp. She didn't use a pick, just her fingers. I didn't know how she did it, but it was a thing of wonder to watch.

Then I spotted Liz in the crowd with our mutual friend Angelica. Liz shouted, "Fuck it up, Lyric!"

Then Angelica shouted, "Don't fuck it up! I want to hear *good* music!"

Liz playfully shoved Angelica and said, "It's a figure of speech, dumbass."

Angelica went, "*I know*, but don't encourage him."

Then I spotted another couple of friends of mine – Josie and Jess, the only lesbian couple in all of New Freedom as far as I knew, sitting next to Jimmy. Jess was a sweetheart and Josie knew how to take care of business. She was short, but I'd seen her throw down before. She shouted at Angelica and Liz, "Shut the hell up so they can get on with it!" then gave me and Jazz a wink. The bouncer – a bald man in his late thirties or early forties named Wayne – sat with the two of them and his wife Crystal. They were almost always together, even when he was here, and even though I didn't know them too well I always thought that was sweet. He crossed his arms and shook his head laughing at Josie's forwardness.

I looked over at Jazz, who was laughing into the microphone, audible over the din of the revelrous crowd. "Thank you all, you're far too kind – well, maybe not *too* kind, but certainly kind enough," she said with a smile. Her voice carried like it was in an amphitheater. There was a gentle rasp to it that hit the ears with all satisfaction. Then she said, "Without further ado...."

She closed her eyes and leaned into the microphone as she began singing. Softly, in a low tenor, I added the timbre of my voice to hers as we began acapella:

*"Dellll-ta-a Dawn, what's that flower you have on?*
*Could it be a faded rose from days gone byyyyy?*
*And did I hear you say...?*
*He was meetin' you here today...*
*To take you to his mansion in the skyyyyy...."*

Then she strummed the first chord and I began an arpeggio to complement it, while her hand intermittently drummed on the body of her acoustic as she played, creating a sound that was something beautiful to listen to.

I don't think there was ever such a perfect moment in my entire life.

\*\*\*

Our set went on until about nine o'clock and we were finally wrapping up. Jazz said into the microphone, "Alright, ladies and gentlemen, we're gonna take a quick break then we'll be wrapping up here shortly. I hope everybody is enjoying the show."

She set her guitar down and stepped away from the mic. I asked, "Taking a break at the end of the set?"

She made an embarrassed face and said, "I *really* have to pee."

I let out a laugh and replied, "As you were."

She wandered off toward the bathroom and I sat there keeping my fingers primed. I had almost finished my whiskey during the set but it was finally starting to hit me. Suddenly there was a sense of shame. My mind pictured Jazz coming back and me being too fucked up to play the last song.

I glanced down at the bourbon resting beside me.

*C'est la vie.*

Then I downed the rest of it in one gulp.

"Wow," a girl's voice came. "You couldn't wait till you were done to get back to drinking, huh?"

I looked up. Makenna was standing in front of me with something between a grin and a smirk. "You know this place is for adults, right?"

"I'm eighteen," she protested.

"Drinking age is twenty-one, kid."

Makenna looked over at Lorraine behind the bar and Rust on a stool in the corner. "They said I could come in and watch you guys play as long as I don't try and order a drink," she said, then looked back at me. "So deal with it."

I chuckled and said, "Fair enough. What are you doing here, anyway? Won't your parents be pissed?"

Her face fell. "Well, considering my dad's off sailing the ocean somewhere, I don't think he'll notice. Me and my mom got into a fight about it last night and she tried to kick me out again, but I told her 'no,' so *she* left instead. She's staying at my aunt's house until *I* apologize – so she's gonna be there a while."

Her sardonic attitude didn't hide the fact that she was hurt. I told her, "I know what absent parents are like. But it's alright. It makes you tough. You could survive in the wild. Most of your friends? They'd be dead in a day."

Her face lit up but she didn't say 'thank you.' Instead, she pulled out a piece of paper from her back pocket. "Here."

"What's this?" I asked.

"It's your song. I came up with a tune."

"Oh, shit – that was fast." I took the paper and looked it over. She wrote out notes for the vocals under the lyrics on the front, then tabbed out a guitar melody on the back.

"It's not much, but I think it's within your self-taught ability," she teased. I listened to the tune in my head.

"This... This is good. You came up with this in a few hours?"

"Well, yeah," she almost laughed. "What else was I gonna do today?"

"Makenna, you were at work."

She shrugged. "I got bored."

There was a sense of proudness I felt when I looked at her. "You're gonna go far, kid."

Then Jazz came back from the restroom. "Well hey, beautiful," she beamed at Makenna. "What are you doing here, baby? Shouldn't you be home?"

Makenna sort of shrugged and said, "Nobody's there, anyway."

Sympathetically, Jazz touched her shoulder. "I'm sorry. Your parents acting up again?"

"Always," she sighed.

Then I handed Jazz the paper. "Change of plans," I said. "You think we can do this?"

She looked it over and said, "It's only a couple of stanzas, but yeah, I can sing this. Can you play it?"

I practiced the rhythm Makenna had written. It paired perfectly with the lyrics in my head. "Yeah, I can play it."

"Well, in that case...." Jazz smiled.

"Oh, real quick –" Makenna added, " – the beat is like a *duh, duh, duh-duh, duh, duh, duh-duh*." She leaned forward and drums her hands on top of the amp beside me as she speaks. "You got that?"

Jazz picked up her acoustic and drummed the beat on the hollow body of the guitar. "Got it."

"Now go sit down, Mozart," I told her.

Makenna grinned proudly and I gestured with my head toward a couple empty stools at the corner by Rust. She scurried away, then I said into the microphone, "Alright, boys and girls, we're gonna do something a little different for this last song. A friend of mine helped me write this – and it's still a work in progress, so if it sucks then blame her." There was a laugh and Makenna made a pouting face. "Kidding, kidding. The only one who can fuck it up is me." Then I looked at Jazz. "You ready?"

She held the paper and went over the lyrics again. "Sure am."

I turned back to the crowd. "This is *Step into the Sound*."

Instantly, I began strumming the melody. It was sad, it was sweet, and it had the cadence that matched what it felt like to be beaten, bruised and broken, frustrated beyond heartbreak, yet to still keep going.

Then Jazz began to sing.

*"I just killed a friennnnd, said I took his life,*

*I became a cowarrrrd when he caught me with his wife,*

*The barman said 'Your karmaaaa, when it finally comes around,*

*When it's time to face up to the musiiiic or get into the ground,*

*Just pick up your guitarrrr and step into the sound,*

*Step into the sound.*

*So I picked up my guitarrrr and I started down the road,*
*Hidin' out in old dive barrrrrs with the lawman on my coat,*
*'I shot a man in my hometownnnn,' I said, she asked me, 'why?'*
*I looked at the bartenderrrr and I said, 'to watch him die.'*

*She said, 'Your karmaaaa, when it finally comes around,*
*When you know that it's overrrr 'cause the lawman's coming down,*
*Just face up to the musiiiic and step into the sound,*
*Step into the sound.'*

*When he gave me fifty yearrrrs, the Judge, he asked me, 'why?'*
*I looked at hiiiiiii-im and this was my reply:*

*The man I called a friennnnd, you know he killed his wife,*
*Found out she was with meee-e, then he took her life,*
*And when I found herrrrr, you know I asked him 'why?'*
*His eyes became colderrrr and he said, 'to watch her die.'*

*If my devils ever leave meeee, then my angels will as well,*

*Find my penance here in Countyyyy while I'm climbin' outta Hell,*

*And your karmaaaa, when it finally comes around,*

*You can make a deal with the Devillll, and get into the ground,*

*Or sing along with your angelssss, and step into the sound,*

*Step into the sound.*

*Step into the sound."*

The bar went silent for a moment. Jasmine's voice faded as it held that last note of the somber yet triumphant melody Makenna had written. All eyes were upon her, then I strummed the last notes.

From the crowd, Red's voice cried out, "Hell yeah!" and he led the patrons in a round of applause.

"Thank you so much, everybody," Jazz said into the microphone. "We've been Lyric and Jazz, and we hope you had as much fun as we did."

Then Red's friend Roy yelled out, "Encore! Encore!"

And Liz yelled, "Play Freebird!"

So I leaned into the mic with a grin and replied, "Fuck all of you."

There was a laugh and Jazz shook her head. I gave her a mischievous grin and then looked at Makenna sitting in the corner of the room, away from the crowd. Silently, I mouthed the words *thank you*. She smiled back at me, then Lorraine went over to her and said something. I'm gonna guess it was a gentle push to get the hell out of the bar now that the set was over and the real drinking was about to commence. Makenna got up, waved at me and Jazz, then walked out the door through the pool room.

"Oh, hey," her voice came as she walked out the door. Puzzled, I thought about who Makenna might have run into on her way out. But I didn't have to wait for long.

Alita walked into the bar.

She looked terrified.

# Chapter 13

"Hey, are you okay?" I asked as I set my guitar on the stand next to me and hopped off the stool. Alita stood there looking frightened, glancing around – probably looking for Huck.

"He's lost it, Lyric," she said.

I grimaced. "What did he do?"

Alita gathered her thoughts as Jazz came by, her own countenance mirroring mine. "Alita, what's wrong?"

"Is it that obvious?"

"A little bit," Jazz replied worriedly.

Alita took a deep breath, then said, "He threatened me. He saw me at the Shell and told me if I came near you again... he'd kill you."

My brow twitched angrily. "I'd like to see him try."

Jazz interjected, "Well *I* wouldn't! Lyric, this is serious!" Then she looked at Alita. "Did you tell your dad?"

"Yeah...."

"And?"

"And he said that's just Huck puffing his chest, standing his ground. That Lyric oughta learn how to stay away from a brewing storm."

I scoffed. "Fucking unbelievable."

"He said as long as you don't violate that restraining order then you've got nothing to worry about," she remarked bitterly. "He's so goddamn out of touch, I can't stand it."

I studied her for a moment, then gently placed my hand on the small of her back. "Come on, let's get you a drink."

The three of us sauntered to the bar through the crowd as the jukebox kicked back on, serenading us with today's hits and yesterday's favorites. We stood next to Red and Roy – who was older than Red by a good ten years, with hair in a ponytail and a gray beard. Swear to God, half the men in that town had ponytails. He said, "You guys absolutely killed it up there, seriously."

"Thank you," Jazz smiled politely, trying to shake the nerves from Alita's revelation.

"No, I'm serious," Roy went on. "You two have something special, man, I'm telling you. I love it, I love to see it."

"Thank you, Roy," I replied dryly. My heart was pounding and all I wanted was a drink to slow it down.

Roy got real close and put his hand on my neck – amicably, not like the old pervert Rick who was sitting in the corner – but it still bothered me. It triggered some deep-seated anxiety from childhood, one of the many lessons my father must have taught me growing up. "Seriously, you guys –"

"Roy, read the fuckin' room," I snapped suddenly. He recoiled. Guiltily, my face fell. "Sorry," I mumbled over the music. "Just... nerves." I patted him on the shoulder. "I appreciate you."

He took a step back and said, "All good, brother," then shot Red a look that said *sheesh*.

Roy removed himself from the vicinity and Madeline came over and got me and Alita our usual drinks. The bourbon did little to quell the anger or anxiety stirring inside me.

My ears caught the sound of arguing a few feet down and I looked over. Red had been pulled into a heated conversation with Liz and Angelica. He said, "I didn't do *any* of that and you know it. I never put my hands on her and I've never hit a woman before in my life." There was indignation written on his face.

"Well that's not what Layla said!" Angelica shot back.

"You mean that's not what a lying whore said?" Red feigned dumb, looking at Roy – who began to chuckle. "Roy, can you believe it? The woman who cheated on me with five different dudes said *I'm* the bad guy! Well jeepers, we better believe her!"

Angelica huffed her breath. "You're not slick, Red. I see you."

"Angelica, with all due respect: please, fuck off."

She stared at him incisively for a moment, then she and Liz returned to their corner. I said, "Damn, Red. You sure have a way with the ladies."

He rolled his eyes and replied, "Tell me about it."

Then Josie came up to us. Her speech was a little slurred and there was a can of Miller in her hand, but she was still lucid. Her partner Jess was the designated driver, so Josie could cut loose a little bit. She put her arms around me and Jazz. "You guys are phenomenal," she said. "Seriously."

Jazz smiled her gorgeous smile and replied, "Thank you, baby. Music is the quickest path to the soul."

Then Josie looked at me and said, "And you... Lyric, you could be great. You've got hustle, you're smart, you're talented. You just need to get out of your own fuckin' way." I held her look for a moment, then she reached up and tousled my hair despite being almost a foot shorter than me. "I love you guys."

I squeezed my arm around her shoulder. "Love you too, Josie."

The second she released us and walked back to Jess, Wayne, and Crystal, the door swung open and Layla walked in.

"Fuck," Red muttered.

I put my hand on his shoulder. "It's all good, man. Just don't worry about it."

"That's kind of hard to do when she's walking toward me."

Suddenly Layla was standing in front of us. It was strangely relieving to see her now, knowing that I didn't break my bond with Red for a night of physical release. Timidly, she half waved and said in a small voice, "Hey."

Red took in a deep breath. "You got a babysitter?"

"Of course I did."

He let the air out and nodded solemnly. Then he looked at her. "Buy you a drink?"

She sort of smiled. "Sure."

Red turned around and ordered her a cocktail. "It's a little noisy in here," he said to her over the sound of the music. "You wanna...?" He jabbed his thumb toward the back door.

"Yeah, we can do that."

He handed her the drink with a conflicted expression, then placed his hand on her lower back and walked her to the door. He shot me a grim look as they left my line of sight.

"Jesus Christ," I muttered to Alita and Jazz as I snuffed my cigarette in a nearby ashtray. "Small fucking towns."

As if on cue, the door opened again and in walked Will and Misty.

"And here we fucking go," I raised my hand and dopped my palm to the bar.

Will spotted me at the bar and came over with his date. "Well fancy meeting you here," he said, almost nervously. His face was bruised from earlier.

I looked at the girl; she seemed just as plastered as she had been on the train. Out of habit and civic duty, I shot Lorraine a look and gestured with my hand across my throat – it was code for flagging a patron, meaning you probably shouldn't serve them. Then I said to Will, "Just a heads up, Red's out back."

Will sort of shrugged and said, "That's alright. I'm sure we can all act like adults for long enough to have a few drinks without resorting to violence."

I mimicked his shrug and replied, "Well, you fucked his wife, so I don't know about that."

"Yeah, but... So did you. Didn't you?"

I frowned and shook my head. "Turns out it never went that far. I thought it might have, but she left me off the list. So she really did just walk me home that night."

Will nodded, surprised and almost disappointed, and said, "Well that's good."

I peered at him through my glasses. "Yeah, it is. Thanks for throwing me under the bus to try and save your own ass, though. Really appreciate that."

For once, Will said nothing, just rubbed his beard.

Then his date drunkenly peered down the other end of the bar. Her speech was badly impaired. "Hey, isn't thatthe angry les– HICCUP –bian who triedta fight me?"

I snapped my head toward the other end of the bar. Josie was down there.

Will said, "Probably. Not a lot of angry lesbians in this town."

"Fuck that bitch," the girl spat as Angelica and Liz got up and went through the back door.

Josie must have had the ears of a bat because she was suddenly looking down at our end of the bar. "You say something?" she asked sharply.

"Ah, shit," I grumbled.

Misty leaned forward and shrieked, "Yeah! I said *fuck you, bitch!*"

Jazz and I exchanged wide eyed glances while Alita nervously sipped her beer as Josie got up and made her way toward us.

She shouted, while gesturing emphatically: "You got a fucking problem, you drunk ass skank?"

Will interjected. "Ladies, ladies, calm down. Let's not make mountains out of mole hills."

"Oh, fuck you, Will!" Josie roared. "How drunk did you have to get *this* one before she'd touch your cock?"

Misty argued, "I'm not cock at all and I ain't touchin' his drunk!"

Will frowned and said to Josie, "Okay, harsh. Clearly you're intoxicated, so I'm gonna give you a pass on that one."

"I don't give a shit about your pass!" Josie shouted. "Control that bitch before someone knocks the last three fuckin' teeth out of her head!"

The girl jumped from her barstool and Will quickly grabbed her small frame as she swung her arms wildly. I couldn't help but think of Scrappy-Doo raising his fists and yelling *let me at 'em! Let me at 'em!*

Will said forcefully, "Misty, stop!"

Then Wayne came over. "The hell are you people screamin' about?"

Misty pointed at Josie and shouted, "This butch ass bitch wants to fight!"

"I don't want to fight, I want you to shut the fuck up so we can enjoy our drinks in peace!"

Wayne opened his mouth to speak, but a shrill shriek from the back patio cut him off.

*"You know what?!"* Angelica's voice came. *"Fuck you, Red!"*

Then we all heard the sound of glass breaking and hitting concrete.

195

Wayne rolled his eyes and sighed heavily. "God damn it."

Just as he moved toward the back door, it opened and in walked Red, soaked from head to toe in what must have previously been a full bottle of beer. He had sort of a stunned look in his eyes. Layla walked in with him.

Wayne asked, "Red, what the hell happened?"

Red sighed and said, "Don't worry about it," then looked at Lorraine, who stood at the ready to break up a fight. "Can I get my tab, please?"

She narrowed her eyes in puzzled confusion. "Sure, baby. You two separate or together?"

Red glanced at Layla, then said, "Together."

Lorraine walked down to the register and the back door opened again. I stood in the middle of the bar, watching everything unfold. Angelica and Liz came back in. Liz looked like she couldn't believe what just happened, and Angelica's lips quivered angrily.

Wayne asked quickly, "The fuck did you do?"

Angelica pointed at Red and yelled, "Gave him a taste of his own medicine, that's what!"

Wayne glanced between the two of them quizzically, then asked, "Miller Lite?"

"She broke a fucking bottle over my head," Red said loudly but calmly. "So I'm gonna go home and sleep off this forthcoming concussion."

Wayne gave Angelica a look that said *really?* then let out a sigh. "You gotta go, Angel."

Before she could retort, Red noticed Will down the bar. "Oh, and here we fucking go," he said angrily. In a flash, Red was standing in the midst of the screaming match between the women flanking Will.

I glanced at Jazz and blurted, "Shit!" as I ran to intercept him. Alita had shrank into the corner, quietly watching the confrontations unfold from the safety of a table. Old man Rick leaned toward her to say something, but she shot him a look of daggers and held a warning finger that shut him up before he even spoke.

"You've got a lot of fucking nerve, my friend," Red began, puffing his chest. Will gripped the bar nervously, struggling to look casual and unafraid.

"It's a bar, open to the public," he replied steadily, slowly, keeping his breath from shaking. "I have as much right to be here as you do."

Red scoffed. "Right? Sure. That's not in question. The question is whether or not it's the *smart* fucking thing for you to do."

Layla stood behind Red and I landed in between him and Will. Will's eyes flicked towards hers and she looked away guiltily. "Layla," Will began, "could you please tell your man here that it would be better for you to go home together than for him to spend the night in jail?"

Layla shrank into herself timidly, barely visible behind Red. I interjected. "This is stupid, both of you. Just let it go, Red. As much as it sucks, he's right. We're not in the wild west – there are consequences to this shit." Suddenly I could hear Jazz's words coming out of my own mouth.

Then Will's date shrieked, "You're damn right there are!"

Josie rejoined irritatedly, "Will you shut the hell up already?!"

Then Will said, "You're lucky I didn't press charges on you on the train."

Layla looked at Red dumbfounded. "What the hell did you do on the train?"

Red frowned. "I clocked him."

Will sort of shirked and said, "I wouldn't say you *clocked* me, but it was definitely worthy of an assault charge. Notice how I didn't call the cops? You're welcome."

There was an electric silence as the two men stared at each other, Will fearfully gripping the wooden bartop. I placed my hand on Red's shoulder. "Red, man, come on. Go home to your kid."

For a moment, he was statue still. Then he finally let the air out. "You're right, you're right," his head fell. Then he picked it back up and pointed a finger at Will. "You're lucky I actually have something to lose."

Those words brought back the ones Sheriff Swanson had told me earlier.

*In my experience, that's the most dangerous thing a man can be.*

*What? Free?*

*Alone.*

I snapped out of it just in time to watch the tension in the place finally snap.

Misty shrieked, "Oh would you *just – fucking – hit him already!*"

Without warning, she hurled Will's beer bottle across the room. It shattered against the brick wall right beside Alita and old man Rick. She screamed and shielded her face from the broken glass, while Rick scurried away and stood next to the jukebox.

All of our heads snapped toward Alita. Jazz ran to her instantly, and just as I turned to shout, "What the hell!" at the drunk woman, Josie came roaring over. Right before fists began flying, I heard a familiar drum beat take over the jukebox. I glanced over and saw Rick standing there with a mischievous grin as The Sweet's *Ballroom Blitz* began to play.

*Oh, mother fucker.*

As the guitar riff kicked in, Josie didn't waste her time on words.

"You crazy bitch!" Misty screamed as Josie pulled her by her deep red hair. Misty stumbled backwards onto the floor, her barstool clanging against the hard wood ground, and in a matter of seconds, the bar had broken into a brawl. Fists were flying left and right, coming from people who weren't even a part of the ordeal. Red clocked Will in the jaw again, then a friend of Will's jumped in and started throwing blows at Red. I grabbed the stranger by the back of his shirt and pulled him off, then he turned and shoved me into the bar before assailing Red again. Will ran around the other side of Red, so I leapt toward him and rammed my shoulder into his gut.

"You had it coming," I muttered as he fell down, winded. Up ahead, Jimmy jumped on somebody like a spider monkey and pulled him to the ground, wrapping his arms and legs around him with a wrestling pin. I turned around and saw another guy I only knew in passing choking out Roy, who had a terrified look in his eye. Quickly, I pulled his arm off of Roy's neck and we grabbed each other by the shirts. Then Red pushed his opponent off of him, turned and socked the choker in the back of the head. He collapsed and hit his head on the bar, then clutched himself in pain as he rolled around on the ground. Rick stood by the jukebox, tapping his feet and clapping to the music while Josie dragged Misty by her hair. Then the drunk woman jumped up and started futilely clawing and scratching at Josie. She tried instinctively to pull her hair, but Josie kept it buzzed. And she didn't play around with catscratches and hissing.

Josie cocked her arm back and drove her fist right into Misty's face.

"Oh, *damn*," I recoiled at the sight as the woman fell on her ass, holding her face.

In a deep, nasally voice, she yelled, "You crazy bitch, you broke my nose!"

In the struggle, Red took the man who jumped on him and spun around, then threw him into a window when his balance went off. A loud crunching *crack* drowned out the music spilling from the jukebox.

Then a gunshot went off.

Everybody was silent.

Out of instinctive fear, I checked to make sure the revolver was still in my back pocket. *Whew, okay, so that wasn't me.*

We all craned our necks to see a decently intoxicated Colton Rust standing at the entrance to the pool room, a revolver in his hand pointing at the ceiling with a bent elbow. His face looked unconcerned, but there was an unmistakable sense of warning about it.

He nodded to Lorraine to turn down the jukebox. Once the music was quiet, he said with his slow drawl: "Now that I have your attention... Ladies and gentlemen, I do believe we're gonna call this one an early night. I'd like to ask that you all calmly, politely, and *quietly* pay your tabs so I can assess how much it's gonna cost to repair the damage y'all just did." Rust glanced up at the bullet hole in the doorway trim as sawdust fell down. "And that I just did, I guess. If y'all would be so kind as to get the hell out of my bar in an orderly fashion, then, well..." he sort of checked out the revolver, "...this here is an antique, so I'd really rather not have to fire it again. If you've got any questions, keep 'em to yourself. I prefer not to be bothered."

With that, Rust casually sauntered through the pool room and up the stairs.

My eyes scanned the aftermath. Red was making up with the guy he was fighting, Will was rubbing his face and pulling out his wallet, Josie was regrouping with her partner and friends, while Wayne was corralling everyone to the bar to pay up. Jazz and Alita sat anxiously at their table by our equipment. Jazz was comforting her, letting her maternal instincts kick in.

Misty stumbled as she got up, holding her face. "Will, she broke my fucking nose."

"Yes, dear, I noticed," Will breathed sardonically, unconcerned as he set money on the bar. He looked at me. "I'll catch you later, Lyric."

"Yeah," I sighed. "I'll see you when I see you."

Will and Misty walked past Layla without looking at her, while Misty continued to mumble about her fucked up face. Josie was surveying her knuckles at the other end of the bar. After a few minutes, it was down to me, Jazz, Alita, Red and Layla – plus the ones who worked there.

"Guess we should probably hightail it out of here," I remarked, pulling out my wallet. Lorraine made a sympathetic yet amused face.

"Yeah, probably." Then she started laughing. "God damn, just another night at the Clawhammer."

I laughed with her. "That's gotta be one for the record books."

Layla, still timid, strolled toward the front door through the pool room, glancing at the bullet hole in the trim as she passed through the doorway. Red came over and put his hand on my shoulder as Jazz and Alita came by. Alita handed me my guitar and Jazz had her instrument in its case slung over her shoulder. With a wild look in her eye, she asked, "So what the hell just happened?"

"Drunk bitches and bad friends," Red replied dourly. Then he patted me on the back. "Thanks for having my back, Lyric. I appreciate you."

"You would do the same for me."

Red nodded silently. Then Layla's voice hit our ears. It was shrill and concerned. "Hey, Alita – isn't that your car out front?"

Alita furrowed her brow. "Yeah? Why?"

Layla's face tightened. "It looks like someone went through it."

My heart dropped. Immediately, I grabbed my instrument and all four of us hurried to the door.

All of Alita's personal effects were strewn about the sidewalk.

She burst through the door. "What the hell!"

I followed her. "Alita, wait –!"

"Who the fuck –?!" she stopped on the porch suddenly, gripping the white railing as Red, Layla and Jazz joined us. "Why do I even have to fucking ask...." she mumbled to herself. I took off my glasses and slid them into my pocket as another flash of lightning crossed the sky; anxiously, I awaited the thunder that never came.

*Am I imagining things?*

Jazz asked, "You know who did it?"

Alita almost glared at her. "Who do you think?"

Almost forebodingly, I took a breath. "You guys go on and get out of here – I'll help the lady pick up her things."

"You sure?" Red asked.

"Yeah," I sighed. "You've got something to go home to. Plus, no telling if Will goes home and calls the cops or not."

Red studied me for a second, then nodded. He addressed Layla: "Come on, babe."

It was strange to watch the two of them walk down the steps together. Sometimes there's an inexorable pull toward each other, even when it's gonna kill you both – like two stars ensnared in a binary system, spinning around each other and inching closer over millions of years, until they finally collide and obliterate one another.

Vaguely, I wondered if the stars ever regretted it.

Jazz put her hand on my arm worriedly. "You sure you'll be okay? If Huck is out to get you, then –"

"Then I'll take care of it," I replied distantly. "Get out of here, Jazz. I'll call you later."

"From home or from jail?" Her words were sharp but her eyes were soft.

"Home."

After a moment, she nodded. "Okay." Jazz wrapped her arms around me in a hug. Faintly, I could smell the scent of patchouli and something else, maybe lavender. Then she hugged Alita. "Be safe, okay?" she said to her.

Alita nodded quickly and quietly.

Then Jazz took one more look at us and walked off to her bright red van, the only color I could see save for the tail lights of the exeunting cars. With a heavy sigh and leaden feet, Alita and I descended the steps and began putting her things back in her car. She grumbled aloud, "I hate this, I hate him, I wish I never dated him."

"At least you don't have to sleep in your car tonight."

She paused and shot me an angry look. "I never *have* to sleep in my car, Lyric. I choose to. If this is how I have to make it on my own, then this is how I'll make it on my own. I don't need my idiot father and I don't need my psycho boyfriend. I don't need anybody."

"What about me?" I asked suddenly.

Alita froze. Then she resumed gathering her things without looking up. After a moment, she finally said, "I don't need you. But I like having you around."

I think there was some glimmer of love in my eyes when I looked at her.

Another voice broke the silence.

"Yeah, I bet you fucking do, you cheap whore."

It was Huck.

Instantly, I leapt to my feet as he marched angrily toward us.

Alita spoke first. "You mother *fucker!*" she shrieked, throwing a hairbrush at him.

Huck dodged it, then scoffed and said, "What? I'm not the one who threw all your useless shit out onto the ground. Maybe it was one of the other ten guys you fucked."

"I didn't fucking cheat on you!" she yelled.

"*Stop!*" I shouted suddenly. "Fuck!"

Huck took a step toward me. "The fuck are you gonna do about it? Mind your own goddamn business, Lyric. Or step up and do something." His chest was heaving; he was beyond angry. Immediately, it was like I was a teenager again, staring down my father in one of his blind, drunken furies. I remembered the lessons he taught me those nights.

"I'm not gonna fight you, Huck."

"That's because you're a fucking *pussy* and you know it," he snarled.

Calmly, I shook my head. "No. It's because I don't wanna kill you." He recoiled at that and his breathing halted. "And I'm afraid that, the next time you touch me, I'm just gonna... *snap*. And then that loaded .38 in my back pocket is gonna have one less bullet in it." There was a long, tense silence as Huck stood there with balled fists, trying to tell if I was bluffing or not.

He knew that I wasn't.

Then I said, "I'm through with this, Huck. No more. You got your restraining order, now just leave me the fuck alone. Leave *her* alone. I'm not from the same world as you – my dad taught me there's no such thing as a fair fight. When a man gets angry, *real* angry, it's kill or be killed. That's where we're at now, man. And *this* –" I motioned to the few remaining items on the ground. "It makes me real angry. It either ends like this… or I guess we oughta start diggin' that grave. Take your pick."

For what could have been minutes, Huck just stared at me. Then he pointed his finger. "You're a fucking psycho, Lyric."

I looked him in the eyes. "Then you best stay the hell away from me."

The tense silence that followed was cut by the sound of a man whistling on the porch. The three of us craned our necks to see Rust standing there, surveying his antique pistol, smoking a cigarette. "This is one of my favorites," he mused aloud. "1884, Colt .45, four and three quarters barrel… No tellin' how much killin' it's seen. 'sGot character. Single action, army issue… Means you've gotta cock the hammer before the firing mechanism will engage. Kind of outmoded – double action's usually faster, 'less you know what you're doin'. But I could probably empty that cylinder 'fore someone even got to thinkin' about running." He shot a glance at Huck, who swallowed nervously.

"How you doin', Rust?" Huck tried to feign being nonchalant with a desperate smile. He didn't know Rust was standing there when he let his mask slip. But he was scared – Rust knew it.

Huck's biggest fear was being seen for who he really was:

A coward.

"Oh, not too bad, not too bad," Rust replied casually. "But I'm not gonna lie to you, Huckleberry: it really ruffles my feathers when a man goes around a woman's back to give her a hard time. You got something to say to her, you say it. She don't wanna listen, then, well, guess you're shit out of luck."

"Rust, I didn't –"

Rust just frowned and shook his head. "Save it, my friend. I've been around too long for you to bullshit the bullshitter. Normally, I would kindly request that you help the young lady load her car back up, but going off that look on her face, I'd say you're probably better off just... walking away."

Huck scoffed. "You know what this piece of shit did?" he pointed at me.

"Nope, and I don't particularly care," Rust dismissed. "I'll tell you what he's *gonna* do, though: he's gonna make good on that promise about the revolver in his back pocket if you keep pushin'." Huck's face fell and the fear he was trying to subdue broke through. "There's a lotta men out there that'll threaten to kill you till the day God does it for 'em. That one –" he gestured with his head toward me, " – he ain't one of them. Do yourself a favor, Huck. Go home. Nobody's gotta go to prison tonight."

For a moment, Huck stood there, glancing between the three of us. Then, finally, he looked at me and said, "Empty fuckin' threats, that's all you are. Can't even make good on them."

I held his look as I spoke. "Sure I can."

With that, the man finally left. I let out a sigh of relief. Alita screamed out, "Fuck you, Huck!" then angrily threw a handful of clothes into the backseat.

My head turned toward Rust at the top of the steps. "Thanks, Rust."

"Don't mention it," he replied. He tossed the cigarette down the steps then went inside. "You kids be safe now."

But as we finished putting Alita's things back, I couldn't shake the feeling that the night wasn't over.

# Chapter 14

Alita drove us back the short distance to my house. Neither of us spoke. Her hands quivered against the steering wheel as her car came to a stop.

"You're shaking," I said. "There's nothing to be scared of."

"I'm not scared. I'm angry."

I tilted my head. "That – yeah, you've got some things to be angry about. But put it out of your mind, alright? Being pissed off all night isn't gonna do anybody any favors, least of all you."

She gave me a look and replied, "You just don't want to have to deal with it all night."

I couldn't help but smirk. "I mean, yeah, if we're being honest. You're kind of a lot when you get mad," I chuckled softly.

"What, and I'm a little when I'm calm?" she retorted. "I know what people say about me, Donovan. People don't want me around here."

I shook my head. "That isn't true."

"Sure it is. They think I'm crazy."

"Well, you do scream a lot," I teased.

A smile cracked across her face and she shoved me playfully from the driver's seat. "Shut up!" she laughed. "I'm being serious. People think I'm crazy and they don't want to be around me. They don't need me. I'm not stupid."

"No, you're not stupid. And you're not crazy. And for what it's worth, I don't need you. But I like having you around."

She smiled for a moment, but in an instant it broke and gave way to tears. Suddenly, she was sobbing into her hands.

"Alita, it's okay –"

"I just... God, I don't know why I'm still here," she bawled. "I don't want to be here anymore, Lyric, I just don't. Either I go out on the streets to sleep or I go out on them to work. I can't do it again. I don't want to be in this town with *him* stalking me and hanging over my head like a bad cloud. I'm so sick and tired of waking up and feeling like this – like there's nowhere to go, like my life is already over. Every day I wake up and I just want to fucking die. How do I fix that? How do I fix my crazy fucking brain? I don't fit into this world and this world doesn't want me here." She cried some more, then looked at me. "You were a psychology major, right? Tell me how to fix my brain. I'm going fucking insane and I can't take it anymore."

For a moment, I thought about what to say to the woman. Then I stopped thinking and just spoke.

"Maybe your brain is fine. Maybe it's your soul that's killing you. This constant pursuit of happiness we've all been sold, where we never grow up and life is always a party and it's worse if it's not... It just isn't true. Yeah, insanity happens in the brain, sure, but the void that creates it is a lot deeper than that."

Her tears slowed as she held onto my words.

I continued. "If you feel like killing yourself, that means something is wrong in your life – according to how *you* want it to be. It could be a lot of things. It could be everything. But you have to understand what those feelings really mean."

"Yeah?" she sniffled. "What's that?"

"They mean you want to live. They mean you'll want to live again tomorrow, no matter how bad you feel. Take a step back and see the forest for the trees. You're alive because you want to be, so the hardest part is already over. You're free, Alita. You're free to do anything you want to. The only question now is: what will you do with that freedom?"

Alita sniffled again and wiped the sleeve of her jacket against her eyes. "How dare you cut to the core of me like that, sir."

Our eyes met and we held it for a while. Alita glanced from my eyes to my lips three times. My eyes glanced at hers, too – bright red, ruby lipstick standing out in the black and white darkness like a beacon from Aphrodite herself. My eyes rested on her, studying the side of her face until I committed every detail to memory, every flaw and imperfection in her skin that made her human.

And every imperfection made her more beautiful.

In an instant, I leaned forward and pressed my lips against hers. Her tongue met mine and my hand gently held the back of her head, running my fingers through her soft, straight hair that still caught the light even in darkness. Then I pulled away with a small smile.

"What?" Alita tittered, her eyes reddened but drying.

"I think I like you."

She looked away for a second like she was blushing, then looked back at me. "Really?"

"Really."

She smiled. "I think I like you, too."

"Well that's convenient, because we're at my house," I replied, opening the passenger door. Alita laughed as she got out of the car and I slung my guitar over my back. "Ladies first," I gestured up the handful of steps on my porch.

"You're just trying to look at my ass."

"Yup," I replied as I watched her hips sway going up the stairs. I opened the door and we went inside the living room. Red light bathed the house until Alita turned on the lamp next to the sofa with a soft white bulb, evening everything out. I threw on my glasses to block out the light. Out of habit, I popped a tape in the recorder and started rolling.

"What are you doing?" Alita asked. "Am I being interrogated?" she sort of winked.

"No," I grinned, flopping down onto the couch with my guitar in front of me. "I like to record my practice sessions. Lets me know where I need improvement."

Alita grinned, then leaned over the cassette recorder on the coffee table. "Testing, testing, one-two-three."

With a grin, I leaned in and said in a slightly deeper voice, "Hello, I'm Johnny Cash."

Alita giggled playfully, then said into the recorder: "Good evening, folks, and welcome back to *Southern Sound Radio* with your hosts, Donovan Lyric and the wonderful Alita Swanson." I laughed with her, then she looked at me and asked, "So, Mr. Lyric, what are your thoughts on the events that transpired tonight?"

I leaned over the box. "Well, Ms. Swanson, tonight was what I would call, 'a whole lot of bullshit.' We had bullshit from the blue corner, bullshit from the red corner, even bullshit out on the street."

She exclaimed in a throaty, muppet-style voice: "It was total calamity!"

I laughed and said, "Almost." Then I reached for my cigarettes in my breast pocket. "Fuck," I mumbled.

"What?"

"I left my smokes at the bar."

Alita sort of smirked, then leaned back across the sofa and put her feet in my lap. "Then I guess you better go get some more."

I waved my hand over her feet. "What are you, a fucking cat?"

"Something like that."

I rolled my eyes behind my shades and picked up her legs. My intoxicated hand couldn't help but travel up the length of her calf to her thigh, then back down from her inner thigh. She almost purred with excitement.

"That feels good," she whispered.

"Mmmm, I really need cigarettes, though," I said softly back.

She reached out and put her hand on top of mine. "They can wait."

I glanced at the clock. "Only for a quick one – Shell closes in fifteen minutes."

Suddenly Alita sprung up and sat on top of me, taking my guitar and setting it on its stand gently. She straddled my groin with her legs spread out to the side, her jeans tightly hugging her hips and her ass as she rubbed her hands up and down my chest. I glanced down at the red *S* and, vaguely, I wondered to myself: *how am I doing today?*

Sensually, she whispered in my ear, "Then give me five."

Like two wild animals, our mouths were joined and our hands explored each other's bodies in a frenzy. In no time, I unbuttoned her jeans and pulled them down to reveal a bright red thong underneath. "You wore those for me, didn't you?" I asked coyly.

"Maybe," she moaned as I bit into her neck. Like a ravenous creature in need, she took my dick from my jeans and pulled her panties to the side. She was already ready to go, and it slid inside her like a key made perfectly for one particular lock. "Oh, *fuck!*" she moaned loudly as her hips began to rock back and forth. I grabbed her by her sides and lifted her slender frame up and down, each movement feeling better than the last. My fingernails clawed into her back and hers into mine. My eyes spotted the bruises on her forearm; I held her as tightly as I could.

She was safe now.

Her cries of pleasure drifted through the open window into the quiet nighttime air of New Freedom as I took her ass in my hands and squeezed firmly, each of us going faster and faster and deeper and deeper, until finally –

"Oh my fucking *God*," she collapsed onto me breathlessly as we finished simultaneously. "Fuck, I needed that."

Her hair smelled like flowers as she rested her chin in the crook of my neck and shoulder. "Now I *really* need a cigarette," I remarked.

She pulled back with a smile, then lifted herself off of me. I made an uncontrollable noise from the sensation of her body sliding against mine, and she smirked proudly. "When you come back, be ready for round two," she commanded as she laid on her side on the sofa. I rose to my feet and stared at her perfect half-clothed body, carved from marble by the greatest artists in Heaven.

"I don't think that'll be a problem."

She gave me a cute look and tightly hugged the couch pillow. "Hurry back."

With an undeniable sense of the greatest form of exhaustion there is, I hurried out the door and up to Main Street where the gas station was.

"How's it going?" the night time cashier greeted me in an almost stilted fashion, like an announcer on a TV commercial. He always said the same thing no matter how many times he saw you. It was kind of nice, in a way – you could always count on it, even when everything else in life was nebulous and changing. Interactions with him were always exactly the same. Quickly, I asked for a pack of cigarettes and stood there while he rang them up.

Then something caught my eye.

It was a pamphlet resting in a stand by the register. It read: *THIS SUMMER come check out the Ashville SUNFLOWER FESTIVAL! From August 3rd to August 18th!*

"Will that be everything for you then?"

For a moment, I was elsewhere in my mind. "Huh? Oh, yeah, sorry." I handed him the cash, then grabbed a pamphlet and stuffed it into my inside jacket pocket and walked out.

But I didn't go home yet.

Instead, I sat myself down on a concrete half-wall surrounding the gas station and lit a cigarette.

Lightning flashed once again, and I waited for the rain that would never fall. Somberly, I looked back on my busy day.

Aloud to the sky, I asked casually, like greeting an old friend: "How're you doin' today?" Then my eyes fell to the pavement. "How am I doin' today?"

There was nothing but silence. Always, nothing but silence.

But this time, I looked back up and I kept talking.

"I'm probably looking in the wrong spot," I said to the sky. "Makes more sense that you'd just be sort of... everywhere – you know? I mean, why would you be in outer space, anyway? In a galaxy far, far away..." I softly chuckled to myself. "Or the great firmament, as you called it. Well, as *someone* called it, claiming they were your words. Talk about a farce – trying to write dialogue for God...."

My gaze was held in the clouds for a moment, then I looked at my black shoes shamefully. "I got mad today. I don't know why. I can be better than that – I *should* be better than that." Then another silent strike of lightning arrested my attention back to the horizon. "I don't wanna be like that. There's a lot to judge people for, but I don't know if it's right. A lot to fight people for...." I thought back to Huck. "We're all wicked sometimes. Least everyone *I've* ever met is. On one hand, you're a bastard if you judge them, because sometimes you're just like them. But on the other, you're a coward if you don't, because then you'll never do better than them, and they'll never have anybody to watch and learn from. So I guess it boils down to what you'd rather be – a bastard or a coward." For a while, I awaited an answer.

As usual, it never came.

Meekly, I mumbled, "Lemme know if you ever figure it out."

Then I withdrew the pamphlet from my pocket, and just stared at the photos of sunflowers surrounded by a white-picket perimeter.

My memory did the rest.

# Chapter 15

## August 13th, 1995
## The Day After Red's Bonfire

"Fuck...." I groaned as I woke up in bed. Light broke through the blinds, blinding me as soon as my eyes were open. One hand snapped to my face to shield them, the other searched desperately for my sunglasses. When they were on my face, I opened my eyes.

"Oh, what the hell...." I muttered. My room was a mess; a mostly empty beer bottle had been knocked over, along with a lamp, and my sheets were in total disarray. There were streaks of blood along the door and the wall. My heart tightened. "Oh, shit, is that –?" I lurched forward. *"Ow, fuck!"*

Quickly, I glanced down at my arm, the source of the pain. My knuckles were all cut up and there was a four inch long, two inch wide patch of skin missing from my elbow down the forearm, like I took a fall across my rugged carpeted living room floor. It had scabbed overnight. *I guess that explains the blood. But what explains the injury?*

*Oh, fuck...*

Suddenly the memories of Red's bonfire the night before hit me. *I remember Alita calling me the Devil, then...*

*Layla.*

*Did she come over last night?*

Desperately, I racked my brain searching for the answers. But it was like they were hidden behind an iron curtain. *I remember she was the last one still up, I sat down and had a few more drinks with her, it got... weird. Something was uncomfortable. I said something to her that I shouldn't have, I think... Then...*

*She walked me home.*

*Did she leave me at the door or did she come in?*

I checked the clock on my nightstand. It was eleven in the morning on a weekday. Red would probably be at work and the kid would be in school.

*Please tell me I didn't have sex with my best friend's wife.*

A nervous pit formed in my stomach as I threw the sheets off me and stepped through the door, across the kitchen and into the living room. "Oh, shit...." I gasped softly.

Everything was scattered about. The heavy TV set lay on its side on the floor, while the coffee table had been pushed so hard it was all the way on the other side of the room. My couch had been practically dismantled, with cushions and pillows strewn about. My VHS and cassette tapes were tossed about, too, and the record player was on its side, still spinning as it searched for the needle.

"Did I get fucking robbed?" I blurted out. A cursory scan told me I didn't; nothing was missing, just thrown about. Everything but my guitars.

Sorely, I knelt down and reached my hand below the TV stand through the crack, and pulled out a few tapes and my cassette recorder, then put them back on the table.

With a heavy sigh, I sauntered over to the phone and dialed Red and Layla's house.

*"Hello?"* Layla's voice answered.

"Hey, Layla, it's Lyric," I began anxiously.

*"Oh, hey,"* she replied brightly.

For a moment, I considered what the best option was. I didn't want to come out and ask, *hey, did we fuck last night?* because I didn't want her to feel like I thought lowly of her on the chance that infidelity wasn't actually in her nature. But I couldn't pretend like I wasn't suspicious. So I decided to be as honest as I could. "Thanks for walking me home last night," I told her. "I just woke up and my house is a complete fucking mess. It looks like I got robbed and then they decided to stop halfway through when they realized most of my shit is worthless."

She laughed through the phone. *"Well, your balance was a* little *off last night, so that's not surprising."*

Feebly, I laughed. "Yeah, yeah I guess it was. If I'm being honest, I sort of blacked out right around the time I was bringing the whiskey back inside."

*"Oh, shit, really?"* her tone changed.

"Yeah," I replied shamefully. "It hard cuts from you on the porch to you walking me home. That's the last thing I remember – standing in front of my house with you. So thank you for making sure I got home safe."

*"Yeah, yeah, of course."* Pause. *"You were really that drunk?"*

"Yeah," I replied with gravel in my throat. "It was a rough night, apparently."

*"Yeah, I'll say...."* Another pause. *"I had no idea you were blacked out. Other than the stumbling, you were so... cogent."*

Shame gripped me again. "Yeah, it's something of a problem in my life." She laughed. "I call it 'functional blackouts.' I'll get so hammered that I don't remember a single thing, but somehow people can't even tell I'm more than just sort of drunk."

*"Yeah, damn... Everything good, though?"*

I sighed with relief. It sounded like nothing happened. "Yeah, everything's good."

*"Cool, cool. Could... Could you do me a favor, though?"*

"Yeah?"

*"Don't tell Red I walked you home."*

My heart stopped. I should have asked her to elaborate, but like a coward, I refused to look a gift horse in the mouth. If I had, maybe I could have seen the Trojans in there. "Yeah," I said after a while. "I won't tell Red."

*"Thank you."*

\*\*\*

Later that night, Red and I were sitting on his porch. Layla had made herself scarce; I wasn't sure what I said or did the night before, but things were different. There was a different energy when she looked at me now.

"Quiet night," Red mused aloud as we listened to the crickets chirping.

"Peaceful night," I replied. "I like it."

He took a drink from his whiskey and I did the same. I was limiting myself to just a few – lest I black out again. Suddenly, Red blurted out, "I've been thinking a lot about the Devil talk from last night."

"Oh yeah?" I cocked my brow, then glanced guiltily at the tattoo on my arm. If I looked for long enough, I swear I could see it move.

"Yeah," he stared out into the distance. "About the nature of truth, free will, what to do with knowledge. I know a lot of things about this world, Lyric. Even some esoteric shit that most people won't ever hear of. Rome never ended, consciousness is the ego death of God, time is a flat circle…" Then he looked at me. "But you know what the bitch of it all is?"

"What's that?"

He shrugged. "None of that really matters."

Curiously, I asked, "How do you figure?"

He surveyed his decently large lawn with trees on the one side. "How does knowing about God help you plant a tree? What does the knowledge of death and evil do for someone with their boots on the ground, putting food on the table for his family? Not a damn thing. It's all play. We have the luxury of getting to play in the psychosphere, but it isn't real – none of that matters. People matter. *Your* people matter. Other than that…" he shrugged. "Fuck 'em."

I studied him in admiration. "Yeah, well, your kid is gonna grow up knowing a hell of a lot more than the guys around him."

Red shook his head. "No he won't."

I raised my brow again. "Why's that?"

Red thought for a moment, sipping on his bourbon. He inhaled sharply through his teeth as the smooth burn caressed his throat. "Damn, that's good bourbon."

"Better than what I can afford," I toasted him with a grin.

He grinned back and said, "You'll get there one day. You're still young." Then he went back to his thoughts. "I don't want Daniel to know me. I've seen a lot of bad shit, Lyric. I've *done* a lot of bad shit. My kid? He doesn't see any of that. He sees a man who loves him and provides for him. Why would I want to go and ruin that? If he wants to know how fucked up the world is, he'll have to figure out the way we did – the hard way."

For a moment, I bonded with the drink in my hand and took a long gulp. Then I asked, "What about you?"

"What about me?"

It took a second to gather my thoughts. "If there was some great truth, some horrifying reality – something that could take apart your family if you knew it – would you want to learn the hard way? Would you want to know? Basically, would you bite the apple?"

Red took a long drink from his glass. "No."

\*\*\*

The next day I called Alita. I hadn't talked to her since the bonfire.

"Hey...." I said into the phone.

*"Hey...."*

"How... are you?"

She sighed. *"Been better, been worse. I finally got the last of my stuff moved into Huck's place today. I guess it's all official now."*

I nodded even though she couldn't see it. It was more of a bitter, reluctant nod, though. "That's good, that's good, better than living in your car I suppose...."

*"Is it?"*

There was a long silence.

"I'm sorry about how things happened, Alita. I... I do feel some type of way about you, but I just can't do that to Huck. We would need to wait. What I did was shitty and it was a betrayal, but I still consider him a friend."

*"Yeah, I know... He doesn't know it was you, by the way. I told him I hooked up with somebody while we were broken up but I wouldn't say who. He thinks it's you, but I doubt he'll ever admit it."*

I sighed into the receiver. "Thanks, I suppose. Christ, this is all fucked. When did life stop being easy?"

*"It was never that easy, Lyric,"* she replied, almost amused.

"Fair enough."

We went silent again. Before I could speak, Alita abruptly asked, *"You wanna go to the Sunflower Fest?"*

"What?" I chuckled in bemusement. "When is it?"

*"Today."*

"Let me check my schedule – yup, I'm free," I smiled to myself.

*"Okay, good. I'll be there in fifteen minutes."*

In no time at all, Alita was at my doorstep and I bounded into her car. "Took you long enough," I teased.

She rolled her eyes and turned up the music. Crosby, Stills, Nash and Young kept us company as she drove. "You know, everybody remembers Crosby, Stills and Nash, but nobody ever remembers Young," she mused.

"Bullshit," I laughed. "Neil Young is the most famous out of all of them."

"Exactly. That's why nobody remembers he was part of Crosby, Stills and Nash," Alita laughed sweetly. Then the radio began playing a familiar tune, upbeat and bright with a sort of *caliente* style. The voice of Johnny Cash poured through the radio, singing about a ring of fire.

I leaned toward Alita and deepened my voice a little, then said, "Hello, I'm Johnny Cash."

She giggled and glanced at me. "You definitely dress like him, *man in black*."

I glanced down at my shirt; it was the one with red *Superman* decal on it. "Well, not quite today, but I'll take that as a compliment."

"You should," she grinned.

I grinned back. "Now I just need to learn how to play like him and I'll be set for life."

She laughed again and replied, "Keep at it. You'll get there." She gave me a look that melted me like butter in the sun and I had to look away.

A few miles outside of town, we pulled into a lot at the edge of an expansive field of sunflowers, with a renovated barn serving as the ticket booth. "Have you ever been here before?" she asked as we got out.

"Don't think so."

"Don't *think* so?" she tittered as we walked. "How could you not remember going to a literal field of sunflowers?"

"I drink a lot."

She playfully smacked me in the arm and we both laughed. The place was more crowded than I expected; it was a beautiful day out and the sun was shining down on all our smiling faces.

"You grab the tickets, I'll grab the beers."

"Sounds like a plan," she smiled at me.

In a shady pavilion right in the center of the lot was a band playing Grateful Dead tunes. They looked the part, too. Long hair and beards, hippie clothing, tapestries hung up over the makeshift stage. And they sounded just like them.

"Oh, I *love* these guys!" Alita commented as she met me by the beer kiosk under the pavilion.

"You know it's not actually the Grateful Dead, right?"

"Yeah, no duh," she laughed. "I've seen these guys cover them before. They're amazing."

"Because of course you're already familiar with the local Grateful Dead cover band," I teased.

She made a pouty face, trying not to smile but failing. The beerkeeper handed me two drinks.

I grinned. "Let's go, dead-head."

"I hate you," Alita laughed, walking ahead of me, her black dress with white polkadots swaying in the breeze as she glanced back. "Come on, *Superman*."

Grinning to myself, we trekked beyond the white wooden fence, about three feet high, and moved slowly through the never ending field of flowers for a long time. She stopped and looked at almost every single one of them. Meanwhile I was busy staring at her every chance I could. In that moment, it didn't really matter to me if it made me a bad friend.

*I think I'm in love.*

She waved me over excitedly. "Lyric, look!"

"What, is this sunflower doing something different than the rest?"

She shot me that same pouty face again when I teased her. "Don't be a dick," she replied humorously. "Look at the bees." She gestured subtly to the face of the flower. A handful of bumblebees had made it their resting spot, crawling around and enjoying the warmth just like the rest of us. "I wanna keep one."

I laughed and said, "You got the equipment for that?"

"Pft, I don't need a beekeeping hive. I'll just let them live inside with me."

I laughed again and said automatically, "Yeah, see how Huck likes that."

Suddenly the mood changed. We both felt it. For a moment, we had completely forgotten about the real world on our fake date. And a part of me didn't want to go back.

"Oh, my God," a girl's voice said quickly. I turned and saw a young woman with a polaroid camera around her neck, standing there with her boyfriend watching me and Alita interacting with the bees on the flower. "You guys are like the *cutest* couple."

"Actually, we're –" I began, but Alita interjected.

"Thank you so much!" she beamed, then glanced at me from the corner of her eye. I couldn't help but smile.

"And I love that you've both got, like, the dark aesthetic going on when you're out here in a bright yellow field."

"Is that what color these things are?" I asked. "I've got a rare form of color blindness – all I see are shades of gray and red."

The girl's eyes lit up. "Really?"

"Yup." Then I glanced around the field, shining brightly with white light that I could only imagine would be gold if I shut my eyes and played some music. Then I looked at Alita. "Believe it or not, it's still beautiful."

She began to blush and the girl put her hand on her heart. Her boyfriend even grinned at that one. Then she asked, "You want me to take your picture?"

"Sure," I replied, pulling out my wallet.

She scoffed and said, "Oh, put that away. A moment like this deserves to be captured."

Alita and I exchanged glances, then I shrugged.

The girl glanced around for a second, then found an ancient looking front end to a car – undoubtedly placed there by the owners of the land to drive home the old-timey farm experience. "Ooh, why don't you guys sit on that car?"

"Probably runs better than mine does anyway," I joked as we sat down.

The girl readied her camera and Alita looked right into the lens. "Okay, say *sunflowers!*"

"Sunflowers!" Alita smiled.

The camera clicked and whirred as it slowly produced a white square of film. She handed it to me and said, "Here you go. It'll be finished developing in a couple of minutes."

"Thank you so much!" Alita said with gratitude.

As the image slowly faded into existence, I looked at it. Alita was staring into the camera, but I wasn't.

I was just looking at her.

***

The sun was setting by the time we left. "That was *so* much fun!" Alita exclaimed as we got into the car. "We should do it again soon!"

I smiled but there was a weariness to it. "That would be lovely."

As she drove back toward New Freedom, she studied me. I had been silent the whole drive. "Everything okay?"

"Yeah," I breathed. "Everything's okay."

"You know you can't lie to me, Lyric," Alita grinned mischievously. "I see *right* through you."

"Oh yeah?" I asked. "What do you see?"

She thought for a moment. "I see a man who's got almost his whole life ahead of him still and doesn't know it. I see a man who could go on to do great things, but he doesn't realize it. I see someone tortured, but tries not to make it anybody else's problem. I admire that about you. That's where most of us go wrong, I think. We get so caught up in ourselves that we forget other people have their own lives, but you... You don't do that. Whenever you look at me or you talk to me, I feel like... All you see is me."

Her car rolled to a stop in front of my house as her words finished.

Then I said:

"I think I'm in love with you."

Suddenly her demeanor changed. Her smile vanished, and her hands gripped the wheel of the parked car. "Lyric...."

"I'm sorry," I interrupted. "I know I'm flighty and I know I go back and forth because of how complicated everything is, but Alita... I really do." There was a painful silence. "I think you do, too."

For a moment, she didn't say anything. Then: "I'm committed to giving things with Huck another chance."

"Oh, fuck him!" I rejoined. "Does he do *any* of that? Do you think he's ever once in his life seen you? Really seen you?"

"Maybe...."

"Alita –"

But she stopped me. "You should go inside, Lyric." She averted her eyes with something between guilt and shame. "I don't want to have this conversation right now."

I let out a heavy sigh. "Then when?"

"I don't know..." she replied quietly. "Maybe never... I don't think you'll ever really be ready to take that leap."

For a second, I looked her over. She looked like she wanted to cry. Then I nodded and said, "Okay," and stepped out of the car. "Call me when... Whenever you want to."

"Bye, Lyric. Thank you for today."

And then she drove off.

I stood there on the sidewalk watching until she vanished. Then I went inside and I started to drink. I started to drink and I didn't stop. The half bottle of bourbon I had was empty and I was out of beer by the time the sun came up.

*Fuck it, Shell's open. I can just go get more.*

So I staggered out of my house back onto the sidewalk. The world spun around me quickly and I said aloud, "Whoa, shit –"

Suddenly, I was sitting in my car.

*Wait, wasn't I going to the gas station? I don't need to drive there, I can just wa–*

And then in an instant, I came to, driving down the road.

*Dammit, why am I driving?* Where *am I driving? Gotta turn aro–*

And suddenly, I was miles away.

I had driven back to the Ashville field of sunflowers.

*Huh, go figure.*

As if on its own, my foot pressed the gas pedal down and I sped up toward the rising sun. I took the polaroid of me and Alita out of my back pocket and stuck it on the dashboard.

Our last conversation kept replaying itself in my head.

*Then when?*

*Maybe never.*

Those words did something to me.

It was like this imaginary future I had built in my head came tumbling down.

*Why didn't I just take the leap when I had a chance?*

And then suddenly I didn't really care whether the future had me in it or not.

The road curved sharply up ahead with the sunflowers on the left side of the road, past the white wooden fence.

My foot held the gas down all the way as Elvis belted out his song about burning love in my ears. That angle of the curve on the road, the speed of my car against its weight –

*Betcha I can flip it, wake up in the next life.*

And as the sun rose above the horizon, that's exactly what I tried to do.

As fast as I could, I sailed that piece of shit up the road and lurched the steering wheel as hard to the right as it would go.

But my car didn't flip.

Instead, it lost traction and went straight off the road. My body lurched as the car plowed right through the white picket fence surrounding the flower farm, and in an instant I was flying through the field of sunflowers. I must have driven through a couple hundred feet of flowers at least before I came to my senses and turned back toward the road. I had to break through the fence a second time to get back out.

Weary, defeated, drunk beyond belief, I limped that old car back home, went inside and passed out.

A few hours later there was a knock at the door. Stumbling out of bed, still a little drunk, I opened it. It was Sheriff Swanson.

# Chapter 16

## August 15th, 1995

"Thought I might find you here," Swanson remarked as I opened the door.

"Well, I live here, so...." I retorted as the afternoon light shone on my face, piercing my shades.

"You have any idea what I'm doing here, Mr. Lyric?"

I let out a worried sigh. "No, but I'm sure you're gonna tell me." Suddenly I noticed he was holding something at his side.

He lifted it up. It was a sunflower.

"This look familiar to you?" he asked pointedly.

For a second, I hesitated. "Yeah, it does."

"Figured it might," the Sheriff said. "I did a preliminary investigation. Not sure if you noticed this, but your car back there –" he nodded up the alley to my garage, " – has a few dings in it, couple of busted headlights, and a hell of a lot of sunflowers in the undercarriage. Mind explaining to me how they got there?" I didn't say anything at first. "Couple people saw your car leaving the field. Must've been around six-thirty or seven o'clock this morning. Sound like somewhere you might have been?"

I let out a sigh. "Yeah. Yeah, that was me."

He looked me over for a moment. I knew I looked like shit. I was hungover and drunk at the same time. "You wanna go ahead and tell me what happened?"

The thought of calling Carl crossed my mind, but maybe I didn't deserve to get out of this one. "I went for a drive this morning, went a little too fast, went off the road. Honestly, it didn't even occur to me that what I did was property damage – I was a little shaken by the whole ordeal, so I went home."

"I see, I see...." Swanson stroked the scruff on his chin. "Were you drinking?"

Again, I hesitated. *I should lie.*

Then I glanced down at my shirt.

There was a stain across the red *S*. All of a sudden, shame rested itself on my shoulders.

So I told him the truth.

"Yeah. I was."

Swanson let out a deep exhale. "You know I'm gonna have to arrest you, right?"

I nodded. "I figured." Then I looked down at myself again. I was in my boxers. "You... mind if I go get changed real quick?"

Swanson studied me for a second, trying to figure out if I was the kind of man to come back out with a pistol and start blasting. Then his nostrils flared and he replied, "You've got five minutes."

I nodded curtly, then went back inside. When I returned, I was dressed head to toe in black – black button down tucked in, black slacks, nice shoes.

"You know this ain't a funeral, right?" he asked.

"Maybe it is."

He pulled a sympathetic frown, then removed the handcuffs from his belt. "Turn around for me."

I complied. The cold metal of the cuffs almost cut into my wrist, they were so tight, but I didn't mind. Pain was always a good reminder that you're real.

Swanson guided me down the steps to his patrol car parked out front and placed me in the passenger seat. "What, you're not putting me behind the cage?" I mused.

"Nah," he replied casually as he got in. "You don't strike me as much of a danger."

"Hooray for small victories," I remarked dourly.

We drove in silence for a minute, then he asked me, "So what the hell possessed you to drive like that?"

I frowned almost imperceptibly. "I think it was the Devil."

The sheriff studied me for a moment.

"You're the guy who's been runnin' around with Alita, right?"

"Kind of. We're friends."

"Friends?" he raised his brow.

"Yeah. Friends."

He mulled over my words. "She talks pretty highly of you. Not gonna lie to you, son, I wasn't expecting this to be how we officially met. I'm Jed."

"We've actually met before. You gave me my first charges ever back when I was in high school."

"No shit?" he asked in surprise.

"No shit."

"Hm," he kind of recoiled in amusement. "What were the charges?"

"Disorderly conduct and assault. I got into a fight."

He clicked his tongue. "You weren't the one that broke the kid's nose in the bathroom, were you?" Then he took a look at me. "Oh hell, that *was* you, wasn't it? I remember the sunglasses. You've got something wrong with your eyes, right?"

"Achromatopsia, yeah. But I didn't break his nose. Just... bloodied it."

He sort of snickered in good humor. "Yeah, I remember you."

"Good to officially meet you," I remarked dryly. "I'd shake your hand, but I'm kind of tied up right now."

He chuckled to himself. "Props for your attitude. Most guys in your position tend to get a little bitter, kind of cynical."

"What makes you think that I'm not?"

He glanced at me. "I think you *act* like you're bitter and cynical, but I don't think you really are. Hell, I could be wrong. Maybe you're a raving lunatic under that facade. Maybe you're a killer waiting to happen, just needs the right bar fight to set him off. But shit, at least you're honest."

"How far does honesty take you for a DUI?" I asked glumly.

Swanson clicked his tongue. "Not as far as you might think." Then we rolled into the parking lot of the police station. "Lucky for you, you're not being charged with a DUI."

"What?" I asked. "But I told you I was drinking?"

He half-shrugged. "Ain't no way to prove it. Courts need hard evidence and blood-alcohol tests to figure things like which tier to place you in and how to convict. I could put it in the report that you admitted you were drunk and drove through a field, but... Hell, I may as well save us all some time. Look, my daughter vouches for you. I'd say she might even think the world of you. But this shit...." His tone became more serious. "I'll play ball with you if you play ball with me. My only concern is that you'll end up putting me or mine in harm's way, and that's something I just can't abide. Give me your word you'll cut back on the liquor – and I ain't sayin' you need to stop cold turkey altogether or nothing – but give me your word as a man you'll cut back, and I'll make sure this little incident doesn't throw a wrench into the rest of your life." He surveyed me carefully as he spoke. "Deal?"

With a heavy sigh, I said, "I don't want to hurt anyone."

The sheriff nodded. "Good man." Then he got out of the car and came around to open my door. "I'll have my eye on you, too. So if you start fuckin' up or you start slidin', or I start hearin' shit around town about you being up to no good... I will make it my *personal* mission to keep you as far away from my daughter as possible – understand me?"

His eyes were threatening when he spoke. I wasn't afraid, but a part of me probably should have been.

"I understand."

\*\*\*

"Lyric, your ride's here."

"Thank fucking christ," I blurted in the jail cell at the Sheriff's Department. My feet were in shackles and I had been booked hours ago. It was a zero dollar bail, they said, but because it was a driving offense, they needed to release me into someone else's custody. I turned and looked at the few other men in the drunk tank with me. "Well, gentlemen, it's been a pleasure. Hope to see you on the other side."

One of them groaned tiredly and said, "Just get the fuck out of here, Johnny Cash."

I grinned mischievously. I had been sitting in the corner singing *Folsom Prison Blues* to myself on and off for the last hour. When they took my mugshot, I did my best to make the same face Frank Sinatra made. If you're going to jail, might as well make the most of it, right? I sauntered over to the heavy metal door and a police officer opened it for me. "Hold out your hands," he demanded. Roughly, he slapped a pair of cuffs on me, cutting into my skin just like the last pair.

"Goddamn, why do women like this so much?"

The cop looked at me weird but I could tell he was trying not to grin. In a low voice, he replied, "To be honest, I couldn't tell ya."

I smiled faintly as he escorted me to a nearby bench and removed the shackles. Then he led me down the hall where the receptionist gave me my release forms and arraignment dates. "Agricultural vandalism?" I read aloud, amused. "I didn't know that was a thing."

"Neither did we," the receptionist said. "Congrats, you're our first." She handed me a pen to sign a few forms, then the cop took me out the door. Carl was standing by his Volkswagen in the parking lot, dressed casually and smoking a cigarette.

"Why hello," he waved with a grin.

"Man, am I glad to see you," I began as Carl came over to us. The cop undid my handcuffs and gave Carl something to sign.

"He's all yours," the cop said. "Good luck."

"Thank you, officer," Carl replied. I rubbed my wrists as I followed him to his old Volkswagen. "So how was your morning?" he asked with humor in his tone.

"All things considered? I've had worse."

"That's the spirit."

When I got home, I thought about what Swanson had said about the drinking. I didn't want to quit. He didn't even ask me to. But I knew the moment I went off the road that if I didn't stop, then eventually I *would* do something there was no going back from.

So I grabbed the bottle of bourbon, took one last swig, and poured it down the drain.

It wasn't until March that I relapsed.

\*\*\*

**New Freedom, May 17th, 11:00 PM**

My cigarette dwindled to a smoldering ember as I thought back to that day at the field of sunflowers. Those seven months or so where I was sober were enlightening; they made me realize how much I hated being sober. When you have a drinking problem, then you stop, suddenly there's all this pressure on you to stay stopping. Each day that passes is another day lost if you fuck up and fall off the wagon. Eventually, it hits you – *this is the rest of my life*. And that feeling doesn't sit well. It makes you nauseous – almost as nauseous as the liquor used to.

You start running through scenarios in your head, like *what if I hit twelve years sober and then relapse? What would that do to my self-esteem? I can never have another drunken movie night, or play a show fucked up, absorbed in the music. Can't do bar hookups because she's drunk and you're not. Can't do fucking anything, can't fucking go anywhere. We quit drinking to preserve life, but goddamn, is this the life I want to preserve?*

So eventually I caved. And that chain of events led me right to this stone half-wall outside the gas station, drunk and caught up in trouble with the law again, starting fights I wasn't sure I could finish, lashing out and burning bridges.

*Does it have to be this way? I'm not even two months on a bender and I'm one bad step away from prison.*

I took a last look at the bright red dying ember of the cigarette and thought about Alita lying on my couch. *I should go be with her. It's what I've wanted for a long time.*

*I can take that leap.*

Galvanized, I tossed my smoke and pulled myself out of the pity party. I looked up at the sky full of distant lightning again and said, rife with good-natured sarcasm, "Good talk, God. A little one sided – maybe wanna work on that. But otherwise – two thumbs up." My feet carried me confidently back to my house, picturing the rest of the night with one of the most beautiful women who ever walked out of the Garden, who understood me, laughed with me, with a light that shone so bright you'd think it would hurt to look at, but it never did.

It was the only light I think I could have stared at forever and not went blind.

But something tightened in my gut as I approached my house. I couldn't place it, not until I was up the steps and on my porch with my hand reaching for the doorknob.

Then it hit me:

The door was slightly ajar.

Anxiety ripped through me like a bullet through the chest. I took a deep breath and held it as I pulled the revolver from my belt and cocked the hammer.

It was ready to fire.

Then, slowly, I pushed open the door.

My mouth fell open in horror.

Everything in my living room was in disarray. The coffee table was flipped on its side, the record player thrown off of it, my guitars were knocked over, my tapes and records scattered about like an earthquake had shaken them.

And on my couch sat Huck, with his hands clasped together, staring at the floor. It looked like he had been crying.

Next to him was Alita. Her eyes were open.

But she wasn't moving.

She wasn't breathing.

She was just... limp.

"Huck..." I stammered as my arm went weak and the revolver hung at my side. "What did you do...."

He didn't look at me, just kept staring at his hands. Weakly, he muttered, "She said something and I... I just snapped. I lost it, Lyric...."

Then he looked me in the eye.

"I strangled her."

Quietly, I breathed the word: "Why?"

He looked me in the eye and said, "Just to watch her die."

The revolver rested at my side as my body froze and shook at the same time. I couldn't stop looking at her. That divine spark was gone from her eyes.

The only light that would never make me blind had gone out.

A tear rolled down Huck's cheek and he sniffled. "I told her," his voice cracked. "I told her to stay away from you. I didn't... I didn't think it would get this far...."

His voice faded beneath a loud ringing in my ears, like a trumpet or a horn slowly rising to a crescendo in my head. In shock, I took three steps into the living room, standing at an angle to the sofa, unable to believe my eyes.

She was really dead.

The horn grew louder until it was almost all I could hear.

"Stand up," I commanded.

Huck hesitated. "What, are you gonna shoot me?" he asked feebly.

"Stand *up*."

Fearfully, he rose to his feet. "Kill me, call the fuckin' cops, I don't care anymore...." He looked down at the dead woman. "I used to think she was perfect."

When I looked at her dead, lifeless form, and all of the choices that we three had made to lead to that moment played back in my head, I noticed all the small imperfections on her face that made her human.

The sound inside my head was deafeaning. I could barely hear myself as words softly escaped my lips:

"The Devil never whispered 'perfection....'"

Huck screwed up his face and looked at me in terrified confusion. "What?"

Then the horn became silent.

I looked the man in the eye and the devil in my skin pointed the .38 at his heart.

"He whispered 'freedom.'"

The gunshot made a deafening *boom* inside the house.

Blood spattered on the wall behind him as the bullet ripped through Huck Singer's heart and exploded the soft white lamp beside the couch. Everything was suddenly bathed in red.

He collapsed backwards onto the sofa.

Shocked, mortified, horrified, he touched his hand to his heart and gazed at the blood it was soaked in, then looked back up at me.

I stood there and gazed at the sight until all the light went out of his eyes.

Just to watch him die.

# Chapter 17

## River Sound County Courthouse, Hannover-Fist, Ohio
## May 08th, 1997

The entire courtroom falls silent at the revelation. Carl takes a deep breath from the lectern. I can feel Judge Thomas' eyes upon me, and I'm trying not to look at the crowd.

But I can't help it.

I scan my eyes over the shocked and heartbroken faces of my friends in the audience. Lorraine, Rust, Jazz, Red in the back corner, so many people from town. I can only imagine it must be hard to hear that your friend put a bullet through your other friend's heart, warranted or not.

A lot of people loved Huck. Of course, most of them didn't know him the way I did.

Carl regains his poise.

"So the night of the murders, you left your house and came back to find Huckleberry Singer sitting next to Alita's dead body, correct?"

"Yes, that is correct."

"And, to the best of your memory, can you repeat again what Mr. Singer said when you found them?"

My body tenses up as the memory plays back in my head. "He said he strangled her, he killed her. Just to watch her die." My voice breaks for a second, then I regain my composure. "And when he said that, something inside of me just... snapped."

Suddenly a shrill voice cries out from the benches. "You rotten *liar!*" a woman screams. I glance up; it's Mrs. Singer. A plastic water bottle sails from her hand as she cocks back her arm and hurls it toward me. I dodge it by an inch and it slams against the wall behind the witness stand.

The judge slams his gavel. "Order! Order! Bailiff, could you please –?"

"On it, your Honor," the bailiff responds immediately, hurrying through the rows of benches toward Huck's mother. "Come on, ma'am, you've got to go."

"*You* killed her!" she screams through tears. "You killed her, and then you killed my son! You ran from the cops because you know what you did! You killed them then you just slithered away!"

"Ma'am –"

She yanks her arm away from the bailiff and gives him a stern look, the kind only a mother could give. "I'll walk myself out, thank you," she huffs at him through tears. Then she turns back to me with shaking hands and wet eyes. She extends her finger toward me. "May God have mercy on your soul; Lord knows you won't find it here on Earth."

Then she storms out of the pews and through the large doors back to the outside world.

Judge Thomas rubs his temples exhaustedly, then addresses the court. "I believe this would be a good moment to take a brief recess; court will reconvene in fifteen minutes, counsel," he says to Carl and the DA team.

"Thank you, your Honor," Carl replies. The bailiff comes and escorts me off the witness stand back into Carl's custody. I take one more glance at the crowd as they disperse. Rust stops and looks at me, and our eyes meet across the room for a second. Wordlessly, he nods, then walks out the doors.

In a moment, Carl and I are back in the small room we were in before. He lets out a heavy, frustrated sigh and removes his blazer. "Well shit," he says. "Hell of a time for a recess."

"They call it 'recess' but I don't see no swingset," I attempt to smile. It fails. All I can do is think about the knot in my stomach, and the look on Mrs. Singer's face. "She really thinks I killed her, Carl."

"Who?"

"Huck's mom. You saw the look on her face. She really thinks I did it. How many other people you figure think I'm guilty?"

"Doesn't matter," Carl dismisses. "The only ones that matter are the twelve people in that jury box."

"Oh, how reassuring. I have to trust that a bunch of strangers think I lost my faculties in order to avoid dying in prison."

"Well fuck, Donovan, maybe you should have just called the fuckin' cops then!" Carl snaps.

"Would *you* have called the cops?" I argue sharply. "Because I *know* you wouldn't. You woulda shot him, too."

Carl sighs again and sits down at the small desk, running his hand through his short, slicked hair. "It doesn't matter. What matters is that we get through the rest of the story."

"I wasn't too long-winded up there, was I?"

He gives me a look that asks *are you serious?* "It's a long story to tell, don't worry about the jury's attention span. They've got nothing else going on today, I *promise* you."

I let out a sigh. "I really don't want to have to talk about this next part...."

His expression changes and studies me carefully, stoically, but warmly. Then he puts his hand on my shoulder. "It'll be alright, man. Like you said before – the music's here. You just gotta face it."

We share a look full of fear and hope for a moment, then the door opens. It's the bailiff. "Judge Thomas is ready to reconvene."

With a heavy sigh and heavier feet, we march back into the courtroom and I resume my place on the witness stand. After a moment, Judge Thomas appears and takes his seat.

"Sorry about that, folks," he says. "It's not entirely unusual for emotions to run high in cases like this. I would ask that any other members of the general public, should you begin to feel your composure slipping or emotions taking over, that you politely and quietly excuse yourself from the courtroom before throwing projectiles at the defendant." The crowd softly chuckles, but it's underpinned by the morbid reality of the case. Then he addresses Carl. "Mr. Hoskins, you may continue with your direct examination."

"Thank you, your Honor," Carl rises to his feet and returns to the lectern. "Now, Mr. Lyric, how would you describe the feelings you felt upon finding the scene of the murder?"

My body trembles and my lips quiver. I take a long, slow breath. "It was... world shattering. That's the best way I can describe it. Alita and I had a tumultuous friendship, there's no doubt about it. The stars never seemed to align with us, but she was my –" My voice cracks. I grit my teeth and clear my throat into a balled fist. "I fell in love with that woman the day that I met her. Seeing her body lying there on the couch, next to that fucking madman –"

"Language," the Judge interjects.

"Sorry, your Honor. Just... the look on his face. He knew what he had done. And when I saw the scene, there was some kind of old-world idea of justice that sparked back up in my head. Like, 'if I don't do what I have to do, who else could he hurt?' Probably nobody. If I had been thinking rationally, I would have called the cops. But when the woman you love is strangled to death – because you went out for a pack of *cigarettes* – the world just quits making sense for a moment. And all it took was a moment for me to pull the trigger."

There's another tense silence. Then Carl asks, "Did it seem wrong to you at the time?"

I shake my head. "No. It seemed, in a warped way, like the right thing to do."

Carl nods and takes a breath. He knows the next question is the big one – almost bigger than the question of Huck's murder.

He looks me in the eye behind my dark glasses and asks:

"So why did you run?"

# PART II

# Chapter 18

## Driftwood, Ohio, March 1983

My dad drove the beat up old truck in silence. We were leaving my high school; I was sixteen at the time. The entire ride, he held an incredibly pissed off look on his face.

"This might be the stupidest fucking thing you've ever done."

I didn't say anything back.

He was a big man, taller than me by a few inches and outweighed me by eighty pounds. A gray beard grew from his chin, underneath a shock of unkempt hair on his head. There was a constant look of coldness in his eyes that didn't warm up until he had some smoke or a drink in him. At that moment, they were hidden behind sunglasses just like mine.

"Assault, disorderly conduct – I mean, for fuck's sake, Donovan. You know what we call your situation? 'Proper fucked.'"

Meekly, I muttered, "He started it."

"Well you sure as hell finished it," my dad snapped back. He kept his eyes on the road. "You're lucky Officer Swanson didn't take you to jail."

"It wasn't that bad," I retorted.

"You damn near broke the kid's nose," he shot. "Kid said he didn't even land a punch on you, and you just kept going."

My face twisted into an indignant snarl all on its own. "He called us 'poor.'"

My dad let the air out from his nostrils. "You've gotta be careful with that anger, Don. It'll land you in prison someday."

The rest of the ride was silent. In a couple minutes, we made it back to our old farmhouse. The farm wasn't exactly in working order – mostly just empty fields that were used for grazing once upon a time, with a few wooden buildings scattered around the yard. Patches of dead grass littered the pasture and bony barren trees climbed toward the sky across the yard, surrounded by more dead grass. Nothing had grown there for a long time. It didn't matter if it rained or we were in a drought, the land refused to yield any life.

Out in the corral by the barn, if you walked across the cracked concrete floor sunken into the ground, broken by tenacious weeds desperate for the sun, you could find the skeletal remains of a dead cow.

Around the chicken coops, every once in a while I'd find old bones from the dozens of chickens that got killed by the foxes digging under the wire fences, no matter how hard we tried. An old cat and a couple of dogs were buried out there, too. Even around the house, in a little garden embedded with store-bought soil, we couldn't never get anything to grow. We'd plant crops and flowers every year, every season for a long time, and nothin' would ever sprout up. If it did, a cold snap came through and made sure it died.

There were even a couple of tombstones out back behind the house. They were moved from somewhere else on the property, decades ago by the looks of it. No telling where the bodies might actually be buried, but sure enough they were out in that ground somewhere.

The appraiser told my dad there was some kind of toxic spill out in the soil, and Lord only knew how long it could be before anything would grow there again. Figured that was probably how we got the place so cheap – ain't nobody got a use for a farm that don't grow shit anymore.

Sometimes when I was out there, I'd look around and try to picture what it used to be – a Garden of Eden, back in the day, decades, maybe even generations ago. Now, it was like the land was poison, and anything that touched it surely would die.

For a while, I figured I'd die there, too. Right in that house, during one of my dad's drunken fits of rage.

The rusty old pickup truck came to a halt in our driveway, but we didn't get out quite yet. Instead, my dad sat there mulling something over in his head for a moment.

"What's up...?" I asked.

"I ever tell you about your great-grandpa?"

I thought for a moment, then shook my head. "I don't think so, no."

My dad chewed the inside of his mouth for a second. "He was a violent man. Least that's what my dad told me – he never met the guy. Heard it all from his kin growing up."

"He never met him?"

My dad shook his head. "Your great-grandpa died in prison. Got locked up when your grandpa was a baby."

"What was that, like a hundred years ago?" I blurted out. My dad shot me a stern look. "Sorry," I mumbled quickly. "What was he in jail for?"

There was a silence. "He killed a man. Shot him in the heart."

"*Seriously?* Why?"

He shrugged. "Nobody knows. Rumor had it the man he killed was talking a little too much to his wife, getting a little too friendly, but she said she barely even knew the guy. Your great-grandma didn't talk about it all that much, but from time to time she'd open up about it. She told me once she thought it was just to see the other man die."

"But... Why?"

My father looked at me. "Because he was angry."

Another hush fell over me.

After a minute, my dad went on. "She told your grandpa that his dad was a good man, but I'm pretty sure that was all bullshit. He was a musician – that old piano upstairs belonged to him, once upon a time. Came over from Ireland – that's actually how we got our name, 'Lyric.' His accent was so thick that the immigrations people misheard 'Donovan Lee Rick' for 'Donovan Lyric' and he kept it. Then she'd tell my dad when he was a kid –" for a second, he affected a heavy southern accent, " – that his daddy was sitting in jail, pickin' and grinnin' on his *gui*tar all day long. Me, personally, I think that was bullshit, too."

"How come?"

He looked at me. "They don't let you play guitar in prison."

I didn't know what to say. So I said nothing, just sat there staring out the window at the black and white fields of dying green.

"If you don't nip this shit in the bud quick, while you're still young enough to do it, then you might end up there some day, too. We've got a lot of anger, Don. It's built into us. Hell, I don't have to tell you," he glanced away shamefully. "You've seen how I am when I drink too much. You know exactly what we are. We're a little fucked in the head, I think. We don't see the world the way a lot of your friends see it."

"How do they see it?"

He gave me a look of warning. "Like it's a nice, safe place. You know it ain't. I've made damn sure of that." He let out a sigh. "Violence is something our family has to be careful with. Like that kid you beat the hell out of today. He didn't really do nothin' to you, and you could have settled it with a couple of love taps, probably. He looked kinda like a wormy little fuck. But you didn't. You got angry, and you hit him hard. Not as hard as you *could*, but harder than you had to. That anger... It'll kill you just as quick as it'll kill the other guy. Violence is life and death to people like us, even when it isn't, because you never *know* when it will be. We aren't made for this world, not this century at least. But we're stuck here, and we've gotta play by their rules – understand?"

I mulled it over, staring down at the black and gray *Superman* T-shirt I was wearing. It was my favorite shirt when I was sixteen, but I felt like an imposter wearing it. Then I nodded. "I understand."

"Good. The world is a cruel place; only way you'll ever win it is to be cruel right back. But you gotta know your limits." He opened his door and stepped out of the beat up old truck. I followed suit as the sun began to dip low over the fields. "It should go without saying you're grounded. No Atari, no TV, no comic books."

"Not even comic books?!" I whined loudly. He gave me a swift palm upside the head.

"That's what the fuck I said, ain't it, *Superman?*"

With a grumble, I replied, "Yes, sir."

We trekked through the long yard and went up the couple narrow stone steps into the farm house. It opened into a sunroom a kitchen adjacent to a dining room and a living room. The bedrooms were all upstairs. Everything in the house looked as old as it was. Every floorboard creaked, every window was brittle, the old wood stove in the kitchen had years of tarnish on its brass handle and soot blocking the window inside. It's funny, when I was a kid, I hated that place. Now I would do anything for a house like that for myself.

My mother came down the stairs with a disappointed scowl. "Of all the fucking things, Don," she began. But my father held up a hand gently to silence her.

"We went over it. The boy doesn't need any more chastising. Not yet, anyway." Automatically, my father strolled over to a cabinet and pulled out a bottle of bourbon. I had never tried the stuff – at that point, I had drank maybe once in my life, and it was vodka and fruit punch. Not half bad.

He set a rocks glass down and three ice cubes clinked as they hit the glass, then he filled it with the dark liquor. My mom held her disappointed stare at me with her arms crossed, then finally softened her stance. "Are you hurt?"

My dad answered for me. "The other kid didn't even land a hit."

My mother shook her head frustratedly. "That would explain why the school used the word 'assault' when they called."

"He could have tried a little harder to defend himself," I mumbled with a smirk, then put up my fists in a boxing stance. "Dude's apparently never seen a boxing match in his entire life."

My mother rolled her eyes. My dad said, "Don't be too proud. There's a reason the Devil's greatest sin was pride."

"Shouldn't we be proud, though?" I asked.

"Only if you've earned it. Otherwise, it's arrogance. The Devil thought he knew better than God, thought he could usurp him, thought he knew what was better for us than He did. *That* kind of pride is arrogance."

I was skeptical. "Okay, but didn't the Devil kill a lot of people in the Bible? Wasn't *that* his greatest sin?"

"The Devil never killed nobody. That was God's department; the Devil was just an arrogant little shit. Look where that got 'im."

"What about Job?" I asked curiously. "He killed his children."

"Yeah, because God told him to," my father answered as he stashed the bottle back in the cupboard. "Then they all got resurrected when Job refused to break his faith. Again, proving the Devil wrong – circles right back to that pride thing I was just talking about."

Keenly, I watched him. I was always trying to gauge his mood when he drank, whether or not he was likely to fly off the handle, start screaming and throwing shit, or worse – putting his hands on my mother. That had only ever happened a handful of times, but sometimes it was bad.

And it was always terrifying.

Growing up, I always figured it'd be my father who killed me – just like a book straight out of the Bible.

My mom let out a sigh through her nostrils and said, "Dinner will be ready in a bit. Go up to your room and wait for me to call you down. And put your comics outside the door – *all* of them. I'll be counting."

I did as she asked, but I never came out when they called me. I wasn't hungry. Adrenaline, shame, fear for the future – they all rattled my body like an anxious maraca. There was nothing to do but listen to the wind and stare at the white walls.

Cautiously, while they ate, I pushed open the door and looked outside my room; the comics were still there. *Guess she forgot to come get them.* So I swiped one of them off the top of the pile, conspicuously placed there on purpose for just that scenario. It was the most recent *Superman* adventure – Action Comics no. 541, written by Marv Wolfman that month. In the story, a sorcerer named Satanis had split Superman's powers in half, and absorbed half of them while taking the facsimile of the hero. In this one, Superman wasn't invincible – for the first time in his life, he was mortal.

My eyes were glued to the colorful pages even though I couldn't see most of the colors. But Superman always had a lot of red; that helped him stand out to me. Straining my ears to make sure my parents weren't coming up the stairs, my eyes rested on one of the hero's speech bubbles on the fourth page.

*"Don't like this feeling of impotence! Don't like being half a superman! I want my other half back! And I want him now!"*

For a moment, I thought about that line. It reminded me of something I had read in Literature class earlier in the year, a quote from a poet named Rainer Maria Rilke:

*"If my devils are to leave me, I'm afraid my angels will take flight as well."*

Still listening closely, I continued on.

Naturally, Superman overcomes the sorcerer, and his two halves become whole again.

But one more passage stood out to me. It wasn't from the hero, it was from the narrator, when the villain is taunting the hero, hitting him with everything he's got, trying to get a rise out of him as he flies in to deal the victory blow:

*"But the Man of Steel doesn't respond...*

*Instead, he simply...*

*Acts!"*

There was something to that brief passage. As I finished the comic, I wondered if a human being could ever live up to the Man of Steel. Maybe we weren't supposed to. Maybe what mattered is that we tried, even when we failed.

Maybe what matters is that we act.

Footsteps creaked near the stairs and my heart skipped a beat. Quickly, I opened the door in silence and replaced the comic book. I could hear my mother's steps as she stopped by my door, followed by the rustling sound of paper, then her footsteps disappeared down the hall.

*Welp, there go my comics.*

By a quarter after eleven, the boredom overtook me. Carefully, I listened for the telltale sounds of what my parents were up to in the living room. Indistinct laughter carried throughout the house. They were probably stoned by now, watching something on the TV or listening to a radio show. It was strange, I only ever really heard my father laugh when he was with my mother, but I also only ever heard him scream when he was with her, too. He would accuse her of cheating one day, then the next he would talk like they had been soul-bonded across multiple lifetimes.

The absolute duality of man.

Quietly, I crept across my bedroom and slowly pulled open my door, straining my ears to hear their conversation. I'd been keeping track of how many times I heard the clink of ice cubes for a fresh glass; by my count, he was on his fifth whiskey of the night. That meant the conversation could be going one of two very different ways.

*"Letterman* wishes *he could be Johnny Carson,"* my dad was saying as a crowd laughed on TV. *"He's just an imitation – Carson's a comedic genius."*

*"I don't know if I'd say 'genius,' but he's sure as hell funny,"* my mom laughed.

*Okay, they're distracted. They're happy, and they're distracted.*

As noiselessly as I could, I crept through the upstairs hall toward my father's den, thinking that's probably where my mother stashed my comics. Silent as a breeze in the night, I opened the door and flicked on the lamp resting on his desk. Soft light bathed the room, peeking through my dark glasses. There wasn't really much entertainment to be found in there, as far as I was concerned. Certainly not any comics, I realized with an internal groan.

There were some old books, a Bible, some equally old vinyls, a bunch of rifles and handguns mounted on the walls – most of them loaded – then a few sports magazines on the coffee table in the center of the room and some dirty magazines in the desk drawer he didn't know I knew about. I thought about taking one and perusing through it, but I'd seen all the pictures so many times they had sort of lost their luster.

Tucked in the corner of his den was a small, black briefcase. I already knew what was in it – it was my dad's old poker set. A complete stack of chips, allegedly all different colors, and a couple decks of cards. When I was a kid, he'd play Texas Hold'em all the time, and I'd sit there and watch enraptured as his buddies lost every other hand to the man. He taught me how to play, and a couple times a week for a long time, he'd let me in on his games.

Of course, eventually, his buddies all quit coming over one by one. I used to think it's 'cause they were tired of losing, but the older I got the more I realized he just stopped inviting them, or they'd start to get put off by the man's intensity and constant switching between the Devil sitting on his one shoulder and the angel on the other.

Sometimes, that angel was so quiet I wasn't even sure she ever existed.

My eyes shifted away from the poker set and my attention was drawn to the grand piano in the corner of the room. Nobody in my family actually played anymore, but when my great-grandma died, someone had to take it. My heart began pounding as I walked over to it. Gentle as a mouse, I pressed my finger down on a key.

Very softly, a high pitched note struck my ear.

It sounded a little out of tune – and there was no way in hell my dad would pay to get a piano tuned for nobody to play. But I could make do.

I moved my finger down the piano, playing each white key as I went. Quietly, I said aloud, "C... B... A... G... F... E... D... C."

Quickly, I craned my neck and strained my ears to make sure nobody was coming. My dad might literally kill me if he caught me in his den.

Nothing but laughter and Johnny Carson.

So I turned back to the piano. I had been trying to learn for a while with the one in the school's music room, but it was hard to steal time. For a moment, I studied the pattern of the keys. I couldn't name any chords, but I had seen enough people play to figure some things out.

Carefully, I spaced my fingers with alternating keys on either hand, then pressed them down. The sound that came out was still a little off tune, but it was such a wild thing to hear. My hands played that chord. I couldn't tell you what it was, but I could tell you it was a chord. When I think back on it, I can't help but wonder if it was that secret chord David played that pleased the Lord.

So I kept at it. I'm not sure how long I was playing for, but after a few minutes, it sounded to an untrained ear like I knew what I was doing.

Music might really be the quickest path to the soul.

*"Oh God DAMN it!"* my father's voice yelled. I missed a key and the sound became sharp. Suddenly I froze, straining my ears to hear over the sound of adrenaline abruptly shooting through me. *"Can you get me a fucking paper towel?"*

My mom tried to stifle her stoned laughter. *"What happened?"*

*"I knocked my fucking drink over."*

More stifled laughter.

*"What?"* my father asked humorlessly. *"What's so goddamn funny?"*

*"Nothing,"* she laughed. *"I'll get you a towel."*

*"Goddamn better, woman…."*

Sometimes he called her 'woman' affectionately, like an old school bit of slang you can never drop.

I didn't think this was one of those times. There was vitriol in the way he said it.

*"Honey, calm down. Jesus."*

The silence that followed was sickening.

I could feel a knot tighten in my stomach as I braced myself for what was about to happen.

When your house is a tornado, you get pretty good at spotting a brewing storm.

Then –

*CRACK!*

The sound of glass shattering split my ears. My mother cried out, *"Samuel!"*

I couldn't hear what my father was saying – something about 'cheating whore' this and 'lying bitch' that. For a moment, I froze. It had been almost a year since the last time he had gotten violent, and the sounds of bodies slamming into walls told me that streak had just been broken.

*"Sam, stop!"* Her screams were enough to curdle my blood.

I had to do something.

*Just act.*

Quickly, my eyes darted around the room. Then I spotted his revolver, fully loaded, and snatched it from its spot on the wall.

I ran downstairs.

Bursting into the living room, I stood there defiantly. The man hadn't noticed me yet; my mother was pinned to the wall, my father's right hand holding her wrist and his left clutching her throat.

*Oh my God, he's going to kill her.*

*"Sam– Samuel!"* she sputtered.

The look of wild fury in that man's eyes could have made me shrivel.

But it didn't.

Instead, with a shaky hand, I raised the revolver.

"Let her go!" I shouted, my voice wavering.

And suddenly he stopped. He was looking at me, pointing the gun at him. A calculation seemed to run through his brain. He scoffed condescendingly. "You can't even use that thing, can you?"

When I looked him in the eye, I didn't see any angels sitting on his shoulder.

Just the Devil.

So I said, "Sure I can."

But he saw right through the veneer of confidence. He let her go and she collapsed to the floor, then crawled away with her back against the base of the sofa, coughing and rubbing her throat. The man took a step toward me. "Then do it."

For a moment, I hesitated.

Then he took another step.

So I pulled the trigger.

Nothing happened.

My eyes went wide.

I pulled the trigger again.

Still nothing.

Like lightning, he snatched the gun from my hand and shoved me backwards. I landed on my ass and scurried back to the wall by the doorway, then leapt to my feet.

*I'm going to die.*

He took a look at the revolver and said, "See, Don, this is a *single action* revolver." Then he looked at me. The fury and fire in his eyes hadn't abated. "So when you want to fucking *fire it at somebody*...." He pointed it at me.

"Dad, don't –!"

"You have to do *this*."

He cocked the hammer back and pulled the trigger.

The kitchen window shattered through the doorway behind me.

Then he fired again into the wall beside me.

And again into the heavy CRT a few feet away.

I squeezed my eyes shut, my entire body quaking, praying I didn't die.

When I opened my eyes back up again, there was no remorse in his. The fury had turned into sour disappointment.

With his hand, he pressed on the base pin latch beneath the barrel, withdrew the pin, then popped out the cylinder and tossed it to me. I flinched as I caught it in my palms and looked down at shell casings inside.

*.38 SPL.*

He glared at me and said, "There's that pride again."

Then he just... walked out the door. The sound of his truck starting up could be heard from inside, and the man drove off. Probably to some sleazy bar out in town.

My mother's tears still flowed quietly and she whispered, "Thank you."

I spent the rest of the night sitting on the steps, chain smoking cigarettes I bought from a friend and waiting for my nerves to calm, even though I knew they never would.

That night replayed itself in my head while I stood over Huck's dead body, slumped and bleeding out on my couch next to Alita's still warm, yet all too lifeless form.

# Chapter 19

## New Freedom, May 17th, 11:07 PM

*Angels, what have I done?*

My body shook as I stood there, smoke pouring from the barrel of the revolver. A pool of blood slowly emanated from Huck's cadaver, spilling onto Alita's pale skin.

For a moment, I thought I could see the light flicker out of Huckleberry's eyes in real time.

As if the weight of the world just fell upon me, I sank to the floor, kneeling like Atlas as he shrugged. *What have I done?*

Almost on its own, my hand touched the black cross hiding beneath my shirt.

*What do I do?*

My eyes surveyed the scene and thought it through. This was the sheriff's daughter. This was her boyfriend, whom most of the town knew had been feuding with me over the girl. He had been abusing her, treating her like shit for months, but nobody else was privy to that as far as I could tell.

Nobody but the sheriff, and he was convinced she was crazy. Huck could do little wrong in his eyes.

He took care of the sheriff's little girl, after all. Kept her off the streets and in a casket.

Jedediah would come in, find the two of them dead. He would ask why they were in my apartment, and I would tell him Huck broke in when he found Alita's car outside my place.

Except I forgot to lock the door; there were no signs of forced entry anywhere. She had scratches on her back from *my* fingernails. My DNA was literally inside her body, and she was in a state of half-undress. Me and Huck were about the same size, too; any bruising that might show up around her neck could be pinned on me. After all, I'm the one who had her skin cells embedded in my nails. And the sheriff already thought I was one bad day away from losing my shit.

Today had been one *very* bad day.

My eyes scanned over Huck's dead corpse. There were no defensive wounds – she didn't scratch him, bite him, hit him when he got ahold of her. That meant he probably restrained her wrists with one hand and choked her with the other.

It also meant there was even less way to prove he did it.

Meanwhile, my body was bruised and scratched from the brawl at the tavern and the fight the night before.

What seemed more likely? That the sheriff would take my word for it that she came over, I stepped out for ten minutes and came back to a brutal murder?

Or would he take a look at this crime scene and surmise that Huck had come over to parlay, things went south, so I shot him – then raped and murdered his daughter in a drunken fit of rage?

My temper was practically famous in this town.

Occam's Razor suggested the simplest answer was most often the correct one, and I was living through the exception that proved the rule.

Even if they got my alibi from the Shell, it would just look like I had gone out for a pack of smokes to *create* an alibi.

There was only one other person on the planet who knew how Alita died.

And he was lying on the couch with a hole the size of a finger in his heart.

*I can't call the police here. They'll pin both of these murders on me.*

*I have to call Carl.*

My hand refused to move for a moment, still struck in awe and tragedy by the sight. But I tucked the smoking gun into my belt and hurried over to the phone on the wall, then spun the dial through Carl's number.

"Come on, come on, come on, pick up, Carl…." I muttered to myself in a frenzy.

*BEEP!*

*"Hey, you've reached Carl Hoskins, attorney at law, go on ahead and leave a message and I'll get back to you whenever I can."*

"*Fuck!*" I roared into the receiver. Then I slammed it back down on the hook. Then again, and again, and again and again until bits of plastic debris were flying off the wall and the guts of the circuitry were exposed. "*FUCK, FUCK, FUCK, FUUUCK!*"

The phone fell from my hand and dangled by its cord.

*What do I do now?*

With a sharp inhale, I thought about the only other people I could turn to in a crisis like this.

*Rust. He can help me.*

My breath left my body slowly. I took a look around my house; I knew I would never be coming back here, I think.

So I stepped over to my guitar at the other end of the sofa and strapped it on my back.

I paused as I tightened the strap and looked down at Alita. Her eyes were stuck open, frozen in horror. My lips quivered as I looked down at her, her normally rhythmic and gentle breathing having ceased entirely. I took my hand and gently closed her eyes, leaned down, and softly kissed her forehead.

I whispered, "I'm sorry…."

Then I turned around and walked out the door.

Out in the distance, my ears caught the sound of sirens.

My blood froze in my veins.

Bouncing off the walls up Main Street, I could see red lights intermittently cut out by bright whites. People told me those ones were blue, but all I saw was bright white. They were getting rapidly closer.

Someone must have heard the gunshot.

Swiftly, I turned and I ran down North Bethel Street, unable to outrun the sound but fast enough to get out of their sight. Behind the house on the corner of Bethel and Garden, I stopped and peered out toward my house, taking off my glasses. The lights stabbed my eyes but I had to make sure they were stopping.

Two squad cars came to a halt in front of my place.

Sheriff Swanson stepped out of one of them.

His eyes rested on Alita's car for a moment. Even from that distance, I could see his fear rising.

I had locked the door behind me – figured it could buy me some time.

*Knock, knock, knock!* The sheriff rapped his fists against the door. "Mr. Lyric – this is the Sheriff's Department, open up!"

The sheriff glanced at the other officer who had been riding with him as the two in the second car got out. "Jed," the other cop at my door began, "I don't think he's gonna open up." Their voices were faint from the distance, but my ears were sharp and I made my heart stand still.

"Someone starts firing off bullets in their home, there ain't too many ways this goes down," Swanson replied gruffly. He withdrew his own revolver. "What in the hell is my daughter's car doing here? I don't like this." Then he knocked again. "*Lyric! Open up!*"

The other cop went over to the wide living room window and tried to peer past the curtains into the dull red light. "Caller only said one gunshot. Maybe he finally manned up and took himself out," he mused sickly.

"Doubt it," Swanson curtly dismissed. He looked back at the other two deputies standing by their car. "You two, go around back – check for signs of B-and-E, unlocked doors, footprints – anything. I don't know what we might be walking into."

"Yes, sir," they complied, running around to my backyard.

"Donovan!" Jed shouted again. "You've got thirty seconds before I break down this door!"

Then the other deputy stooped low by the window with his hands cupped around his eyes like binoculars. "Oh, *shit!*" he suddenly exclaimed.

"What is it?" the sheriff asked quickly.

His deputy gave him a dire look. "I think I see a body."

The sheriff's face fell. Then the deputy drew his own sidearm and the sheriff roared, "Lyric, we're coming in!"

With a heavy foot, he kicked the door three times before it snapped through the frame.

The moment he was inside, I could hear a blood curdling, heartbroken cry. *"No, no, no, no! God please, no!"*

My throat burned and my eyes stung. It was the wrong way to find out you just lost your only daughter.

But the time for sympathy would be later.

Right then, I had to run.

So I did.

As lithely as I could, I cut through the darkness across Garden Street onto Water, through a few yards past the front of the bar. Couldn't go in through the front, too much light. So I turned and ran up the alley until I was at the tall fence behind the Clawhammer. Rust usually didn't bother with padlocking the gate; I slid my finger between the gate and the latch and flipped it open, then crept onto the patio and hurried to the back door, careful to keep my guitar from hitting anything and making noise.

My fist knocked against the glass. In a loud hush, I called, "Rust, it's Lyric! You in there?"

Nothing.

Desperately, I yelled louder, "Rust!"

Then the silhouette of the tall, lanky man and his wild beard and hair strode through the darkened bar. He peered through the glass curiously. "Well, how do you do, Mr. Lyric?" Then he opened the door.

My face said it all.

"Ah, shit..." Rust exhaled. "What happened?"

Anxiously, I swallowed my throat. "He killed her, Rust. He killed her in my house. Then I shot him in the heart."

Rust studied me for a moment, then shook his head and sighed. "I tried to warn him. Some men just can't be reached. Come on, get in here before the cops make their way down."

Quickly, I stepped into the darkened Clawhammer. "I don't know what I'm gonna do, Rust," I began frantically.

"My advice would be to get ahold of Carl, first and foremost."

I shook my head. "I tried that. I think he's passed out."

"Yeah, figures," he said, stepping behind the bar. He glanced at me as he set down two rocks glasses and a bottle of bourbon. "Not used to seeing your eyes," he said. "Guess the place is usually a little brighter than this."

He poured two singles and slid one toward me. My hands shook as I set my guitar down on the bar and picked up the shot, then poured it down my throat. "Thank you," I said with a burn.

"So I take it that's what those sirens I was hearing were for?" he asked. His nonchalant coolness never left him as he spoke.

"Yeah," I breathed shakily. "Jed is at my place right now, with at least three other cops. I give it maybe another minute or two before the place is swarming with them."

"Shit," Rust clicked his tongue quietly. "Rotten way for a man to find his kid." Then he poured another shot.

"Yeah, I know...." He held the bottle toward me, but I dismissed it with a wave of my hand. "I need to sober up," I said. The room was spinning but I anchored my concentration on making it stand still. Nothing kills your high quite like leaving a murder in your wake.

"Good man," he breathed, then downed his own shot. "You passed the test."

For a moment, he and I were both silent. Then I said, "I can't turn myself in, Rust. There's no way in hell they're gonna believe I didn't kill Alita. My DNA is all over her, and a prosecutor would have no problem at all painting up a motive for me to do it."

Rust mulled it over for a moment, then asked, "What exactly happened?"

I took a deep breath. "Alita came over after we left, we had sex, I went out for a pack of cigarettes. I couldn't have been gone longer than ten minutes. When I got back, Huck had broken in and he was sitting next to her dead body on the couch. I think he strangled her."

Rust nodded to himself. "Then what happened?"

"I told him to stand up so he could die on his feet, then I shot him in the heart. I think he died before I left, but I don't know. He might still be *bleeding to death* as we speak. *Fuck!*" I ended with an eruption, throwing the rocks glass across the room. It shattered against the wall with a familiar sound. Rust studied me carefully. "Sorry," I muttered.

"If anybody gets it, Lyric, it's me. The question is now – what the hell are you gonna do about it?"

For a moment, I paused and ran through my options. "I have to lay low until I get ahold of Carl, at the very least. Once he talks to the cops for me, and can make sure I have a chance to fight the murder I *didn't* do, then... well...."

Rust gave me a knowing look. "Then you've gotta face the music."

I said nothing.

He went on with a sigh. "Well, this is probably damn near the first place Jed is gonna look for you, so you can't stay here too long. I can make a couple of phone calls, figure out somewhere you can lay low for a few days. But you're gonna have to figure out how to get there on your own, Lyric. That's gonna be the hard part."

I nodded humbly. "I appreciate you, Rust."

Just as he opened his mouth to reply, a sound interrupted him.

There was a knock at the door.

# Chapter 20

Everything went still except for my beating heart. Were the cops already out looking for me? How long had it been since they got to my house? It couldn't have been longer than five, ten minutes.

Maybe that's all the longer it took. They stumbled into a double homicide, after all.

Curtly, Rust shot me a look and gestured with his head for me to hide.

I mouthed, *where?*

Then he nodded toward the kitchen. I couldn't hide upstairs; I would have to walk by the front door with its pane of glass to get there. The kitchen was the only option.

But even then, if they rounded the side of the building, they would stop at the kitchen door leading into the alley first.

I had to stay low, keep quiet. So I crept around the bar and into the small, gritty kitchen, ducking down beside the inactive fryers.

Gently, I brushed my hand against the revolver in my back pocket just to make sure it was still there.

Would I really use that against the police? That would be suicide, I reasoned.

But you back a wild animal into a corner, sometimes it goes for the kill – even if it knows it won't survive, either.

Straining my ears, I listened to Rust's footsteps as he approached the front door. My hand reached around my back to steady my guitar.

And then I realized I left it on the bar.

My heart dropped.

They would know I was here.

Then a rapping came at the door again – this time, with a voice.

It was a woman's voice.

"*Rust? You in there?*" the sound of Jazz's music hit my ears. "*I left my amps behind.*"

My breath escaped me with relief, but I didn't leave my hiding spot. All I wanted was to see the light in her eyes shining, to make me feel like everything would be okay for just a minute, but I couldn't drag her into this.

I heard the front door creak open. Rust said, "*I figured you'd come back for that tomorrow, to be honest with you. Wasn't expecting any late night visitors.*"

Jasmine's footsteps entered the building. "*I was gonna, but I was still in the neighborhood and I know you're a night owl. Sorry if I'm intruding.*"

"*Not at all, ma'am.*" The way he said *ma'am* had a layer of old-world respect to it, like it was as dignifying as the word *queen* or *highness*.

Then Jasmine's tone changed slightly. "*You see all those cops on Bethel Street?*" she asked. My heartbeat kicked up. There was heavy concern in her voice. "*They're all over Lyric's place. What happened?*"

Rust took a moment, then replied, "*Couldn't tell ya. I heard the sirens, figured they were close, but I haven't seen him since y'all left earlier,*" he replied coolly.

Jazz's feet stopped. "*Really? Because that looks an awful lot like his guitar lying there.*"

My chest contracted tightly with a sharp wind.

There was a long pause.

Then she asked, *"Is he in trouble?"*

Rust told her, *"Jazz, the less you know about the ongoing predicament, the better."*

I heard a soft gasp escape her. *"Oh my God... What happened?"*

*"I am not at liberty to say, and I advise you to respect that. Your amps are over in the corner where you left 'em. Get 'em and head on outta here, or you'll be caught up in something you want no part in – I promise you."*

She ignored him. *"Lyric?! Where are you?"* she called out.

*"Jazz –"*

*"I want to know what happened! Is he alright? Is Alita okay?"*

Total silence.

Then she whispered, *"Oh my God... Please don't tell me..."*

*"Jasmine –"*

Before he could continue, I stepped out from the kitchen.

"Hey, Jazz."

She stood in the middle of the bar with a torn look of worry all over her face. "Lyric, what happened? There's half a dozen cop cars at your place right now. Where's Alita? Did Huck do something?" She began to pace around anxiously. "I knew I shouldn't have left you alone tonight."

"Jazz…" I began with pain in my throat. "Alita's…."

Her eyes widened. "Please, don't say it...."

"Alita's dead."

Like a boulder landed on her shoulder, Jasmine slowly sank to the floor. "Oh, my God..." Then she looked up at me with glistening eyes. "Lyric, what happened?"

I walked over and knelt beside her. "Huck broke into my place when I went out for a pack of cigarettes. He strangled her to death."

Her eyes widened with horror at first, then creeping realization. "Lyric... What did you do?"

I said nothing.

She gasped softly. "You killed him... didn't you?"

My silence answered her question.

Like a mother bear protecting her cubs, she threw her arms around me and spoke while biting back tears: "It'll be okay. We'll figure this out, alright? It'll be okay."

Gently, I pushed her away. "I don't think it will."

She studied me carefully for a moment, then rose to her feet. I did the same, and she asked: "What are you going to do? Did you call Carl?"

"He's either asleep or not home tonight," I replied.

"Well you can't run from the cops!" she protested. "What are you doing here? You have to turn yourself in, Donovan! The longer you hide from them, the worse it's gonna be!"

I shook my head and began pacing. "I can't do that, Jazz – not until they know I didn't kill Alita."

She gave me a dumbfounded look. "How are they supposed to know that if you don't talk to them?"

"Jazz, it's the *sheriff's* daughter!" I exclaimed. "Lying dead on my couch next to her boyfriend! With *my* DNA all over her!" Anxiously, I ran my hand through my hair. "If he sees me, I promise you, he *will* kill me on sight."

Jazz crossed her arms as a fearful tear rolled down her cheek. "Why do you think that?"

My thoughts echoed back to what the sheriff had said to me earlier. "Because he thinks I just made him the most dangerous thing a man can be."

"Angry? Hurt?"

"Alone."

A heavy silence fell over the bar. She mulled my words over as Rust sauntered to the phone on the wall. After a moment, he broke the silence. "I'm gonna make a phone call or two. You kids sit tight. Stay away from the windows. They'll be looking for you here soon, I bet."

Rust lifted the phone and dialed a number. He spoke softly; I couldn't make out what he was saying. After a minute, Jazz said, "This is a nightmare...."

"God I hope so," I replied. "But I don't think we're gonna wake up."

Fraught with worry, biting her nails, she looked at me. "Why did you do it? Why'd you have to kill him?"

I thought for a moment. "Because in a twisted way, I think it was the right thing to do."

"Lyric, I told you this isn't the wild west! You can't have a standoff at sunset like it's gonna solve all your problems!"

"It's too late for that now," I exhaled. "There's no going back from this."

Rust's voice loudened slightly. "Alright... Alright... I'll let him know. Thanks, partner." Then he hung up the phone.

Jazz gave him a curious look. "Who was that?"

"Red Sutherland," he answered. Then he looked at me. "Can you make it to Killdevil?"

I took a sharp breath and thought for a moment. "Possibly. I can get there in a couple hours going down the trail, but... They'll be lookin' for me everywhere."

"I can take you," Jazz suddenly offered.

"Absolutely not," I replied staunchly. "You shouldn't even *be* here. You've gotta leave, Jazz."

"Hell no I'm not leaving!" she protested loudly. "If you try to walk to the next town over, they'll catch you for sure!"

"Yeah? And what happens when they spot a bright red van heading for Killdevil? They'll pull you over, lock me up and charge you for assisting my escape. There's already blood on my hands. You're not coming with me." Then I looked at Rust. "What's Red thinking?"

Rust stroked his long beard and lit a cigarette. "He's got a safehouse just over the state line in West Virginia. It's out deep in the woods – ain't nobody ever gonna find it without a map."

"Shit..." I mumbled. "He was telling me about that earlier."

"You get to him," Rust went on, "he can give you the map with its location marked. Trick is, you gotta be quick, and you gotta be quiet. Keep in mind, man's got a family to look after. It don't matter how good of friends you may be, the sheriff's department comes knocking at his door while you're there and all bets are off. Between you and his kid, it ain't much of a competition."

Solemnly, I nodded. My heart was racing and my brain was on fire, but I could see clearly. *Get to Killdevil, get the map, get across state lines.*

*That almost sounds doable.*

*Almost.*

"Alright," I exhaled. Then I looked at Jazz. "I'll call you as soon as possible." I glanced at Rust. "Is there a phone at the safe house?"

He nodded. "Red's got a communication rig set up there. It's old school, military radio – might take you a minute to figure out how to use it, but it oughta fare well enough against the woods. You ain't got much time, and every second you sit around here is another second you're more likely to end up in prison, or six feet under it."

I nodded again. "Understood."

Jasmine glanced at my guitar lying on the bar and muttered, "Of all the things to bring with you...."

Nervously, I told her, "If I end up in prison for the rest of my life, then tonight might be the last night I ever get to play it."

She frowned sympathetically, then embraced me tightly. "Please, be careful."

"I'll do my best."

Finally, Rust looked at me and said, "Just remember, Lyric: this is gonna end one way or another, and no matter what, eventually your karma's gonna come around – good and bad. When that happens, when the music's here, well... You just gotta face it."

My face morphed into a deep, grim frown as I reached for my guitar. "I don't know if I can do that, Rust."

But then a loud banging came from the front.

*"Rust, this is the Sheriff's Department. Open up!"*

# Chapter 21

Jazz snapped her head toward me with a look of borderline terror. My hand froze in place.

I would guess my face matched hers.

Silently, she mouthed, *what do we do?*

And I replied, *don't follow me.*

Calmly, Rust shot me a look and nodded toward the patio. He held up a finger and mouthed the words, *one minute*, pointed at the front and made a gesture toward himself with the other hand, then made a semi-circle motion with the first hand, like drawing a trail with his finger.

*Go outside, wait one minute, he'll get them in the door, then I book it down the alley.*

*How hard can it be?*

Anxiously, I swallowed my throat and pulled my hand away from the guitar. I didn't know if that would be the last time I ever got to see that instrument. Silent as a phantom, I knelt down and crept to the back door, opened it, and slinked out onto the concrete patio filled with wooden picnic tables. I kept my body low and stayed near the six-foot high paneled fence.

There were footsteps all around me, and voices in the alley.

"You really think he would be dumb enough to hide out here?"

"I don't fuckin' know, Tarlton. It's a small town – where would you start?"

"*Damn, Jones, don't bite my fuckin' head off. I'm just thinking out loud.*"

"*Well stop.*"

The voices stopped by the back patio gate. I strained my ears over the sound of my rapid heartbeat.

"*You gonna open it or what?*"

"*Can't open it. Not without a warrant.*" Then, loudly, the voice called out, "*You out here, Rust?*"

*Fuck. I'm trapped.*

Then another voice sounded off. "*Hey, come back to the front. Rust is at the door.*"

The footsteps shuffled off toward the front of the bar and I let out a quiet breath of relief. As soon as they rounded the corner, I hurried to the tall gate and slowly opened it.

I could hear the voices of Rust and the police on the porch.

I stopped and began counting to sixty in my head. That's about how long Rust figured it would take for the coast to clear and the cops to be inside.

Gently, I touched the cross beneath my shirt.

Rust said, "*What's going on, fellas?*"

"*You happen to have seen Donovan Lyric lately?*"

Rust took a moment to respond. His voice was as nonchalant as ever. "*Well, he was here earlier. Ol' Huckleberry came up and started threatening him. I settled that one right quick. No idea where he went afterward.*"

"*Who was he with when he left?*"

"*He was seeing off the sheriff's daughter. Huck was trying to intimidate her, the way the insecure men among us are prone to do. We scared him off. Couldn't tell ya where he went after that. Wouldn't tell ya if I knew, either.*"

"*And why is that, Colton?*"

"*Call it an occupational hazard, call it a force of habit. Unless someone's trying to hurt me or mine, well, it ain't really none of my business, is it?*"

There was a pause. My eyes focused on the train platform, down the alley and across Water Street, mapping out the quickest line in my head for when it was time to run.

"*Well, there's a double homicide on our hands and right now, and Lyric is our only suspect. You happen to know anything about that?*"

"*No sir, I do not.*"

Under my breath, I counted silently: "Eighteen... Nineteen..."

Another pause. "*What about that van there on the street? That belongs to Jasmine Garcia, doesn't it?*"

"*I believe it does.*"

"*She here right now?*"

"*Yessir.*"

"*You mind if we talk to her?*"

"*Well, that's up to the lady, now ain't it?*"

The officer grumbled. "*We're just trying to touch base with Lyric's affiliates. People he might trust to help him on the run. As of now, he's a suspect. Pretty soon, he don't turn up, well... He'll be a fugitive from the law.*"

Before Rust could reply, Jazz's voice hit my ears. *"What's going on here?"* she asked.

*"Ms. Garcia, you happen to have any idea on the whereabouts of Mr. Lyric? We've gotta ask him a few questions concerning a couple dead bodies on his couch."*

My throat tightened as I thought back to Alita, lying there lifeless.

Jazz paused, then asked, *"What happened?"*

The cop sighed. *"We're not too sure yet. But it looks like a love triangle gone bad. Sheriff's daughter's been killed. Same as her boyfriend."*

*"And you think Lyric killed them?"*

*"Well, we don't have too many other suspects to go on. Given his recent behavior... It's starting to look pretty likely."*

*"No, he wouldn't do that,"* she protested. *"He might be reckless, he might be a rebel, but he's not the Devil. He wouldn't hurt a woman. Especially not one he cared about."*

There was a pregnant pause. Then the cop asked pointedly, *"What about a man?"* Jazz fell silent. After a second, the cop went on. *"Look, Ms. Garcia, if you've seen him or if you know anything, you'd do best to tell us about it now. 'Cause if the sheriff – and my god, my heart goes out to him – if the sheriff finds out later that you knew what was going on, it's gonna be that much worse for you. You might find yourself in a cell right along with him."*

At that point, Rust spoke again. *"That's a coward's tactic, my friend – threatening a woman."*

*"Look, I'm not threatening her, we're just –"*

Rust interrupted. "*Come on inside and take a peek around if it suits you. I ain't got nothin' to hide. Nothin' you'll ever find, anyway.*"

"*Sure thing. We won't be too long.*"

"Fifty-seven... Fifty-eight... Fifty-nine..."

Then I heard footsteps entering the bar.

"Sixty."

The door closed.

There was nothing left to do but run.

Keeping my breath still, I quickly hurried down the alley. The trail and train were right across the street from the bar, and the expansive woods surrounding the town were just past that. All I had to do was get across the road without being seen.

*And it sounded so easy in my head.*

The second I was in the road, red lights flashed off the walls coming down Garden Street.

A cop car turned and faced me.

For a moment, I froze, blinded in the bright white headlights.

Then, through the loudspeaker, I heard the sheriff's voice. It was strained with fury, barely staying level. "*Donovan Lyric, stay where you are!*"

Immediately, Jasmine burst through the front door of the Clawhammer. "Lyric, *run!*"

I stole a single glance at her and the frantic look on her face as the cops tried to push past the slender woman. She held her hands in the doorframe to stop them, but it barely bought me a second of time.

And then I ran.

Quickly as I could, I cut through the park by the train platform and booked it down the trail. A horde of footsteps charged after me.

*Shit! There's no way I can outrun them! Fucking idiot!*

I couldn't run all the way to Killdevil, and I couldn't turn myself in.

My dad once told me the term for my situation was "proper fucked."

And then an idea struck me as I sprinted up the trail.

The train and its half-a-dozen cars were parked on the tracks, just a hundred feet ahead.

Then the sheriff cried out, *"You evil bastard!"*

A gunshot rang out into the night.

I cried out in pain as hot metal embedded itself into my right tricep.

*"FUCK!"*

*Ignore it!* I thought to myself. *Keep going!*

Jasmine's voice shrieked in terror. *"Don't kill him!"*

And one of the deputies yelled, *"Dammit, Jed! Don't shoot!"*

Clasping my hand against the wound, I kept running until I reached the train.

Swiftly, I ran around the side so the cops couldn't see me. In a few moments, they would all catch up to me, but they didn't see me board the train. I hoped against hope they would think I ran into the woods.

*They need a reason to think that's where I went*, I reasoned, gritting my teeth as my arm throbbed. *I gotta give them one.*

So I leaned out of the rearmost train car, picked up a heavy stone from the ground and tossed it into the bushes. The blood on my hand stood out bright red in the black and white darkness as I receded into the train car.

Then I heard one of the cops shout, "Over there! He went into the woods!"

Ducking down, I crept through the train into the second passenger car in the rear and strained my ears. Another cop yelled, *"Fan out! Don't let him escape!"* Then the thundering stampede ran for the woods.

But before I could breathe any relief, the sheriff yelled, *"You two! Stay back and search the train!"*

*"Yes, sir!"*

Tears stung my eyes as I tried to forget the burning lead in my muscle. The sound of footsteps boarding the rear car hit my ears.

They would find me in seconds.

Silently, I crouched down and scurried the length of the car, opening the door quietly and closing it again. Then I went through the third and the fourth, until finally I hit the luxury car where Red clocked Will. I ran past the red leather seats toward the bar at the end and knelt down behind it, listening closely for the rising sound of footsteps.

*"Mr. Lyric!"* one of the deputies called through the train cars. *"We know you're in here!"*

My teeth gnashed down on themselves, biting back any sound that might escape my lips. I glanced down at my right hand; blood began to trickle from the beneath the sleeve of my jacket.

Fear gripped me like the Devil folding his wings as he fell. I scanned the darkness. Flashlights shone through the windows of the doors, getting brighter with each passing moment. Soon they would be upon me, and the story would be over. I'd spend the rest of my life in prison for a crime I didn't commit, and never be believed about the one I did.

*It can't end here. This can't be it.*

My eyes rested on a mini fridge behind the bar.

*Hell with it. Might as well have one more drink before I go.*

The footsteps grew louder and louder. They couldn't have been more than one car behind me now. My good hand reached out toward the fridge – but then something caught my eye.

There was a maintenance hatch in the floor beneath it.

*Holy shit.*

As quickly and noiselessly as possible, I slid the small refrigerator to the side to reveal the foot-by-foot square hatch in the floor. Four heavy screws held it in place. Immediately, I took out my knife and started undoing the screws.

"*Donovan Lyric!*" the deputy shouted again. The knife slipped from the screw and I cursed silently, panic creeping up on me as the cops got closer.

The other deputy shouted, "*Come out with your hands up, or we* will *shoot!*"

*Come on, come on, come on!*

Then, finally, the fourth screw came out. It hit the floor with a quiet *thud* just as the door to the luxury car opened. I grabbed the four screws and stuffed them in my pocket so they wouldn't give away my escape, then frantically lifted the hatch and crawled headfirst through it, praying I didn't make a sound as I hit the gravel and tracks below it.

Pain shot through my arm as I landed but I ignored it, then gently lowered the hatch back down.

I could hear the footsteps right above me.

"*Lyric, we know you're in here!*" one of the deputies called. His flashlight swung across the windows of the car like a lighthouse spinning in the dark as they looked for me. "*Tarlton, check the conductor's car. If he ain't in there, then he's not here.*"

"*Roger that.*"

A pair of heavy footsteps crossed over me as I laid in the dirt and gravel, with crossties pressing into my back. The second pair of feet hovered just behind the bar.

Light shined through the cracks in the hatch and, for a moment, I went blind.

My heart raced as I heard the muffled sounds of a man kneeling down.

*Fuck! Fuck! They know I'm here!*

But the hatch never opened.

Instead, all I heard was the *hiss* of a cold beer can cracking.

"*What the hell are you doing?*" the other deputy asked as he regrouped with the first.

"*Might as well have a drink. The guy isn't in here. Looks like Nelson was right – he ran off into the woods.*"

The second deputy let out a sigh. "*Gimme one of those.*"

Another *hiss* and *crack* hit my ears, then the faint noise of the beers being drunk quickly. The first deputy spoke into his radio, "*Sheriff, this is Tarlton. Doesn't look like our suspect is on the train – we searched every compartment. What's your status? Over.*"

The radio crackled, then I heard the voice of the sheriff. He sounded distraught, with a note of fury underpinning his voice. "*We've got all boots out in the eastern woods following his trail. You two get on back to your cruisers and patrol the area. He can't have gone far. Over.*"

"*Copy that. Over.*"

Then the other deputy said, "*Between you and me, I think they oughta boot the sheriff off this one. Man can't think clearly after a sight like that.*"

"*You ain't wrong. Soon as he hears about it, the chief deputy's probably gonna send the man home. I give it ten minutes 'fore we get that order radioed in, tops.*"

Their voices became quieter as their footsteps retracted. "*Ten minutes? Hell, I'll take that bet. I say they do it in five, shots fired 'n all....*"

"*I can't believe he really shot the man....*"

Their voices trailed off as the two deputies stepped out of the luxury car. From beneath the train, I watched their footsteps until they made it back to their patrol unit, turned over the engine, and drove off.

296

For another five or six minutes, I waited under the train. I could feel my sleeve getting wetter and wetter from blood.

As soon as I was sure enough time had passed, I rolled out into the open.

Hesitantly, I rose to my feet and looked around the serene, placid darkness.

I was the only one there.

Alone in the silent night, I walked down the trail toward Killdevil.

# Chapter 22

"How much further?"

"Not much," Alita replied, looking back at me with a slight grin, the sun beaming down on us. The light always hurt to look at, even when it was just at a glance or coming from up high. "It's worth it, I promise."

"Worth it, huh?" I said back, mirroring her expression. "Worth walking in this eighty-five degree weather when I could be at home with a cold drink in an air conditioned room?"

"No wonder you're so pale," she teased. "Have you ever even been outside before?"

"I grew up on a farm – I love the outdoors. In the early spring, and then again in the fall. Not a big fan of summer heat."

"Well, get used to it. There's not a whole hell of a lot else to do in New Freedom."

My eyes were fixed on her as we walked down the trail toward Killdevil. It was maybe a month after I moved into the place in New Freedom, five years ago. I had never been down the trail before. "You know, we could have taken the train."

"Where's the fun in that?" she grinned, doing a pirouette in her long, hippy-patterned skirt with a tube top covering her torso. Her hair moved gracefully in the wind like it was as much a part of Mother Nature as the trees and the creek.

"Where are we going, anyway?" I asked, hiding my impatience.

"My second favorite spot in the world – the swimming hole."

"Second favorite?" I asked with a wry smile. "What's your first?"

She looked back with a grin. "You'll figure it out."

"How very mysterious of you, Alita."

The tree branches hung over the trail like bony fingers shielding us from the sun. Even through my sunglasses the light still burned, but I didn't mind it too much when I was with her. Just up ahead was the road leading in and out of town, north through New Freedom to Killdevil.

"'Mysterious' is my middle name," she replied with a goofy look on her face as we crossed the street that intersected the trail, the left hand leading to the road and the right hand leading to a small group of houses tucked back almost out of sight. Lorraine lived in one of them, I was pretty sure.

When Alita looked at me, I felt like I was glowing.

She gave me one more smile, then pointed up ahead a small ways. "There it is – the spot where the creek settles for a moment in its journey from the river."

Gleefully, she trotted – almost pranced – over to a concrete tunnel built into the trail, a little spot overlooking the shallow water. Water flowed incessantly into a small basin, coming from the creeks and streams produced by the dam carefully corralling Mother Nature, lest she unleash a flood upon Southern Sound County of Biblical proportions.

I said to Alita, "I thought you called it a *swimming hole*? How you gonna swim in two feet of water?"

She pursed her lips as her feet landed on the top of the tunnel and said, "You've gotta get here after it rains, genius, when they let up the dam."

I glanced up at the clear white sky – blue, I think it was to her – and replied, "Might have picked a bad day to bring me here, then."

She smiled and said, "There's never a bad day to be with nature."

"Well you've clearly never seen a tornado," I winked at her behind the shades.

She tried to make an irritated look, but couldn't help her smile. "Pft, have *you?*"

"As a matter of fact – no, no I have not."

She laughed with me, then sat herself down on the concrete with her feet dangling over the edge. I stood beside her and looked down at the stream. Beneath the endlessly rushing fluid were carefully placed, large stones. It seemed to have been built with some idea of reverence and beauty in mind. Water bubbled and babbled into the brook through the tunnel, but at the small basin it was peaceful. Little fish could be seen slicing through the ripples with surgical precision, barely disturbing the water. The drop was maybe ten or twelve feet down – on that bed of rocks and stone, it wouldn't kill you, but I'm sure it'd hurt like hell. "You ever fall in?" I asked.

"No," she tittered. "What, you scared of heights?"

"Only a little," I breathed as I sat down beside her. She gazed out over the field beside the road, stretching out for hundreds of feet before it turned back into woods. A large, steep hill was on the side behind us, covered in forest for miles. Someone could hide out in those woods for days and not be found, I figured.

"A little fall like that ain't gonna kill you," she said. Her voice was sweet; it blended into the sound of the breeze almost naturally, like she was where she belonged. She gave me a quick smile, then stared out over the verdant field, where I saw only white and gray. If I closed my eyes, I could almost picture it as a sea of green. I opened them up again and my eyes rested on her, studying the side of her face until I committed every detail to memory, every flaw and imperfection in her skin that made her human. Then she turned and glanced at me. "What?" she cracked a self-conscious grin.

"Nothing," I replied, quickly turning away. "You have something on your face."

"Fuck – is it a pimple?" She touched her cheek quickly and brushed the nothing away.

I laughed. "Don't worry, you got it."

She held her look on me for a minute, then said, "You're weird."

"I guess I'll go fuck myself, then," I grinned.

"Weird is good. I like weird."

"Well, I hope so, because you're definitely weirder."

"Oh, coming from you? Sure I am," she replied slyly.

I smiled a broad, beaming smile, and the two of us fell silent. Then Alita reached into the deerskin purse draped around her shoulder.

"Can I show you something?" she asked.

"Sure."

"Just... Don't laugh, okay? Or judge me or whatever. I'm not shy about a lot of things but this is one of them."

"You can't start off by saying 'don't judge me' before I know what it is," I responded. "What if you pull out a human head?"

She screwed up her face and made a confused laugh. "It's not a human head, you jerk!"

"Animal bones?"

Then she shrugged one shoulder. "You're getting warmer."

I recoiled a little bit and my mouth fell open slightly.

Alita burst out laughing. "Oh my God, I'm fucking with you, Lyric. Actually, now that you mention it...." She pulled out a small, flat wooden box with a glass top. Inside it was a preserved monarch butterfly, with black and white spots. She handed it to me.

"You carry around a dead butterfly?" I asked, bemused. "This is what you wanted to show me?"

"It belonged to my mom, before she died a few years back. She had tons of them – that was her hobby. Don't worry, she didn't kill them." She added that part when she saw the look of concern on my face. "She would spend her days in the woods, in the garden, anywhere outside that she could be," Alita went on, taking the wooden box back and gently caressing the glass. "People always thought she was crazy. I don't think she was. Nature is kinder than people; the trees don't judge you for seeing the world differently. Birds aren't interested in what you watched on the TV last night. And butterflies don't care who you are or what you've done. All they see is another creature, just like them."

I didn't know what to say. A part of me was in awe of the young woman beside me, and another part was terrified I wouldn't be one of the kind people in her life, and someday this moment would be soured. "She sounds... unique."

"She was." There was a creeping sorrow in her voice.

Gently, I asked her, "How did she die?"

Alita frowned with melancholy lips. "My dad had her medicated," she said. "Whatever they put her on... It ruined her. All the light in her eyes was just... Gone. It was like she was dead inside. Long before she took her life."

With empathy, I frowned too. "I'm sorry."

"It's okay... Everything happens for a reason." Alita was quiet for a moment, staring at the casket for the butterfly. "It's blue, by the way."

"What?"

"The butterfly." She pointed at the white spots on its wings. "It's blue. I know you can't see it, but... You said you remembered what colors looked like, right?"

My eyes went from her to the butterfly. I stared at the black and white spots for a second and committed its shape to memory, then I closed my eyes.

I could picture the blue in its wings.

My eyes opened back up. "Thank you," I whispered.

Alita smiled, then she tucked the box back into her bag. "But that's not what I wanted to show you." She pulled out a small, leather bound book and held it toward me. "Here."

"What's this?" I asked, taking it curiously.

"Poems. It's sort of like my own private journal, just... artsier, I guess. No, wait, that sounded pretentious – forget I said that."

I sort of laughed, opened the book and flipped through the pages. There had to be dozens of short stanzas scrawled throughout. "You wrote all these?"

"Mhm," she nodded. She took it back for a second and opened to a particular page, then handed it back to me. "This is one I wrote when I was out in Colorado."

"When was that?"

"I just got back a couple months ago. I looked around at where I was and I just... I wanted to be somewhere else. I wanted to get away from here."

"What, you got friends out west?"

She shook her head. "I was alone. I prefer it that way. All my life, I've had people like my dad telling me what I can and can't do, what's realistic and what's just fantasy. That I need somebody to take care of me, that I need a man or a husband or – God forbid – a shrink. I wanted to prove them wrong. So I got in my car and I just started driving until I came across a sight I'd never seen before."

"Damn," I breathed with admiration. "You just... packed up and left?"

"Yup," she nodded.

"Where did you stay when you were out there?"

She shrugged again. "I just slept in my car at first, till I made some money."

"Seriously?" I asked in sharp disbelief.

"Yeah," she kind of laughed. "That's the thing people won't ever tell you – you don't need money to be free, you don't need a house to be independent. Out there, completely on my own, having to figure out how I would eat every day with what money I could scrounge up working a few nights at clubs, getting to decide what to do with every minute of every hour of every day, sleeping underneath the stars, no taxes, no TV, no politics, no news... I don't think I'll ever find that kind of freedom again. And people called me crazy for it."

Rapt in awe, caught in her shining eyes behind the circular frames of her glasses, I hesitated. "Working at clubs?"

She kind of frowned embarrassedly. "Surprised you haven't heard – tends to be one of the first things people like to talk about when I'm not around. I worked as a dancer a couple weekends a month to get by." She kind of scoffed to herself. "I hate that term. 'Dancer.' As if people don't know what it means. I was a stripper. And then after that...."

"After that what?" I asked, taken aback.

She took a breath. "One thing led to another, a few of the girls showed me what they were making by doing a little... *extra* work, and –" She stopped abruptly and looked at me. "I don't know why I even bother with the euphemisms. I was a prostitute, Lyric."

"Shit, wow," I breathed in surprise.

Then she noticed the crestfallen look on my face. "The money I made from that was enough to survive for the next year or two back here. But anymore I do what God-fearing people call 'honest work.' Cleaning hotel rooms, trying my hand at tattoos on the side. A few of the girls out west taught me some basics and I really loved it."

"Basics of tattoos or of stripping?" I teased wryly.

She laughed and shoved me a little. "Tattoos, you jerk. Well, both, I guess." There was a moment of quiet. "Guess this is the part where you tell me I'm a sinner, huh? Or that I'm 'used up,' 'no good anymore,' yadda yadda yadda, right?"

For a second, I held my eyes on her. "No."

She was the one taken aback that time. She kind of brushed the hair from her eyes. "Well thanks."

It took me a moment to gather my thoughts. "I think you're better than a job like that – hell, most women are better than that. But struggle is real – you did what you had to do to get by, in the name of freedom. Sometimes freedom makes us do things we might think are evil or soulless, but that doesn't always *make us* evil. I don't think it makes you lesser; I just think it means you know why people shouldn't put a dollar sign over their bodies, because a piece of your soul goes with it. If there's really such a thing as the soul, you can't put a price on it."

There was a peculiar look on her face, and I couldn't quite place what she was feeling. Sadness, maybe; the look you give somebody when you feel like they've seen you for who you are and admire you all the same. She said, "Well, things would have to get pretty bad for me to ever dance again. In the stripping variety, of course." She sort of smiled at the end.

"For what it's worth, I'd love to see you dance – clothes on or off, dealer's choice," I joked and she laughed warmly.

"I can't stand you sometimes," she smiled.

I smiled back. "What made you come back to New Freedom?"

Her demeanor shifted and she grabbed her arm with her other hand. "I guess I got... lonely, I think. It's stupid, I know, I've already heard it." She mimicked her father's voice: "'Oh, well what did you expect, Alita? You drove a thousand miles away from everyone you know.'" Then she let out a sigh and went quiet for a moment. "I guess home really is where the heart is. But I don't wanna be here forever. There's so much more to this world than we ever get to see."

As I stared in black and white at the woman with red lips, for the first time in my life I felt like somebody else really understood what it meant to be free. "Trust me, I know what you mean." She half smiled and half frowned, then I looked down at the book in my hands. "Can I read it?"

"Only if you don't judge me."

"I guess we'll find out," I replied coyly. Her handwriting was curvy and artistic, almost leaping from the page. The poem read:

*In starry skies and darkened nights,*
*With wings of white we'll all take flight,*
*Never to be arrested, yet always are we tested,*
*To be brought back down to earth, we are bested;*

*Yet while we grieve our lost reprieve,*
*Fearful not, though all we've seen*
*Has cost a lot, still we have our fields of green;*
*And though it's rock, this coarse and rugged desert bed,*
*With just a thought, the fields of green will spring again.*

My eyes must have scanned those lines three or four times before I finally looked up from the page.

Alita shirked away with a look of embarrassment. "I told you they weren't very good."

When I looked up at her, I wasn't sure what to say. "Alita, it's beautiful."

She rolled her eyes. "You can't flatter your way into my pants, Donovan," she said with the hint of a smirk.

"Believe me, if that were my angle, I would be trying a lot harder," I fired back. Her face darkened and she began to blush, taking the book back.

"I couldn't think of a way to rhyme 'bed' with anything relating to 'green' so I kind of just had to half-ass that last line, and –"

"Alita," I interjected. Her voice stopped and she looked at me. "You have talent."

Then she smiled. It was a warm smile without any caveats or compromises. "Thank you," she said. She took the book back and returned it to her deerskin purse, then stared back over the field and I could have sworn I was in love.

*Well, if ever there were a moment...* I thought to myself as my heart pounded.

Just as my body began to lean toward hers to steal a kiss, she spoke again:

"So I think I'm getting dinner with Huck tomorrow night...."

That memory replayed itself in my mind as I crossed the street intersecting the trail by the swimming hole, carefully stealing away the darkness, blood still trickling down my arm. It had slowed down – for the last two miles, I kept my hand clutched around the wound, ignoring the searing, throbbing pain it caused. Through the night time air, I could hear the sound of that same stream and brook creeping through the tunnel just up ahead. I could almost still see her sitting there, her long skirt hanging down to her ankles as they carelessly swayed over the water.

And suddenly it dawned on me that I would never see her again.

Wearily, I decided to stop for a moment. I glanced around quickly to make sure the cops weren't in the area, then staggered with heavy feet to the spot I had been sitting that day and lowered myself to the cool concrete, letting my feet hang over the side as I pulled out a cigarette with my teeth and struck a match.

Even in the darkness, the place was beautiful. Eventually the town would probably build something on that plot of land – a park, a bar, a brewery, or some other eyesore – but that night it was just the same as it was the day Alita took me there.

As smoke caressed my lungs, I said aloud softly:

> *"Yet while we grieve our lost reprieve,*
> *Fearful not, though all we've seen*
> *Has cost a lot, still we have our fields of green;*
> *And though it's rock, this coarse and rugged desert bed,*
> *With just a thought, the fields of green will spring ag–"*

I couldn't finish the last line. My voice cracked and broke and my eyesight became blurry as tears welled up. For a moment, I sat there and I let myself feel the pain.

As I looked up at the sky, I caught a flash of lightning and I asked quietly, "How're you doing today?" Then I let out a heavy, pained breath and looked down at the water. "How am I doing today?"

Another light in the distance caught my eye.

Down at the end of the trail from the direction I came, I could see the faint spark of flashlights. Muted voices followed.

The cops were walking the trail.

As I leapt to my feet, suddenly a bright pair of headlights turned down the small road intersecting the trail, and with a skip in my heartbeat I turned, ready to run.

But before my feet began to move, I heard a familiar voice.

It was Jazz.

"Lyric!" she called in a hushed whisper from the driver seat. "Come on, get in!"

# Chapter 23

"Jazz?!" I blurted out in surprise, my voice hushed.

"Dude, hurry up!" she waved me over frantically with a look of distress. Her dreadlocks slipped from her headwrap and hung over her shoulder out the window.

Cautiously, debating for a split second if I should take the chance, my eyes darted around. There were no other cars in sight, but the police down the trail would be upon us in a matter of minutes.

So I ran around the side of her bright red van and got in the passenger seat.

Without wasting a second, Jazz backed out and drove down the road, staying under the speed limit, heading north to Killdevil.

"What the hell are you doing here?" I asked sharply.

"Saving your ass, apparently," she remarked impatiently. "What the hell are *you* doing? Stopping for a freaking smoke break?"

Guiltily, feeling dumb, I picked at my beard with my good arm, my left hand. "That was one of Alita's favorite spots."

Jazz fell silent. I felt her eyes boring into the side of my face as she drove toward Killdevil. "She's gone, Donovan. Reminiscing right now won't do anybody any good. I shouldn't even be doing *this* but here I am."

After a moment, I said quietly: "Thank you."

There was another pause, interrupted only by the churning of the old engine. "I thought they killed you, you know. They shot at you."

"They didn't shoot *at* me."

She made a puzzled look, then her eyes widened. "Oh my God – did you get *shot?!*"

"Little bit," I grumbled.

Quickly, she flicked on the overhead light to look at my arm, with a bullet hole in the sleeve of my jacket.

"Ow, *fuck!*" I winced, shielding my eyes.

"Shit, sorry!" she hurriedly apologized. I took my sunglasses from my pocket and put them on. Jazz split her attention between the slowly winding road and my slowly bleeding arm. "Lyric, you need to go to the hospital!"

"Well obviously I can't do that," I replied caustically. "Sort of defeats the whole purpose of running from the cops, don't it?"

"Hey, don't get shitty with me," she chastised. "I'm risking my own freedom by helping you here."

"You're right, you're right," I breathed. "Sorry." The van slowed down at a stop sign and she leaned in for a closer look.

"It looks like the bullet embedded itself in your tricep," she said.

"Yeah, I noticed."

"I could probably suture it, but we can't do anything while the bullet is still in there. Hang on –" She reached into the back and pulled up a bandana. "Here – tie this above the wound."

Immediately I took off my dark denim jacket – now with a frayed hole in the sleeve where the bullet shot through – and wrapped the bandana around my arm as blood leaked its way toward the red *S* on my chest and down to the devil on my forearm, then pulled it tight with my teeth. "See? All better," I remarked, turning off the light and tucking my glasses back into my jeans pocket.

"No, we still need to get that bullet out and patch that hole up before it gets infected. You can't go out hiding in the woods for God-only-knows how long with a wound like that."

"Think you can jimmy it out with a knife?"

She gave me a wild look as she resumed driving. "Are you out of your mind?!"

"Hell, probably."

"You're not Rambo! You stand more of a chance of pushing it further in than anything by doing that!"

"Well I'm all out of ideas then, doctor!" I rejoined.

"Well fuck!" Jazz exclaimed, hitting the steering wheel with the palm of her hand. The cab went silent for a moment as we both tried to figure out what to do.

"You think Red might have what you need?"

Jazz tightened her lip, then said, "I doubt it. His place is still only half moved in to – I don't wanna take the bet that he packed a first aid kit. I watched the man clean a wound with *dirt* one time, so…."

"God fucking dammit," I muttered. "I wish EMTs didn't have to report things."

Then suddenly it hit me.

"Wait," I began. "Makenna lives in Killdevil. She was an EMT for a year – she might be able to help."

Jazz turned and looked at me with borderline shock. "Absolutely not, Lyric! We can't drag anymore people into this than we already have!"

"Well we're sort out of fucking options! So unless you like having *blood* all over your seats...."

Jazz grumbled in her throat. "We don't even know if she's home – and if she is, what are the chances she actually helps? What if she calls the cops and turns you in?"

"She won't."

"You don't know that!"

"Yes, I do." I held my gaze on Jazz's face for a moment. "Look – we're in *your* van, right? And as far as I can tell, the cops aren't gonna be looking for *you*. They don't know that I'm with you. They were still searching the trail. So even if they start patrolling Killdevil, they have no reason to look at wherever you're parked – right?"

She frowned tightly. "Okay, sure – but what if the sheriff decides to anyway?"

"I overheard a couple deputies talking. The sheriff's being pulled from the case. Even if a few deputies show up, they won't get through the door. They don't have a warrant and Makenna isn't a suspect in any crimes."

"Maybe *I* am."

"If you were, then they would have detained you at the Clawhammer."

Jazz huffed anxiously. "What about her parents? You think they're just gonna let us walk right in?"

"Her parents skipped town again, remember? She was talking about it at our set tonight. Her dad bailed and her mom stormed out after one of their fights. Far as I know, Mrs. Dryer is at her sister's house until further notice."

"We don't even know if *Makenna* is home!" Jazz protested.

"If she's not home, then we're shit out of luck and that's that," I argued. "But right now, I think it's our only option. You're the one who wants the bullet out of me, anyway."

"Because you'll *die* in the woods if you don't get it out!"

"Exactly," I replied. "It's our only option. If the cops show up, I have a gun –"

"*Lyric!*"

"To say I *forced* her to help me. And you. I'm a lunatic, remember? They'll buy it."

Jazz let out an anxious breath through her nostrils. "Fine. You're right. We don't have a choice."

Her van slowed down as we rolled past a white sign with red letters that read: *WELCOME TO KILLDEVIL.*

We would be at Makenna's house in just a few minutes.

Idly, I thought aloud as we drove past the tightly packed old looking houses and apartments, "You ever wonder why Puritans named all these towns such metal shit like 'New Freedom' and 'Killdevil?'"

"Smalltalk? Really? Now?"

"I'm just trying to keep my mind off things," I replied softly. Jazz frowned with the corner of her mouth. Then I asked, "What happened at the bar after I left? Is Rust alright?"

She didn't take her eyes off the road as she spoke. Mine were drawn to her ruby red lips. "He's fine; the cops didn't ask him too many questions after they started chasing you. A deputy came back while they were searching the train, tried to get him to turn you in, but it's Rust we're talking about. He wouldn't speak to the Devil even if he were in Hell."

"What about you?" I asked. "They didn't give you too hard of a time, I hope."

"They didn't believe me at first that I didn't know about the murders. Which, I mean, I guess yeah, they were right. But I told them the truth – I went back to the Clawhammer to grab my amps. It had nothing to do with you. Of course," she added, craning her neck briefly to look in the back of the van, "I fudged the details a little bit and said you left your guitar there earlier."

Quickly, I turned in my seat. Pain shot through my arm but I ignored it. Lying flat on its back was my guitar. "Oh, *thank you!*" I breathed excitedly. "I was really bummed about having to leave it behind."

She shook her head. "I can't believe you even brought it with you. How are you gonna run from the cops with a guitar slung across your back?"

"I didn't think I would be doing any *literal* running. I didn't think any of tonight would ever happen." Just to make sure it was still there, I brushed my fingertips against the handle of the revolver tucked into my belt.

"Amen to that," Jazz mused dourly. "Rust called Carl before I took off, left a message for him."

"Well, the voicemail I left him screaming 'fuck' over and over again might clue him in that something is up," I remarked glumly. "Rust didn't say anything that could incriminate himself, did he?"

Jazz cocked her brow almost playfully. "Have you met the man? He was practically speaking in code."

I couldn't help but grin. "That's Rust for ya. What did he say?"

"Told him he ought to call Red tomorrow, made a vague hint at needing to get himself a radio receiver, said the cops came by and you were in trouble. That was it." Then she looked at me, her face stricken with concern. "How do you think this is gonna end, Lyric?"

Anxiously, I swallowed my throat as Jasmine pulled the van to a stop in Makenna's driveway. Her car was still there. "One way or another."

Jazz threw the van into park and held her concerned look for a moment, then killed the engine. Quietly as we could, we both stepped out of the van and hurried to the front door. Jazz knocked gently a few times – no answer.

Then I loudly banged my fist against the door.

"Shhh!" Jazz hushed frantically. But before she could say anything, the door opened. Makenna stood there in her pajamas and a tank top underneath dim, barely visible lighting, looking like we had just woken her up.

"Lyric? Jazz?" she asked in surprise. "What are you – ?"

I cut her off.

"I've been shot."

# Chapter 24

Makenna's eyes widened and her jaw fell agape. "You what?!"

"I got shot, Makenna. I thought I made that pretty clear the first time." I said hurriedly. "And you might want to keep it down – the cops are looking for me."

Wide eyed in disbelief, she looked at Jazz. "Is he serious right now?"

"Painfully, painfully serious," Jasmine replied grimly.

I gave the girl a look. "Emphasis on *painful*."

Then Makenna looked back at me and her eyes rested on the makeshift tourniquet around my bicep, with blood still trickling down to my fingers. "Oh my God," she gasped quickly, covering her mouth. "Get in here!"

Without waiting another second, we hurried through the door. Makenna locked it behind us. "Thank you –" I began, but she interrupted.

"What the hell happened?! Who shot you?!"

"A particularly unhappy sheriff."

Her jaw fell slack. "The *sheriff* shot you?!"

"He thinks I killed his daughter."

Makenna blinked twice and shook her head curtly. "*What?* Why?! What the actual Hell is going on?!"

I glanced at my wound, getting a good look at it for the first time since the bullet hit me. The back of my arm was swollen and purple, and coagulated blood had created a foul ring around the bullet hole. "Why don't I explain while you're taking this fuckin' bullet out of me?"

Makenna clasped both hands over her mouth and stared at the wound in awe and wonder. "Holy *shit*, you really did get shot!"

"Yup, sure did – and believe it or not, it isn't getting any better while we stand here." I winced as I twisted my arm around to get a better look.

"Kitchen, *now!*" Makenna barked, pointing down the hall. I exchanged a glance with Jazz, then the two of us strode down the hall.

Makenna's house was nice – I'd never seen the place before, but her parents certainly had more money than they knew what to do with. *No wonder they can afford to disappear all the time.* A chandelier hung in the living room as we walked past the entryway, with pristine, almost new-looking furniture decorating the place. A lot of it looked like it was scarcely used, I noticed, and a grand piano rested in the back corner of the living room; it reminded me of the one my father used to have.

We burst into the kitchen and Makenna flipped on the light. Bright white light, almost brilliant, shone down from the ceiling. "Jesus fuck!" I shielded my eyes. "Give a guy a warning first!"

"Newsflash, *Superman* – not all of us have superhuman night vision," she shot back impatiently.

I grumbled to myself as I put my glasses on and opened my eyes. The kitchen was every bit as pristine as the rest of the house. It was probably three times the size of mine. It even had an island with a second sink and stove. "If the tile was any whiter I think it would literally blind me," I remarked, trying to inject humor into my voice as I ignored the ever-growing pain in my arm.

"I don't care," Makenna rejoined crassly, pulling a wooden chair into the middle of the room. "Sit."

I didn't argue with her. Wearily, I sat down on the chair while Jazz stood with her back against the counter facing me. Makenna disappeared down the hall and up the stairs for a minute, then returned with a decent sized first aid kit. Jazz said, "The bullet's lodged in there, I think. I would have taken it out myself but I don't have the right equipment."

With laser focus on the wound, Makenna unlatched the kit and rolled up my sleeve, revealing one of the sharp black wings etched in ink there. "Yeah, it's in there alright. Does it feel like it hit bone?" she asked.

"I don't think so," I replied. "I feel like I'd be in a hell of a lot more pain if it did."

"Well, you're about to be in a hell of a lot more pain regardless." She handed me a wooden bit. "Here, you're gonna want this."

"What for?"

"So you don't break your teeth."

"Why would I –? *Mother FUCKER!*" I cried out in pain. Cold metal cut into the wound.

"Because this is gonna hurt *really* bad."

As fast as I could, I put the wooden bit in my mouth and gnashed down, clenching my jaw in agony as I felt a metal pair of pincers pry open the bullet hole. Jazz nervously bit her nails as I leaned forward and gripped the island counter with left-handed with white knuckles; idly, I noticed there was scarring on them from years of violent use.

Then I felt another piece of cold metal enter my arm.

All things considered, I think I would rather just get shot again.

"Hold still, you big baby," Makenna scolded. "If you're man enough to get shot, you're man enough to get unshot."

I squeezed my eyes shut and bit down as hard as I could – I think I would have whether I thought about it or not. Something about that kind of pain sends all of your muscles screaming. Even my legs were trembling as my nerves wrestled with the various pieces of metal duking it out in my tricep. The long tweezers cut against the singed muscles in my arm as they fought to grab the bullet. My muscles tensed and flexed as I balled a fist and glanced down at the underside of my forearm, facing up at me as blood trickled around the blackened creature's wings, and I could have sworn I saw the devil move.

Instantaneously, my mind flashed back to when I got it. There were no words in the memory, just an image: Alita looking up and smiling at me as she wiped the blood away from my skin, the needle gun whirring in her hand.

"Hold still!" Makenna admonished again. I snapped back to the present. "I've almost got it!"

Then –

"*Got it!*" she exclaimed triumphantly.

"Mother of *fuck!*" I yelled as the bit dropped from my mouth to the floor.

Makenna stepped out in front of me with a sort of entertained grin, clasping the deformed piece of lead between the tweezers. "See, look at that," she cooed patronizingly. "Congratulations, Lyric – it's a bullet."

"Ha-ha, very funny," I grimaced as she dropped the bullet into the palm of my hand. "Now could you stitch me up, *please?* I'm beginning to feel bad about all the blood on the floor."

"You might wanna put the bit back in," she replied as she went around me.

"What? Why?" Then I felt the sensation of liquid fire pouring into the wound. "God *dammit!*" I yelled.

"Because I have to disinfect it." I could picture her trying not to smirk back there. Even Jazz cracked a bit of a *schadenfreude* grin at my loud reactions. My fist clenched tightly around the bullet as I pounded against the countertop. "Alright, the hard part is over. I just have to sew you up now."

"Thank Christ for that...." I muttered. Makenna rifled through the first aid kit for a second, then pulled out her suture equipment and got to work. Slowly, I unclenched my fist and looked down at the bullet. I recognized the caliber. ".38 special – go figure."

"Thank your lucky stars for that," Makenna remarked. "In the city, the cops are all issued semi-automatic nine-millimeters. One of those rounds would have probably cut right through the bone. I saw that a few times while I was in the field."

"Guess the old world still has its perks," I remarked back.

After a few minutes, Makenna was done and the wound was stitched up. Irritatedly, she packed up the medkit, then set it on the counter and crossed her arms next to Jazz. Makenna could have burned a hole in me with the look of disapproval in her eyes. "Okay – now tell me what the hell happened."

I took a deep breath and told Makenna the story. Her face changed and morphed with surprise, shock, and then heartbreak with every sentence until I finally finished.

"Oh my God..." she breathed. "Huck's really... He's really dead?"

Grimly, I nodded.

She placed her hand over her mouth and her eyes glistened. Jazz put her arms around her shoulders to comfort her. Makenna asked, "Did he... Did he tell you why he did it?"

My jaw trembled imperceptibly as I replied: "Just to watch her die."

Her feet almost frantic in their pace, Makenna began walking back and forth across the kitchen. "Holy shit. Lyric, this is bad. Like, *really* bad. The entire sheriff's department is gonna be looking for you."

"Already are," Jasmine interjected. "They were heading down the trail when I caught up to him. Means it won't be long till they're canvassing Killdevil."

I rose to my feet. "Exactly, which is why I need to leave, *now*."

Makenna's eyes widened with fear. "Well where the hell are you gonna go?!" she protested. "There's a fifty-

fifty shot they'll nab you the second you walk out that door!"

"Better that than they start *knocking* on the doors," I rejoined. Then I looked at Jazz. "Red isn't far from here. I can hoof it."

"Like hell you can!" the woman and the girl responded in unison.

Then Makenna added, "Just stay here until daybreak! They won't be looking for you here."

"Yeah, until they spot Jazz's bright red van in the driveway," I replied. "You think they're stupid? They'll stake out and watch every door. The longer I'm here, the worse it's gonna be for both of you. And you are *way* too young to go to prison, little Mack."

For once in her life, she didn't have a response. She just crossed her arms and glared at me.

I slid the chair back to its place at the table. "Once I get to Red's, he's got a map to a safehouse out in West Virginia. I can hide out there, communicate with Carl by radio until I've got a fighting chance at being charged with only the murder I actually committed."

Makenna grunted sorrowfully. "Why'd you have to go and do this to yourself?"

Bracing myself for the danger I was about to step out into, I slowly let the air out of my lungs. "Penance."

Then I turned and headed for the door.

"You're not going by yourself," Jazz practically barked.

"Jazz –"

"No," she cut me off sternly. "I'm already in this with you. I'm not taking this exit. I'll get you to Red's, then we'll head to the River Sound Dam *together*. Once we're over the state lines, then..." She swallowed her throat. "Then I'll let you go your own way."

There wasn't any arguing with her. "Okay," I said after a while.

"Wait!" Makenna called suddenly. I stopped. "Let your arm rest for a few minutes – okay?"

"Makenna, I don't –"

"I don't care!" she retorted. "If I screwed up your stitches and they start coming out early while you're in a freaking *cabin* in the *woods*, then it's gonna be *my* fault when you *die* from an infection!" Her mouth was pulled in a tight frown and there was a look of desperation in her eyes. "Please?" she pleaded. "Just long enough for me to make sure it doesn't start bleeding again...."

Frustratedly, I sighed through my nostrils. "How long?"

"Fifteen minutes. Tops." The look of fear in her eyes broke my heart.

I breathed in deeply and exhaled slowly. "Fine. Fifteen minutes. As soon as that clock hits midnight, I'm walking through the door. Got it?"

She tried to smile – the same innocent, triumphant smile she had every time she worked me over for food at the Blacktop. "Got it."

\*\*\*

Jasmine sat on the pearly white sofa in the living room with Makenna. Meanwhile, I paced around, unable to bring myself to sit down. Jazz chewed her lip nervously and Makenna watched me like a hawk, as if she was worried I would bail the second she looked away. My eyes scanned the photos and fixtures on the wall behind the piano as I paced. A generation of family vacation pictures hung amongst a myriad of guitars. The older the photos, the happier the family looked. By the time Makenna was in high school, her father was absent from a third of them, and her mother absent from another third. Makenna's smile never faded, though. Across all the photos, she was smiling. She was the spitting image of her mother, almost, except her smile – she had her father's smile. I surmised that's where she got her bravery and spirit for adventure from, too, as I tried to count the number of framed photographs with the man taking his family to exotic places. Eventually, I asked, "Where'd your dad go, anyway?"

Makenna shrugged on the couch. "Somewhere on a boat."

I didn't turn my head. "Yeah, that figures."

"It'll be a real shock to him when he comes back and I'm in Boston," she added.

Then I turned. "Wait – you got accepted?"

With a wry smile, she nodded. "I'm going to Boston for biomedical engineering. They gave me a four year scholarship."

Jazz put her hand on the girl's shoulder and said, "That's incredible!"

My head turned back to the photos, vaguely wondering about all the times one of her parents was absent from one of them. Without looking back, I said, "I'm proud of you."

A few seconds went by in silence, then my hand gravitated toward a sleek black acoustic guitar hanging on the wall. "May I?" I asked.

"Just don't get your blood all over it," she remarked with a faint grin.

"Jokes on you, you're the one who did the stitches."

Her grin widened as I carefully pulled the guitar down and sat myself on the end of the piano bench, facing away from the keys. I dug my finger into my fifth pocket and pulled out my bright red pick with the guitar resting on my thigh. My fingers trembled and I struggled to find a tune. "Dammit...." I cursed under my breath. "I need a fucking drink...."

Makenna watched me as though she were studying me for a moment, then got up and sat beside me on the bench, facing the piano. Her eyes scanned over the keys for just a moment, then she began to play.

The tune was instantly familiar.

Proudly, she glanced at me as she continued to play the notes of *Stairway to Heaven*.

"Impeccable taste," I remarked.

"Good music is good music," she echoed my own words back to me.

We sat there and listened to the melody as the girl played it perfectly, note for note from memory.

And then my fingers found the tune.

I began strumming along in sync with the keys, then Jasmine began to sing.

*"There's a lady who's sure...."*

I closed my eyes and played the set of arpeggios of the song, and then the magic happened.

In my thoughts I could see, like smoke forming rings, ethereal sprites in all the colors of the rainbow; drawing shapes out for me glean, they drew leaves and trees and grass and bees, flowers and a phoenix rising through a plume; I saw clouds and lakes all in blue, and as the sprites danced with the tune, in their wake they left their colors like an echo.

*Music really is the quickest path to the soul.*

For a while, nothing else mattered. It was just us three and the music we played.

But a song is only beautiful because it ends.

And as we struck the last chord, my hands began to tremble and shake again and I felt my eyes sting. As the music stopped, the sprites vanished.

Our fifteen minutes were up.

Midnight was here.

With a deep breath, I opened my eyes and regained my composure, then replaced the guitar on the wall. I looked at Jazz. "It's time."

Stoically, she nodded and rose to her feet.

Makenna jumped up from the bench as I strode to the door. "You don't have to go!" she protested. "You can stay here! You'll be safe here."

Jazz stood beside me at the door as I looked at the girl. "But you won't."

Her lips started to tremble. "God dammit," she sniffled. "Why couldn't you have just stayed sober?"

I frowned with the corner of my mouth. "I am what I am, Makenna. I can't change that."

"Sure you can," she pleaded. "I don't want you to go to prison...."

I took a deep breath and told her, "Whatever happens... happens. I'll be okay."

As my hand reached for the door knob, I paused, then looked back at Makenna.

I might never see her again.

"This world will eat you alive if you let it," I said. "Your life is about to change, hopefully for the better. You're gonna meet a lot of new people in college and in your career and wherever life takes you. But don't ever let them break you. Most of them won't tell you that's what they're trying to do, but that's what they'll be doing. Something they never teach you in school is what people who live in darkness do when they see light in your eyes..." Her expression softened as I continued. "They try and snuff it out. They try to clip your wings, to convince you that there's something wrong with you and you're broken. You're so bright, Makenna. You could do just about anything you want to. Don't let the world take that away from you."

Suddenly, I found myself thinking about my father.

Then I said, "And you aren't your parents. You don't have to be like them, just because they're your blood. You can be better. You *are* better. But you have to keep being better every day, especially when it's tough. Don't take the easy way out. Don't sell yourself short. And don't forget the most important thing about people."

The girl sniffled and wiped back a tear. "Yeah? What's that?"

"They *want* to be good, even if they fall short of it most of the time." I glanced at the bright white light from the chandelier above her. "All they need is a light to show them the way. The world's gonna try and break you, so you've gotta show it you'll break it first." Then I shot a look at Jazz before my eyes returned to the girl. "But you have to break it with kindness; break it by *being* unbreakable."

Makenna frowned and her eyes glistened. "But the world is cruel... How can you win if you aren't cruel right back?"

For a moment, I could hear the memory of my father saying those same words to me when I was about her age.

*The world is a cruel place; only way you'll ever win it is to be cruel right back.*

I looked at Makenna and told her, "If that's how to win, then I'd rather lose."

Then I opened the door and stepped out into the night.

Cautiously, my eyes scanned the neighborhood. No headlights, no sounds of cars. In the darkness, I could see everything, like it was bathed in a light only I could see.

We were in the clear.

Jazz looked back at Makenna and said softly, "Thank you," then shut the door as the girl stood there in the hall. Quickly, she and I jumped into the van and she turned over the engine. "Where's Red's new house?"

"Cherry Lane," I replied. Then I pointed out the windshield as she backed onto the road. "Three blocks that way, hang a right. It's the only house on the road."

Her face fraught with worry and sympathy, Jasmine looked at me and said, "Everything will be okay."

Anxiously, I took a breath. "Eventually, everything always is."

# Chapter 25

*Dear God, is this what my life has come to?*

Those were my thoughts as I strolled up the brick steps to the Clawhammer and walked through the door the first time in my life. I was twenty-four, fresh out of a bad relationship, and ready to go ahead and tie the knot on this bizarre dream we called life.

It was summer, late in the evening but not too late. I had eight hundred dollars to my name, and I was ready to spend it all on however much liquor it took to kill me. That was all the money I had saved up from the diner I had been working at. I was still wearing the uniform – black slacks and a black button down to match.

Cigarette smoke and musical notes filled the air – Rolling Stones, I think it was. The sharp sound of a cue ball breaking the billiards struck my ear as soon as I walked in.

"Ooh, good break!" an older woman said to the man shooting.

He didn't take his eyes off the table. "Could've been better," he replied nonchalantly as he rounded the table.

The woman looked up at me and smiled, taken aback. "Well hey, Johnny Cash."

Self-consciously, I looked down at my attire. "I'll take it."

She kind of studied me for a second. "You new here? I don't think I've ever seen your face before."

"I'm from Driftwood," I replied. "Never been here before, but I hear it's cheap so why the hell not."

"Really depends on how much you drink," she replied with a sharp smile.

The man looked up at me and said, "You look like you just walked out of Folsom Prison, I'll be damned."

"Maybe I did," I replied as I sauntered past them into the bar area.

The place was surprisingly packed for a weeknight. A large man wearing suspenders sat at the bar, talking to the bartender. "Lorraine, I swear to Christ this place will be the death of me," he chuckled.

"You sure it ain't gonna be the Red Bull that kills you, Carl?" she grinned back, pouring an energy drink into a glass of vodka.

"Either or," Carl laughed as he took the drink. Almost timidly, I sat down between him and another man. The other one was tall and broad, if a bit doughy, with light-colored long hair hanging down in a ponytail.

The bartender greeted me plainly. "Whatchu drinkin', baby?"

I thought for a second. I wasn't a big drinker. My favorite "liquor" at the time was Kahlua, if that tells you anything. "Black Russian, please."

She sort of smiled and replied, "Name for the tab?"

"Lyric."

She raised her eyebrows at me. "A real name."

"I'm not making that up, I promise."

She eyeballed me suspiciously. "You got your ID?"

I fished it out of my wallet and handed it to her. "See?"

Lorraine chuckled and said, "Well, sonuvabitch. Coming right up, Lyric."

Carl sized me up as he took a drink. "That's a hell of a name. What're the glasses for? You a rockstar or something?" he laughed.

"No," I laughed with him, a little nervously. "I dabble with the piano, that's about it."

Then the other guy turned and said with a slight grin, "Pardon my eavesdropping, but did you really say your name is *Lyric*?"

"Last name. First name's Donovan, but I don't like shortening it to 'Don' and 'Donovan' is just too long."

The ponytail guy laughed heartily and patted me on the back. Instinctively, my muscles tensed like I was ready to fight. At that point in my life, I hadn't been around people much since high school. My dad taught me not to trust them – "you don't trust anyone, not the cops, your teachers, firefighters, even your own family outside of the house." The only friend I had all through college was the woman I'd been seeing and living with, and when we split, I guess it was safe to say I had nobody.

It made me the most dangerous thing a man could be – alone. And in that isolation, I was hellbent on a path of self-destruction.

But as the guy laughed, my muscles eased up. He wasn't trying to hurt me. He held out his hand. "I'm Will, good to meet you."

I shook his hand, then Carl introduced himself too as Lorraine set down my drink. Carl asked me, "So what's up with the shades? You look like a narc."

Amused, I replied, "Achromatopsia."

Carl said, "A chroma what now?"

"Achromatopsia – total color blindness. It also means my rods work overtime, which makes everything brighter than hell."

"Oh, damn," Will stroked his trimmed beard. "Isn't that the thing that one singer has? Shit, what was his name...."

"John Kay," I answered. "Lead singer of Steppenwolf."

"That's it!" Will grinned. "You born to be wild?"

"Born to be wild, racing with the wind on a magic carpet ride," I chuckled back. My stomach rumbled as the Kahlua and vodka began duking it out in an empty gut. As Lorraine walked by, I flagged her down. "Kitchen open?" I asked hesitantly. I never liked ordering food late. It's an industry faux pas.

"Sure is. Whatchu want?"

"Bacon cheeseburger? Medium rare if the cook will do it."

"You got it."

She jotted the order down on a ticket and strolled down the long, winding bar into the kitchen. Will said with a faint smile: "This place has some of the best food in town, believe it or not." Then he nodded toward the kitchen. "Huckleberry back there will fix you up good, trust me."

"Huckleberry?" I smirked. "And y'all think *I've* got a stupid name?"

Carl and Will both laughed. Then Carl said, "Yes, yes we do."

For the first time in a long time, I felt at ease. My eyes glanced around the bar at all the people. They might have walked straight out of a hunting magazine. Heavy duty work jackets, hands blackened from motor oil and lubricant, long beards and untrimmed hair. But there was a strange sense of honesty that came with it. Nobody was trying to impress anybody else.

Some of us came there to die, but most of them were just there to forget about the troubles of the world we were in.

They were there to live.

After ten or fifteen minutes and another drink, the burger came out. Most people can't cook one for shit. They smash the patty down, get rid of all its flavor. That red shit that comes out isn't blood, it's myoglobin – a type of protein found in muscle. That's where most of the flavor comes from, that slight taste of iron in the beef. Let's you know something had to die in order for you to live. There was respect in that, I felt. Food isn't human fuel, it's sacred. It's a sacrifice that has to be made for you to see another day.

I devoured the thing in a few bites.

Carl looked over and laughed with a hint of disgust. "Jesus Christ, man. Unhinge your jaw some more why don't ya?"

"Sorry," I laughed through the last bite. "Forgot I was in public."

"You just get out of prison or something? 'Cause if you did, give me a call next time you need an attorney."

I wiped my mouth with the napkin and laughed. Will had disappeared somewhere in the process, I realized as I looked around, thankful nobody else saw me eat like a wild animal. "No," I grinned. "It was just really good."

Carl laughed as Lorraine poured him another drink. "Give your compliments to the chef."

I took my drink and rose to my feet. "There a patio out back?" I asked the bartender. "I could use some fresh air after that."

"Yup, right around the corner."

My feet stumbled a bit as the alcohol sailed through my bloodstream and I found my way outside. There were five or six picnic tables arranged on a concrete floor, with a tall white fence surrounding the perimeter. There were almost more people outside than in, all vying for that impossibly nice June summertime air.

I sauntered over to an empty table and sat down on the top, rested my feet on the bench, pulled out a cigarette with my lips then struck a match. Then I heard Will call out, sort of drunkenly, "*Lyric!*"

My head snapped toward the sound. He was sitting at a table with a few other people. I don't remember who all was there, except for one girl. She had round glasses and straight hair hanging halfway down her back, with mousey features and bright eyes.

Suddenly I felt my heart pounding.

Nervously, I got up off the table and walked over to theirs. "Lyric!" Will shouted again with a sloppy grin.

"Why do you keep saying that?" the girl asked, somewhere between nervous and irritated.

He looked at her and said, "Because that's his name."

"No it's not," she said immediately. "No way his name is 'Lyric.'"

"Surname," I responded. "My family came here from Ireland a few generations back. Story goes the immigrations guy misheard 'Donovan Lee Rick' as 'Donovan Lyric.' My great-grandpa liked it so much he just didn't bother to correct him. Hence, 'Lyric.'"

She studied me for a second, then said skeptically, "Well that seems improbable. Why are you wearing sunglasses?"

Will kind of laughed and looked at her. "He's colorblind. Settle down, Alita. He's cool."

Suspiciously, she narrowed her eyes behind her glasses. "I'll be the judge of that."

Then Will groaned and said, "Not everyone is out to get you, Alita. Just relax, alright?"

With one deep swig, she finished her silver bullet and rose to her feet. "I am relaxed. I'm also out of beverage." Without another word, she turned and went inside.

Will gave me an exhausted look, then circled his finger by his temple and whistled. "She's a little crazy, that one."

My eyes followed her back inside. "I don't think she's crazy."

Will peered at me, then replied with a smirk, "Give it time, buddy. Give it time."

I took a drink and asked, "You two dating?"

"Pfft," he blew a raspberry. "Hell no. I don't think I would survive that." Then his eyes traveled to the center table where a man sat in a tie-dye shirt by himself, smoking a cigarette and drinking a whiskey and a beer. His hair was short and dark and his chin was covered in scruff. "That's Huck, by the way. Huck!" Will called out.

Huck sort of side-glanced at him with a look somewhere between *how you doin'?* and *please leave me alone*. "What's good, Will," he replied unenthusiastically.

I took a drag from my cigarette, then asked, "You're the one who made my burger?"

"Yup," Huck replied without looking up.

"It was a good burger. Thank you."

Crassly, he scoffed. "How do you fuck up a burger?" Then he smashed his cigarette into the ashtray, got up and went inside.

"Seems like a nice guy," I remarked, peering through the door. Alita smiled at him from her barstool and he gave her a polite wave as he walked by.

Will waved his hand. "He's just in a bad mood. He's about had the shits of this place, I think. He's been talking for a while about wanting to cook somewhere else – something about late night drunks, I guess. Don't take it personally."

"Well, I'm one of the late night drunks, so I don't think he's gonna like me."

I went back to the Clawhammer the next five nights in a row. I would be lying to you if I said it wasn't in the hopes of seeing Alita again.

As Jasmine's van pulled up to Red's house, a part of me wondered what would have happened if I just hadn't gone back.

"Okay," Jazz said, her car idling at the end of Cherry Lane in front of a newly built home. "Take your time in there, but don't take *too* much time. We're still a good twenty minutes from the state line – a lot can happen in twenty minutes."

"I'll be quick," I breathed. My arm still hurt but it wasn't nearly as bad since Makenna had taken the bullet out.

"And I'll be here," she added with warmth as I opened the passenger door.

I paused and looked back at her. "You always are."

Then, with nerves tightening and a sick feeling in my stomach, I marched up to Red's house and knocked on the door.

After a moment, it cracked open and he appeared, glancing around to make sure no one was watching. "Whose car is that?"

"Jazz," I replied. "She's my accomplice now, I guess."

Red's nostrils flared and he kind of frowned. "Alright. Get in here. Quickly."

Hurriedly, I stepped through the door and followed Red into his living room. The place was sparsely decorated – it could use a woman's touch, so to speak. But in a few years, it would look like a home. "Layla with you?"

"No," he said curtly. There was something off about his demeanor; I couldn't put my finger on it. "Over here." He led me to a table with a map sprawled out over it and turned on a dim light. "Rust gave me the lowdown on what happened. He left out a lot of the details, but I think I picked up on the gist of it." Red looked me in the eyes. "You didn't kill the girl, did you?"

"Of course not," I replied weakly. "I killed her killer."

He let out a slow sigh. "I would have done the same thing."

"I know you would have," I said. "I don't think we were built for this generation, Red. It's in our blood to take matters into our own hands – kill or be killed, an eye for an eye, no more knives in the back, just a bullet to the heart."

"Yeah," he breathed. "Something like that. Okay," he laid his hands on the map. "So I've marked down where we are *here*," he ran his finger along the creased paper. "You follow *this* road and get to the dam –"

"I'm familiar."

"And then this is where it gets tricky," he went on, speaking clearly but quickly. "Once you're across the second bridge, you've gotta cut through the woods right at *this* turn, bearing north through West Virginia. There's a hidden trail – and by hidden I mean it's *really* goddamn hard to find. I made it myself, walking back and forth for miles over and over again to make it look like a deer trail. You follow that for about seven miles –" he ran his finger along the trail on the map. "You'll come across a creek that looks like you can't cross it, but there's a handful of stones laid out that you can use to get to the other side. Once you're across, go up the hill and bear *east*. Walk for another mile and a half, you'll come to a clearing in the heart of the forest. The cabin is there. It's stocked up with enough food for a month, but you'll have to get water from the stream. The radio there has enough battery life to operate for months without fail. The frequency you'll want to tune it to is written down in a notebook in the cabin; I'll be able to pick up your signal."

A hint of admiration crept across my face as Red finished speaking and we made eye contact. I wasn't sure what to say. So I just said, "Thank you."

He nodded stoically and rolled up the map, then handed it to me. "You've gotta be quick. The minute Jed catches wind you've crossed state lines, you can bet your ass all of West Virginia's gonna be looking for you. Then the feds. I hope you realize how serious this shit is, Lyric." He paused and looked right at my soul. "The whole country is gonna want to know where you are."

Anxiously, I let out a shaky breath. "Makenna always said I should be famous."

Grimly, Red nodded once. "Godspeed, brother." Then he led me through the sparse hall and out the front door. I pulled out two cigarettes and handed him one. As he lit it, he spoke. "There's something we need to talk about before you go."

Curiously, I raised my brow. "What is it?"

Red took a moment to breathe, gazing out over his new found land. "It's about Layla." Then he looked at me. "She told me something."

Before he could say anything else, I already knew. Guilt wrapped its steely fingers around my heart. "Did what I think happened... happen?"

"She fucked another one of my friends." His gaze didn't break. "I'm not talking about Will."

For a moment, we held the look.

Then I said, "I know."

"It was you."

My throat tightened. I wasn't sure what to say. Rust's words crossed my mind again.

The music was here, all I had to do was face it.

So I told him. "I know... I was afraid that's what happened." Red's eyes narrowed with curiosity. I went on. "That night I blacked out, when I woke up and my apartment was torn to hell... I knew she made a pass at me, but I didn't know how far I let it go. I had this sick feeling in my stomach, but then, when she confessed to cheating on you and I wasn't on the list, I thought that meant the best – thought it meant it didn't get that far."

"Yeah, well... it did." There wasn't any anger in his voice. Instead, it was... somber. Sad. Like watching an old friend leave for the last time. Both of you know it's the last time, but neither of you can bring yourself to say it.

"Deep down," I went on, "I knew what I did, I think. There was a lot of denial, a lot of caveats and maybes. But I knew. And I should have told you. I'm sorry. I think... I think I just got tired of convincing my friends to bite the apple."

Red's face tightened as he pushed back his emotions the best he could. "Yeah," he finally said. Then he looked at me again. "You know, with Will, I wasn't surprised. He's soft, he's sneaky. He's the kind of person who waits till you turn around to shoot you in the back. I was angry – hell, I almost killed him. But when she told me about you, it was... different. It broke my heart, Lyric. You were one of my best friends. Some of the conversations we've had... I can't talk about shit like that with most people. I can't talk about esotericism and philosophy and magic with people like Will. But you got it. You were always on the same page as me. And that's why it hurts so much."

"Yeah...." I replied, my throat sore from biting back my emotions. "I know, Red."

Red took a drag from his cigarette. "I'll help you out with this, but when it's all over... We can't be friends, Lyric. We just can't."

I nodded my head slowly. He was right. Just out of principle, we couldn't ever have the same relationship we had earlier that day.

Then I held out my hand.

He did the same, and we shook hands. "Just know," I told him, "if anything ever changes... This is one bridge I won't ever burn. If you ever need anything and I can help...."

There was a moment of silence before he said, "I know."

And then we let go.

With one fewer friend, and the weight of the world on my shoulders, I got back in Jasmine's van.

"Are you okay?" she asked softly.

My voice was harsh and graveled. I didn't look at her when I replied.

"I'll be fine."

Her eyes rested on me for a moment, and her hand laid across mine. "You will."

Then she backed out of the driveway and down the road, leaving Killdevil and cutting through the backroads of the outskirts of New Freedom, heading toward the river as lightning danced in the sky for the rain that would never come.

Bright red letters on a sign caught my eye as the River Sound distantly played its music in my ears:

*You are now leaving New Freedom, Ohio – We hope you come back soon!*

# Chapter 26

Lightning flashed in the sky as I stood in front of the Clawhammer on the fifth night I ever went there, donned in black. Lightning every night, but never any rain. Idly, I wondered if that was something God liked to do just to fuck with us mortals, if there were such a thing as God.

I stood on the brick steps for a moment, watching the sky. Each flash hurt my eyes, but the sights were worth it. There was never any thunder, either. It was like the lightning was coming from somewhere we could never reach, and its thunder in turn could never reach us.

*Am I imagining things?*

Then a woman's voice hit my ears. "You better get inside before it rains."

I turned around. Alita was walking up the steps. My heart began to beat louder as I looked back to the sky. "I don't think it's gonna," I replied distantly. "It never seems to rain here."

"Sure it does," Alita responded nonchalantly as she sauntered past me and opened the door. "You just haven't been here long enough."

I looked at her, her bright red lips standing out in the black and white darkness. She held the door open expectantly.

"Age before beauty," she teased.

With a grin, I walked inside. She followed right behind me.

"How come you always dress like you're going to a funeral?" she asked as we stepped through the pool room.

"Never know when you're gonna die," I replied slyly. She gave me a look, then I grinned and said, "I work at the diner out in Driftwood."

"That makes more sense," she grinned back. "You oughta consider the place up the street from here – you'll make way more money. Closer, too."

"Noted," I said with a smirk.

The sound of an electric guitar – clean, no distortion – filled the bar along with a man's voice singing. It wasn't bad, but it wasn't anything special. He could hit notes but it wasn't the type of voice that would ever sell a show.

The guitar, on the other hand – that was something special.

Alita and I walked into the main bar area. Tucked in the corner sat Huckleberry on a stool, playing a six-string and singing into the mic. "Damn," I remarked aloud as we took our seats. "I didn't know he played."

"He's pretty good," Alita chimed. Madeline strolled over.

"Whatchu drinking, guys?"

"Silver bullet," Alita responded.

"Bulleit, neat."

Madeline cocked her brow below her head of light, wavy hair. "Can you handle that?" she asked as she poured the bourbon. "It's a pretty big step up from Kahlua and vodka."

"Sure I can." I took the glass and drank a quarter of it in a swig and coughed forcefully. My mouth, my throat, and my gut all screamed at me as the acrid liquor went down. I tried to hide it on my face, but Alita laughed softly.

"Looks like you're loving it," she said.

Madeline cackled joyously as she set down Alita's beer and walked away.

My throat burned and my voice was raspy as I battled the whiskey settling in my stomach. "It's an acquired taste," I replied. "I intend to acquire it."

She and I both turned to watch Huck play. It was really something to behold. He held that instrument with the kind of care you'd see from a father cradling his newborn. Then the song finished. With a grin, he said into the microphone, "Thank you, thank you. I hope nobody noticed that note I fucked up in the middle. Actually, I don't care. Let's see *you* all do better." The bar collectively let out a laugh. "And on that note, no pun intended, it's time for me to get as drunk as you filthy degenerates. Fuck the man, fuck society, and thanks for comin' out, everybody."

A round of applause was given to the man as he set his guitar down on its stand, then casually strode over to me and Alita. She said playfully, "Ya did good, kid."

He scoffed with a grin. "Like you would know – you just got here."

The three of us laughed and I said, "Hey, that was the best final sixty seconds of a show I've seen all day. Cheers."

Madeline set a beer and a whiskey in front of Huck and we clinked our glasses together. "I'm surprised this place hasn't scared you off yet," he said, then glanced around. "Buncha filthy animals in here."

I shrugged. "I grew up on a farm. Me and filthy animals tend to get along."

He laughed curtly and replied, "Amen to that, brother."

Alita said, "I wish I got here sooner. I was really looking forward to watching you play."

Huck shrugged casually. "Too bad. I don't do encores and I don't do *Free Bird*."

I laughed with him. "Man, I wish I could play."

"So what's stopping you?" Huck asked pointedly.

I counted on my fingers sarcastically. "Lack of an instrument, musical talent, the ability to do different things with both hands –"

Huck mimicked my finger counting. "Excuses, excuses, excuses," he said. "You wanna do something, then just do it. Nobody's stopping you but you."

"Well if you ever need a keyboard player, I can do Hot Cross Buns."

Huck scoffed and chuckled. "What, you think I was born knowing how to play guitar? It's all about practice, man. Practice and passion. If you don't have the passion, then don't fuckin' practice. And don't bitch about it, either. 'Cause then you don't really give much of a shit about the music, you just want to be able to say you did something cool. If you've got the passion, then get out of your own way."

I wasn't sure what to say; he was right.

Then Lorraine came over to us. "Hey," she said to Huck, "I'm having a little get together at my place after we close up. You down?"

He thought about it for a second, stroking the scruff on his chin, then said, "Fuck it, why not."

Lorraine grinned, then gave me the stink-eye. "You can come too, I guess." Before I could respond, she broke into a laugh. "Sorry, I just love fuckin' with you, Lyric. Idunno why."

Huck laughed and said, "He's an easy target."

"You know," I began, taking a sip from my glass with a laugh, "I'd love to counter that, but you're not wrong." Then I glanced at Alita. "You coming?"

"Am I invited?" she asked.

"Sure, baby," Lorraine said sweetly. "Just don't let your dad know."

Huck, Lorraine and I shared a laugh and Alita rolled her eyes.

As the night carried on, the three of us found ourselves sitting at a picnic table out back. "The fuck did you just say?" Huck scoffed with an incredulous laugh.

"I said I want you to hit me," I replied, dragging my cigarette. "You know how long it's been since I got hit in the face?"

Huck scoffed again and said, "No, but I'll tell you how much longer it's *gonna* be – not tonight, for starters."

"Oh, come on," I argued with a devilish grin. "I don't wanna forget what it feels like."

Alita gave me wide eyes and protested. "That's absolutely nuts, Lyric. Nobody's gonna hit you."

Huck looked at her coyly and said with half a grin, "He keeps it up and I might."

"See, that's the spirit," I laughed drunkenly. "Pain reminds us that we're real – I don't wanna forget what it feels like."

Huck cackled loudly. "Look, don't take this the wrong way, but I don't know if you could handle it."

I scoffed and waved my hand. "Believe me, I can handle it."

"Yeah, see, you *say* that," he replied, rubbing his chin, "but if I comply with your dumbass request and you end up lyin' there on the ground crying, then *I'm* gonna look like the bad guy."

Alita crossed her arms and huffed. "I can't believe you're even entertaining this," she said as the voices around us blended together.

Huck replied, "Well it's certainly entertaining."

"Okay," I began, "what if I prove that I can handle it? Then will you hit me?"

He cocked his eyebrow. "How the hell are you gonna prove you can take a hit before I hit you?"

For a moment, I scratched my beard and thought about it. "Pain is pain – right?"

Bemused, Huckleberry chuckled. "Generally speaking, yeah."

Then I held my three-quarters-smoked cigarette straight up in the air like a bullet. "Observe."

Without hesitation, I held my forearm straight out and slowly pressed the burning tip of the cigarette into the top of my arm.

Alita's eyes shot wide open and she yelled, *"Lyric! Are you fucking crazy?!"*

"Probably," I grinned as the cigarette burned my flesh. I held it there until it went out completely. Huck bore a look of amused surprise as he rubbed his chin. "That good enough for you?" I asked proudly.

He stared at the fresh burn on my arm for a moment, then said, "Hang on." Without another word, he got up and went inside the bar.

Alita grabbed my wrist and looked at the wound. "Jesus Christ, Lyric! You're a freakin' *loon*, a regular madman."

"Madman? Maybe. Regular? Well I've never been accused of that before in my life."

Then the door opened again and Huck came back out, wearing an oven mitt and holding a fork. "Come on, stand up," he said with a humored smirk.

My face matched his as I got to my feet. "What, you gonna stab me with that?"

"Nope," he replied. He held the fork up. "*This* was just in a five hundred degree oven. You think you can handle pain?"

I looked from him to the fork, then back to him. "Alright – if I can handle this, then you gotta clock me. Got it?"

Huck clicked his tongue. "You're not gonna like it."

"Believe me, man – it ain't gonna bother me."

He tilted his head and made a face like *if you say so*, then I held out my left forearm with the bottom facing up.

My skin began to melt instantly as he pressed the hot fork into my arm.

353

Painfully, I winced and made a fist. But there was a grin on my face the entire time.

After a few seconds, Huck pulled the fork away. There was a large patch of burned skin on my arm where it had been pressed. Almost proud, I said, "See?"

He nodded a couple times in mild disbelief, then said, "Alright man, you got it. Not in the face, though." He turned and went inside, then came back out a second later without the mitt and fork. "And not out here. You know, cameras and everything. Meet me in the restroom."

"*Gay*," I coughed into my hand, then looked at him with a laugh.

"Huck!" Alita shouted.

"What?" he grinned. "It's not like I'm gonna kill him."

We marched inside the bar toward the bathroom while Alita sat on the bench with her arms crossed in a huff, judging the hell out of us but we didn't care. The door swung shut behind me. The bathroom was small and shitty, with a pair of urinals surrounded by wood disintegrated from years and years of drunks with bad aim. The wooden door of the stall was carved all to hell with graffiti and names. One caught my eye: *Alita SLUTson.*

I was so drunk that my first thought was *huh... I thought it was 'Swanson.'*

Then Huck took a boxer's stance.

"Hold up," I said. "Lemme just...." I shook my hands and moved my head side to side a couple times. "Alright, I'm ready."

"You sure about this?" he asked with an anticipating smirk.

"Never been more sure about anything in my life. Probably. Go for it."

"If you say so."

He cocked his fist back then slammed it into my sternum. I flew backwards into the door and it swung open as the wind sailed out of me, landing flat on my back.

"Shit, you good?" he asked hesitantly.

"Yup, I'm good," I wheezed from the ground. I felt my rib *crack* with a sharp pain as I sat up slowly. Huck couldn't stop laughing. He held his hand down and helped me back up. My rib was probably broken, but I didn't care. With a grin, I said, "I almost forgot what that felt like."

"Yeah, well, make sure you remember it this time, psycho. Next time you might not get up."

"That's the thing about me, Huck – I don't know how to stay down."

Huck kind of laughed with amusement and said, "Yeah? Well I could keep knockin' your ass down all day."

With a grin, I replied, "Then you're just gonna have to kill me." Holding my chest as I opened the door, we sauntered through the bar and back outside to our table.

Alita just shook her head in judgmental shock. "You two are gonna be the death of me."

A few hours later, Lorraine and Madeline were closing up the bar while a few of us stood around the brick patio out front. I sat on top of the picnic table out there, smoking a cigarette and staring out at the train platform right across the street. Near the sidewalk, Alita and Huck were talking in low voices, laughing with each other. I'd be lying if I said I wasn't a little jealous, but I didn't let it bother me;

she was a free spirit and she could choose whatever she wanted in life. Like the Stones always said, you can't always get what you want.

Then the two bartenders stepped out of the now dark building and locked the door. I asked, "So where's your place?"

Lorraine nodded toward the trail. "Up there a little ways."

"You live in the woods?"

Madeline rolled her eyes to the back of her head. "What do *you* think, dumbass? There's houses back there."

"That makes more sense."

The two women laughed, then we all began walking toward the trail. I moved stiffly; every time I turned or leaned over, it felt like my rib was cracking all over again. My eyes were fixated on the bright red train engine as we passed it. "This thing ever run?" I asked.

Huck replied. "Fuckin' barely. It goes a few towns over and comes back. People actually pay money for that shit."

I laughed to myself. Then I asked him, "Oh hey, you know you left your guitar back there, right?"

He shrugged. "It'll be there in the morning. I'm not worried about it."

Alita grinned mischievously and said, "Unless someone breaks in and steals it."

"Yeah, *that's* what they're gonna steal," Huck grinned back. "Not the hundreds of dollars worth of liquor or the thousands in the safe."

"You never know – maybe they're a very *particular* kind of thief."

"What, a thief of joy?" Huck sneered playfully. "Because that's what you're sounding like right now."

Alita crossed her arms and huffed her breath as we walked, pretending to be angry.

And I thought to myself, *so this is what having friends feels like.*

It only took maybe twenty or so minutes before we reached a small road intersecting the trail that led to a couple of houses. You could hear the sound of a stream just up ahead. I followed the group and we entered through the basement door of one of the houses. My feet were already shuffling from the liquor, but I was ready to drink more.

"Alright," Lorraine announced, "just nobody break anything."

"Just because you said that, now I'm gonna," Huck grinned.

Lorraine turned and cocked a fist, trying not to smile. "Bitch, you better not."

I didn't really know most of the dozen or so people there. Faces I'd get accustomed to over the years, but that night they were practically strangers to me. I found my spot in a chair across from a sofa, sitting with Huck and Alita as I passed around my dugout full of weed and slowly got stoned from cannabis and liquor. There was laughter and music all around.

At some point, I said, "Man, you know I went to the Clawhammer to *drink* myself to death?"

Alita's eyes widened behind her glasses and Huck laughed incredulously. "How's that goin' for ya?" he asked.

I took another drink. "At this point, I'm kinda hoping it doesn't kill me," I laughed with him. "Life's a drag, but I'm diggin' it."

"Why in God's name would you want to do that?" Alita asked.

I shrugged. "Life don't seem to be going anywhere. Figured I might as well tie the knot."

"Well don't!" she protested.

Huck thought for a moment, then pulled out a film canister, popped the top off and dropped some buds in his hand to pack his own bowl. He took a hit then handed it to me and said, "Life never goes anywhere. That's the point of it. It just is what it is. You're not supposed to try and make something greater of it than that – that's what fucks us all up."

I coughed forcefully with excruciating pain as the smoke left my lungs and handed it back to him. I didn't let the agony show on my face; I could handle it. "How do you figure?" I asked, almost short of breath.

He took a hit and held the smoke for a second. "We're all born into this world screamin' and crying," he said, smoke filling the air. "That's how a lot of us die, too – screamin' and crying. Doesn't matter what you do, we all gotta die someday. So why not make the most of it?"

"Yeah, that's the part I'm stuck on."

"So don't think about it. It's all about experiences, man. Like this – this is an experience. We might not remember too much of it, but that's what it is."

"Sounds like we're just spinning our wheels to me."

"So let 'em spin," he replied. "How the fuck else is a car supposed to move forward? We're free to do whatever we want to, man. Hell, look where you're at. This town is called *New Freedom*, for God's sake. Because that's what it is. You were in a bad spot, so you chose to leave, and now you're here. It's *literally* new freedom." He took another hit and handed the bowl back to me. "We're free to do whatever we want; live the life you want to live. The only question is: what will *you* do with your freedom?"

The sound of the rushing River brought me back to the present, along with Jasmine's voice as sweet as honey: "We're almost at the dam."

I snapped back to the interior of the van as she drove cautiously toward the West Virginia state line. Soon, I would be on my own.

An unease settled in the cab. I think she was as nervous as I was. My head turned toward her. "Thank you, Jazz." She shot a glance at me, mixed with worry and love. "I mean it. No matter what happens after this, if I end up dead or in prison, just know that –" My voice stopped suddenly. I actually wasn't sure what I wanted to tell her. So I quit thinking, and just said what my soul wanted to say. "Just know that, if when life is over we come back to this Earth reincarnated, as ourselves or anybody else… I hope I have the privilege of knowing you in every lifetime I ever live."

Her response was silence, but it was the sort of caring, calm silence where you both know that the feelings you want to express are beyond words.

I was okay with the silence.

Slowly, driving just under the speed limit, Jazz rolled the car onto the dam.

"Stop here," I urged gently.

"What for?" she asked. "I can take you all the way to the line."

I took a deep breath. "This is as far as you need to take me. I want to pay my respects." Then I looked at her. "This was Alita's favorite place in the world."

Jazz frowned sympathetically with the corner of her mouth, then pulled onto the shoulder of the bridge. "Okay," she said.

I pulled my jacket over my torso and winced at the pain in my arm, then opened the passenger door and rounded the side of the vehicle to the back. The double doors popped open. I grabbed my guitar and slung it around my back. Jazz opened her door and met me by the rear. "You should hurry back," I told her as I sauntered to the rail, looking out over the vast River Sound. "The sheriff's men might be looking at these parts soon."

She followed me to the rail. "Then I guess we'll meet them together."

There was a beautiful kind of stoicism in her eyes – the sort you might see from a mother bear who's just been shot, but saved her cubs from the hunter, then watches them in her last moments just to let them know her soul will always be with them. The spirit of Mother Nature lived in that woman's heart; I was sure of it.

Together, she and I gazed out at the dark wonder of the rushing river. For once, I wasn't afraid of falling over the edge of the bridge. Lightning flashed in the sky again, and I could hear the echo of raindrops all around me, yet felt none of them, saw none of them. It was as if the rain were coming from a different time, long ago, and all we could glimpse was its memory.

I looked down at the red *S* encased in a diamond on my shirt, like a serpent coiled in crystal, and I remembered the day with the sunflowers.

At that moment, I realized nothing could ever tarnish that memory – not life, not death, not even change.

All of our time together flashed before my eyes, every moment of laughter, pain, joy and sadness, each and every sight of her gazing in wide wonder at the beautiful world we were given; standing on that bridge with her, desperately fighting my fear of falling over.

A twinge of sorrow struck my heart as it suddenly hit me:

I never read *The Prophet*.

Then, quietly, Jasmine began to sing.

"*Dellll-ta-a Dawn, what's that flower you have on?*
*Could it be a faded rose from days gone byyyy?*"

My lips quivered, my eyes stung and my throat tightened as I listened to the woman sing.

"*And did I hear you say...?*
*He was meetin' you here today...*
*To take you to his mansion in the skyyyy....*"

And for just one moment, we found peace.

Then the sound of tires coming down the road from the direction of the state line hit my ears, and my head snapped toward a pair of headlights. They blinded me in an instant; automatically, my hand pulled my glasses from my pocket and put them on my face.

Suddenly bright red lights began flashing on the top of the car.

My heart sank.

It came to a stop on the bridge, and I caught a glimpse of the Sheriff's Department logo on the driver's door as it opened.

Jazz shot me a look of terror. I couldn't make out who it was through the bright lights piercing my dark glasses.

Until I heard his voice.

"*Mr. Lyric!*" Sheriff Swanson boomed with fury. "Just the man I was looking for."

# Chapter 27

My eyes adjusted to the bright lights and the image of the sheriff resolved, standing by his cruiser behind his open door with his revolver drawn, pointing at the sky with a bent elbow as if he were going to shoot down God himself.

Scared as hell, I raised my hands slowly and pushed back the fear as I stepped toward him. "I didn't kill your daughter, Sheriff."

His mouth twitched contemptuously. "Then why's her cold dead body lyin' on your couch?"

I took another step toward him, conscious of my own revolver tucked in my back pocket just behind the neck of my guitar. But I didn't want to use it. "Huckleberry broke in," I told him as quiet lightning illuminated us both. "He strangled her to death. When I came back, I found her like that."

The sheriff scoffed. "Then what, he shot himself in the heart?"

"No. I did."

The sheriff recoiled almost imperceptibly. "You expect me to believe that?"

"As a matter of fact, I do. It's the God's honest truth. Look me in the eye and tell me I'm lying."

Jed clicked his tongue. "That's the thing I don't like about you, Mr. Lyric…" There was venom in his voice. "I ain't never seen your eyes."

For a moment, our gazes were locked. "Kill 'em headlights and I'll show you."

363

He narrowed his eyes at me and stared for what felt like a long time. Then, without looking away, he reached into his car and killed the lights – the headlights and the flashers on top all went dark. The only light now came from Jasmine's van behind us and the intermittent flashes of lightning above.

Slowly, my hand moved to my face. I took off my glasses and carefully handed them to Jazz, who stood just behind me to the left, visibly shaking.

"Huh," the sheriff scoffed to himself bitterly. "Would ya look at that. You ain't gotta soul after all."

Then he trained his revolver on me. I didn't flinch.

"I told you, Sheriff," I said emphatically. "I didn't kill Alita. You can shoot me if you want, it ain't gonna bring her back." His face twisted painfully. "The man who killed her is already dead. I don't know if it was God's will or the Devil's, but she got as much justice as she's ever gonna get. Killing me won't do a damn thing for her."

He studied me for a moment, fury written on his face, then he cocked the hammer.

At that moment, Jazz jumped forward with her hands up. "Wait!" she cried. "He's telling the truth!"

Jed snarled at her. "The hell you think I oughta listen to *you* for?" he sneered. "Aiding a fugitive from the law in his escape? Hell, I should lock you up, too."

"If that's what you have to do, then that's what you have to do," Jazz replied, keeping her voice level despite her trembling body. "Lyric loved your daughter. He wouldn't have killed her."

Jed spat on the bridge. "What do *you* know about what he loves?" he roared. "Man's got a bad reputation from here to Driftwood." Then he looked at me. "How many of your friends have you stabbed in the back for a night with their woman? How many times you sat around, waitin' for your chance to jump?"

Self-contemptuously, my mouth twitched. "More times than I should have."

"Then why in the name of God you think I'm gonna believe you now?"

Calmly, I replied: "Penance."

Jedediah recoiled, and his weapon wavered for a moment before he pointed it at my heart again. "You're a treacherous, lyin', no good fuckin' *snake*, Lyric. Crawlin' on your belly in enmity of all the good men God put in this world."

"Good men like Huck?" I rejoined sharply. The sheriff winced. "You see those bruises on her forearms? Ask the coroner how old he thinks those bruises are. They ain't from today, and they ain't from me."

Jed's face twisted into a vicious snarl. "You watch your goddamn mouth when you speak of the dead to *me*, boy."

"I'm not speaking of the dead," I replied staunchly, taking a step forward. "I'm speaking *for* them. She was trying to get away from the man, Sheriff. He hurt her. She tried to tell you, and the whole town said she was crazy. They called her a liar. They called her a sinner. They called her a whore. But I never did. I just called her what she was."

"Yeah?" the sheriff's voice shook. "What's that?"

Plainly, I said: "Alita."

Faintly, I could see the sheriff's lips begin to tremble. "Don't. Don't you fuckin' dare." There was a crack in his voice as he spoke.

Then I recited:

"*Yet while we grieve our lost reprieve,*
*Fearful not, though all we've seen*
*Has cost a lot, still we have our fields of green.*"

Jed tried to maintain his composure as he spoke again. "What is that? What the hell is that?"

I grit my teeth to push back the pain. "It's a poem your daughter wrote, when she went out to Colorado a few years back. She let me read it once, and it's stayed with me forever." The Sheriff's eyes glistened against Jasmine's headlights. I took another step forward. "I didn't kill her, Jed. She was something special to me."

Lightning brightened the sky for a moment. The sheriff said, "You got two witnesses to your crimes, Lyric – one up in Heaven and the other down in Hell. 'Less God starts speaking to me real quick, I suggest you make your peace with him. Admit what you did and maybe I'll make it easy on you."

Without breaking eye contact, I took another step and shook my head. "Then you're just gonna have to kill me."

I could hear Jazz's terrified breathing a few feet behind me to my left.

The sheriff glanced between the two of us, his gun still pointed at my heart. A wild fury gleamed in his eyes.

Then he said, "That'd be too easy for you. You took one of mine, well... Only makes sense that I take one of yours."

My eyes widened with shock. In an instant, the sheriff swung his revolver over and pointed it at Jazz.

"*No!*" I cried out.

In a single move, I turned and grabbed the frightened woman with my back facing the sheriff.

His revolver boomed deafening thunder as the gunshot made a spark in the darkness.

Jasmine screamed and I felt a dull pain in my back, preceded by a *thudding* sound like lead striking wood.

My body hurled both Jazz and I to the ground and I laid on top of her, trying to figure out if I was dying or not.

But there was no time to think, no time to respond.

There was only time to act.

In a flash, I rolled over onto my back, skidding my guitar against the pavement, and drew my revolver from my belt.

*Angels, let my aim be true.*

My right hand pulled the trigger as my left palm struck the hammer, and I fired a single shot toward the sheriff.

Then all went quiet.

Peering through the darkness, I scanned the area out ahead of us, trying to spot my combatant.

His feet were visible beneath his cruiser's open door, pointing straight up and moving weakly.

Quickly, I looked at Jazz, lying on the road next to me. "Are you okay?"

"I'm fine," she panted. "Is he –?"

"I don't know," I sprang to my feet. My thumb cocked the hammer back again and held it pointed at the sheriff's hidden body as I slowly made my way over to him.

Grief struck me when I saw him.

He was lying by his vehicle, blood pouring out of his neck. My bullet had ripped through his jugular.

He was dying.

Immediately, I fell to my knees, laid the revolver and my instrument next to me then clasped my hands over the wound. I turned my head and shouted, "*Jazz!*"

She ran towards me and stopped with a gasp. "Oh my God...."

Frantically, I called out, "I can't stop the bleeding!"

"Hang on!" she yelled back. "I'll find something!"

"Hurry!" My voice was harsh and my head snapped back toward the dying man as blood rushed through my fingers and over my hands. Jed sputtered weakly as his lifeforce spilled into his throat and onto the pavement, through my fingers. He was going to die and there was nothing I could do to stop it.

Panicked, as seconds went by, I turned my head and called out, "*Jazz!*" one more time.

But my voice stopped short as her headlights struck my eyes.

I saw something I couldn't explain.

As the two bright white lights poured from her van, I saw broad, shimmering rings with the texture of fingerprints appear around them in the shape of halos.

But the halos weren't white. They weren't red, either. They were golden.

My voice went still and my mouth hung open, rapt in awe.

*Am I imagining things?*

As I stared at them, they began to move – morphing and breathing like two living things, with the same sort of cadence as a bird when it flaps its wings. There was some kind of warmth to them, and in my head I could have sworn I heard the angels sing.

The rings danced like fired to the rhythm of the voices, folding and unfurling but never breaking.

When I stared at those shimmering golden rings of light, something stirred inside me that I didn't know was there before.

I think it was my soul.

And then they vanished, and the choir silenced.

My head turned back toward the man dying below me, and I knew there was nothing I could do.

A silver crucifix hanging just beside the wound glinted as lightning struck the sky.

It looked just like mine, hanging from my neck outside of my shirt, only brighter.

I didn't know if prayer would do anything besides provide Jedediah comfort as he passed on to the next life. Maybe that was all it needed to do. I didn't know many prayers, but there was one I still remembered my father teaching me.

Softly, I recited it:

"Our Father, who art in Heaven, hallowed be thy name... Thy kingdom come, thy will be done... On Earth, as it is in Heaven... Give us our daily bread, and forgive us our trespasses, as we forgive those who trespass against us... And lead us not into temptation, but deliver us –"

My voice cracked and my eyes stung.

I set those emotions aside and finished the prayer.

"But deliver us from evil."

Then, the light went out in the man's eyes.

Jazz hurried over to us, carrying a shawl. "All I could find was –" Her voice ceased suddenly, then came back in a fearful whisper: "Is he...?"

Solemnly, I nodded. "Yeah." Then I picked up the revolver, uncocked it and tucked it back into my belt.

An array of emotions colored her face all at once – grief, sorrow, relief, mourning, and then hope. She wrapped her arms around me. "Thank you," she whispered.

We held the embrace for a moment, then I pushed her away gently, staining her jacket with the blood on my hands. "You're not hurt, are you?"

She shook her head curtly, "Mm-mm. Are you? Did you get shot again?"

With something of a wince, I lifted my guitar up from the pavement. My back hurt, but it was the dull pain you get with a bruise, not the searing pain from a gunshot, and as I looked down at the guitar, I realized why.

There was a .38 caliber bullet hole in the body of the instrument.

"Looks like music saved my life."

Jazz looked at the instrument in wide-eyed wonder. "Divine intervention...." she whispered.

"Maybe," I said quietly. "Maybe not. Maybe I should be dead. Maybe it was a cosmic accident that I'm still alive at all."

Jazz turned her gaze toward me. "Do you really still believe in cosmic accidents?"

As I stared down at that sleek black beauty with the bullet hole, I didn't know how I was still alive. "No, I don't think I do."

Jazz studied me for a second, then asked somberly, "This is where we part ways, isn't it?" Her eyes focused on the woods leading to the next bridge and then the state line. "You're just half a mile from freedom now."

As I looked down at the body of the sheriff, everything suddenly made sense. "I've always been free, Jazz. I think that's part of the problem." Then I looked at her. "And yes, this is where we part ways. But I'm not going to West Virginia."

She furrowed her brow for a second, then her eyes lit up with fear as she realized my meaning. "Lyric, you can't...."

I shook my head. "I have to. I don't wanna hurt people anymore, Jazz."

"But they'll lock you up for the rest of your life!"

I just shrugged. "Whatever happens... happens."

She hugged herself, then somberly asked, "What about me? What if they lock me up, too?"

I shook my head briefly. "Carl's good with the DA. It won't be hard to convince them not to press charges on you. All you've done is the right thing – you never hurt anybody."

With a deep look in her eyes, she wrapped her arms around me again and hugged me tightly. It hurt, but I didn't mind the pain. "Okay," she whispered.

Gently, I pushed her away, then reached over the sheriff's body and picked up the radio handset in his cruiser. I gave Jazz one last look. "The music's here – all that's left to do is face it."

Her eyes glistened as lightning flashed in the sky. She nodded slowly; she understood. "Just step into the sound."

With a deep breath, I pressed the button on the radio to speak.

"Hey," I began, "this is Donovan Lyric. I think you guys are looking for me. I'm out on the River Sound Dam… the sheriff is here, I think he's… I think he's dead. You should probably send somebody to pick me up. I won't put up a fight."

The radio sizzled with static, then a voice came through: *"Mr. Lyric, stay right where you are. A unit will be with you shortly."*

"The woman who's with me…" I went on, looking at her. "She didn't have any part in this. If I let you catch me, then… I want you to let her go. Okay?"

There was a pause, then the voice simply said: *"Okay."*

I dropped the handset onto the driver's seat, and for a minute, me and Jazz just stood there on the dam, listening to the music of the river as lightning flashed above us.

Then, finally, it started to rain.

The bridge turned red as the sky washed away the blood from my hands.

# PART III

## РАЗДЕЛ III

# Chapter 28

### River Sound County Courthouse, Hannover-Fist, Ohio
### May 08th, 1997

The court goes silent as I finish my story. In the crowd I spot a few wet eyes; several people got up and left sometime during. I can't say I blame them – I wouldn't want to hear about my friends dying, either.

I don't dare look at the jury box. It doesn't matter what their faces say. It doesn't even really matter what their verdict says, either.

I told my story.

There's more freedom in that than all the world can ever offer.

Carl takes a deep breath at the lectern. "Mr. Lyric," he begins, "is it true to say that you only fired your weapon at Jedediah Swanson *after* he made it known his intentions were to kill Jasmine Garcia?"

I lean toward the microphone in the witness stand. "That's correct."

Then Carl looks at the judge. "Your Honor, I would like to present Exhibit 26 to the jury."

Judge Thomas nods. "You may proceed."

Carl gestures at a few other court officials, and they quickly wheel out a projector. Another one pulls down a white screen. Carl then addresses the jury. "The following is the dashcam footage obtained from Sheriff Swanson's police cruiser on the early morning hours of May 18th, 1996. It has been analyzed and verified by the River Sound County Sheriff's Department as intact and unaltered." Then he pauses. "I would like to warn the court, some of the footage is difficult to watch due to its nature."

He gestures to the man operating the projector, and he slides a tape into the machine.

I see myself and Jazz on the white screen, and I hear my voice. *"I didn't kill your daughter, Sheriff."*

*"Then why's her cold dead body lyin' on your couch?"*

The entire scene plays out again, beat for beat. It's difficult to watch, harder to relive. Then the sheriff says, *"You took one of mine. Well... Only makes sense that I take one of yours."*

*"No!"*

Gunshots ring out in the courtroom in low-fidelity audio. I grit my teeth as I watch it play out. Jazz shoots me a look from the audience that tells me *it'll be okay*. Carl lets the reel run all the way to the point where I radioed the department to come and get me, then nods to the operator to stop the tape.

Carl addresses the jury again: "You can clearly see in the police footage that Jedediah Swanson unambiguously threatened, then attempted, to execute Jasmine Garcia in cold blood. My client made no threats of violence against him, indicated no level of threat at that moment, and certainly neither did Ms. Garcia. Had Mr. Lyric not done what he had, then Ms. Garcia would have been killed – for the crime of being a close friend of my client."

Finally, I let myself glance at the jury. They look sick, distraught even. It's a hard thing to watch, a man of honor falling down.

Carl scans his eyes over the jurors, then rests them on the judge. "No further questions, your Honor. The defense rests."

Judge Thomas nods as Carl takes a seat. Then he looks at the prosecution team. "Counsel, you may begin your cross-examination of the witness."

The older prosecutor in the middle of the three at his table rises. There's a look of determination in his eyes. "Thank you, your Honor." He approaches the lectern Carl just left, then turns his attention on me. "Mr. Lyric, when the sheriff stopped you on the bridge, did you have any intention of turning yourself in?"

For a second, I hesitate. "No. Not until I had a chance to clear my name."

"In the footage we just saw, you can be clearly seen walking toward the sheriff. You were aware of the revolver in your back pocket at that time, correct?"

My eyes narrow behind my glasses. "No, I suddenly remembered it was there *after* he shot me," I reply sardonically. "What do *you* think?"

The judge snaps his head toward me and Carl shoots me a baffled look.

Quickly, I murmur, "Sorry, your Honor." Then to the prosecutor, "Yes, I was aware of the revolver."

He stares me down. "What was your plan if the sheriff wouldn't listen to your plea?"

"What was my *plan?*" I repeat. "Didn't have one. I was playing an empty hand."

"Then why did you step toward Jedediah Swanson?" he asks incisively.

"To put myself closer to him than Ms. Garcia was," I respond. "A man who's alone in the world is a dangerous thing; I knew there was a chance he would use her to hurt me."

"So you entered that confrontation ready for combat?" He holds his look on me like it's a great *gotcha* moment.

I try to subdue my anger, but some of it leaks through. "If you're trying to say my plan was to kill the sheriff all along, then, well... You can walk right into Hell, and I'll see you there."

"Mr. Lyric!" the judge scolds. "Keep your answers civil or I *will* hold you in contempt of court."

The prosecutor clicks his tongue and pauses for a moment. "You are the only one Ms. Swanson told about the *alleged* abuse sustained from Mr. Singer, to your knowledge – is that correct?"

I take a deep breath. "As far as I know, yeah. Half the town thought she was crazy, but she knew I wouldn't. She trusted me to protect her. And I failed."

"We've already seen from the coroner's report that Mr. Singer sustained no defensive wounds – something fairly uncommon for a murderer. Yet when you were arrested that night, it was recorded that you had many bruises and scratches on your person. How do you explain that?"

"Probably something to do with that multi-man brawl that broke out at the bar. Alita was a skinny girl. It wouldn't take much for Huck to restrain her, especially if he caught her by surprise."

He continues. "And *your* DNA was found on her body, in her genital regions, and under her fingernails. How do you explain that?"

"We had sex."

"Consensually?"

"Oh, *fuck* you."

"*Mr. Lyric!*" the judge slams his gavel furiously. He glares at me, then looks at the prosecutor. "Counselor, I would ask that you stop attempting to get a rise out of the defendant or you'll *both* be held in contempt."

The prosecutor shifts uncomfortably. Then he says, "You made it known to Huckleberry Singer earlier that night that you intended to kill him, didn't you?"

"No," I answer staunchly. "I made it known that, if it came to a life or death situation, I would choose life – *her* life, and mine."

"And then when you shot him, was that you choosing life?"

Carl leaps up. "Objection, your Honor – the prosecutor is asking an argumentative question."

"Sustained," Judge Thomas says. "Counsel, move on."

I interject. "No, I'll answer it." Carl shoots me a dumbfounded look. I give him a plain one back, then look at the prosecutor. "When I shot him, there didn't seem to *be* any other choice. Life, death, it was all the same. When you come home to find the woman *you* love lying dead next to the man who killed her, then maybe you'll understand. There isn't a second choice to make in that situation... Not one that you can live with. I hope to God you never have to know what that feels like."

The prosecutor studies me for a second. "It's been established by several witnesses that, while Ms. Swanson and Mr. Singer had many arguments, they had reconciled numerous times. What made you think *that* night would be any different?"

Carl leaps up again. "Objection – my client has no way of knowing what might have been going on in the deceased parties' heads."

*Deceased parties.* Tremors shake my heart with sorrow.

"Sustained," the Judge rules. "Counsel, please rephrase your question in a way that allows an actual answer from the defendant, or move along to the next question."

The prosecutor thinks for a moment. "Why did you feel that Mr. Singer was a threat against your life or hers, despite the months-long entanglement never previously indicating a life-or-death response?"

For a second, I thought back to the serpent in the Garden. "Because that night, he knew I was in love with her. Knowledge changes everything. It informs every decision that we make, and there are things we can't ever go back from. Whatever good might have been in his heart, it was gone that night – long before I shot him there. I turned him into the most dangerous thing a man can be."

"And what is that, Mr. Lyric?"

"Alone."

A somber hush falls over the courtroom. Finally, the counselor says, "One final question: do you regret what you did?"

Alita's smile flashes across my mind's eye, her bright eyes and ruby lips shining in the white light of the sun. The world would never get to see that again, and neither would I.

"No."

Triumphantly, the prosecutor tries to hide his smirk. "No further questions. The prosecution rests."

As he returns to his seat, the judge rubs his temple. "Well, I believe we could all use a break." Then he looks between the Carl and the three prosecutors. "Court shall be adjourned for today; it will reconvene tomorrow at nine A.M. so that you may present your closing arguments to the jury." Exhaustedly, he slowly lets out a breath then raps his gavel. "Dismissed."

I look at Jazz one last time as the crowd rises and the bailiff comes to escort me. She gives me a look of deep compassion.

As the bailiff takes by the arm, my heart skips a beat.

Hope is standing in the back of the room, looking at me with a mixture of sadness and something else.

I think it was pride.

# Chapter 29

Sitting back in my cell, there's nothing to do but think.

Prison is nothing like the movies – everyone always tells you that, but you don't really believe them till you get there.

The thing movies always leave out is how utterly boring it is.

River Sound County Prison isn't exactly Alcatraz; most people would probably rather just do their time than try to escape. Most of us are only in here for a couple of years; the rest of us are here waiting to find out how much longer we have to stay.

I'm in the latter category.

My cell is small with a pair of uncomfortable bunkbeds for me and my theoretical cellmate. The room is only six by six, with blank white walls and a sink and shitter on the side opposite the beds. You and your cellmate get to take turns trying to ignore the other one taking a crap. Of course, I haven't gotten a cellmate yet. Not a lot of crime happens in this neck of the woods, and this ain't one of those prisons at max capacity. If anything, it almost feels a little empty.

Hell, sometimes I wish I had a cellmate. Then I'd have someone to talk to.

Sitting with my legs over the side of the bottom bunk, I look up at the ceiling. Light shines down from a fluorescent fixture, but I don't particularly mind the pain. At least it's something to feel.

My mind flashes back to the look of sad pride Hope was giving me when they took me out of the courtroom.

I pray I did the right thing; I pray I finally became an example she can learn from on how to walk in the light rather than a portrait of how to live in the dark.

But I don't know.

Out loud, staring at the ceiling, I ask, "How're you doin' today?" As always, I wait for the mute response. "I'm not doing so well myself, thanks for not asking," I breathe. "I told the truth. Sometimes I think that's all I wanted to do, just let the world know who I really am. Doesn't really matter what happens to me now. That jury's gonna make up their own minds about me, so's everybody else if they haven't already. But I can't really control that, can I? Hell, I don't even think *you* can control that. That's why you were so pissed off about that little *snafu* in the Garden. Only way you could control us, keep us out of trouble, is if you kept us in the dark. Then the ol' lightbringer came slithering in." My eyes fixated on the light for a moment. "Well, I'm sitting in the light now. For better or worse, that's where I am."

Then the voice of the ward's correctional officer calls out: "Lights out in five minutes!"

My face pulls a frown. "Isn't that ironic."

The light turns off a few minutes later as I lay me down to sleep. And as I try and put aside the sick feeling in my stomach, the nerves of the unknown, my mind wanders back to that night I turned myself in.

\*\*\*

Rain poured around us as Jasmine and I sat in her van, waiting for the cops to come. Neither of us said a word; we just sat there silently as I smoked a cigarette and looked out the window to the expansive, dark river.

    I couldn't stop thinking about the halos.

    I think I'd seen a miracle.

    Then a pair of headlights, mixed with red and white flashers, slowly pulled up behind us. I looked at Jazz.

    "Music's here."

    She pursed her lips and nodded, then we both stepped out of the van and the rain slowed to a drizzle. Immediately, I raised my hands in surrender, letting the cigarette dangle from my lips. The police cruiser stopped and two deputies stepped out. "Mr. Lyric?" one of them asked, his hand resting on his sidearm in its holster.

    "Don't shoot," I said calmly. "I surrender."

    He looked me up and down for a second, then motioned for the other one to go check out the sheriff. "Do you have any weapons on you?"

    "Revolver, tucked in my belt around my back," I replied, keeping my hands raised, puffing on the cigarette. The deputy walked over quickly and pulled it from my belt.

    "It loaded?" he asked.

    "Four shots left."

    Then the other deputy, kneeling by the sheriff, called out, "Shit, I can't find a pulse!"

    I told them, "He bled out a couple minutes ago. I'm sorry."

The deputy holding the revolver looked at the gruesome scene and exhaled deeply. "Ambulance will be here in a minute," he said, almost to himself.

Jazz spoke up. "He tried to kill me," she said sorrowfully. "I think finding his little girl like that just... broke him."

The first deputy eyed her skeptically, then said to his partner, "Jones, search the woman."

"On it, Tarlton."

Jones got up from the sheriff's side and hurried over to Jazz, patted her down quickly and asked, "Any weapons in the car?"

She shook her head. "Just a friend's guitar."

"Okay," Jones said. "Wait by the cruiser." Jazz complied, then both deputies were upon me.

Tarlton handed Jones the revolver, then said to me, "Turn around, put your hands behind your back."

"Yeah, I know the drill," I replied dully. My hand took the cigarette and tossed it on the pavement then I put them behind my back in one motion. In an instant, a pair of metal cuffs were bound tightly around my wrists.

Jones fumbled with the gun, trying to unload it. "How the hell –?"

"It's a single action," I remarked. "There's a pin you have to unlatch under the barrel. Then you can pop the cylinder out."

Jones followed my instructions and popped out the cylinder. Then Tarlton asked me, "Where'd you get the revolver?"

I took one last look at it before the deputy put it in his car. "It belonged to my father."

"He still around?"

"Nah," I replied. "Died a few years back."

"Well, I'm sorry for your loss." Tarlton looked back as a swarm of lights approached the bridge. There were a few more cop cars and an ambulance, all rushing onto the scene. Then the deputy said, "Jones, take Ms. Garcia home – we'll have to search your car before we can release it back to you, but you're free to go. I'll take Mr. Lyric here to the station."

Jazz and I both made incredulous looks. She asked, "You're really not charging me?"

Tarlton sort of shrugged. "Way I see it, you held a fugitive under citizen's arrest till we got here. Ain't nothing to charge you with. Besides..." he paused, looking at me, "I'm a man of my word."

I couldn't help but think back to that line about people wanting to be good.

"Come on, Ms. Garcia," Jones said to Jazz. She stopped, then stooped down and picked up my cigarette butt, tucking it in the breast pocket of her light denim jacket.

She stole one more glance at me as Tarlton put me in the car, telling me with her eyes that it would be okay.

Tarlton took me down to the station. There weren't any jokes to make this time, no poses for the mugshot. Everything felt dark and bleak, and I lacked the energy to so much as smile.

"You get one phone call," a deputy told me as they put me in that all-too-familiar cell with a payphone on the wall. Then he handed me a dime.

I held it in my palm for a minute.

I knew who I needed to call.

As the coin slid into the phone and I dialed the number, I held my breath anxiously.

Finally, I heard a tired, half-asleep voice on the other end.

"*Hello?*" Layla greeted.

My hands shook and I took a deep breath. "Hey, Layla. It's Lyric."

"*Oh... Hey....*"

There was a pregnant pause. Then I finally said, "Can... Can you tell me what happened that night? I need to know."

"*Lyric –*"

"I know that Red knows," I cut her off, sensing the hesitance in her voice. "It's okay. I'm not mad at you. You did the right thing." My voice was deep with gravel as I spoke. "But I don't remember what happened or what I said to you, and I've been avoiding it out of sheer guilt ever since. And that's me cutting myself slack that I don't deserve. I've put it off for too long. You can tell me to go fuck myself if you want, but I don't want to keep hiding from the bad things I've done."

The silence that followed was unbearable.

Then, after all, she said, "*I didn't want to tell Red about you, but... I got tired of lying to him, you know?*" There was heavy guilt laden in her voice. "*I was really drunk, too. But on the back porch you were giving me advice about what it would be like to stay with Red or to leave him. Then you said you were kind of into me and we... fooled around a bit, a lot of making out. Then before I walked you home, you said you weren't gonna do any more than that – which I was totally fine with. But when we got to your place it just kind of... happened."*

Painfully, I grit my teeth and gripped the phone. Fragments came back to me as I listened to her speak, but only fragments. I still couldn't remember – and I had to live with the fact I probably never would.

She continued. *"I'm honestly really sorry we ended up doing that... It was a terrible feeling for me when you said you didn't remember...."* There was a long silence. *"I hope you don't hate me for it."*

It felt like a long time before I could speak again, and when I did, my throat hurt. "Christ, I'm a terrible friend...." Her only response was the sound of her breathing. "I don't hate you. It wasn't your fault. You know, I've been trying to figure out why, when you saw me at the gas station earlier, you asked me if I was proud of you for moving out. And the more I thought about it, the more I realized what probably happened, and what I probably said that night.

"When I get that drunk, I have a habit of cutting right to the core. And I figured I probably said something to you about Red, about how deeply unhappy you both were. And then the caveman part of my brain jumped to 'woman, oonga oonga yes,' like it always does."

Layla laughed softly, almost sadly.

I went on. "I don't blame you for telling Red, either. If you hadn't, I never would have known the truth, because I would have stayed too much of a coward to face it. You did the right thing. Thank you for telling me; at least now I never have to wonder."

There was one more silence between us, until at last she said, "*Have a good night, Lyric.*"

Then I hung up the phone.

\*\*\*

They kept me in the drunk tank for a couple of days until I could get in to see the magistrate Monday morning, nine A.M.

Go figure, right on time for the arraignment they had already scheduled for the assault charge.

The cops escorted me to the magistrate's office a few miles away from the sheriff's department. There was an officer by my side every moment that I wasn't in a cell. We sat in the muted, gray building for a while before Judge Swinton was ready to see me; I was still in the clothes I had been wearing at the time of arrest. At least they had the decency to wash them for me.

Then the door to the judge's courtroom finally opened, and a very familiar young face greeted me with a look of disappointment and relief.

It was Hope.

I had wondered if she would still be there that day for her internship – a part of me was wishing she wouldn't, but another part was glad that she had. I expected her to look at me with judgement, maybe even anger. But all I saw was disappointment and worry. She said, "I thought I told you to wear something nice."

The deputy motioned for me to stand up, so I rose to my feet. "It was between this and a jumpsuit," I replied.

She looked at me the way I imagined God looked at Lucifer when he realized what he had done – with forlorn heartbreak. Then she said to the deputy, "The judge is ready to see you."

"Thanks, Hope," he replied, then we followed her into the courtroom.

Carl sat in the room at the defense table, the only other person in the room besides me, the deputy, and Hope, and I took a seat next to him, my hands cuffed out in front of me. "How you doin', buddy?" he asked with a firm pat on my shoulder.

"All things considered? Not too bad," I replied meekly.

"That's the spirit."

Then Judge Swinton marched into the room through a door beside her spot at the judge's bench, carrying a small stack of papers. We all stood up. "You can sit down," she said plainly.

We complied, then she flipped through the papers. "Well, Mr. Lyric, here we are again. Before we get started with your arraignment, I would just like to clarify a few things:

"What we're here for today is not to determine your guilt or innocence in any crimes. I won't be asking you any questions regarding the circumstances of your charges, outside of clarification questions that require a 'yes' or 'no' response. This is to determine the validity of the charges being pressed against you, to determine your necessity for bail, and to clarify any details such as where you're living and where you'll be staying as you await trial. Do you understand?"

"Yes, your Honor."

"Just as well, I am aware that you and Hope are friends, just as you're probably aware that she's an intern here at my office and sits in on most of my cases. She requested that she could sit in today specifically, and as this is a public preliminary hearing, I granted her permission."

My heart skipped a beat. It was a feeling somewhere between shame and gratitude. *She asked to be here today. Even after what happened at the restaurant.*

The judge continued. "Considering those circumstances, anything talked about today must remain confidential; you are not to seek from her, or pressure from her, any sort of legal advice regarding your charges. You may also not discuss matters regarding this case with her outside of this courtroom, unless it is in private – do you understand?"

There was an indescribable feeling of warmth that washed over me in waves. Sitting beside Carl, with Hope in the benches just behind me, it dawned on me:

After everything I had done, even after the trail of destruction I had left in my wake, I still wasn't alone.

And I never had been.

"Yes, your Honor."

The hearing went by swiftly – I was to be held at River Sound County Prison until my trial. As we walked out of the courtroom, Hope said to me quietly, "It'll be okay."

And I replied, "You have no idea how much I appreciate you."

She just smiled and said, "I gotchu, Lyric."

They didn't let me ride shotgun that time when they put me in the cruiser. I was in the back, behind the cage with my head resting against the window for the long drive to Hannover-Fist. *Maybe this was a mistake after all.*

But as we rolled through the barren land of Driftwood, I could have sworn I saw a miracle.

When we passed the old farmhouse I grew up in, abandoned and dilapidated all to hell, that land where nothing would ever grow was teeming with life.

In the pasture behind and around the house was a thick, lush, thriving field of some kind of crop climbing toward the sky, a few inches high and rising.

It was as if they had finally purged the poison from the soil.

Quickly, I asked the deputy driving me, "Hey, you know what they planted here?"

Casually, he replied, "Sunflowers."

\*\*\*

The sound of a machine beeped rhythmically in the hospital. Memories had a funny way of replaying themselves in your dreams. And as I looked around the hospital room, I knew exactly where and when I was.

My father lay on the bed in the room. He looked old, haggard, worn down. Time had been unkind to him, the same way he had been unkind to time.

Anxiously, I slowly paced around the room.

"Would you knock that off?" he coughed. "It's driving me fucking crazy."

"Sorry," I murmured. He looked odd in a hospital gown. I never thought I'd see him in one of those. The man had barely gone to a doctor in my entire life. Now, there he was, all gowned up with tubes coming out of his nose and patches on his arm, with an IV sticking from his vein.

"God," he groaned. "I hate this."

"I don't think anybody's ever loved their hospital experience, dad."

"Well you've clearly never heard of Munchausen's, then." He cracked a feeble grin and laughed, then it morphed into a cough. I never wondered where I got my smart mouth from – even on his deathbed, the man had a comment for everything. "God fucking *dammit*," he swore as his chest heaved.

I guess that's also where I got my sailor's mouth from.

Quickly, I handed him a glass of water. "Quit fuckin' cracking jokes and maybe you'll cough less."

"Oh, yeah, a glass of water," he remarked as he took the cup with trembling hands. "That'll fix me right up."

"It'll definitely shut you up for a minute," I grinned wryly. Time had softened his personality; I hadn't seen him get violent since that night he shot at me.

For all that mattered.

He quit drinking on and off for the last decade of his life, but he never went back to whiskey. He'd drink enough beer to give himself a headache for a couple months, then let it go for a while till he started back up again. But the Devil never sat on his shoulder the way it used to. He still held onto it, I think; maybe he was just as afraid as I was that, if his devils ever left him, his angels would as well.

"Yeah, well," my dad mused, turning his head toward the window. "Your mother tried to shut me up for thirty years. Never worked for her, God rest her soul."

"Looks like God finally found a way to do it," I replied.

He sort of chuckled. "Nah, it wasn't God. It was the Bulleit and Maker's Mark and all the beer. You know, when I pictured drinking myself to death, I imagined it would be a lot quicker than this."

"Trust me, I understand the sentiment."

He chuckled again, then turned his head toward me. "Yeah... I figured you would." Suddenly his face became... pensive. Like he got lost in time for a moment. "My God, you're just like me."

"Christ, I certainly hope not."

He laughed weakly again. "Well, not *just* like me. You never did get quite as tall as me, did you?"

"Ha-ha, very funny."

He grinned. "I thought it was kinda funny." Then he went quiet for a moment. "You look just like I did when I was a kid – well, I guess I can't say 'kid' anymore. You're, what – twenty-five?"

"Dad, I'm twenty-seven."

He dismissed it with a wave of his hand. "Eh, same thing. Your jaw is shaped the same as mine. You can probably take a hit pretty well, can't you?"

"Like you wouldn't believe."

He snickered humorously. "Yeah, you're definitely my kid. Never had a doubt about it. You look just like I did when I was your age."

"Well hopefully that trend doesn't stick – you don't look so hot these days."

He grumbled and laughed simultaneously. "Tell me about it. World finally broke me."

Looking down at him, I shook my head. "No it didn't."

We held eye contact for a moment, then he glanced away. "I know it wasn't easy, the way I raised you. Hell, I'm not surprised half your friends are veterans. Livin' with me, the way I was, I wouldn't be surprised if you've got some of your own PTSD. People who've been in life or death situations probably just make more sense to you, and you probably make sense to them. I know what it feels like not to make sense to people."

"Dad, you don't have to –"

"Shut up. I'm talking."

With a frown, I complied.

He went on. "You saw a lot of things you shouldn't have had to see. And for that, I am sorry."

His words struck me. I don't think he had ever apologized for anything before. I didn't know what to say.

He took a deep breath, coughed it back out, then continued. "But you grew up strong. You grew up right.

Make no mistake, Don – you *are* strong. Stronger than me. This is probably a fucked up take in this day and age, soft as everybody is now, but I think you got exposed to just the right amount of violence. I taught you what words really mean, and you know where the time for words stops. Where you have to quit talkin' and just... act.

"I don't know if I ever told you," he went on, "but I was proud of you that night. After you did what you did, I think a part of me quit layin' hands on your mother because I knew the next time it happened, you'd make damn sure you knew how to use that weapon."

There was a moment of silence. Then I said, "Yeah."

He looked me over with a glimmer of pride. "I wasn't ever gonna kill you," he said. "But you didn't know that. You had all the reason to think I would, yet you rose to the occasion anyway, and you didn't back down. Don't ever back down. Don't let the world break you. You gotta make sure it knows it's gonna have to kill you first." He coughed ferociously for a minute, a look of pain on his face, but he bit it back down and got himself under control.

He said, "People aren't all bad, Don. They *want* to be good. Even I *wanted* to be good, I just wasn't ever any good at it."

Remorsefully, I frowned with the corner of my mouth. "You weren't always so bad at it."

"Yeah I was," he replied calmly. Then he looked at the ceiling. "I don't know what I believe in anymore. I used to talk to God but He don't really answer me. If He's out there somewhere, though... I think that's why he put us on this Earth – to show each other what good can look like. That's why he put *you* here. You can be better than anything I ever was. You already are. You've got friends, you've got women chasing after you, you're independent. You're kind – most of the time, anyway. Sometimes you're an asshole, but that's probably the me in you," he sort of laughed.

I laughed with him, trying not to focus on the pain. "Yeah, yeah I suppose it probably is."

"Ah, well, what can you do...." He took another drink of water and smacked his dry lips. "Water here tastes like shit," he remarked. "Nothin' like the well water back at the house." We both went quiet for a moment.

"Dad –"

He cut me off. "People fail, Don. People fall down, sometimes they don't get back up. But I think you can show them how, 'cause all your life you've always gotten back up. Don't ever forget that. I never gave much to this world – Shit, I probably took a hell of a lot more than I ever gave. Maybe that's why I'm here right now. I never really gave anything back to the people around me. Instead, I just cut 'em all off, isolated myself out in a house where nobody could bother me and nothin' could grow."

"Dad, you're gonna knock yourself out if you keep talking," I remarked, trying to be light hearted to mask the sincere fear of his impending passing.

But he said one more thing.

"I thought people were bad, but anymore I think maybe... they just need somebody to hold the light sometimes. And for all I took from this world, from these people... the greatest thing I ever gave them is you."

Before I could respond, another voice broke through.

"Mr. Lyric, you've got a visitor."

My head snapped toward the door of the hospital room, then suddenly I awoke.

I'm sitting upright in my cell bed, and the CO is standing behind the iron bars.

"What?" I ask, rubbing my eyes.

"I said you've got a visitor."

I glance at the clock on the wall. It's 7:30 in the morning. Carl won't be here until 8:00. Confused, I ask him:

"Who?"

# Chapter 30

I'm sitting in the relatively small visitor's room, anxiously picking my beard and rapping my fingers against the metal bench. Guards are posted at each entrance – the one for the visitors, and the one for the inmates.

*It must be Jazz. I can't think of anybody else who would go out of their way to see me the day of the verdict.*

A sick feeling enters my gut as I think about the closing statements ahead, followed by the jury's deliberation.

*Christ, I hope the jury doesn't take too long. What if I'm one of the cases that takes them days and days to decide? I'd probably wanna hang myself in my cell just to relieve the anxiety.*

*But if they come back after twenty minutes, that probably won't be a good sign either.*

*Christ. I really am proper fucked, aren't I?*

My eyes glance down to the underside of my forearm, facing up at me with the sleeves of my black prison jumpsuit rolled up, and my eyes rest on the devil there.

Then the visitor's door swings open and I wait with bated breath, wondering who's about to walk through.

For a second, I think I must be seeing things.

Makenna walks in, wearing a nervous look on her face and glancing around, clutching her purse tightly like she 's afraid someone's gonna accost her in the practically empty room.

Then she spots me.

Her eyes light up, but her expression wavers as the reality of where we are dawns on her.

"So," she begins, scanning the room as she walks to my table. "This is prison."

"Sure is," I remark, attempting to smile.

She stares at me like a hawk, then shakes her head. "My God, what a shame." Her tone is playful and teasing. She looks genuinely happy to see me, despite the circumstances.

"Yeah, well, what can you do?" I reply as she sits down.

"You could stop drinking, for starters."

"Been there, done that. I'm a year sober," I grin wryly.

She rolls her eyes. "It doesn't count if you're in jail."

"Well I know a group of anonymous alcoholics who would beg to differ."

Then she kind of smirks. "Do they have AA here?"

"Idunno," I shrug. "I never asked."

She cocks her brow. "You're not doing like group therapy or something? Oh God, don't tell me you went for the toilet hooch."

I laugh warmly. "Nah, I was never a big fan of wine. They tried to offer me some, but I turned it back into water."

She tries not to smile and fails. "You're stupid."

"Trust me, Makenna, I'm realizing that more and more every day."

Then she laughs and asks with sing-songy sarcasm, "Sooo, how are things?" Her face stretches into a broad grin and she rests her chin in both palms, with her elbows on the table. It's been a year since I've seen her and it's like we haven't skipped a beat.

"Eh, fair to middling, I'd say. Prison's not so bad. Except everybody keeps calling me 'Roy Orbison' and 'white Ray Charles.' and 'white Bobby Caldwell.' Not a single 'John Kay.'"

The girl strikes a confused face. "Bobby Caldwell *is* white, though?"

Taken aback, I physically recoil. "Wait, really?"

With a bemused grin, she laughs. "Yeah…?"

"Shit," I mutter to myself in surprise. "Better not tell Deon that."

Makenna grins some more. "Hey, at least it's better than 'prison bitch.'"

"Makenna, I'm in *county* jail. Pretty sure rape usually doesn't happen until you get to somewhere you're never getting out of."

Suddenly the tone changes as we both realize that's where I might be heading, and there's a long silence.

Finally, she says, "Just kill somebody on the first day, I'm sure that'll get the message across."

"Hey, here's an idea," I reply, "maybe don't encourage me to murder people while I'm surrounded by prison guards."

She scoffs good-humoredly. "As if you've ever needed *me* to encourage you to self-destruct."

"Yeah," I breathe, "fair point. How's Boston?"

"I'm loving it," she smiles. "Got A's in all my classes for the whole first year."

"I knew you would. Just don't get cocky – it's not a good look for you. Pride is pride, but unearned pride is arrogance. Look how well that worked out for Lucifer."

"You're one to talk," she chides.

"Exactly – take my fucking word for it," I chortle, finally feeling at ease.

She narrows her eyes and tries not to grin, but a smile breaks through. Then she says, "Sorry I couldn't make it for the first ninety-nine percent of the trial. I just finished my finals yesterday, took the first flight in. And *boy* are my arms *tired*."

"Settle down, Seinfeld. That's not even how the joke goes," I jab playfully. "You didn't miss a whole lot. I mean, other than one hell of a testimony. That and the footage of what happened with the sheriff. That was… grim."

Her expression sours. "I still can't believe you did that. I can't believe you did *any* of that. Like, even for you and how insane your life tends to be, it's like –" she gestures with both hands, "– *wow*."

"Yeah," I scratch my beard, "I'm still not sure how I'm alive."

"You've got a freaking guardian angel, that's how."

I glance up at the ceiling. "Something like that. Lotta good it's gonna do me. I don't think I'm walking away from this one, Makenna. I saw the look on the jury's faces – they think I'm dangerous."

"Well I think you're paranoid," she argues. "No sense in imagining outcomes that haven't happened yet. You're kind of a nut, but you're not *that* crazy."

"Aren't I, though?"

"No," she declares emphatically, "you're not. You're intense sometimes, but you've spent a lot more of your energy trying to protect people than hurt them. Remember old man Rick?"

"You say 'remember' like he's dead."

Her face changes. "Oh, right," she says after a second. "You probably don't get the paper in prison."

I make a puzzled expression. "What?"

"Rick died," she says. "Like, six months ago."

"Oh, shit," I respond, taken aback. "What happened?"

"Fell down drunk and hit his head," she says plainly.

I think about it for a moment. "Good. Hell got another demon."

"I'll say," she replies with a sick look on her face. "A *bunch* of stuff came out about him right after he died. Lorraine told me he was facing child molestation charges."

"No shit?" I ask, unsurprised.

"No shit," Makenna echoes. "Apparently he touched the daughter of the woman he was living with – when she was *eleven*."

My gut tightens into a knot of disgust. "I wish that were shocking to me."

Makenna continues with a look of bewilderment. "It was so crazy, Lorraine said people were actually toasting him at the bar after his funeral. People were *mourning* him."

Casually, I shrug. "They didn't know. Most people didn't know he was evil. They just thought he was a harmless, kind of creepy old pervert. There's a reason I tried so hard to protect you girls at the restaurant. People get the benefit of the doubt when sometimes they shouldn't. Personally, I never had any doubt about that one."

Makenna watches me, then half frowns. "I miss that place."

"Yeah," I sigh. "Me too. Probably wouldn't be the same without you and Hope. God willing, maybe I can go back there someday."

She tries unsuccessfully to force the frown into a smile. "I'm sure you will."

"That makes one of us."

There's an uneasy pause in the conversation.

"You really think they'll find you guilty?" Makenna asks softly.

A moment goes by before I respond. "There's no evidence proving I didn't kill Alita, and nothing proving I didn't kill Huck in cold blood out of jealousy. All they have is my word and the people who vouched for me. I don't think that's gonna be enough. I mean, I *admitted* to killing the man. What are the chances they decide that I'm not just making up a tall tale to cover my ass?"

Her eyes fall to the table. She says in almost a whisper, "I don't want you to go away forever...."

My heart breaks in real time as I watch her start to tremble. There isn't anything I can say to comfort her – nothing I can say that isn't a lie, anyway. Instead I simply ask, "So to what do I owe the prison visit? You just figured I was lonely? Came by to brag about school? One last goodbye before they cart me away?"

She looks up at me. "I finished your song."

I raise my brow. "Really?"

Proudly, she grins and nods. "Mm-hm!"

"Only took you a year," I tease.

She scoffs. "You could've finished it. What, you been busy?"

"Not exactly," I grin. "Let's hear it."

Almost fearfully, Makenna glances around at the few other inmates in the room, talking quietly to their loved ones. "You want me to *sing? Here?*" Then she crosses her arms and clicks her tongue as she leans back. "Are you crazy?"

"Jury's still out on that one."

She gives me a look as I smile at my own double entendre. Then she reaches into her purse. "I'm not gonna sing it, but I recorded it for you."

"Really?"

"Well yeah," she replied obviously. "How else are you gonna listen to it? Last I checked, you're not a mind reader."

Warmly, I smile. "No, no I am not."

She pulls out a cassette, then says, "I didn't have a tape player, so I sort of broke into your place – well, not *broke* into. You really shouldn't leave the spare key on top of the doorframe, by the way. That's like the second place anyone would look."

"Yeah, that's kind of a recurring theme in my life. Thank Christ Carl's kept up with the mortgage for me. I'm gonna be giving him my paychecks for the rest of my fuckin' life if I don't spend it in prison."

"Yeah, probably," she says as she pulls out a very familiar cassette recorder. "Your place is still trashed, by the way. It took me like half an hour to find this thing."

"Where was it?" I ask curiously.

"It got knocked all the way under your entertainment center," she tells me. "All the way back by the baseboards. Your record player is broken, just FYI. Also – I can't believe you have The Cranberries on *vinyl*." Her grin stretches from ear to ear as she laughs.

"Hey, good music is good music, god dammit," I laugh with her. Then she sets the battery powered cassette player on the metal table and pops it open.

Suddenly my heart stops.

I think hers does, too.

"Wait…" she stammers. "Is that…?"

There's still a tape inside.

Slowly, our eyes meet.

My hand is trembling.

Shaking, unable to keep it steady, I press the opaque top back down until it clicks, then I rewind the tape to the beginning. Fear stays my hand as my index finger hovers over the *play* button.

My eyes meet Makenna's again through my dark glasses. She puts her hand on top of mine, then together we push the button.

I hear the sound of Alita's voice.

"*What are you doing?*" she laughs. "*Am I being interrogated?*"

My hand clasps over my mouth to silence a gasp.

Then my voice comes in. "*No, I like to record my practice sessions. Lets me know where I need improvement.*"

"*Testing, testing, one-two-three.*"

"*Hello, I'm Johnny Cash.*"

My mouth drops. Makenna's face matches mine.

Quickly, I fast forward fifteen minutes into the tape.

Then I hear Huck's voice.

"*She said something and I... I just snapped. I lost it, Lyric.... I strangled her.*"

My voice is barely audible in the tape. "*...Why?*"

There's a pause.

Then Huck says:

"*Just to watch her die.*"

I can hardly believe my ears. My finger hits the *stop* button. Barely able to contain my breath, I jump to my feet. The CO by the door snaps his head toward me.

"Something wrong over here?" he asks in an authoritative tone as he saunters over.

Makenna looks up at me in wide-eyed disbelief, and I think I can see a glimmer of hope in them.

Then I look at the guard through my glasses and tell him urgently:

"I need to make a phone call!"

# Chapter 31

*"Kill me, call the fuckin' cops, I don't care anymore.... I used to think she was perfect."*

There's a long pause in the tape. Then my voice speaks softly. *"The Devil never whispered 'perfection....'"*

*"....What?"*

*"He whispered 'freedom.'"*

*BANG!*

Carl lets out a long exhale and stops the tape, then leans back in his chair as we sit in a large conference room with the DA's team of prosecutors. I'm sitting in the same black suit I wore yesterday. Even that, full dark, doesn't quite describe the feeling of the room after what we just listened to.

The lead prosecutor strokes his chin in deep contemplation as his two cohorts sit beside him, one woman and one man, visibly uneasy. "Well, God damn...." he finally says softly. It's mere minutes before the trial is set to resume for its conclusion; the tension in the air could be photographed, it's so palpable.

Carl replies. "Look, you heard the same tape I did." He leans forward confidently, but I can see the painful discomfort on his face. Those were his friends who died, too. "The entire murder of Alita Swanson was recorded. You can have experts come and make sure that tape isn't doctored all you want, I won't fight you on that. But Bruce... We both know that Lyric didn't kill the girl."

The woman leans in and says something indiscernible to the prosecutor. He nods, then returns his attention to Carl. "Christ, that was brutal." There's a look of horror creeping through the lines carved in his face. "But that doesn't change the fact that it *also* proves your client murdered Mr. Singer."

Carl makes a dumbfounded look. "Well yeah, no *shit*. In case you haven't been taking notes, that was never in question. The question is *why* he did it. And when a jury hears what *you* just heard... I don't think they're gonna have a lot of sympathy for Mr. Singer."

Bruce puts his hand over his mouth in serious contemplation. The clock ticks loudly on the wall – never ceasing in its eternal march. Then finally, he asks, "What do you propose?"

Carl leans back into his chair. "Drop the charge for the murder of Alita. There's no sense in even asking the jury to consider it at this point – this recording exonerates him of that completely."

Then the woman beside the prosecutor looks at her boss. "I think he's right, Bruce. If we tried to push all three homicides after *that* goes into evidence, it'll make us look vindictive. Imagine what the press would do with that information."

Then the other man goes, "Keep in mind, too, that even though we're dealing with the court of law, a jury is still more inclined toward the court of public opinion. They're human beings. If it looks to them like we're refusing to budge after obvious evidence *dramatically* changes the circumstances, they might vote *not guilty* out of sheer empathy." Then he glares at me. "Everybody loves the underdog."

My face doesn't even twitch. "Not everybody."

Then Bruce rubs his forehead and lets out an exhausted sigh. "Son of a bitch...." He raises his eyes to Carl and frustratedly asks, "Where the hell was this the last twelve months of discovery? If I find out you've been sitting on this –"

I interject. "A girl found it in my house." They look at me.

The woman asks, "A girl? What was she doing there?"

With a faint smile that evaporates quickly, I reply, "She was helping me finish a song I wrote. She's a good kid. Said the tape recorder got knocked behind the TV. Guess the sheriff's department didn't do as thorough of an investigation as they thought they did."

Then Carl puts his fingers through each other and says confidently, "Like I told you, you can have the tape audited if you want. But we both know it's legit. Drop the homicide charge in the case of Alita Swanson, drop the double-murder love-triangle-gone-wrong argument. You want my client locked up? Argue what's there to argue – whether or not the murder of Huckleberry Singer was justified under the defense of temporary insanity. Otherwise, well..." He clicks his tongue and leans back, sliding his hands into the pockets of his slacks. "I guess we'll see you at the mistrial."

The three members of the prosecution team exchange glances. Then the woman says, "A mistrial would look *really* bad. The chances of us being able to convict if we have to come back with one, maybe even two fewer homicide charges – given the footage of the encounter with Mr. Swanson...." She trails off for a second. "Bruce, I think we should take this road. Drop the charge regarding Alita Swanson."

Beads of sweat form on the lead prosecutor's forehead. Minutes go by it seems. Then, finally –

"Alright, Hoskins," he says. He extends his hand forward. "You've got a deal."

Gladly, Carl shakes his hand. "Thank you, Bruce. We'll have to set the trial back by maybe an hour to get Judge Thomas up to speed and fill the jury in on the change of plans." Then he puffs his cheeks and lets out the air. "It ain't gonna be pleasant listening to that thing again in the courtroom."

"Yeah, well..." the prosecutor frowns. "God willing, this ordeal will be over soon." He grabs his stack of papers, taps the bottom of them against the table, and he and his cohort stand up.

Then he looks at me and says:

"One way or the other."

\*\*\*

It's another agonizing hour and a half before the trial begins for the day. We all go through the usual motions I've gotten used to – stand up, sit down, let the judge remind the court of the rules of courtesy and the jury of what we're there for.

He tells them, and the several faces in the benches behind me as I sit next to Carl at our table, in a booming voice: "Now, as the jury is aware, but for the benefit of the court I will make clear now – given new evidence obtained by the defense, the charges against the defendant have been amended." There's a surprised murmur through the crowd. I look back and spot a handful of familiar faces: Lorraine, Madeline, Rust, Jimmy, Liz, Angelica, Josie, Jess, CJ, Hyde, Jazz. Even Red is sitting in the stands.

This time, Hope and Makenna are there, too.

They're sitting next to Jazz, and all three of them look sick with worry.

I want to tell them I'll be okay, but to be honest I don't know if I will.

Judge Thomas continues. "The prosecution has dropped the charge of murder in the second degree of Alita Swanson."

This time, the murmurs are louder.

I glance back again and a quick, proud smile flashes across Makenna's face like her heart just skipped a beat.

The judge raps his gavel. "Please, I ask that those in the audience remain quiet. The jury is instructed to disregard any testimony made in an attempt to demonstrate the defendant's guilt of the murder of Ms. Swanson. However, all other charges – murder in the second degree of Huckleberry Singer and of Jedediah Swanson, as well as resisting arrest – have not been amended. With that being said..." He motions to Carl, "...Mr. Hoskins, you may proceed."

Carl takes a quick breath and says, "Thank you, your Honor," then rises to his feet and marches to the lectern. "I would like to enter into evidence Exhibit 27."

The judge looks at the prosecution team. "Counsel, any objections?"

The prosecutor responds, almost reluctantly, "No, your Honor."

Then the judge turns back to Carl. "You may enter into evidence Exhibit 27."

Carl looks at one of the court officials and gestures. The man complies immediately, bringing out a speaker and cassette player.

My tape with the murder on it is in his hand.

Carl then addresses both the jury and the audience. "In an unexpected turn of events, we have managed to procure an audio recording of the events that transpired at 10 North Bethel Street, New Freedom, Ohio, the night of May 17th, 1996."

A collective, quiet gasp escapes many of the lips in the crowd. The members of the press begin taking notes furiously.

Anxiety rips through me; I don't want to have to listen to it again.

But it needs to happen.

The world needs to know what happened.

This is my penance.

*Bite the fuckin' apple, everybody.*

Carl continues. "This tape, which was found at the residence of Mr. Lyric by a party who both the prosecution and the defense have agreed shall remain anonymous, has been examined by experts for the prosecution, and has been found by the state of Ohio to be untampered with and undoctored in any way. In simpler terms, it is a genuine recording of the murders of Alita Swanson and Huckleberry Singer."

I half turn my head to glance at the crowd; they look about as sick as I feel.

Carl takes a long, deep breath. "I must warn you, what you are about to hear is... shocking. Any person who does not want to hear what we are about to play for you..." Suddenly, he becomes very candid. "Nobody will hold it against you if you want to step out of the room."

He waits. The entire room goes so still I think I can hear Jasmine's heart beating as I look back at her. She's biting her nails, and for a second, I think she's gonna leave.

But she just looks at me with a face that says *we're still in this together.*

Nobody gets up; everybody stays.

Then I return my attention to Carl. He takes one more look around, then addresses the court official. "You may play the tape."

There's a sound of hissing and static for a moment, and then I hear the voice of an angel for the last time.

ALITA: *"What are you doing? ...Am I being interrogated?"*

LYRIC: *"No... I like to record my practice sessions. Lets me know where I need improvement."*

ALITA: *"Testing, testing, one-two-three."*

LYRIC: *"Hello, I'm Johnny Cash."*

ALITA: *"Good evening, folks, and welcome back to Southern Sound Radio with your hosts, Donovan Lyric and the wonderful Alita Swanson."* *LAUGHTER* *"So, Mr.

*Lyric, what are your thoughts on the events that transpired tonight?"*

LYRIC: *"Well, Ms. Swanson, tonight was what I would call, 'a whole lot of bullshit.' We had bullshit from the blue corner, bullshit from the red corner, even bullshit out on the street."*

ALITA: *FALSE VOICE* *"It was total calamity!"*

LYRIC: *LAUGHTER* *"Almost…. Fuck."*

ALITA: *"What?"*

LYRIC: *"I left my smokes at the bar."*

ALITA: *"Then I guess you better go get some more."*

LYRIC: *"….What are you, a fucking cat?"*

ALITA: *"Something like that."* *LONG PAUSE* *"That feels good…."*

LYRIC: *"Mmmm, I really need cigarettes, though…."*

ALITA: *"They can wait."*

LYRIC: *"Only for a quick one – Shell closes in fifteen minutes."*

ALITA: *"Then give me five."*

The tape proceeds to belt out the sounds of me and Alita's last time making love. The court looks slightly uncomfortable by the graphic sounds of sex, but as I hear it play back, all I can think about is how much I should have cherished that moment.

I wish I had given her all fifteen of those minutes so that maybe I could have given her the rest of the years of my life. I wish I didn't get up and leave for something as mundane as a pack of cigarettes. I wish…

Then it hits me –

Would she want me to wish things were any different?

When she told me about her mother's suicide, she said everything happens for a reason.

Maybe there was a reason for this, too.

ALITA: "*Oh my fucking God…. Fuck, I needed that.*"

LYRIC: "*Now I REALLY need a cigarette.*" *SHUFFLING*

ALITA: "*When you come back, be ready for round two.*"

LYRIC: "*I don't think that'll be a problem.*"

ALITA: *PAUSE* "*Hurry back.*"

As I hear that sound again, it strikes me that was the last thing she will ever say to me.

And suddenly my eyes become hot, and everything is blurry.

Sitting at the defense table, my head falls into my palm.

Silently, I start to cry.

In the background of the tape, the sound of movement can be heard, then a moment later the warm sound of a vinyl spinning, then music comes out. It's a familiar, old song sung by Tanya Tucker, the first track on the album – *Delta Dawn.*

But just as she begins to sing, the sound of the door opening is caught on tape.

ALITA: *"Well that was quick – What the fuck?!"*

The music stops suddenly.
Then a man's voice is heard.

HUCK: *"I fucking KNEW I'd find you here!"*

The entire court lets out a choked gasp. Fury stops my tears dry.

ALITA: *"Huck, what the hell –?!"*
HUCK: *"You lyin' fucking WHORE!"*
ALITA: *"Get out! Get the FUCK away from me!"*
HUCK: *"Oh, I'm sorry – were you busy fucking someone else for a place to stay? Pretending you're a good person covered in a layer of shit and makeup, trying to hide the grotesque fucking manipulative ABOMINATION you are on the inside?!"*
ALITA: *"What the fuck is WRONG with you?! Just leave me alone! I'm done!"*
HUCK: *"Oh, you'll be alone alright! No wonder your daddy doesn't like you, you untrustworthy fucking LIAR!"*
ALITA: *"I'd rather be MILES away and alone if it means I don't have to stay with you!"*
HUCK: *"Yeah, typical small town fucking skank! Average looking fuckin' bar floosie's what you are!"* *PAUSE* *"Just know, I've told probably seven people in the last hour what a fuckin' whore you are, so enjoy the fame. Maybe you can break THEIR fucking hearts, too!"*

ALITA: "*I don't care, just get OUT of here!*"

HUCK: "*Don't worry, I will. And I'll be periodically bringing your things home to you – AKA the fucking trashcan! You can pick them up on the side of the road, where you'll probably be working in the future!*"

ALITA: "*I'll get them tomorrow – you don't have to be like this.*"

HUCK: "*Yeah, I'M the bad guy who got cheated on, so now I'M a fuckin' threat. Fuck you!*"

ALITA: "*I didn't fucking cheat on you!*"

HUCK: "*Yes you did, Alita! Yes you fucking did!*"

ALITA: "*You're acting like a literal fucking PSYCHO right now, Huck!*"

HUCK: "*Oh, I'M the psycho? Not Mr. Fucking Damaged you're sleeping with?!*"

ALITA: "*I don't care if he's damaged, he LISTENS to me! He cares about me!*"

HUCK: "*I fucking cared, too, Alita! I fucking cared, too!*"

ALITA: "*Bullshit! All I ever was to you was fucking property! You never even read a single thing I wrote! You don't care about me and you never did!*"

HUCK: "*HA! You're not fucking special! Nobody is going to read an author who lives on a fuckwalk!*"

*SLAM*

ALITA: "*Fuck you!*"

HUCK: "*Yeah, throw your fuckin' shoes at me! Piss me off some more, see where the fuck it gets you!*"

ALITA: *"Get the fuck out of here before I call the cops, you fucking lunatic!"*

HUCK: *"The fuck you think daddy's gonna do?! You're fucking crazy, Alita. You're a crazy fucking WHORE and everybody fucking knows it! I won't miss your sorry fucking ass while you're busy shacking up with that fucking loser! So goodbye forever, you stupid, STUPID bitch!"*

ALITA: *"Yeah? Well while you're busy thinking about it tonight, sobbing in your fucking bed, let me go ahead and answer the question you'll be stuck on when you cry yourself to sleep – yes, he's bigger than you."*

*LONG PAUSE*

HUCK: *QUIETLY* *"What the fuck did you just say to me, woman?"*

*ANOTHER LONG PAUSE*

HUCK: *"What the FUCK did you just say to me?! You filthy fucking WHORE!"*

*CRASH, SLAM, ALITA SCREAMS*

ALITA: *"Huck, no –! STOP!"*

HUCK: *"THE FUCK DID YOU JUST SAY TO ME?! YOU FUCKING WHORE! HOW'S THAT FEEL, HUH?! YOU STUPID BITCH! HOW'S THAT FEEL?!"*

There's an overwhelming feeling of sickness as Alita can be heard choking and sputtering through the tape. It takes everything in me not to vomit on the spot.

For two full minutes, all that can be heard is the sound of Alita slowly choking to death.

Then the tape goes quiet for a moment.

HUCK: "*Alita…? Hey – hey, come on, wake up! Alita, quit fuckin' around! I didn't mean it!*" *SILENCE* "*Hey! Wake up! Wake up! Oh my God… Oh my God….*"

The tape is silent except for white noise for several minutes. Softly, Huck can be heard sobbing in the background.

Then the sound of the door creaking open comes from the speaker.

LYRIC: "*Huck……. What did you do?*"
HUCK: "*…….She said something and I… I just snapped. I lost it, Lyric…. I strangled her.*"
LYRIC: "*….Why….*"
*PAUSE*
HUCK: "*Just to watch her die.*"
*LONG SILENCE*
HUCK: "*I told her…. I told her to stay away from you. I didn't… I didn't think it would get this far….*"
LYRIC: *BARELY AUDIBLE* "*Stand up.*"
HUCK: "*…..What, are you gonna shoot me?*"
LYRIC: "*Stand UP.*"
*SHUFFLING SOUND*
HUCK: "*Kill me, call the fuckin' cops, I don't care anymore…. I used to think she was perfect.*"
*LONG SILENCE*
LYRIC: *BARELY AUDIBLE* "*The Devil never whispered 'perfection….'*"

HUCK: *PAUSE* "*What?*"

LYRIC: "*He whispered 'freedom.'*"

*BANG*

*THUDDING SOUND*

The tape plays on for another several minutes, capturing the sound of my attempt to call Carl. Then the sound of me destroying the phone on the wall in a fit of brokenhearted rage.

*CRACK, CRACK, CRACK*

LYRIC: "*FUCK! FUCK, FUCK, FUCK, FUUUCK!*"

There's one more long silence, before finally, just before the tape cuts out:

LYRIC: *BARELY AUDIBLE* "*I'm sorry....*"

As the tape comes to a close, Carl turns and faces the jury. His eyes are as red as mine, and his voice cracks as he says: "The defense rests."

# Chapter 32

They let me out for a smoke while the jury deliberates. I couldn't focus on anything when Carl gave his closing argument; the court had to take a fifteen minute recess after the tape was finished. Some people were sick, some people were crying. Most of us were silent.

It didn't much matter to me whatever the prosecutor said in his closing argument, either. The truth was out. Even if I wound up in prison for the rest of this life and the next, there was freedom in that.

People finally knew she wasn't crazy.

And they finally knew who I was.

Two cops are standing next to me, one on either side as we step just outside the back of the building. They don't take me out front for fear of being swarmed by reporters. Turns out my case really caught a bit of attention.

I guess triple homicides will do that.

I'm all nerves as the smoke fills my lungs, and the tobacco does little to change that. The jury's been at it for an hour already – so much for a quick verdict. Maybe that's a good sign. Maybe there's twelve angry men in there, indignant about the injustices the same as I am. Or maybe there's only one lone holdout who thinks I ought not to rot.

Half-heartedly, I chuckle at that.

Standing out behind the courthouse, all I wanna do is play my damn guitar. It's been so long now I can't even imagine how rusty I would sound.

If I ever get to play again, anyway. My dad told me they don't let you play guitar in prison – so far, that seems to be the case.

Then the familiar voice of a man strikes my ear through the door. "You got one of those for me?"

I turn around sharply.

It's Red.

Immediately, one of the cops says, "Sir, you can't be out here."

Red sizes him up real quick. "Your supervisor – that's Chief Wilson, right?"

Subtly, the cop recoils. "As a matter of fact, yes sir, it is."

Red nods with his face almost in a smirk. "Why don't you go ahead and call him on your radio and tell him that Red Sutherland would like to share a cigarette with an old buddy of his?"

The cop takes a hard look at Red, then acquiesces curiously. "Hey chief, it's Sergeant Downy here. You happen to know a 'Red Sutherland' by any chance? Over."

The radio sizzles for a moment, then another voice comes through. "*Old Red? Yeah, I know him. Why? What's up? Over.*"

With a surprised look on his face, the sergeant radios back, "Says he'd like to have a smoke with Mr. Lyric. We're out back of the courthouse right now. Over."

Compressed laughter can be heard through the radio. "*Ah, hell, why not? I owe him one. Keep your eye on him, though. He's a tricky bastard.*"

Red smiles and laughs, then gestures for the radio. Apprehensively, the sergeant complies. "How you doin', Wilson? Stayin' out of trouble?"

There's laughter again, then, "*Stayin' out of it and catching it in the act. Take her easy, Red.*"

"Only way I know how to take her."

Then he hands the radio back to the sergeant. The two cops give Red a puzzled look.

He says plainly, "We served together back in the day. Good guy."

Then the cops ease up and let out a soft chuckle. "As you were."

Red looks at me and cocks his brow. "See – I told you I've got friends all over the place." Then I sort of laugh and pull out my pack of cigarettes. "Cowboy killers still?" he asks.

"Yup," I reply. "I keep hoping they'll kill me but it turns out I ain't much of a cowboy."

Red laughs heartily and lights his cigarette. For a minute, we stand there looking out at the road across the vast parking lot. He says, "It's like a sea of concrete. You know this used to just be a field?"

"Figures. Mankind doesn't know when to stop building. That's what I like about New Freedom – they figured the fifties was a good place to stop."

Red sort of snorts humorously, then says, "Give it time. They'll keep building it up. Some day, when you and I are old fucks, we won't even recognize it anymore."

I take a long drag. "Sometimes I wish time would wait." Then I turn and take a look at the courthouse.

"Maybe not today, though. Kinda wish they'd get on with it." Anxiously, I let out a shaky breath.

Red studies me for a moment, but doesn't speak.

So I ask him, "How've you been?"

He shrugs. "Fair to middling, I'd say. Daniel's doing good. He saw *Star Wars* for the first time the other day."

"No shit?" I ask with a faint grin.

"No shit," Red beams.

"What'd he think of it?"

"Loves it. The first one is his favorite."

I crack a grin. "Smart kid." Then I take another drag and, almost hesitantly, I ask, "How's Layla?"

Red frowns slightly, but nods. "She's... better. We're still separated. I don't see that ever changing. She's kind of a succubus, that one. But it's my own damn fault for giving into it for so long."

Guiltily, I half shrug my shoulder. "You love her. The hell else are you supposed to do?"

"Amen to that, brother."

A minute goes by in silence.

Then Red says, "I've been meaning to tell you something for a while. I don't know if you're aware of this, but you've been kind of hard to reach this last year or so."

"Yeah, something about being in prison, I think," I joke.

"Yeah, something like that," Red grins slightly until it fades. He looks out over the concrete sea filled with cars idling like boats tied to a pier. "When I confronted you about what happened – about what you did... You know, it killed me a little bit, Lyric. That was probably one of the most unpleasant conversations I've ever had to have with a friend."

Guiltily, my face falls. "Yeah... Me too."

"But it wasn't like it was with Will," he continues. "You know, Will did everything he could to deny it. Told me she was lying, called her crazy, called *me* crazy, threw you under the bus... But when I told you I knew what happened, you didn't try to fight it. You didn't run from it. I could've killed you out there and you knew it, but you you got up anyway. You took accountability for your own actions. And it's hard not to respect you for it. You were a man. That's something we don't see a whole lot in this day and age."

Letting his words run around in my head, I inhale and let it back out with a nod. "We're from an old world, me and you. A lot of people don't see things the way we do."

"No, no they do not," he replies emphatically. "I just wanted you to know... No matter what that jury in there decides, you did what you had to do."

He and I share a look of understanding. His stoicism never breaks, not even for a moment.

I reply, "Yeah, well... It took a lot of wrongdoings to get me there."

"Still," he says, taking one last, long drag of his cigarette. "You did the right thing."

Then he tosses it out to the pavement.

He gives me one last look as he opens the door and says, "Eventually, you always do."

He disappears inside, and I'm left finishing my smoke in between the two cops. My eyes are drawn to the smoldering cigarette butt a few feet out in front of me. I glance at one of the guards. "You mind if I...?"

He raises an eyebrow, then says, "Go right ahead."

I take a few steps forward, snuff the burning remnant of his cigarette and mine, then put both of the butts back in the pack.

"Sorry," I tell them. "I have a friend who would kill me if she caught me tossing cigarette butts on the pavement."

The cops both let out a bemused, quiet laugh. A plane flies overhead and it catches my ear, then I'm suddenly staring in wide wonder at the bright white sky, barely discernible from the clouds.

If I close my eyes, I can picture it as blue.

But I keep them open and I ask aloud softly, "How're you doin' today?" I keep my eyes up there for what feels like a long time before I ask, barely audibly, "How am I doing today?"

Then the door opens again.

This time, it's Carl.

"Lyric," he says, suppressing his own anxiety. "It's time."

\*\*\*

I'm back at the defense table as the audience shuffles back into the courtroom. As if it's the last time I'll see them, I take a look back at my friends.

I only wish they knew how much I appreciated all of them.

Judge Thomas enters and we all do the rise-and-fall routine, and then a minute later the jury comes in from a door by the jury box.

It's like they've all been trained in the art of not displaying a single goddamn emotion. I'm shaking with nerves, trying to get a read on the future.

And then I remind myself, it doesn't really matter.

No matter where I end up, I'll always be free.

That's all life really is, isn't it? An overwhelming amount of freedom, where you wake up every day and have to make the choice if you'd rather live or die, despite knowing just how evil the world can be.

I don't really think there's anything that could make me choose the latter anymore, because I also know just how good it can be.

Judge Thomas begins speaking as the jurors take their seats. "Mr. Foreman," he addresses the head juror, who rises to his feet, "has the jury reached a decision?"

He clears his throat, then calmly but clearly replies, "Yes, your Honor."

Judge Thomas nods and says, "You may deliver your verdict, then."

The air intensifies with electricity as the foreman speaks into a microphone, reading from a small piece of paper. "On the count of resisting arrest and obstruction of justice, we the jury find the defendant...."

My leg starts to shake. *Good God, get on with it.*

"Guilty."

A few people make a sound; I half expect the judge to rap his gavel again, but he lets it pass.

My gut tightens as I make peace with my impending prison sentence.

The foreman continues.

"On the count of murder in the second degree of Sheriff Jedediah Swanson, we the jury find the defendant...."

*Here it comes.*

"Not guilty, by reason of self-defense."

A collective sigh and gasp hits my ear from the benches behind me. Carl exhales sharply in relief beside me. He and I exchange glances as we prepare ourselves for the big one.

Then the foreman says:

"On the count of murder in the second degree of Huckleberry Singer, we the jury find the defendant..."

It's mere seconds between the end of that word and the beginning of the next one, but I could swear my life flashes before my eyes. So I close them, and I just picture that day at the swimming hole with Alita.

*Everything happens for a reason.*

"Not guilty, by reason of temporary insanity."

Suddenly the people behind me erupt in cheers and applause. I could have cried with relief at the sound of it as my breath escapes me.

This time, the judge uses his gavel. "Order, order," he says almost lackadaisically. He lets out an exhausted sigh – it almost looks like relief. He gathers his thoughts, then says, "Well, I see no reason to drag this ordeal out any further." The court lets out an almost giddy laugh, like they've all been just as frightened and anxious as I've been.

Then Judge Thomas looks at me and says, "Donovan Lyric, for the crime of resisting arrest and obstruction of justice, I hereby sentence you to eighteen months in River Sound County Prison, with twelve months time served. Upon your release, you are sentenced to twenty-four months of supervised probation, with a suspended sentence of an additional twelve months incarceration should you violate your probation." Then he gives me a stern look. "This will include a mandatory two years of abstaining from the use or consumption of alcohol. Do you understand?"

My jaw trembles from both excitement and relief. I don't really mind the six more months in prison.

And I sure as hell don't mind another two years sober.

All I can say is, "Yes. Thank you, your Honor."

The judge studies me for another moment, then says, "Very good," and strikes his gavel one time. "Court is adjourned. Have a good day, everyone. And God bless."

I look back to see a plethora of smiling, relieved faces. Jazz has tears in her eyes and I could melt when I see her smiling for the first time in what feels like a year. Then my eyes travel and rest on Colton Rust.

He simply nods.

# Chapter 33

## River Sound County Prison, June 22nd, 1997

The other inmates eye me suspiciously, sitting in a circle. *Fuck, they're gonna kill me. This was a bad idea.*

One of them, a big burly black man who could probably murder me with a couple hits, stares through my dark glasses right into my soul. The scrawny, tatted up white guy sitting next to him isn't looking at me any kinder. A few other guys sit in the circle, all of them staring anxiously.

*Welp, guess this is it. So much for the cowboy killers.*

Then the big guy's face changes and he goes, "Ah, God *dammit!* Fold."

The circle lets out a collective groan.

Then the scrawny white dude clicks his tongue and smacks the air, throwing his cards down. "Mother of fuck, fuck it, I fold too."

My face stretches into a wide grin as I look down at the river – five cards laid out in a row on the table in the rec room at the prison. I set my cards face down and pull the pot toward me. "Let's see," I begin, "five smokes, a Little Debbie snack, a bottle of Coke, and – man, who the fuck put their shoelaces in the pot?"

The circle lets out a laugh, then a guy named Dominick says, "Well shit, man, I ain't have nothin' else to bet with."

The big black guy, Deon, picks up the shoelaces and tosses them back to Dominick. "Mutha fucka, you *still* ain't got nothin' to bet with. Dusty ass bitch." He cracks a big grin and everybody laughs again.

Then the scrawny guy, Gary, goes, "Aight, white Ray – whatchu playin' with, anyway?"

"Wouldn't y'all like to know?" I retort with a smirk as I lean back.

"Gotta be kings, *ay?*" a latino fellow named Jefe says with a heavy Mexican accent. His name isn't actually *Jefe*, it's *Jeff*, which sounds the same in Spanish as it does in English. But Gary called him *Jefe* one time without realizing it means *boss* in Spanish, and he was too embarrassed to admit it so he just rolled with it and acted like he meant it as *boss* in the first place. So now we all call him *Jefe*. "Homeboy bet hees last cigarette on it. They got two kings in de river already – ees gotta be kings."

Deon grins again and goes, "Let's see 'em, Ray."

I let out a laugh and flip my cards.

Dominick looks pissed off and stunned all at once. "You bet your *last* cigarette on a fuckin' *two* and a *five?*"

"Sure did."

Gary leans back and tosses his hands up. "Man, you can't do that!"

"Sure I can – I just did, didn't I?"

Then he clicks his tongue and says, "Man, you crazy."

Proudly, I sort of shrug. "I've been called worse."

Then Deon leans forward and points at my glasses. "Nah, see man," he chuckles, "you playin' with a *handicap*. It ain't fair."

"Deon," I reply, "you understand that I'm *literally* handicapped, right? Like, visually impaired?"

"Visually impaired my ass," Dominick goes with a laugh. "You got X-Ray vision or somethin'?"

I can't help but grin. "Nah, I ain't got superpowers. Just used to play Texas Hold'em with my dad a lot when I was a kid."

Gary scoffs with a smirk. "Oh yeah? Where he at now? Playin' the big leagues?"

I glance up at the ceiling. "Maybe – depends on if God lets you play cards up there."

Then Gary clicks his tongue and dismisses me with a wide wave. "Get the fuck outta here with that religious shit, man."

I sort of laugh and shake my head quickly. "I ain't religious. Just too damn lucky to be a coincidence, is all."

Deon laughs and says in his deep voice, "Lucky? Man, you see where you at?"

"All things considered?" I respond. "I think I like the hand I was dealt."

"Pft," Jefe goes. "Nothin' hand, what you got dealt, *hombre*."

Then I grin. "What's the line from that movie? 'Sometimes 'nothin' is a pretty cool hand.'"

"Uh huh, uh huh," Deon replies skeptically, grabbing the cards and shuffling the deck. "Whatever you say, James Dean."

Gary shoves the big guy and says, "That ain't James Dean in the movie, dipshit. It's Paul Newman."

Deon gives him a look of playful contempt. "Man, I know you ain't tryna say Paul Newman was the rebel without a cause."

"No, I ain't," Gary responds staunchly, "'cause he ain't talking about *Rebel Without a Cause*. That was *Cool Hand Luke*."

I grin and say, "A man of culture, I see."

Deon shakes his head and clicks his tongue. "Shit, ain't my fault all y'all look alike." We all laugh, then Deon looks at me and goes, "Alright, Roy Orbison. Ante up."

Just as I go to put a couple cigarettes in the pot, the door to the rec room opens and a correctional officer steps in. "Lyric, you got visitors."

Jefe quickly goes, *"Ohhhhh,* you got a *lady friend, sí? ¿Tienes una chica hermosa?"*

I hop off the bench and toss my cards down with a wry smirk. "I'm not *that* lucky. *Quiero una Mexicana mamacita, mi amigo.*"

Jefe grins and Gary goes, "Man, quit speakin' in tongues."

Jefe shoves him and says, *"¡Es español, estúpido!"*

They howl with laughter at each other as I step away. When I take a look back, I notice the old 1978 *Superman* movie is playing on the TV, suspended below the ceiling behind a metal grate, and I can't help but smile.

*Prison ain't so bad.*

I follow the CO as he leads me through the prison toward the visitor area. "So did you happen to check the names on the sign in sheet there, Cody? Or does it get to be a surprise again?"

"For the last time," the CO responds dryly, "it's Officer Nash. I ain't your buddy. And no, I didn't check the sign in sheet because I ain't your mom, either." There's humor in his voice as he speaks.

"Sure thing, Officer Nash... ol' buddy ol' pal."

We get into the visitor area and I take my seat at a table. Idly, I glance around at the other inmates in black jumpsuits the same as me – well, I guess they were probably navy blue, but it was all the same to me.

They're all talking to friends and loved ones, each of them with a face that, whether happy or sad, cherishes that moment.

*Five more months*, I remind myself.

I only have to sit there for a minute before my visitors arrive.

It's Jasmine and Makenna.

Immediately, I burst into a smile. "Well hey," I greet cheerfully.

Jazz sits down across from me with a look of apprehensive surprise, and Makenna does the same. Jazz says, "Well hey yourself...?" then kind of giggles. "I'm sorry, I didn't expect you to have such a... sunny disposition."

Makenna grins and says, "It's because he's around his kind now. You know – criminals."

I let out a laugh and reply, "Oh ha-ha. I mean, that actually was kind of funny, but *ha-ha* to you anyway. How's your summer treating you?"

"Pretty good," she says. "Just enjoying the fresh air, summer breeze, and all the freedom in the world." Then she props her elbows up and rests her chin in her hands. "How's yours?"

"I've already got all the freedom in the world," I grin back, then look up at a small window near the ceiling, watching the clouds drift by. "Nobody can ever take your soul, and that's all you need."

"That's what *you* think," Makenna grins mischievously.

Jazz gives her a look but can't help but laugh. "We've got thirty minutes with the guy and you're spending it torturing him?"

Makenna shrugs with her hands out and says, "Well if prison won't do it, how else is he gonna learn not to run from the cops?"

She gives me a look and I grin. "And I would have gotten away with it, too, if it weren't for you meddling... well, *me*, I guess."

Makenna giggles and says, "I still can't believe you called the cops on yourself. All that trouble you put Jazz through, just to pull *that*." She crosses her arms and shakes her head.

"Don't worry – I've already got my escape planned out."

Jazz laughs incredulously and I turn around to look at Officer Nash.

"That was a joke!" I call out. "Don't worry, that was a joke!"

He shakes his head and tries not to crack a grin.

Then I return my attention to the woman and the girl in front of me and say, "We're good friends, me and that guy."

"Yeah, I'll say," Makenna remarks with heavy sarcasm. "Seems like a real big fan of yours."

Then Jazz eagerly clasps her hands together and says, "Speaking of real big fans...." Almost like asking for a green light, she gives Makenna a look and she returns with one that says *go for it*.

"What?" I ask with a faint laugh, kind of confused.

Jazz practically jumps up and down in her seat. "I'm doing an album!"

My eyes light up with excitement. "Oh, shit, really?" I exclaim. "It's about damn time. See, I knew I was holding you back."

Makenna interjects. "Well, I wouldn't quite say *that*."

I give her a puzzled look. "What do you mean?"

With a look of sheer enthusiasm, Jazz tells me, "So one of my friends out in Tennessee – real big in the music scene down there – invited me out to record some songs with him, so I did. Then I told him about our little gig in Southern Sound County, and he wants to sign me to his label."

I click my tongue. "Well, I knew it would happen sooner or later. Finally off to the big-times."

"Yeah," Jazz says with a broad smile, "and when you're out of here, you're coming with me."

Skeptically, I scoff. "Yeah, okay. Someone who's never even heard me play is just gonna invite me in on your record deal because, what, you made a really convincing argument?"

Then Makenna goes, "Welllll, about that...." and cracks a sly smile.

For a second, I study her quizzically. "You didn't."

"Yup, sure did," she replies.

Jazz says with excitement, "She gave me a bunch of your tapes to bring with me when I went, and I got him to listen to them. He wants us both – Jazz *and* Lyric."

Taken aback, I sort of smile. I'm not sure what to say. "You know, 'Lyric and Jazz' *really* has a better ring to it."

Jasmine rolls her eyes but keeps smiling. "You can't say no to this, Lyric. I mean, you can, but... Do you really want to?"

I can't help but smile. "I guess I've got about five months to think about it."

Makenna then says, "You mean you've got five months to say 'yes.' You want people to hear your guys' work, don't you? Besides, you owe me *big* time." She raises her eyebrows at me.

I give her a proud look. "Yeah, I guess I kind of do. You did good, kid."

Jazz smiles her bright white smile behind ruby red lipstick. "Things are gonna change, Lyric. Everything changes eventually. This is *good* change. Sometimes, change is okay."

Then I glance around the muted gray walls around me and picture stepping out of this place for the last time. "You know, I suppose you're right about that." Heavily, I let out a sigh. "I'm not thrilled about replacing my guitar. That one was my favorite. I mean, it died for a good cause but *damn*. You can't replace a memory."

Then Jazz suddenly turns and gives a look to Officer Nash standing beside the visitor's entrance. He nods at her and steps out the door. I furrow my brow in confusion. Then she looks back at me and says, "Lucky for you, you don't have to."

Then the guard comes back in.

He's carrying a guitar case.

Quickly, he brings it over, sets it on the table and says, "You've got five minutes. Don't make me regret this."

Sweetly, Jazz says, "Thank you, officer." She looks at me and I give her a dumbfounded look. "What?" she asks defensively. "I'm a pretty woman in a *prison* – how hard do you think it is to get what I want around here?"

Suddenly, I just start laughing.

Makenna says, "It might not be *perfect*, but we found a place that does *really* good work on instruments."

Almost nervously, my heart pounding with anticipation, I unzip the case.

It's my guitar, the exact same as it used to be – save for a small imperfection where the bullet used to be.

Grinning like a child, I pull it gently from the case and rest it on my lap.

Then Makenna adds, "Don't worry, I tuned it for you. By ear."

"Settle down there, Mozart," I respond with a wink behind my glasses.

My hand travels the neck of the guitar for a moment, then I press the eighth fret on the bottom string and strum using my index fingernail for a pick, working my way down until the open note after the first fret.

C... B... A... G... F... E.

Beaming, almost a tear in my eye, I'm at a loss for words as my friends smile with me.

They find the words for me.

Makenna begins drumming on the table with her hand. It's a familiar beat for a familiar tune.

It oughta be. It's one of ours.

My fingers find the music and I start strumming the arpeggios she wrote for me and Jazz to play. The strings are quiet without the amp, but that's okay. It feels the same as it ever does. Through dark glasses, I glimpse the devil on my forearm as I strum and I swear I see it move.

As I close my eyes, I watch as a golden light bursts forth in the darkness and loops around quickly in a spinning ring.

It looks like a halo.

With the voice of an angel, one so special it sounds like music even when she's talking, Jasmine begins to sing.

*"If my devils ever leave meeee, then my angels will as well,*

*Find my penance here in Countyyyy while I'm climbin' outta Hell..."*

I join in almost a low hum, adding my timbre to her voice as Makenna drums the beat.

*"And your karmaaaa, when it finally comes around,*

*You can make a deal with the Devillll, and get into the ground,*

*Or you can sing along with your angelllls, and step into the sound..."*

Jazz finishes off with one more refrain as my voice diminishes and I strike the final note.

*"Step into the sound."*

### *A note from the author:*

I'm sure many of you noticed the numerous references to Johnny Cash, as well as a couple to the biopic of his life, *Walk the Line*.

However, the scene in this novel where Alita gives Lyric a copy of Kahlil Gibran's *The Prophet* was *not* a reference to the similar scene from that film.

That actually happened in real life, with the real life inspiration for the character of Alita, and when I rewatched the movie about five years ago, I about shit myself when I saw that.

The only difference between the scene in the novel and the real life event is that, in real life, it happened at the swimming hole – not the dam.

All of the characters and most of the events in this novel, heroes *and* villains, good *and* bad, were inspired by my own experiences and the people I've known.

All of Donovan Lyric's sins, barring murder, are sins of my own; so is his penance.

Even though this is a work of fiction…

You wouldn't believe how much
of this story is true.

Lucas James

*"And he said to them, 'I saw Satan fall like lightning from Heaven.'"* ~*Luke 10:18 ESV*